AT THE EDGE OF THE UNIVERSE

Also by **SHAUN DAVID HUTCHINSON**

The Deathday Letter

fml

The Five Stages of Andrew Brawley

Violent Ends

We Are the Ants

AT THE EDGE OF THE
UNIVERSE

SHAUN DAVID HUTCHINSON

Simon Pulse

NEW YORK · LONDON   TORONTO   SYDNEY   NEW DELHI

SIMON PULSE

An imprint of Simon & Schuster Children's Publishing Division

1230 Avenue of the Americas, New York, New York 10020

First Simon Pulse hardcover edition February 2017

Text copyright © 2017 by Shaun David Hutchinson

Jacket photographs copyright © 2017 by Getty Images (boy and street)

and Thinkstock Images (starry sky)

All rights reserved, including the right of reproduction in whole or in part in any form.

SIMON PULSE and colophon are registered trademarks of Simon & Schuster, Inc.

For information about special discounts for bulk purchases, please contact

Simon & Schuster Special Sales at 1-866-506-1949 or business@simonandschuster.com.

The Simon & Schuster Speakers Bureau can bring authors to your live event. For more information or to book an event, contact the Simon & Schuster Speakers Bureau at

1-866-248-3049 or visit our website at www.simonspeakers.com.

Jacket designed by Jessica Handelman

Interior designed by Mike Rosamilia

The text of this book was set in Adobe Garamond Pro.

Manufactured in the United States of America

2 4 6 8 10 9 7 5 3 1

Library of Congress Control Number 2016956089

ISBN 978-1-4814-4966-3 (hc)

ISBN 978-1-4814-4968-7 (eBook)

For Michael, who held the door open for me

15,000,000,000 LY

I SAT BESIDE THE WINDOW PRETENDING TO READ
Plato's *Republic* as the rest of the passengers boarding Flight
1184 zombie-walked to their seats. The woman next to me
refused to lower her armrest, and the chemical sweetness of
her perfume coated my tongue and the back of my throat. I
considered both acts of war.

In the aisle seat a middle-aged frat bro babbled on his
phone, shamelessly describing every horrifying detail of his
previous night's date, including how drunk he'd gotten the
girl he'd taken home. And he ended each sentence with "like,
awesome, right?"

It sounded less, *like, awesome*, and more like date rape.

"Flying alone?" asked the perfume terrorist. She had a
Chihuahua face—all bulging eyes and tiny teeth—and wore
her hair in a helmet of brassy curls.

"Yeah," I said. "I'm searching for someone."

"And they're in Seattle?"

"I don't know," I said. "Which is why I'm searching for him rather than meeting him." I wasn't exactly *trying* to be rude, but I hated flying. I understood the mechanics, knew my risk of dying in a car was far greater than in a plane, but cramming a couple hundred sweaty, obnoxious people into a metal tube that cruised through the air at five hundred and fifty miles per hour short-circuited my rational brain and loosed the primal, terrified aspect that didn't grasp science and assumed flying the unholy product of black magic. Reading and not having to make small talk kept me calmish. Not that my oblivious seatmate had noticed.

The woman tapped my book with a well-manicured fingernail. "It's nice to see a young man reading instead of staring at a phone."

"Let me tell you about cell phones," I said. "They're two-way communication devices designed to slurp up your private personal information through their cameras and microphones and myriad sensors, then blast that data into the air for any determined creep to snatch and paw through. You believe no one is watching because it helps you sleep at night, but someone is *always* watching. And listening and collecting your GPS coordinates, from which they can extrapolate that you swing by Starbucks every morning on your drive to work, except on Fridays when you take the long way so you can grab a tasty breakfast sandwich. Phones are doors into our lives, and the government keeps copies of all the keys."

The woman smiled, her coral lips taut, and lowered the armrest.

Finally.

But I hadn't really spoken to anyone in so long that instead of returning to my book, I kept talking.

"My boyfriend disappeared," I said. I peered over the seats at a gangly flight attendant near the cockpit who was facing the exit, gesturing at someone with his hands.

"Thomas Ross. He's who I'm hoping to find in Seattle." The flight attendant glanced over his shoulder, his hawkish nose a compass needle pointing directly at me.

"Interesting," the woman said, though her tone said otherwise.

"Tommy vanished two months ago. I'm the only person looking for him. Not the police or our friends. Not even his parents. He disappeared and they've stitched closed the hole in their lives; continued attending their everyone-wins-a-trophy soccer games and forced family suppers, because to them, he never existed."

The flight attendant slid into the galley to allow a

red-faced sheriff's deputy wearing a hunter-green uniform onto the plane. A burnished gold star hung over his left breast pocket, and he carried a gun clipped to a belt strapped around his waist.

The sheriff's officer floated down the aisle, his shiny shaved head swiveling from side to side, scanning each traveler like he possessed a Heads-Up-Display feeding him their names and personal details.

"Tommy'd earned a 3.98 GPA," I said. "He worked as the assistant editor for the *Cloud Lake High Tribune*, kicked ass on the debate team. And I'm certain he loved me. It's the only thing I'm certain of. He wouldn't have just left."

The woman, and everyone else on the plane, watched the cop shamble in my direction.

"Teenagers often make rash decisions," the woman said. "Your *friend* will turn up."

Turn up. Like a missing sock or the Batman action figure my older brother had hidden from me when we were younger. Like Tommy wasn't missing but had simply been misplaced.

"Also," I said, "the universe is shrinking."

The sheriff's officer stopped at my row and faced me. His name tag read BANEGAS. "Oswald Pinkerton? I need you to come with me."

"No Oswald Pinkerton here," I said. "Maybe he's on a different flight."

The cop puffed out his chest, trying to conjure the illusion that he was tough, but his arms looked like the only thing they were used to lifting was a television remote. "Don't be difficult, kid."

"Perhaps you should do as he asks," the woman said. She tucked her legs under the seat so I could, what, crawl over her?

"Let's go, Oswald." Officer Banegas moved aside to allow my seatmates to shuffle into the aisle and clear me a path.

So close. One flight, with a layover in Atlanta, from finding Tommy. Or from crossing off another place he wasn't and further crushing my remaining hope of ever seeing my boyfriend again. If Palm Beach County's Least Competent had stopped for coffee or taken a detour to the toilet to feed the sewer gators, the flight attendant would've shut the doors, the pilot would've taxied to the runway, and I'd have escaped. But maybe this was better. If I'd gone and hadn't found Tommy, I might have been forced to entertain the possibility that he'd vanished for good. This way, I could continue believing I'd find him.

I sighed, grabbed my backpack, tossed the *Republic* inside, and followed the deputy off the plane.

Banegas clapped his hand on my shoulder, leaving me no choice but to accept my temporary defeat. The hatch clunked shut, and I resisted the urge to turn around. My feet weighed a hundred pounds each. Clearly, God had cranked up the gravity.

The terminal—with its gaudy, outdated palm-tree-and-pastel Florida decor—greeted us as we exited the jet bridge. Deputy Banegas guided me to a seat in front of the windows with a view of the runway.

"Wait here," Banegas said. He moved off to the side and mumbled into his shoulder radio.

My plane backed away from the terminal to begin its journey.

My plane.

I'd planned my getaway perfectly. I'd convinced my parents that Lua, Dustin, and I were road-tripping to Universal Studios for the weekend, and I'd begged Lua to cover for me even though I wouldn't tell her where I was going. She'd reluctantly agreed after extracting a promise that I'd explain everything when I returned.

I'd paid for the plane ticket using a prepaid credit card and found a place to crash using HouseStay to avoid having to deal with a front-desk clerk who might question my age. I'd even downloaded Seattle public transportation apps and devised an efficient search pattern that would have allowed me to best utilize my time.

But despite my planning, my plane was flying away without me, and my parents were definitely going to ground me, probably forever.

My life's pathetic theme song repeated in my head. *You failed. You failed. You're a loser and you failed. Dada da doo dee.*

Lua could've written better lyrics, but the beat didn't suck.

Officer Banegas loomed over me. "Come on," he said. "We'll wait for your parents in the security office."

"Can I watch my plane take off at least?" I asked. "Please?"

"Whatever, Oswald."

"Ozzie," I said. "Only people who hate me call me Oswald."

"Fine," Banegas said, annoyed or bored or wishing he'd called in sick. Then he smirked and added, "Oswald."

I walked to the window. My breath fogged the glass as the last feeble rays of the day lit the sky to the west with the colors of orange-and-pink swirled sorbet. I tracked my plane as it turned at the end of the runway. The wing flaps extended. I'd always wondered at their purpose, but never enough to bother looking it up. I considered asking Deputy Banegas, but he struck me as the type who'd cheated his way through college and had only joined the police force because he thought carrying a gun would be cool, then had been disappointed to discover the job consisted mostly of filling out paperwork and offered depressingly few opportunities to actually shoot people.

"How'd my parents find me?"

"Hell if I know," Officer Banegas said.

"Oh."

My plane's twin engines roared. I couldn't hear them inside the terminal, but I imagined their growl as the blades spun madly, faster and faster, struggling to reach critical speed before the road ended. I imagined myself still buckled into my seat, gripping the armrests, trying to ignore my seatmate's fragrance offensive and banal chatter.

The front wheels lifted as the nose pitched up. The air pressure over the top of the wings decreased, allowing my plane to defy gravity. It soared into the sky while I remained rooted to the earth.

Deputy Banegas tapped my shoulder. "Come on, kid."

"Sure." I retrieved my backpack and followed Banegas. We'd reached the lone shop in the center of the terminal when the shouting began. People ran to the windows. I ran to the windows.

Banegas yelled after me, cussing and huffing. I ignored him.

I pressed my face to the glass, crowded on both sides by travelers and airport personnel, and watched my plane tumble from the sky and crash into Southern Boulevard on the far side of the fence separating the runway from the road.

I didn't think about the individuals who died—the perfume bomber, the frat-bro date rapist, the passengers who'd watched Officer Banegas perp-walk me off the plane—only that they burned beautifully.

Then the floor shook; the windows rattled.

Someone screamed, breaking the held-breath paralysis that felt like it had stretched across infinite days though had lasted but the length of a frantic heartbeat.

Officer Banegas's radio squawked. He stood to my right, his arms limp, his eyes wide, watching the nightmare through the glass like it was a TV screen rather than a window.

"Holy shit," he said.

Panic spread like a plague. Rumple-suited businessmen with phones permanently attached to their ears, weary parents and hyper children, heartsick halves of couples desperate to reunite with their missed loved ones, usually ornery ticket agents, and every spectrum of humanity between. None were immune. They screamed and huddled under rows of seats and ran and cried, their actions ineffectual. Their tears inadequate to douse my plane's beautiful fire.

I didn't cry.

Not me.

I laughed.

And laughed and laughed and laughed.

It took two paramedics and a shot of something "for my nerves" to dam my laughter, but far more effort to finally quench the flames.

14,575,000,000 LY

DR. TAYLOR DAWSON REMINDED ME OF BEAKER from *The Muppet Show*—all lanky with wild red hair and bulbous, paranoid eyes. How the hell was I supposed to take a man who looked like a Muppet seriously? Meep meep, motherfucker.

"Do you know why you're here, Ozzie?" Dr. Dawson sat in a spacious flannel chair with a legal pad balanced on his knee. He was the first of my many therapists to favor paper over a touch-screen tablet.

The therapists my parents forced me to see always wanted to know why I thought I was there. Sometimes I claimed my parents had too much money and an overwhelming sense of suburban guilt. Other times I said it was because my brother had freaked out when I'd boarded my windows and taped cardboard over the air vents to keep government

spies from spraying me with poison. I most enjoyed inform-
ing them they were nothing but the next name on a list; an
alphabetical convenience. Everyone deserved to understand
their place in the universe, including two-hundred-dollar-
per-hour psychologists with tacky, generic paintings hanging on their walls.

Which is exactly what I told him. "You were the next
name on the list of psychologists approved by my parents'
insurance. After Conklin, but before Dewey."

Dr. Dawson scribbled a note on his pad. "I see you have
a healthy sense of humor."

"I don't find this funny," I said. "I'm missing work to
waste my time talking to you."

"You believe this session a waste of time?"

"Of course."

"Why?"

I cleared my throat. "This is a waste of time because
we're going to spend the next"—I checked the time on my
phone—"twenty-nine minutes discussing my parents and
my brother and possibly the crash of Flight 1184, because
everyone seems to want to know about *that*, after which I'll
tell my parents you're a quack or that you leered at me or
wore cologne that gave me a headache, and they'll schedule
an appointment with the next doctor on the list, who will ask

me the same stupid questions as you, and to whom I'll give the same stupid answers."

Dr. Dawson's face remained impassively goofy. "Therapy only works if you participate."

"Is that so?"

"It is," Dawson said.

I raised my hands over my head. "Then let's make with the healing, Doc."

Dr. Dawson wrote another note. *Dear Diary, patient is combative and entirely too chatty. I recommend intensive electro-shock treatments and a full frontal lobotomy.*

"Why don't we start with your parents?" he said.

"Fantastic."

"Do you get along with them?"

"Meh . . . ," I said. "The *real* problem is they don't get along with each other. Which is why they're getting a divorce."

Dr. Dawson nodded along. "Does that upset you?"

"Why should it? I'm leaving for college after graduation— probably—and Renny's shipping out for basic training in a month."

"Renny is . . . ?"

"My brother, Warren, but everyone calls him Renny."

"Are you two close?"

"I have this recurring dream where I'm sailing a boat on

a chocolate pudding sea. Renny flies overhead on a missile equipped with a saddle and stirrups, toward a village inhabited by man-sized, flesh-eating emus. He yells that he really loves scrambled eggs before the missile strikes the emu village and explodes."

"Are you worried about your brother joining the military?"

"I'm worried he's going to shoot his foot off," I said. "I'm worried he's going to be the guy everyone hates and who winds up eating his gun from shame. I'm worried the army is going to strip away the things that make him my brother and return him to us as a hollowed-out shell of a human being."

Dr. Dawson's eyebrow twitched, but he refrained from writing down what I'd said, though it probably killed him a little. "It's clear you have complex feelings regarding your brother, and I'd like to unpack those during our next session, but right now I'd like to discuss Thomas Ross."

"Or we could talk about something else." I wriggled in the leather Judas chair I'd been forced to endure, trying to find a comfortable spot. "For instance, were you aware Maya Angelou worked briefly as both a madam and a prostitute? Or that D. H. Lawrence climbed trees in the nude to combat writer's block? I've never had writer's block—not that I write, I'm more of a reader—but I doubt buck-naked tree climbing would help if I did. I should give it a try."

Dr. Dawson nodded appreciatively. "Why do you believe you're the only person who remembers Thomas Ross?" Clearly my non sequitur had failed to deter Dawson. It had worked on Dr. Askari, though it honestly hadn't taken great effort to derail her thought train.

"I'm not crazy," I said.

"No one is suggesting you are."

"Aren't you, though? Isn't that why I'm here? Parents of perfectly sane kids don't send them to therapy."

Dr. Dawson frowned. "Of course they do. Therapy helps people sort through complex thoughts and emotions. Think of therapy as an antibiotic for the mind."

"So you're saying I'm diseased? That I've got a mental infection?"

"That's not what I'm saying at all," Dr. Dawson said. "And I think you're smart enough to know that." He moved his legal pad to the side table, giving me his full attention. "Now, why don't you tell me about Thomas Ross."

Dawson wasn't the first persistent therapist I'd encountered. Dr. Butte had evaded my attempts to dodge her questions too. To fluster her, I'd had to resort to asking her how often was too often for someone my age to masturbate in one day.

"What's to know? I met Tommy in second grade. He kissed me in eighth. He was my boyfriend and best friend.

July third, he existed; July fourth, he didn't. Not even his parents remember him."

"Why do you?"

"Because God has a warped sense of humor? How should I know?"

"Do you have a theory?"

"I have a lot of theories."

"Tell me one."

As therapists went, I kind of admired Dr. Dawson's tenacity, but he wanted to know about Tommy. He'd probably ask about Flight 1184 before our hour was up, which necessitated this being our one and only session. It also meant it couldn't hurt to indulge him a little.

"Have you ever heard of a false vacuum?" I asked.

"I have not."

"The scientific explanation, which I have to admit I probably don't understand as well as I should, describes the stability of our universe as the result of resting in the lowest possible energy state. A false vacuum is one in which it only appears we're in the lowest energy state, until a vacuum metastability event occurs, knocking us into an even lower state." It'd taken me a long time to wrap my brain around the science, and I figured it probably didn't make much sense to Dr. Dawson either. Which he confirmed.

"I'm not sure I understand," he said.

"Imagine the universe is a pot of nearly boiling water. The bubbles on the bottom of the pot are other universes that appear real and stable to their inhabitants, but which, in reality, are not. Eventually, those bubbles rise to the surface and pop. That's a false vacuum."

Dr. Dawson's hand twitched. "And you believe we're living in a bubble on the verge of bursting?"

"It's a theory."

"But how does that account for Thomas Ross's disappearance?"

I'd said more than I'd meant to, but I'd already decided to tell my parents Dr. Dawson fell asleep during our session as my excuse for not wanting to see him again, so it didn't matter.

"If our universe is a false vacuum, then maybe the people living in the real universe are trying to warn me."

Dr. Dawson uncrossed his legs and recrossed them, resting his hands in his lap. "So your theory is that the inhabitants of the true universe have stolen your boyfriend and left you the sole custodian of his memories in order to send you a message?"

"Like I said, it's one possibility. Besides, there are other weird events."

"Flight 1184?"

Shit. I'd walked right into that one. "Sure."

"Do you feel up to discussing it?"

"Why not? I'll always remember those long, meaningful talks I had with the FAA investigators as the highlight of my nearly brief life."

Dawson retrieved his notepad. I swear he actually looked relieved to hold it again. "The police report states you were laughing after the plane went down."

"Went down." I shook my head. "Why does everyone go to such ludicrous lengths to avoid saying 'crash'? They say the plane 'went down' or 'fell' or, my personal favorite, 'attempted an uncontrolled emergency landing.' The fact is the plane crashed. It crashed into the ground, killing a hundred and sixty-seven people. A hundred and fifty-five in the plane, and twelve on the road it crashed into. If Renny hadn't snooped on my computer and ratted me out to my parents, the death toll would've been one sixty-eight."

"Why were you laughing, Ozzie?"

The FAA investigators had asked me the same question a hundred different ways. I think they believed my laughter was an indication I'd caused the crash or been involved in some way, but they hadn't found a speck of evidence I'd been responsible. After they released me, my friends and parents constantly told me how lucky I was fate had plucked me from my uncomfortable seat on the express flight to a fiery death. But I didn't feel lucky.

Dawson patiently waited for my answer. Less than ten minutes of our session remained, and I had nothing to lose.

So I said, "You want to know why I was laughing?"

He nodded. "I do."

"Because I went looking for Tommy and the universe killed a plane full of people to suggest I stay in Cloud Lake. Don't you think that's funny?"

Dr. Dawson glanced at his notepad, then at me. "No, Ozzie, I don't."

"Well, I think it's hilarious," I said. "Especially if it's true."

TOMMY

TOMMY'S SKIN IS HOT. HE IS A HEAT-GENERATING
*star. His radiation accumulates in my cells, breaking them down,
breaking* me *down, twisting my DNA into tight double-helix
knots. His umber skin contrasts against my pale Florida-sun-
defying complexion. Our bodies form a T—Tommy's head on my
stomach—our faces turned toward the sky.*

*"You ever think the moon might want to kill us, Oz?"
Tommy's voice rumbles in his chest, deep as the Mariana Trench,
more buttery than my mom's chocolate chip cookies.*

"Uh . . . no?"

*He glances at me, the whites of his eyes wide. "Come on.
Look at that shifty rock. Are you really trying to tell me she's not
scheming ways to bump us off?"*

*I wiggle left, away from the shell digging into my spine.
Sweat pools on my stomach under Tommy's radiator skull.*

"I'm pretty sure the moon isn't plotting genocide. Because it's a rock."

"Nah," Tommy says. *"She's biding her time, waiting for the perfect opportunity to knock Earth from orbit and take her rightful place around the sun."*

"You're so weird."

"That's why you love me."

A wave splashes over my toes, washing them with the salty aroma of fish and seaweed. We should think about heading home, but it's already so far past my curfew that a few more minutes won't save me from my parents' sensible lecture about staying out too late. Tommy's curfew changes depending on his father's state of drunkenness, and failure to return home by Mr. Ross's whimsical and unknowable deadline could earn Tommy a shiner or worse.

Tommy's father is an asshole.

"You still taking the PSATs Saturday?" Tommy asks.

"Unfortunately."

"Your mom driving you?" I nod. *"Can I catch a ride?"*

"No way. Take the bus, scrub." I laugh and rub my hand along Tommy's bare chest, tracing his dense muscles, pretending I don't notice him flexing. *"We'll swing by around seven."* I twist my neck to glance at Tommy, but he's still staring at the moon. *"What changed your mind?"*

Tommy shrugs. "Pop wants me to work at the garage with him over the summer. He said it's time for me to learn a trade."

"You? A mechanic?" Tommy could recite the names of every US president, explain the differences between parthenogenetic and apomictic asexual reproduction, and whip out an expert essay on the troubling racism present in the works of H. P. Lovecraft in an hour, but his impressive stockpile of knowledge doesn't include how to repair combustion engines.

"Right?" Tommy says. "I don't know dick about cars."

"You definitely know more about dick than cars."

"Never heard you complain."

I grope for Tommy's hand in the dark and lace our fingers together. His hands and feet are always cold. Like his heart and brain hoard his body's warmth, leaving his extremities to freeze.

"You think taking the PSATs will keep you from having to work with your dad?"

"No, but I have to do something," Tommy says. "Sometimes I feel like I'm floating alone in the ocean. Other times I feel like the ocean's in a paper cup." He squeezes my hand. "I refuse to end up like my folks. But what if Cloud Lake's all there is? What if this is it?"

"Would that be so terrible?"

"*Not if we're together, but I'd rather start our lives somewhere else.*"

"*Where?*"

Tommy stretches. He sighs. "Anywhere, Ozzie. Anywhere is better than here."

14,380,000,000 LY

I JERKED AWAKE, CONFUSED AND DISORIENTED. I'D
fallen asleep sitting at my desk, and my stiff neck protested
when I turned it. My laptop's screensaver shone the only light
in my room—the rainbow swirls bouncing from one edge of
the screen to another, morphing and changing colors as they
sought to escape.

I stretched, rubbed the crusty sleep from my eyes. I
checked the time on my phone. 1:43 a.m.

I'd been writing down my memories of Tommy, trying
to recapture the history we'd lost. I'd always kept a journal,
but when Tommy disappeared, the entries had all changed,
and I was determined to record everything I remembered so
I'd never forget. It was more difficult than I thought it would
be. I hadn't safeguarded my memories of Tommy, because I
figured we'd always be together making new ones.

My parents hadn't woken me. Since the oh-God-what-are-you-doing?-Why-didn't-I-knock? incident, my mom rarely entered my bedroom anymore. I think the mess also bothered her. But there's a difference between messy and dirty. Dirty implies used plates under the bed and layers of dust on the furniture and crumbs of past meals embedded in the carpet. All of which described Renny's room, not mine. My room was merely a bit disorganized. Stacks of library books teetered on the edges of my desk, clothes waiting to be folded sat in a lump on the foot of my bed, notebooks and journals and more books stood atop my nightstand and TV and on the floor.

Neatness is the trademark of a boring mind.

I woke my computer and called up the folders containing my where-did-Tommy-go? sites. Links to information about the places Tommy and I had dreamed of visiting. Countries and cities we'd spent hours discussing in hushed voices, planning for the day we could leave Cloud Lake and disappear into the anonymous crowds.

Each folder had a different name. "Maybe" for places Tommy had mentioned. "In the realm of possibility" for vague areas he'd thought had sounded interesting—Meyrin, Switzerland, for example, because he wanted to tour CERN. "Likely candidates" for locations Tommy had spoken of often, which included Boulder, Colorado; Savannah, Georgia; and the Grand Canyon.

Each of the folders contained countless bookmarked sites I'd culled over long, sleepless nights, but the most important folder—named "Tommy's Favorites"—held only two links. One for each of the two locations Tommy had spoken of most frequently. The first was Larung Valley, located in Sertar County of Garze Tibetan Autonomous Prefecture, in China—a makeshift city consisting of thousands of tiny wood houses, home to forty thousand Buddhist monks, and one of the largest Buddhist institutes in the world. The second was Seattle.

Tommy *could* have run away to China, but it was far easier for an unaccompanied teenager to book a domestic flight than an international one.

Sometimes I wondered what might have happened if I'd hopped on a plane to China rather than Seattle. Whether *that* plane would have crashed instead of Flight 1184.

I had another folder with different bookmarked pages. Websites for theories about what might have happened to Tommy if he hadn't run away. Like the one describing false vacuums. Another explained how time travel might work in case it turned out assassins from the future had somehow erased Tommy from the timeline. Still another was all about the existence of the multiverse and how every choice we make causes the universe to split and branch off infinitely. Each theory was less plausible than the last, and it was easier to believe that Tommy had run away and somehow managed to erase himself from everyone's memories but mine because it left me the possibility that I could find him. But the truth was that I had no idea where Tommy had gone or how to get him back.

My bladder ached, so I padded down the hallway to the bathroom. The dark house slept less fitfully than I. Renny's bedroom door stood half-open, his snores a stuffy rumble in the otherwise quiet night. He'd left his TV on again, the volume muted, and the frenetic dance of lights and shadows lit Warren's room enough for me to see him in his bed, tangled in his sheets, still wearing his headphones.

Renny's open door wasn't an invitation, but a remnant of his boyhood fears. When we were younger, he'd forced me to watch scary movies with him. They'd never frightened me, but Renny's imagination conjured glassy-eyed, horned demons from every corner and shadow, and after my parents had gone to bed, Warren would sneak into my room and sleep on my floor. In the morning he'd tell Mom and Dad I'd begged him to do it, and I'd never contradicted him.

Of all the horror movies we'd watched, I loved *The Texas*

Chainsaw Massacre best. And not that craptastic remake, either. My favorite part is the scene where Kirk is peeking through the screen door at the front of the house—during which Renny had screamed "There're skulls on the wall! Don't go in the house, you moron!"—and hears squealing from inside. Then, because, as Renny astutely noted, Kirk's an idiot, he walks into the foyer, past the staircase, to the open doorway in the back. Leatherface appears and—*WHACK!*—nails him once with a mallet. But that's not even the scary part. It's after, when Kirk is on the ground, twitching and convulsing, his face bloody, and Leatherface snatches him up, drags him deeper into the house, and slams the metal pocket door shut. I never forgot the paralyzing finality of that terrifying sound.

It taught me something—something other than not entering creepy houses with animal skulls decorating the walls. The scariest things in life aren't inbred, mallet-wielding psychos or machete-carrying mama's boys or even burned men with razor fingers who kill you in your dreams. Life's truest horror is a door that slams shut that can never be opened again.

When I finished peeing, I headed back to my room to catch a couple hours of sleep before school. Instead of closing my door, I left it open. Just a crack.

"Good night, Tommy," I whispered. "Sweet dreams, wherever you are."

14,000,090,000 LY

I FIRST NOTICED THE UNIVERSE WAS SHRINKING
after Tommy disappeared. After I'd spent weeks scouring the
Internet for digital fragments of him, clues he'd existed that
proved I wasn't delusional.

Tommy *loved* arguing with strangers under the screen
name TommysAlwaysRight, and he frequented dozens
of websites where he'd leap into discussions covering reli-
gion or politics or My Little Ponies. He didn't care what
he argued about or which side he took; Tommy lived for
picking apart the threads of a person's argument until they,
unable to defend themselves from his unassailable walls of
text, dissolved into profanity-laced, frothing-at-the-mouth
rants. He'd claimed he was honing his debating skills, but I
think Tommy enjoyed exposing people to the hypocrisy of
their own sincerely held beliefs.

Of course, Tommy's ability to argue any side of a debate made it difficult to know what, if anything, *he* actually believed.

Sadly, those hilarious manufactured feuds had vanished along with Tommy.

While searching a science message board where Tommy often tried to convince others that humans and dinosaurs had coexisted, I stumbled across a post alleging the universe was thirty billion light-years in diameter. I'd taken astronomy junior year and remembered Mr. Baker explaining that the universe was expanding so rapidly we lacked the ability to accurately evaluate its true size, but what we *could* observe measured roughly ninety-four billion light-years across.

Obviously someone on the Internet was wrong. I Googled "size of the universe," which returned a ludicrous 25,400,000 results. The first few links I clicked supported the thirty billion light-years theory. Even NASA's website confirmed the universe was smaller than Baker had claimed.

But Mr. Baker wasn't a real science teacher. He was a PE teacher who had only wound up teaching astronomy because Mrs. Manivong had won the lottery and skipped town. The most logical explanation was that Mr. Baker had screwed up.

I'd forgotten about the universe thing for a couple of weeks, until I stopped to watch a Hubble telescope documentary because I was too bored to look for anything better, during which the vaguely British, smooth-voiced narrator placed the size of the universe at eighteen billion light-years.

I checked the websites that had previously confirmed thirty billion light-years, but they had all changed to eighteen.

So . . . yeah.

I tiptoed down the stairs to avoid waking Dad, who was snoring on the couch. He was sleeping facing away from me, with his knees bent to keep his feet from hanging over the side. Most of the hair on Dad's head had migrated to his back in thick patches of gorilla fur. Thankfully, I took after our mother while Renny took after Dad, and I'd definitely dodged a genetic bullet.

As I grabbed my keys off the counter and headed out the garage, my phone buzzed and a dramatic guitar riff Lua had recorded to play when she called blared from the speaker. I dropped my keys, which clattered on the glazed terracotta tiles, and scrambled to silence my phone before it woke Dad.

Too late.

"Hey, Ozzie," Dad said. He sat up and knuckled his eyes. Pillow creases lined his left cheek, and patchy stubble covered his face. He looked like a man in need of strong coffee and a new life. "Heading to school?"

"Nah." I retrieved my keys off the floor. "Me and Lua thought we'd ditch and waste the day blowing money on strippers and drugs."

Dad nodded. Either he hadn't heard me or had chosen to tune out my sarcasm. Both my parents had PhDs in willful ignorance. "Sorry I missed dinner last night," he said.

"You didn't miss much," I said. He'd actually missed pork chops, corn on the cob, and—his favorite—fried okra, but his life sucked enough without me making it worse.

"Stayed late grading papers." Dad idly twisted his wedding band on his finger. "Listen, once your mom and I work out this house stuff, I'll get my own place. You and Warren can live with me."

By "house stuff" Dad meant my parents needed to sell the house without losing money, which seemed unlikely. Despite their marriage being deader than the cat I'd dissected in tenth grade, fate and a shitty housing market had forced them to continue living together. I was also pretty certain "grading papers" meant getting drunk and bitching about Mom to his friends.

"I get it," I said. I'd tried my best to play Delaware in the Pinkerton civil war, but Dad had always understood me best. I may have taken after my mother in the looks department, but that was about the only way in which we were alike. Warren, an unapologetic mama's boy, had surprised no one by siding with Mom.

My phone buzzed again; I silenced it. Lua would wait.

"At least you can sleep in a real bed once Renny leaves," I said.

Dad bobbed his head. "Maybe."

"It's your house too." I waited for Dad to agree, to stand up for himself, but my father avoided conflict like a fatal allergy. I jingled my keys. "I should go. Lua waits for no man."

"Hold up," Dad said. "You send in your college applications?"

"NYU, BU, UC Boulder, Amherst, U-Dub Seattle, Oberlin." I ticked the names off on my fingers and could practically hear Dad calculating the cost of my continued education. Because I didn't want to drive the man to start day-drinking, I added, "UF and New College, but maybe I'll kick around Cloud Lake. Take classes at the community college for a couple of semesters." I figured he'd like the idea, seeing as he taught there and I'd qualify for reduced tuition.

Dad tilted to the right and ripped one. "Sorry," he said, but he wasn't. "You're really considering community college? I assumed with everything you've gone through you'd want to flee Cloud Lake the day after graduation."

Everything I'd gone through meant Tommy and the plane

crash and my parents' divorce, even if Dad refused to out-right say so.

"It's only one idea. Why waste the money on an expensive school when I have no idea what I want to study?"

"That's what college is for. I started as a sociology major before I fell in love with literature." Dad furrowed his brow. "There's no shame in feeling uncertain about your future. I have faith you'll find your path."

"Whatever." My phone vibrated, and I imagined Lua yelling at the screen. "I'll be fine. It's Renny you should worry about. He'll be lucky to make it out of basic training with his fingers and toes intact."

Dad's head slumped forward. He stared at his hairy belly. "I worry about both my boys," he said. "Why do you think I'm bald?"

Lua Novak had crawled out of her mother's womb ass first and already a rock star. We met in sixth grade after she moved to Cloud Lake from Phoenix, AZ. She was bossy, foul-mouthed, a part-time kleptomaniac, and she'd fit in perfectly with me, Tommy, and Dustin.

Back then, Lua was "she" full-time. In ninth grade Lua began occasionally dressing like a boy. She informed us we should use whatever pronoun felt most appropriate for how she'd dressed that day. I'd understood the change wasn't a phase and had worried how others would treat her, but most people rationalized her behavior as the eccentricities of a future rock star.

I pulled up in front of Lua's house. He ran down the driveway, opened the back passenger door of my lime-green Chevy hatchback, and threw his bag and guitar across the seat.

"What are you wearing?" I asked.

Lua slammed the back door, opened the front, and slid into the passenger seat. "You don't like it?"

"It" consisted of a rumpled pin-striped brown suit, a blue dress shirt, and a brown tie. Usually when Lua wore masculine clothes, he bound his chest. But his boobs were practically busting out of his suit.

"Come on," I said. "We need to hurry if we're going to stop for coffee."

Lua buckled his seat belt. Without asking, he jacked his phone into the stereo. "Discovered this band last night. French new wave punk. With violins. You'll love them."

I hated them. Aside from not understanding a single word—mostly because I didn't speak French, but also because the band, Genoux Sanglants, didn't sing so much as scream—their voices and instruments bled together and sounded like an army of sadistic dental drills and someone vomiting. In French.

We hit up Dixie Cream Donuts—whose donuts, oddly enough, sucked—and waited in the drive-thru after placing our order. I turned down the stereo and watched Lua air drum on the dashboard until he realized I'd killed the music.

"What the hell, Ozzie?"

"Question: You're wearing a suit, but you didn't bind your chest? Are you more boy than girl today or more girl than boy?"

It was none of my business, but Lua and I talked about everything. At least, we had before Tommy disappeared.

"A little bit of both," Lua said.

I rolled forward, paid the cashier, and took the two Styrofoam cups she handed me, passing one to Lua.

Lua waited until I'd pulled onto Heron Road before peeling back the plastic tab on his coffee, inhaling the steam that rose from the surface, and gulping it down. Lua's tongue was made of heat-dispelling ceramic or something. My own coffee consisted of as much cream and sugar as actual coffee, and I had to let it cool before I could drink it, which usually meant slamming all twelve ounces while walking to first period, because Mr. Blakemore strictly enforced a no-food-or-drink-in-class policy.

"It's just . . . I want to be supportive. You've got it hard enough dealing with Trent and Cody and D'arcy."

"Like I give a steaming corn-filled pile what those inbred sociopaths say about me, Ozzie. People like them are the reason the gene pool needs a lifeguard." Once the first caffeine rush hit Lua, he sipped the rest of his coffee. "But, listen: I'm not going to freak out if you call me 'she' when I'm feeling more 'he.'"

"I guess," I said. "But I want you to know I'm here for you." I didn't add that I wished my friends had been as accommodating after Tommy disappeared.

"Hey," Lua said. "Speaking of being there for me. You're coming to the show at a/s/l Friday night, right?"

"Because you need a ride?"

"For emotional support." Lua grinned. "But if you're offering to drive, I accept."

"I'm working."

Lua frowned. "The bookstore closes at nine. The show doesn't start until ten thirty."

"Maybe," I said. "Why can't you use your mom's car?"

"Dinah? Home on a Friday night?" Lua rolled his eyes. "Get real, Ozzie."

"Just asking."

Lua adjusted his seat belt and angled to face me. "Say you'll come. Who knows, maybe you'll meet someone."

"Someone old," I muttered. "Besides, that new bouncer wouldn't let me in last time, and I don't want to wind up sitting in the parking lot waiting for your show to let out. Again."

Lua pressed his palms together. His short platinum-blond hair made his forehead wide and his brown eyes needy. "Please? You'll get in, even if I have to fold you up and stuff you in my guitar case."

I pulled into Cloud Lake High's student parking lot, which was already packed, and searched for a spot. "Fine. But I don't need to meet anyone."

"You do," Lua said. "If you don't get laid soon, your dick's going to shrivel up and fall off. It's a fact. I read it on the Internet."

"I *have* a boyfriend. Just because no one remembers him doesn't mean he isn't real." I couldn't find an empty space and had no choice but to park in the overflow field, which frequently flooded. Still, better muddy shoes later than a detention now. I grabbed my backpack from the trunk, and we trudged toward campus.

CLH was built like a penitentiary. The various buildings formed a ring around a large open space furnished with benches and palm trees, with gates that shut and locked while school was in session. Once inside, we could only escape through the administration building or fire exits.

Lua and I merged with the hordes of students wandering the quad. When I'd returned to school after Flight 1184, the other kids had treated me like a quasicelebrity. They'd wanted to know what it was like or why I'd gotten off the plane or whether Death was stalking me like in that terrible, not-at-all-scary movie *Final Destination*. But, like with most instances of dumb-luck fame, they eventually forgot about the crash and remembered I was a nobody, which was how I liked it.

We stopped by Lua's locker for homework he'd forgotten to complete. He glanced at me while he dialed in his combination. "Look, Ozzie, even if Tommy is real, and I'm not saying he is, he's been gone five months. It's time to move on."

"Like you and Jaime are moving on?"

"That's different."

"If the rumors are true and he hooked up with Birdie Johnson," I said, "then *he's* definitely moved on."

"My relationship with Jaime is complicated," Lua said. "But at least he's here. Where's Tommy, Oz?"

The first warning bell rang. I shook my head. "Whatever. I've got to get to class." I left Lua standing at his locker and headed across campus to the English building.

Lua should have been the one person who believed in me unconditionally. That he didn't made me question everything.

13,025,000,000 LY

I LOOKED FORWARD TO PHYSICS FOR TWO REASONS: It was my last class before lunch, and it was the only class I shared with my other best friend, Dustin Smeltzer.

Dustin sat at our lab table near the door, resting his arms and head on top of his backpack. He was a study in contradictions. Southern first name, Jewish last name, Chinese features—epicanthic folds over his eyes, straight black hair. The Smeltzers had adopted him as a baby, and as far as I knew, he'd never tried to locate his birth parents.

"What's up, Pinks?" He flashed me his stoner grin, which always brightened my day. It seemed impossible that someone who spent as much time high as Dustin could have earned the grades to be class valedictorian, but he'd held the position since freshman year.

"Same old," I said.

"Yeah." He slapped his thick textbook and spiral notepad on the desk and stuffed his backpack underneath. "My parents are out of town this weekend, so I've got Casa de Smeltzer to myself. You up for some pizza and Battle Gore: Coliseum?"

"Maybe." I slumped onto my stool next to Dustin.

"Don't 'maybe' me. You've been a ghost for months."

I dug my notebook and a pencil out of my bag and flipped through the pages until I found a blank one. "Been busy working. And I haven't been in the mood to butcher cyborg goblins."

"We don't have to game. We can chill. Me, you, Lua. You can't say no to pizza; it'll be like old times."

"Right," I said. "Like old times." Only, Dustin didn't remember that our "old times" used to include Tommy, and they couldn't exist without him.

The final bell rang, and Ms. Fuentes clapped her hands to calm us down. She was tall and bulky—thick arms, thick neck, chipmunk cheeks—but graceful. She was by far my toughest teacher, but she never pushed us harder than she thought we could handle.

"I know you're all eager to begin the chapter on particle-wave duality, but I thought we'd take a break to discuss your end-of-the-year projects."

The awake half of the class groaned. We'd heard

horror stories about Fuentes's final projects. Not only would it account for a quarter of our grades, but past students had referred to it as "the GPA slayer."

Dustin kicked me under the table and then rolled his eyes. He probably figured he could complete the project blindfolded, stoned, and with one hand tied behind his back. I lacked his confidence *and* his perfect test scores.

"Enough griping," Fuentes said. "You're *going* to enjoy this. Not only is it an opportunity for some of you to improve your grades, it's a chance for you to apply the theories we've learned this semester." She paused and looked around the room, her hawkish eyes seeming to say she'd rip anyone to shreds who disagreed.

"This year," she said, "you're going to work in teams of two to build working model roller coasters."

I perked up. A roller coaster didn't sound terrible, and teams were even better. Dustin and I could definitely build a sick ride.

"You'll have until May first to complete your projects, but I'll expect you to bring them in throughout the semester for me to evaluate your progress."

Tameka Lourdes raised her hand. Her wriggling fingers danced like surfacing earthworms. "How are you going to grade us?" she asked when Fuentes called on her.

Ms. Fuentes smiled, though it looked painful, like she'd expected the question. "I'll evaluate your roller coasters based on multiple criteria: the maximum speed your cars achieve, the audacity of your designs, and survivability. I want you to be daring, but to do so without killing your imaginary passengers."

Ignoring the part where the project could potentially destroy my hard-earned B-plus, it sounded fun.

Tameka raised her hand again, but didn't wait for Fuentes to call on her before saying, "Can we choose our own partners?"

Ms. Fuentes shook her head. "No."

It took a moment for her answer to register. Others were already complaining, and Fuentes let them continue a moment before waving us quiet.

"This year, I'm pairing you up based on your test score averages. The highest with the lowest, second highest with second lowest, and so forth."

I wanted to work with Dustin. Aside from being the smartest person I knew, we were already friends, and we could work without the initial awkwardness of getting to know each other.

Surprisingly, Dustin spoke up. "Don't you think that's unfair? I mean, no offense to those at the bottom, but why should I suffer because they don't study?"

Ms. Fuentes clapped her hands twice. The crack cut through the noise and silenced us. "This isn't up for debate, Mr. Smeltzer."

While Ms. Fuentes opened her notebook, the students around me quietly grumbled and shook their heads. No one seemed thrilled with Fuentes's idea; not even those at the bottom of the grade curve who clearly had the most to gain.

"In addition to working together on your final projects, these will also be your new lab partner assignments for the remainder of the year." Fuentes flashed a warning look, daring us to complain. No one did. Not out loud anyway.

"Dustin Smeltzer," Fuentes said. "You're working with Jake Ortiz." It surprised no one that Dustin held the highest test average and Jake the lowest.

"That's so wrong," Dustin said. "Jake's not even here. He's *never* here."

Ms. Fuentes shrugged. "Then you'd better make certain he starts attending class regularly." She smiled before moving on. "Tameka Lourdes, your partner is Martin Burlingame. Ella Boggs, you're with Caitlin Morrow. Oswald Pinkerton, your partner is Calvin Frye."

"Ouch," Dustin whispered. "Sorry about your luck, Pinks." He clapped me on the back.

Calvin Frye? Really? I glanced over my shoulder at the

lab table in the farthest corner where Calvin Frye slept on his desk with his hoodie pulled over his head. Last year he'd captained the school wrestling team and been Coach Reevey's state-level superstar. He'd also skipped eighth grade, so he was a year younger than the rest of us, had started taking college classes in tenth grade, and was voted class president three years in a row. He'd been popular, athletic, and Dustin's only serious valedictory rival.

But something had changed between junior and senior year. He'd quit wrestling, had dropped out of student government, his grades had taken a kamikaze dive, and he'd stopped speaking to his friends. The only time anyone saw his face anymore was in the halls, because he spent class time sleeping. No one knew why, but loads of people had theories.

And Ms. Fuentes had just assigned me and Calvin to work together on a project that could destroy my grade.

Fuentes finished reading off the teams, and informed us she expected us to sit with our new partners next class. Then she launched into a lecture about the dynamics of roller coasters, and how she participated in a club that built them for fun, which was both sad and not unexpected.

I stopped paying attention and began trying to figure out how Calvin Frye fit into the puzzle. It couldn't have been a coincidence that Fuentes had paired us together, but

I didn't understand what role Calvin could possibly have to play in the mysterious shrinking of the universe and Tommy's disappearance. If Flight 1184 had exploded to send me a message to stay in Cloud Lake, what message was I being sent by having to work with Calvin Frye?

12,066,011,000 LY

MRS. PETRIDIS WOULD'VE BURNED THE BOOKSTORE to the ground if not for her justifiable fear of prison. Mr. Petridis had been the one who'd loved books. When he sank their retirement fund into opening Petridis Books and More, which everyone in Cloud Lake simply called "the bookstore," he'd promised his wife he would run the store and she could spend her days in the studio he'd constructed for her in the stockroom working on her true passion: building taxidermy dioramas depicting scenes from Alfred Hitchcock movies.

Morbid, yes, but no one could transform a dead squirrel into Norman Bates like Mrs. Petridis.

Except Mr. Petridis had died. He'd suffered a stroke while arranging the books he'd planned to display for National Pizza Month, and had left Mrs. Petridis as the sole owner of a shop she'd never wanted but couldn't bring herself to burn down.

I worked at the bookstore a couple of nights a week and most weekends, giving Mrs. Petridis the opportunity to plug away on her latest project, which at the moment was a scene from *Spellbound*, created using small birds. Her only rule was that I not bother her, and I never did. She often joked that I ran the bookstore better than Mr. Petridis ever had.

As far as jobs went, I didn't hate it. Mrs. Petridis paid minimum wage, but so long as I completed my duties—which mostly consisted of shelving books, helping customers, and ringing up sales—I could spend my free time reading or studying. She also let me "borrow" books on the condition that I return them in sellable shape. The bookstore functioned as my research center for Operation Find Tommy and was where I'd formulated many of my ideas about what had happened to him.

The bookstore itself was cozy but not crowded, with posters of classic novels framed and hung on the walls. And it was filled with that wonderful book smell that anyone who's ever been near a book will recognize. It's more than the smell of paper; it's the smell of the high seas and adventure and far-off worlds. It's the smell of a billion billion words, each a portal to somewhere new.

In a corner of the store, Mr. Petridis had set off a section and decorated it with tables and chairs and comfy single-seater sofas to encourage customers to hang out. Customers like Skip, one of our regulars. To my knowledge, he'd never purchased a single book, but he lugged a Royal Quiet De Luxe typewriter—which, in defiance of its name, wasn't particularly quiet—into the store most evenings and spent hours pecking at the keys, amassing a stack of pages for his book, which he called *The Countless Lives of August J. Ostermeyer: A Secret History of the Immortal Who Ruled the World*. Mrs. Petridis frequently complained about the noise of Skip's typewriter, but I didn't mind. He was Cloud Lake's own Henry Darger.

Friday nights were usually busy because of the theater next door. Moviegoers often wandered into the store to kill time and annoy me with inane questions about books they had zero intention of buying. After the first premovie rush had died down—it was opening weekend for the second movie based on the Patient F comics: *The Nightmare King and the Horde of Unthinkables*—and I'd finished my shelving, I settled behind the register with the copy of *One Hundred Years of Solitude* I'd been crawling through for the last week. Tommy had frequently "suggested" books I should read, and he'd said *One Hundred Years of Solitude* would change my life, but I found it difficult to lose myself in the many misfortunes of the Buendía family. Maybe the story lost something in the translation—Tommy had read it in Spanish—or maybe the city of mirrors simply mirrored my own life too well.

I stuck a bookmark between the pages, abandoned Gabriel García Márquez for the night, and picked up a book about quantum physics. I was most interested in the idea of the multiverse, as I thought it might help explain where Tommy had gone. I didn't necessarily understand most of what I read—especially the stuff about p-branes and the potential that our universe consisted of seven or more dimensions folded so small we couldn't perceive them—but I imagined the possibility that Tommy had been sucked into one of those other dimensions, that he was still here, maybe even right beside me, but that I simply couldn't see him.

Another theory, equally as unlikely, was that *I* was the one who'd been drawn into a parallel world. One in which everything was exactly the same except Tommy had never been born. Only, if that one were true, then it meant a version of me that had never known Tommy had existed and been displaced by my arrival, and I couldn't help wondering where he'd gone—if we'd switched places and he was in my world, living my life.

Hell, every possibility seemed as implausible as the next, but I kept coming up with them, hoping to stumble onto the truth and find a way to return to Tommy.

The electronic bell at the front of the store chirped, and Trent Williams, D'Arcy Gaudet, and Cody Dawson walked through the door. Trent was a standard-issue jock troglodyte—thick arms, buzz cut, cocky swagger—Cody his parroty sycophant, and D'Arcy a type-A know-it-all with a YouTube channel dedicated exclusively to promoting all things D'Arcy Gaudet.

Trent spotted me standing behind the registers, and a grin broke over his face. "Hey! It's Pink Lady."

Growing up with the name "Oswald" had sucked enough without the added shame of the surname "Pinkerton." I'd spent sixth grade being called "Pink Lady," though most of my peers had stopped using the unimaginative nickname in middle school. Some people, it seemed, never grew up.

"Trent." I glowered at him and walked out from behind the counter. "I wasn't aware you could read."

"Funny," Trent said. "Isn't he funny?"

"Yeah," Cody said. "Too bad he doesn't realize he's the joke."

D'Arcy rolled her eyes. "Ugh, why are we here? If I get stuck sitting in the front row, I'm going to scream."

"See what I gotta deal with?" Trent said.

I detested D'Arcy Gaudet, but she could've done better than Trent. Not only was he messing around with at least three other girls, but everyone knew he had a thing for Lua, though he'd broken a kid's nose in tenth grade for mentioning it.

"Can I help you find something?" I asked, trying to keep my voice neutral.

Trent wandered around the front displays, picking up books and dropping them on the floor. I could've told him to stop or called Mrs. Petridis from the back to kick him out, but it was easier to let Trent be a dick. Eventually he'd grow bored and leave.

"So I hear you're working with Calvin Frye in Fuentes's class," Trent said.

"You heard correctly," I said. I resisted the urge to pick up the books Trent had dropped, knowing he'd only toss them down again.

Trent nodded. Cody shadowed Trent's every move, but D'Arcy stood near the door, her arms folded across her chest.

"You oughta watch out for that kid," Trent said.

"Didn't you guys used to be friends?" I asked, though I already knew the answer. They'd joined the wrestling team together, and had been practically inseparable until Calvin went all black-hoodie-and-no-one-understands-my-unfathomable-pain.

"Only 'cause I felt bad for the kid," Trent said.

D'Arcy let out a high-pitched sigh. "Oh my God! Can we go already?"

The doorbell chirped again. I glanced toward the front, grateful for the opportunity to escape Trent, but was surprised when Mrs. Ross shuffled in. She was wearing loose jeans and a baggy sweater, her hair was springy and big, and she wore oversize sunglasses despite the lack of sun or bright lights.

"Seriously," Trent said, like he was oblivious that another human being had walked into the store. "Calvin's some kind of pathological liar. You can't believe anything he says."

I was only half listening to Trent because I was watching Tommy's mom. I still thought of her as Tommy's mom even though she didn't remember having a son.

"Coach thought Cal was his best wrestler," Trent was saying, "but I always knew there was something off about the kid."

Mrs. Ross glanced in my direction. I couldn't see her eyes, but I imagined them widening slightly when she recognized me, though to her I was no longer the boy who used to play at her trailer and for whose bloody knees she'd kept a stash of superhero Band-Aids, and was instead the crazy kid who'd shown up at her house on the Fourth of July and then called the police when she'd denied having a son.

"I wouldn't spend too much time with him if I were you." Trent really couldn't take the hint that I wasn't listening.

"Sure," I said. "Whatever." I moved past Trent toward Mrs. Ross, but she turned and hurried back out the door.

I wanted to chase after her, but I couldn't leave the store, especially not with Trent hanging around. And what would I have said to her? What *could* I have said?

"And another thing—" Trent started, but I cut him off.

"Look, I don't know what your hard-on for Calvin Frye is about, but we're working on a stupid roller coaster together, and that's all. Okay?"

Trent's mouth hung open. He glared at me for a moment. Then, his eyes locked on mine, he swept the holiday cookbooks onto the floor.

I kept my mouth shut because his psycho smirk made me think he was one insult away from taking a giant crap on the carpet to spite me.

"Come on," he said to Cody and D'Arcy. "We're gonna be late for the movie."

I waited for them to leave before I picked up the books. Trent was a dick, and I didn't care what he said about me or Calvin. It was Mrs. Ross I couldn't stop thinking about. Even though she'd run the moment I'd tried to speak to her, I could've sworn she'd hesitated. Almost like she'd wanted to talk to me too.

But I'd probably just imagined it.

12,000,003,087 LY

DUSTIN CLUNG TO MY ARM LIKE HE FEARED A GAY
riptide was going to carry him out to sea and spit his body
back onto the shore covered in glitter and rainbows. I didn't
learn Lua had invited him to her show until he met us in the
parking lot. Dustin had turned eighteen on Halloween, and
the bouncer checked his ID and drew a fat *X* on his left hand
in black marker. I didn't think the bouncer, a tall drag queen,
was going to let me pass, but Lua managed to sweet-talk me
into the club, just like she'd promised.

The first time Lua had dragged me to a/s/l, I'd expected to
discover my tribe. Instead, I'd found an adrenalized horde of
radically different personalities, bonded only by their status as
outsiders. The club offered them sanctuary. A place where they
didn't have to pretend to fit in. A place to relieve themselves of
their chameleon skin for a couple of hours and dance.

Where I'd hoped to find a unified clan, I found a matry-oshka doll of diversity.

Swishy gay boys trading catty insults and broad-shouldered gay boys in cowboy boots. Butch girls and punk rock princesses. Boys who kissed boys and girls who kissed girls and both boys and girls who believed who they kissed was none of my damn business. Drag queens and transgender men and women and people like Lua who defied labels.

Despite their many differences, they were *my* people, even though I still felt like an outsider. The only person I'd ever truly felt at home with was Tommy.

Dustin tapped my shoulder and pointed toward a dimly lit corner of the bar by the DJ booth. "I think that dude's checking you out, Pinks!" he shouted over a hundred other conversations and the bass-heavy music blasting from the wall-mounted speakers.

I glanced sidelong at my supposed admirer. The guy, who was now smiling in our direction, wore no *X* on his hand, which indicated he was at least twenty-one.

I didn't appreciate the attention Dustin's unsubtle pointing had drawn. The last time I'd watched Lua play at a/s/l, older men in the crowd had smiled and winked at me and grabbed my ass. I'd felt like the last piece of bacon at breakfast. A man my father's age had even tried to stick his hand down my pants on the dance floor, and when I'd pushed him away, he'd called me a tease. As if wearing pants was an invitation for any man with hands to attempt to peel me out of them.

The guy in the corner seemed harmless enough, though. He was tall and wiry with spiky black hair—an obvious dye job—and sleeves of colorful Japanese-inspired tattoos decorating both arms. I couldn't tell from one covert glance whether he was a nice guy or a potential stalker, but thankfully, he wasn't eyeballing *me*.

"Yeah," I said. "I'm pretty sure he's checking *you* out."

"Really?" Dustin stood taller and returned the guy's smile.

"Don't lead him on."

Dustin shrugged. "Sometimes it's nice to feel wanted."

I grabbed Dustin's shirt and pulled him toward the bar to buy a bottled water. On the way we ran into a couple of girls I'd met before—Lua's groupies—and we chatted while waiting for the show to begin. Dustin, ignoring my advice, kept flirting with the tattoo guy, who eventually joined us. His name was Nikos, and he spoke with an accent I didn't recognize. Dustin came clean about being straight, but it turned out he and Nikos were both fans of Akira Kurosawa movies, and they geeked out arguing whether *Rashomon* or *Seven Samurai* was his best film.

The girls—Beth, Blythe, and Mindi—dragged me onto

the dance floor for a couple of songs, and by the time the spotlights flared and the DJ lowered the music, sweat slicked my skin and my brain swam in an ocean of feel-good endorphins, leaving me happier than I'd felt in a long time. I couldn't remember when I'd last allowed myself to think about something other than Tommy, and I immediately felt guilty. But I was there for Lua, so I did my best to stay in the moment and give her my full attention.

Lua stood on the tiny stage behind her keyboard, decked out in a striped corset with sewn-on glittery plastic gemstones, a fluffy pink ballerina skirt, and sheer powder-blue tights. She'd slicked back her hair and layered pale makeup and bright rouge on her cheeks so that she looked like a weirdly sexy porcelain doll reject that had crawled from the depths of my nightmares. Lucky on bass, Poe on guitar, and Claudia on drums wore conservative blacks and grays like they were trying to blend into the background, though it truthfully wouldn't have mattered what they wore. Lua was a star, and everyone else but a dim shadow in comparison.

I didn't know Lua's bandmates well—she kept that part of her life oddly private—but they, along with Lua, played the roles of time travelers who zipped back and forth through history and sang about their adventures. It was kind of a gimmick, but also kind of awesome.

Lua's groupies—who called themselves Lunettes—screamed when she leaned toward the mic, drowning out the smattering of applause from everyone else. Dustin and his new friend pushed their way through the crowd to stand beside us.

"Yeah," Lua said in a disaffected, flippant tone I knew she'd spent countless hours in front of a mirror perfecting. "So we're Your Mom's a Paradox, and we've traveled through time to rock your asses off." Without further introduction, Lua launched into "Heretic in Hosen."

Lua seduced the crowd with her raspy, raw mezzo-soprano. Her voice strutted and clawed into the club's dark corners, daring us not to fall in love with her. Lua inhabited every note, allowed the music to possess her. And we were mesmerized. I'd watched Lua play dozens of times, and even *I* fell in love with her a little more that night.

The crowd bounced to the frenetic rhythm and sang along even though most didn't know the words. They pumped their fists in the air and howled their approval at the end of each song.

"Damn!" Dustin shouted into my ear. "Lua's killing it tonight!"

He wasn't wrong. The band played "Swapping Petticoats for Rifles," "No One Died in the Longest War," and "The

Enchantress of Numbers." Lua had just traded her keyboard for her guitar to play a jaunty song called "In the Future We All Eat Bugs" when the hairs on the tips of my ears rose.

I stood on the balls of my feet and scanned the crowd. I recognized some of the a/s/l regulars, most of whom were watching Lua and definitely not looking at me. The one person I *wasn't* expecting to see was Calvin Frye, leaning against the bar, wearing his familiar black hoodie despite the oppressive heat. He looked like he'd wandered into the wrong club by accident.

What the hell is he doing here? Since Fuentes had assigned us to work together, Calvin had continued his habit of sleeping through class and acting like the rest of us didn't exist. I certainly hadn't anticipated running into him at a/s/l. I considered ignoring him, but I remembered what Trent had said earlier and curiosity overrode good judgment. I zigzagged through the press of bodies until I reached Calvin. He kept his hands buried in his pockets but nodded when I approached.

"What're you doing here?" I asked. When he didn't answer, I leaned closer and repeated my question louder.

Calvin motioned at the stage with his chin. "Came to see the band." He said it casually, like he snuck into club shows every weekend. "They're good."

"I know. How'd you get in?"

Calvin smiled. His front teeth were crammed together and crooked. "Fake ID."

"For real?"

"Uh . . . yeah?"

I pointed at the *X* on his hand. "If you have a fake ID, why not make yourself twenty-one?"

Calvin shrugged. "Do I look twenty-one to you?"

"You barely look sixteen," I said. "Are you really here for the show?"

"What?" he shouted.

The music made conversation practically impossible, and I was torn between watching Lua play the best show of her life and wanting to know why Calvin had invaded my club. "In the Future We All Eat Bugs" ended, and I recognized the opening notes to Lua's cover of "Ziggy Stardust." I made up my mind and tugged Calvin's sleeve. "Let's go outside."

"Why?"

"Glitter cannon," I said. "Lua always brings out the glitter cannon for 'Ziggy Stardust.'"

Calvin nodded. We slid and shoved our way to the back of the club, outside through a door that opened onto a walled patio surrounded by palm trees. The graffiti decorating the walls changed constantly. Last time, a spray-painted anthropomorphic banana had adorned the bricks. Tonight the cast of *The Muppet Show*—gruesome and zombified—loomed menacingly over us.

Though we hadn't completely escaped the music, I could at least hear myself think again. Most everyone was inside, but a few people had migrated to the patio, probably to escape the heat of over two hundred bodies packed together. They relaxed on benches, smoking and chatting. An enthusiastic and oblivious couple pawed at each other shamelessly in a corner.

I perched on the edge of the large circular planter that dominated the patio, and in which grew no actual plants.

"Do they really fire a glitter cannon?" Calvin asked. He sat beside me and folded his hands in his lap.

"They do," I said. "And it's awesome until you spend the next month picking glitter off your skin and out of your hair."

"Oh."

"Why are you really here?" I asked.

"Why do you care?"

Under different circumstances I wouldn't have given Calvin's presence much thought. But we'd hardly spoken during the last three-and-a-half years of high school, and now not only had Ms. Fuentes thrown us together to work on a project, but Trent had specifically warned me about him, and then he'd shown up at *my* club, none of which I believed were coincidences.

"It's just . . . it's weird."

Calvin fidgeted with his hands. "I guess I thought we should discuss our physics project."

"At a gay club? How'd you even know I'd be here?"

"I didn't." Calvin spoke tentatively, like I was a teacher calling on him to answer a question he was unprepared for. "Lua posted the show's details on SnowFlake, and she's your friend, so . . ."

"So you're a stalker?"

Calvin inhaled deeply through his nose and exhaled through his mouth. A vast-ocean sigh I couldn't tell whether he was swimming or drowning in. "I know you don't like me."

"I don't know you well enough to not like you."

"Then we should get to know each other."

The door banged open, releasing a pent-up cheer. The audience's lusty voices surged into the starry night.

There goes the glitter cannon.

Before Calvin's transformation from most-likely-to-succeed-at-everything to most-likely-to-spend-the-weekends-writing-bad-poetry, I'd admired him. According to my journals—the ones written by the me who'd never known Tommy—I'd even crushed on Calvin in tenth grade. But I didn't know him, and getting to know him would distract me from finding Tommy.

"We don't have to become best friends to work on the roller coaster," I said.

"Oh," he said, and maybe I was reading something that didn't exist, but his eyes drooped and I swear he looked disappointed.

"I'm not trying to be mean, but do you even care about the project? You don't seem to care about anything lately."

"I care," Calvin said. "It's just . . . stuff."

"Ah, yes. Stuff does suck." My attempt at a joke fell flat, and I didn't want to miss the end of Lua's show, so I said, "Look, we can work on our project, and I can't stop you from stalking me, but you don't need to pretend to want to be my friend."

"I'm not pretending," Calvin said. "Whatever. You're right. And it's not like the project matters anyway."

"Of course it matters."

"Not if you're going to waste your life waiting around Cloud Lake for Tommy." Calvin stared at me like I alone existed. Like the club and Cloud Lake and the whole of the universe had melted away, leaving us floating together in an empty void.

It took me a moment to process Calvin's words. When my brain caught up, I said, "Wait, what? Do you remember Tommy?"

Calvin stood. I was used to being taller than other kids my age except Tommy, but right then I'd never felt smaller. "I shouldn't have come." He took off inside.

I leaped up and caught the door before it slammed shut. Calvin Frye couldn't just come to *my* club under the pretense of watching Lua's show, drop Tommy's name, and run away. If he remembered Tommy, I needed to know, and I'd yank out his fingernails for the information if necessary.

Onstage, Lua launched into her customary closing song, "Caligula's Horse Was a Senator, Of Course." The heat in the club choked me, and the stage lights cast dancing shadows on the floor and walls, making it difficult to locate Calvin.

I climbed on top of a chair and scanned the crowd until I spotted him near the front door. I shoved and pushed my way toward him, ignoring the curses and grabby hands, and ran into the night. I stood on the sidewalk, looking east and then west, but Calvin had vanished.

I turned to the bouncer, a tall drag queen who used the stage name Bella Donna but whose real name was Adonis, and said, "Did you see a guy leave? Black hoodie, blond hair?"

Bella Donna smiled, her ruby-painted lips revealing glossy white teeth. She laid her hand on my shoulder and squeezed. "Oh, baby. Chasing boys is amateur hour. If he's worth it, he'll find you."

"It's not . . . he stole something from me."

Bella shook her head, looking at me like I was some pathetic, horny kid. "Sorry, baby. I didn't see him."

I missed Tommy so badly that nothing else mattered. I tried to hold on to hope, I told myself I'd find him or he'd return, but my life was crumbling—Warren had joined the army, my parents had fallen out of love, and the future was rushing toward me with ruthless inevitability. I could've handled those things with Tommy to share the burden. Without him, I collapsed under their weight. I crouched on the sidewalk in front of a/s/l and cried. I shook and sobbed, and I couldn't stop.

"Grow up, dude," said a faceless passerby.

"You want me to mess up that pretty face of yours, boy?" Bella said, her voice fierce and protective.

"Faggots," the other voice said, but it sounded farther away.

Bella knelt beside me and wrapped her arm around my shoulders. I got snot on her sequined dress. "It's all right, baby. No boy's worth crying over. Trust me."

But she was wrong. I shed a million tears on the sidewalk that night, and Tommy was worth every one.

By the time I got home, the universe had shrunk to ten billion light-years across.

TOMMY

I CHASE TOMMY DOWN THE SIDEWALK, CALLING
after him to wait. My backpack, riding low on my shoulders,
slaps my spine as I run.

"Come on, Tommy! What's wrong?"

Cloud Lake Middle School is less than a mile from Tommy's
trailer, and Mom lets me walk home with him to play after
school, but Tommy isn't in the mood to play. I knew he was mad
at me when class let out, and I should have ridden the bus home.
But I want to know why he's so angry.

"Tommy? Why won't you talk to me?"

He doesn't answer. Tommy's taller than me by almost half a foot.
I take three steps to every one of his. He grew during the summer
between seventh and eighth grade. Sprouted like a dandelion. His
voice broke into a deep bass, and he grew fuzz on his upper lip that
he refused to shave until Lua told him it looked like worn-out Velcro.

We're both sweaty by the time we reach his trailer. It's actually a manufactured home—not quite a trailer, not really a house, and it rests on cement blocks instead of wheels—but Tommy's always called it "the trailer." The patchy grass out front is littered with cigarette butts and crushed beer cans. A semicircle of beat-up lawn chairs sits off to the side, and Mr. Ross and his drinking buddies will occupy them by sunset. One of my parents always makes sure to pick me up before Tommy's father returns home from work.

Tommy flings open the screen door and lets it slam shut behind him. I stand outside debating whether I should call my dad to see if he can cut out of teaching early to rescue me, which I know he can't, so I end up shucking my backpack onto the dirt and flopping onto one of the chairs. The cheap plastic-woven straps creak, and I wonder how they don't break.

I'm only alone a minute or two before Tommy's mom peeks her head out the door. "Ozzie? That you?"

"Yeah."

"You want to come in?"

"That's okay. I'm good."

Mrs. Ross scrunches her face and then steps out. I once asked Tommy why his skin wasn't as dark as his mom's—I was seven and stupid and Cloud Lake isn't exactly the most diverse town in the world. I thought it was because his father was white, but Tommy said that wasn't it, but he was glad, which I didn't understand at the time because I thought Mrs. Ross was at least as beautiful as my own mother. She's got sharp new-penny eyes and cheeks that honest-to-God glow when she smiles. But she moves slowly, like she's afraid to disturb the air around her. Today she bound her hair in a handkerchief and is wearing frayed, paint-stained overalls. Also, she smells like turpentine.

"You and Tommy fighting?"

"I guess."

"What about?" She leans against the side of the trailer.

"Don't know."

I expect her to keep prying, and I'd tell her why Tommy's angry if I knew, but instead she says, "Want to see what I'm working on?" I nod. "Follow me, then."

Mrs. Ross walks around the side of the trailer. The manufactured homes are set so close together I could reach out and touch them. Behind the trailer isn't exactly a yard, but if you ignore the other trailers and the people peeking out their back windows, you can pretend well enough.

The first thing I notice—because it's impossible to miss—is an enormous crucifix propped against the back side of the trailer. The cross is painted red, white, and blue like the American flag.

"You like it?" she asks.

"I don't get it," I say. "Is it finished?" Jesus is wearing gray

slacks and shiny black dress shoes, but he's naked from the waist up.

Mrs. Ross shakes her head. "I bought the pants at Goodwill for a dollar, but I'm having a devil of a time finding a shirt and jacket that fit." She walks toward the crucifix, which is taller than her, and smooths a wrinkle out of Jesus's pants. "It's an interpretation of the corporate bailouts. How the government shelled out billions to save the folks who drove us off the cliff but didn't give a damn about those of us really hurting."

"Oh." I don't know much about politics. Tommy's interested in that stuff, but it bores me to sleep. "It's nice."

She takes a last look at her work before sitting on a pile of stacked paving stones Mr. Ross has been promising for years he's going to use to build a path to the front door. "You and Tommy have been friends for a long time. You're good for him. Good for each other."

I kick the dirt with the toe of my sneaker. "He's my best friend."

"Tommy doesn't always know how to say what he means. He takes after his daddy that way. Sometimes what's in his head and what's in his heart are too big for words. You know what I'm getting at?"

I shake my head. "Not really."

Mrs. Ross smiles. There are those cheeks, lit up like fireflies.

"*Give him time. He'll work out how to tell you what he's sore about.*"

"*Okay. I think I'll go wait for my dad around front.*"

I take up the same chair I was sitting in earlier. I've got an hour before Dad picks me up, so I dig out my battered copy of The Giver *to start reading the chapters Mr. Strother assigned us.*

I'm lost in the black-and-white world—where life is unambiguous and easy to grasp, everyone says what they mean with clarity and specificity, and each person understands their role in society—and I don't notice Tommy standing in front of me until he clears his throat. I look up. He's holding two plastic cups of apple juice; he offers me one.

"*Thought you might be hot.*"

"*Thanks.*" *I take the juice even though I'm not thirsty.*

Tommy sits, leaving a chair between us. "*You see what Mama's working on out back?*"

"*Pretty crazy.*"

"*Yeah.*"

Tommy's jaw muscles twitch and he bites the corner of his bottom lip. He's gazing into his juice like he can scry the surface for answers. I wish I could help—I wish our lives were black and white, the solutions to our problems readily available—but I don't even know the questions.

Finally, he says, "You really taking Sonia to the Halloween dance?"

"She asked me, so I guess." I sip my juice, which is the cheap kind from the dollar store and mostly sugar. "She didn't really give me a choice."

"Oh."

"It's no big deal."

"You going to kiss her?"

"I don't know."

Tommy throws me side-eye. "Do you want to kiss her?"

At Noah Trumbull's last birthday party—my first boy-girl party—some of the kids played spin the bottle. I sat out the game because the idea of kissing a randomly chosen girl scared me more than being trapped in a car while a rabid, blood-thirsty dog tried to break through the windows to eat me.

I'm not scared of girls—Lua's my best friend, after all—and a lot of my friends are girls, but the boys in my class who joke around about kissing and tell stories about the girls they've kissed—most of which are probably lies—act like kissing is no big deal. Only, I can't help feeling like it is a big deal. Like it's something that deserves to be treated as more than a party game.

I turn toward Tommy. "Is that why you're mad at me? Because you think I'm going to kiss Sonia?"

Tommy shrugs. "No."

"Lua says Kimber's got a crush on you. I bet she'll say yes if you ask her to the dance. Maybe she'll even let you kiss her."

"I don't want to kiss Kimber," Tommy says. He glances my way again. "I was kind of thinking I wanted to kiss you."

"Me?"

Tommy clenches his jaw. "Yeah. You." The way he spits out the answer feels like he's daring me to rag on him for it.

I've never considered kissing Tommy, but the thought of it isn't nearly as frightening as kissing Sonia or a girl chosen for me by a fickle bottle's spin.

"All right," I say.

"All right, what?"

"You can kiss me."

"Right here?"

"Why not?"

Tommy scans the area around the trailer. His father's still at work and his mother's in the back. No one's watching. Tommy slides to the chair next to mine, closing the distance between us. "You sure?"

"Yeah."

He licks his lips, leans over, and kisses me. I'm not sure what I'm supposed to do, so I close my eyes and push my mouth against his. The whole thing only lasts a couple of seconds, but a gentle electric current runs through my skin, and I feel a pleasant stirring in my groin that I like but don't understand.

When I open my eyes, Tommy's staring at me.

"Well?" he asks.

I smile. I'm not sure if I'd feel the same way if I kissed a girl, but I suspect I wouldn't. Kissing Tommy felt important. It felt honest.

"How about we skip the dance, go trick-or-treating on our own—maybe egg Mr. Glass's house for stiffing you after you cut his lawn—stay up all night, and watch scary movies in my room?"

Tommy grins. When he flashes that gap between his front teeth, the world is right. Tommy's smile is, and always has been, my favorite thing.

"And maybe we can try kissing again," I say. "I want to get it right, so I think we should practice. A lot."

9,970,000,000 LY

NOT ALL OF MY THEORIES ABOUT TOMMY'S DISAPPEARANCE were completely fantastical. The most likely hypothesis was that Tommy had simply run away, which was why I'd tried to fly to Seattle to find him, especially since his home life sucked so badly.

Once, when Tommy was nine, he'd left the cap off the toothpaste. Mr. Ross had found it and dragged Tommy out of bed by his ear in the middle of the night, while Mrs. Ross sat in the kitchen unable or unwilling to stop her husband. He screamed at Tommy, and when Tommy couldn't offer a satisfactory reason for not replacing the cap, Mr. Ross threw a plastic brush at him, which missed, hit the wall, and shattered. A plastic chip ricocheted, cutting Tommy below his eye. A millimeter higher and it might have blinded him. Then his father squeezed the entire tube of toothpaste onto the counter and forced Tommy to brush his teeth with it every morning and night until he'd used it all. Mr. Ross didn't relent either, not even when ants swarmed and became trapped in the disgusting glob.

The only problem with my theory about Tommy running away was that it left me with unanswered questions like: Why hadn't he taken me with him? And how had he erased himself from everyone's memories but mine?

There was also the issue of Flight 1184. I didn't believe for a second that the crash had been an accident or a coincidence. The NTSB investigators had recovered the plane's black box, which they said had indicated a mechanical failure of some sort—though I suspected they hadn't been completely forthcoming with the information—had caused the crash, but I had a feeling it was connected to Tommy and the shrinking universe. I just didn't know how.

No matter which way I turned the puzzle in my brain, I wound up with too many questions, exactly zero answers, and more theories than I could hope to test. Like that my life was a dream. Or a computer simulation. I was a self-aware character in a metafictional book à la *The Neverending Story*. Each scenario was wilder and less plausible than the ones before, but any one of them was possible.

Worst of all, I couldn't ignore the most obvious question: *What if I made Tommy up?*

But just because I couldn't ignore the question didn't mean I considered it the answer. Besides, I needed to believe in something, so I chose to believe in Tommy.

I arrived early to physics to talk to Calvin.

If Calvin remembered Tommy—even if he only remembered passing him in the hall or seeing him at some party from across the room—he could prove I hadn't made him up, and then my friends and my parents and the endless parade of therapists would have to believe me. As screwed up as he seemed, Calvin was my first real lead in months.

I'd barely slept Sunday night, rehearsing what to say to Calvin. My stomach had twisted itself into balloon animals through my first four periods, and by the time I reached physics, I wanted to puke. Only, Calvin wasn't there when I arrived.

Ms. Fuentes was standing in front of the whiteboard, and she smiled at me when I threw my backpack on my lab table. "Morning, Ozzie. You're early today."

"Trying to catch Calvin before the bell."

"Good for you." She turned from the board and rested her hands on her lab table. "I expect you boys to build me an exceptional roller coaster."

"No pressure or anything." I sat on my stool as other

students, none of whom were Calvin, filed into the classroom, their faces buried in their phones.

Dustin swept through the door and slugged me on the shoulder. He scanned the room for Jake Ortiz, who had actually made an appearance, though he looked rough and crusty.

"Better go check in with my slacker lab partner," Dustin said.

"Good luck with that."

The final bell rang, and Calvin Frye rode its fading echoes through the door, took the seat next to me, and immediately rested his head on the desk. He wasn't even carrying books, and he smelled like sour gym socks.

Ms. Fuentes launched into our next lesson, and I waited until she turned her back before I elbowed Calvin.

"Hey," I whispered. "Wake up. We need to talk." Calvin grunted but didn't move. I nudged him again. "Don't pretend you can't hear me."

"Ozzie?" Ms. Fuentes asked. I hadn't noticed she'd stopped drawing diagrams on the board. "Is there a problem?"

"No, Ms. Fuentes."

For the rest of class, I chafed at not being able to talk to Calvin. I was so close to maybe getting some real answers, and I couldn't even get him to acknowledge me. I wanted to grab him around the neck and shake him until he told me everything he knew about Tommy, but instead I had to wait. I watched the sadistic clock at the front of the class slowly count down the minutes, and I definitely didn't hear a single word of Ms. Fuentes's lecture.

The bell rang, and Calvin Frye rushed out of the classroom. I refused to let him escape, so I left my bag and chased him into the hallway, ignoring Dustin, who called after me. Calvin walked quickly with his head down and his hands in his pockets. I was nearly carried in the wrong direction by a river of hungry students heading toward the cafeteria, but I saw Calvin duck into the boys' restrooms, freed myself, and followed him in.

"Calvin? I know you're in here." I checked under the stall doors for feet. A pair rested on the floor at the end in the disabled-access stall. "Come on, don't be a dick. Talk to me, all right?"

But Calvin didn't answer, and I'd had enough of his games. I was going to force Calvin to tell me what he did or didn't know about Tommy, even if I had to stuff his head into the toilet until he spilled everything he knew.

I didn't want to catch Calvin with his jeans bunched around his ankles, squeezing out a load, so I shielded my eyes before pulling the unlocked stall door open. I expected him to yell at me, but . . . nothing. No frantic scrambling. No embarrassed shouting. I peeked through my fingers.

Calvin was fully dressed, sitting on the edge of the toilet, staring at his bare arm. He'd pushed back his sleeve to expose the pale underside, and it rested on his thigh. He held a razor in his left hand, lightly between his thumb and forefinger. Slowly he drew the blade across his arm from one side to the other, opening a thin two-inch gash. Tiny glossy red beads welled from the nearly imperceptible line, and from where I stood, it looked like his skin was weeping.

"Jesus Christ!" I rushed forward, smacked the razor from his hand, and grabbed his right wrist. More cuts—some scabbed over, some little more than faded pink slashes—decorated his arm like hash marks carved into a prison cell wall.

Calvin didn't flinch, didn't pull away. He simply looked at me. His face was pasty and pale, but his feverish eyes shone bright electric blue. With his free hand he brushed back his hood, revealing his mop of wavy blond hair, and tugged earbuds out of his ears. I hadn't noticed the black wires snaking up through the neck of his hoodie before, and his teachers probably hadn't either.

"May I have my arm back?" Calvin spoke quietly and calmly, like people caught him mutilating himself every day.

I released his wrist, and he pulled his sleeve down.

"What the hell are you doing?" I asked.

"Inducing endorphin release and inhibiting amygdala activation."

"What the—?"

The outer door slammed open; footsteps echoed against the tile. I caught Trent Williams's reflection in the mirror at the same time as he saw me and Calvin. He was absolutely the last person I wanted to deal with. He lived for making others' lives miserable, and now, after warning me about Calvin, he'd caught us together in a restroom stall. Dad once told me most bullies lash out because they hate themselves, but I was willing to bet Trent loved nobody more than himself.

"Don't you boys look cute?" he said after a nervous pause.

"This isn't what it looks like." Between Calvin cutting himself and Trent busting in, I counted myself lucky I'd made word sounds at all.

Trent craned his neck.

"There's room for one more," Calvin said. Then he snapped his fingers. "Oh, that's right, you only do that when you're drunk."

Calvin's voice was sharper than his razor. Unlike most sensible people, he seemed completely unafraid of Trent.

Trent's face paled—dropping three shades in less than a second—and I worried he was going to kill Calvin and then me for sport. But he said, "That's fucked up. Even for you, Frye," and stomped off.

Calvin stood. He was shorter than me, but not by much. "How about we meet up tomorrow after school?"

"No way," I said. "We're talking about this now."

"I'm not sure the restroom is the most suitable location to discuss our project."

I was shaking, and my voice trembled. "Not the project! Tommy!" I didn't care if anyone heard me yelling. "You brought him up Friday night and then ran, and now you're going to tell me what you know."

In the few short moments since I'd followed him into the boys' room, Calvin had added a slew of new questions to the list of things I wanted to ask him. Why was he cutting himself? What had he meant about Trent only doing *that* when he was drunk? And what the hell did his amygdala have to do with anything? But the only question I cared about at that moment involved Tommy.

"The restroom's not the best place to talk about that, either." Calvin stood and moved toward me, but I was blocking his exit and refused to step aside. "Look," he said. "Tomorrow. We can meet after school."

I'd waited the entire weekend to interrogate Calvin, and now he wanted me to wait another day. I was so sick of waiting, but short of binding his hands with my shoe-laces and torturing him until he talked, I didn't see that I had much choice. The tension fled my body, and I let out a frustrated sigh.

"I work tomorrow."

"Oh."

"We can still meet, though," I said. "Do you know where Petridis Books and More is?"

Calvin nodded.

"Be there at three."

"Cool." Calvin smiled like everything had turned out exactly the way he'd planned.

I stepped aside to let him out of the stall. "You better show up or I'll hunt you down wherever you go."

"I'll be there," he said. "Promise." Calvin brushed past me and left the restroom.

I drove Lua home before my appointment with my future ex-therapist. I hadn't told Lua about Calvin invading a/s/l on Friday night or our encounter in the restroom during lunch. Normally, Lua would have been the first person I told, but I'd felt distance growing between us since Tommy had vanished. It'd started as a small, not-insurmountable fissure in our relationship, but had widened with each passing day into a bottomless crevasse I didn't know how to bridge, and I was tired of shouting across it and her not hearing me. Instead of telling Lua why I'd really been late to lunch, I'd made up a story about eating bad sushi the night before. I'm not sure Lua believed me, but she hadn't pressed the issue, because no one wanted gory diarrhea details.

But I *did* want to tell her.

"Your music selection sucks, Ozzie." Lua scrolled through my phone, mocking every band listed, even though she'd loaded most of them. Her musical tastes evolved rapidly, and bands she loved today frequently became bands she'd ridicule tomorrow. She'd styled her hair messy and chaotic—the cool air through the open windows had blown it wilder—and she wore a corset dress that squeezed her breasts so tightly I worried one speed bump might cause them to burst free.

"Can I ask you something, Lu?"

"If you want to go to prom with me, you'll have to wear the dress."

I rolled my eyes. "I would so rock one of those tight black numbers with a thigh slit. Anyway, you'll probably wind up juggling more than one date, and I refuse to be one of your balls."

"But you're such a cute ball."

"I know," I said. "Now back to my question."

Lua turned toward me. She wiped her hand down her face, replacing her smile with her most mock-solemn expression. "You may ask your question, Oswald Pinkerton of the Cloud Lake Pinkertons."

I almost changed my mind, because Lua clearly wasn't in a serious mood. "What do you know about Calvin Frye?"

"Not much," Lua said. "Smart kid, good at wrestling, had a nervous breakdown over the summer." She shrugged. "Rumor is he's even less likely to graduate than me if he doesn't get his shit together. Why? Do you like him or something?"

"No!"

A grin spread across her face. "Sure."

"It's just . . ." It'd been a mistake to bring up Calvin, so I tried to change the subject. "Fuentes forcing us to partner up made me start thinking about college. Like whether I even want to go. What about you?"

"What about me?"

"You still planning not to go to college?"

"Shit, Oz, all I want to do is make music." She held up her fingers. "These callouses are more than layers of dead skin. They're hours spent practicing. They're my grades; the only ones I care about. Music is my school *and* my life." Lua dropped her hand to her lap. "But I feel like I'm waiting for someone to give me permission. For them to see my callouses and hear my songs, and tell me it's okay to chase my dreams."

I turned down Lua's street and parked in front of her house. The front lawn had grown wilder than Lua's hair, and the driveway was stained with Rorschach inkblots of oil and mildew. But between Lua's hectic schedule and Ms. Novak's two jobs, neither made home maintenance a priority.

"Since when has the Great Lua Novak ever asked permission to do anything?"

"I'm scared, Ozzie," she said. "If I fail, what will I have left?"

"Uh, everything?"

Lua rolled her eyes.

Tommy went through a phase in tenth grade where he read nothing but biographies about great men and women. "You know what's funny?" he'd said to me one night we'd stayed up late talking on the phone. "People like Hillary Clinton and Medgar Evers and Josephine Baker and Ruth Bader Ginsburg. It's like God mixed in something extra when he cooked them up, and the folks around them couldn't help but see it. Like, if people shined, some would shine brighter."

People like Lua.

Lua shone like the sun.

"I envy you sometimes." I said.

"Don't patronize me, Ozzie."

"I'm not!" I needed to leave soon to avoid being late for therapy, but I honestly didn't care. "At least you know what you want to do with your life. You've always known."

Lua frowned, her disapproval searing. "Are we throwing a pity party? Should I run inside and find some balloons?"

"Whatever. Just forget it."

Lua and I squared off, staring each other down. I waited for her to get out of the car, but she remained fixed in her seat. "Yeah, fine, I'm a talented musician. I'm good at exactly one thing. But you, you're good at everything."

I rolled my eyes. "I should get to my doctor's appointment."

Lua got out of the car and grabbed her stuff from the back. She leaned in through the open window and said, "You worry too much, Ozzie. You'll figure it out."

"Thanks," I said. And I meant it, even though I didn't believe her. The sun would never understand. We couldn't all shine as brightly as Lua.

7,956,000,000 LY

THE ONLY SCARY MOVIE THAT HAD EVER TRULY
terrified me was *IT*. And it wasn't even the movie itself, it was
Pennywise the Clown who'd clawed into my nightmares and
liked them so much he'd decided to stay forever. If I thought
about that creepy-ass clown even for a second, I couldn't
shower for hours.

Dr. Andrea Echolls reminded me of Pennywise.

It was her smile.

Or rather, that she never stopped smiling.

She'd walked into the waiting room and called my name,
wearing this crazy rictus she must've thought put patients at
ease but definitely did not. I'd hoped once I plopped down
in the overstuffed microfiber chair opposite the couch she
occupied that her grin would fade, but it didn't. It hadn't.
Not as she went over my history. Not as she asked me the

same basic questions my other therapists asked—How was my mood? Did I get along with my parents? Was I doing well in school?—and not even when she'd asked me why I thought I was there and I replied with my stock answer about being the next name on the list of insurance-approved therapists, which wasn't exactly true since I'd skipped Dr. Norman Dewey.

No matter what, Dr. Echolls kept smiling.

Only weirdos are happy all the time.

"Now that we've gotten the boring stuff out of the way," Dr. Echolls said. "What would you like to discuss, Ozzie?" She said my name so often, I wondered if she thought I'd forgotten it.

"Don't you have questions for me or something?"

Dr. Echolls settled into her couch like we were a couple of old pals catching up. She didn't even have a notepad or tablet. "I prefer letting my patients guide our discussions, Ozzie."

"But isn't that *your* job?"

"You're a comedian, aren't you, Ozzie?"

"No."

"We can chat about whatever you like, Ozzie."

"There's this guy at school," I said. "Calvin."

"Okay," Dr. Echolls said, like this was the most interesting conversation she'd had in months, which was either sad or a lie.

I tried to think of how to phrase what I wanted to say without bringing up Tommy, because I wasn't in the mood to see *that* look on her face. The pitying one everyone wore when I brought him up. "He has information about something—information I need—but I'm not sure I can trust him. I might've been able to last year, but he's different now."

"Why is that?"

"Don't know," I said. "But that's not the point. The point is that I'm not sure I can trust him."

"Why?"

Another question I couldn't answer. I didn't know why Calvin had changed. Honestly, I hadn't known him well enough before, and maybe he'd always been this way and no one had ever noticed. But after catching him cutting himself, I figured there was probably more to it than that.

"Orange juice," I said.

"I'm sorry?"

"Orange juice."

"What about it?" Dr. Echolls said.

"You've eaten an orange, right?" I didn't wait for her to answer. "But I bet there are people out there who have never tasted an actual orange."

Dr. Echolls kept smiling. She didn't interrupt me even

though she must've been wondering what the hell I was talking about.

"So the thing is, all the orange juice you drink is artificially flavored. Even the stuff that says it's not from concentrate. It's a lie."

"I'm not sure where you're going with this," Dr. Echolls said.

Neither was I, not really, but I marched forward regardless. "In order to store OJ for long periods, manufacturers suck the oxygen out of the juice, which also removes the flavor. Then they add these flavor packets when they're ready to bottle and ship it. Many companies base the flavor profile of their packets off the Valencia orange, which is why OJ has such a consistent taste, but at the end of the day, it's all fake."

Dr. Echolls nodded. "That's very interesting, Ozzie."

"Isn't it?" I said. "But it's messed up, too. I mean, what if the OJ companies slowly changed the profile of their juice so that eventually the flavor no longer resembled actual oranges? Someone who'd never tasted a real orange wouldn't know the difference."

"Okay, Ozzie," Dr. Echolls said. "But I'm not sure what it has to do with this other boy. What was his name again?"

Tommy was the one who'd told me about the orange juice. He loved useless trivia like that. He had this whole conspiracy theory about how the government could replace the text of e-books without us knowing, the same way companies could replace the flavor in OJ. But I wasn't planning to tell Dr. Echolls about that.

"Calvin," I said. "And he's like the juice because somewhere over the summer I think someone sucked all the flavor out of *him* and replaced it with something different. Similar to him, but not really."

Dr. Echolls leaned forward. "People don't really work like that, Ozzie."

"What if you're wrong?"

"Okay, Ozzie," she said, her smile wider that I thought possible. "I think that's enough for today. Why don't we pick this up again next week?"

I stood and smiled right back at Dr. Echolls. "Yeah, sure. Next week."

6,089,050,000 LY

MRS. PETRIDIS LOOKED ONE ANNOYING CUSTOMER
away from taking up a machete and hacking us all into quivering bloody chunks.

"Thank God you're here, Ozzie," she said when I walked into the bookstore and tossed my backpack behind the register. "A hundred times today someone's asked me for this cookbook they saw on TV, but no one remembers what it's called and they yell at me because I can't read their minds. Do you know anything about it?"

"*Eat Like It's the End of the World*," I said. "We've got a box of them in the back."

Mrs. Petridis stood with her hands on her hips. "Eat like what?"

"*Eat Like It's the End of the World*," I said again. "It's based off the Apocalypse Diet. Dr. Ness recommended it last week.

It supposedly teaches people to maintain a healthy weight by eating and exercising based on the type of diet and activity they'd be forced to adhere to during a zombie apocalypse. I ordered a bunch; we just need to put them out."

Three different pens were sticking out of Mrs. Petridis's messy gray hair. "That is the most ridiculous thing I've heard in my life, and that includes leg makeup."

I nodded, though I had no clue what leg makeup was, nor did I want to know. "Yeah, but I order every book Dr. Ness recommends, and we always sell out."

"Idiots will buy anything." Mrs. Petridis breathed in and out, her tension fading with each exhalation. "I should sell *you* the bookstore."

"I've got about three hundred bucks. Think that's enough?"

"After the day I've had, Ozzie, I might give it to you for free."

Mrs. Petridis helped me bring out the new books, including the box of *Eat Like It's the End of the World*, and helped me stack them on the front display. As I worked, I noticed Mrs. Ross sitting in the corner, reading.

"How long's she been here?" I motioned at Mrs. Ross, keeping my voice low.

"How should I know? Do you expect me to keep track

of every customer who walks into this godforsaken store?"
Mrs. Petridis broke down the last empty box, added it to
the stack, and picked them all up. "I'll be in the back.
I found a squirrel that's going to make a perfect Scottie
Ferguson."

She disappeared into her studio, which meant I wouldn't
see her until she got hungry, frustrated, or the store closed,
and I busied myself shelving books. My impending meeting with Calvin at three had amplified my anxiety to nearly
unmanageable levels, and working helped keep me from
bursting into flames.

I'd barely paid attention to my teachers during class,
because I couldn't stop thinking about Calvin cutting himself
and Trent catching us together in the boys' room and wondering what he knew about Tommy. He'd ignored me when
I'd tried to talk to him during physics, but I was going to
make him talk when he showed up later, even if I had to take
him into the back and stuff him like one of Mrs. Petridis's
taxidermy animals.

As I worked—shifting books on the shelves to make
room—I kept one eye on Mrs. Ross, though she hadn't
seemed to notice me. I lost sight of her while I was reorganiz-
ing the "Petridis Books Recommends" teen section. I'd made
it my mission to highlight as many non-flavor-of-the-week

books as possible. I'd written all the suggestion cards myself, but had used various aliases. "Liesa" loved books with superheroes, "Jamal" was passionate about books written by diverse authors, "Elisa" couldn't get enough unlikable heroines, and "Anica" adored any book that featured characters who had dogs. I'd tried to recruit Lua to recommend books with a focus on music, but she'd never been able to commit to a book long enough to finish one.

I took a break to peek around the corner and check on Mrs. Ross. Her table sat empty, while Skip was still clacking away at his magnum opus. I hadn't heard the doorbell chime, so she might have been in the restroom or hidden behind one of the shelves where I couldn't see her, but my curiosity drove me to see what she'd been reading.

GED prep books, apparently—four of them—plus, a dictionary and a thesaurus. I picked up the topmost book and flipped through it. Mrs. Ross had never been shy about explaining that she'd dropped out of high school when she got pregnant with Tommy, but I'd never heard her express interest in getting her diploma. Tommy didn't exist here, though, and I wondered why she'd dropped out of high school in the bizarro world in which I now lived, and why she'd decided to pursue her GED.

The doorbell chimed, startling me, as Calvin walked into

the store. He didn't see me and wandered toward the register.

"Hey," I said, approaching from behind him. He didn't hear me, so I tapped him on the shoulder. "Hey," I said again.

Calvin jumped, pushed his hood back, and pulled his earbuds out. His skin was splotchy, his eyes tired and bruised, and he was slick with a layer of sweat. He looked like he'd run straight out of a nightmare.

"You're here."

"Obviously," I said. "I work here."

"Right." Calvin glanced at the GED book in my hand. I'd forgotten I was still holding it. "The pep rallies and prom-mania finally got to you, didn't they?"

"Go, Sea Cows," I said, rolling my eyes. "It's not mine. A customer left it behind." I tossed it on the counter, hoping Mrs. Ross didn't return to her table and wonder why one of her books was missing, and it took heroic effort not to pin Calvin to the floor and threaten to dangle spiders over his face until he told me everything he knew about Tommy. "We can talk here, but I might have to stop to help customers."

"That's fine," Calvin said. "I don't have anywhere to be."

The way he said it, I almost felt bad for him. But not so bad that I was going to let him off the hook about Tommy.

"Last Friday," I said. "At a/s/l. You mentioned Tommy."

"I did?"

"Don't do that. Don't play dumb." My jaw hurt from grinding my teeth. "Tell me what you know about Thomas Ross."

Calvin's expression barely wavered. I thought I saw a hint of genuine recognition, but it might have just been an eye twitch. "Tommy? Does he go to our school?"

"Yes!" I said. "You were on the debate team together! I think. You were on the debate team, right?"

Calvin nodded. "I don't remember anyone named Tommy."

I wanted to crush his fingers in a thumbscrew until he told me the truth. "At a/s/l you told me not to wait around Cloud Lake for Tommy. Why'd you say that if you don't know who he is?"

Calvin was quiet for a moment, and those seconds felt endless. All he had to do was say that he remembered Tommy and it would validate the last few months of my life. I could tell the shrinks and everyone who didn't believe me to go to hell. All he had to do was say the words.

"It was stupid," Calvin said. "I shouldn't have said it."

"So you *don't* know him?"

Calvin shook his head and dropped his eyes. "No."

He was lying. He had to be. "Then why'd you tell me not to wait around for him? How did you even know his name if you don't remember him?"

"I heard rumors," he said. "I have Spanish with this girl whose sister is friends with your brother, I think. I overheard her telling someone about you and this Tommy guy."

"So, what? You heard gossip about me and decided to track me down at a club to offer unsolicited advice on a subject you know less than nothing about?"

Calvin wouldn't look at me. "I really did want to see the band, but then we started talking and you looked so sad—"

But I'd stopped listening. "Who does that? How fucked up are you?"

"Pretty fucked up."

Calvin didn't know anything, and I'd gotten my hopes up for nothing. I was the only person in the entire world, it seemed, who remembered Tommy. I couldn't even stay mad at Calvin for lying about it because he seemed so pathetic. Anyway, he didn't matter; only Tommy mattered.

"You can tell me about him," Calvin said. "If you want."

"I don't want to talk about Tommy. Not with you." I climbed around the register and dug my physics textbook and notepad out of my bag. I didn't want to spend a second longer with Calvin than I had to, but since he was there,

I figured we should start our project so that I didn't flunk physics. "We should work on our roller coaster."

Calvin reached into his back pocket and pulled out a folded wad of graph paper.

"I sort of sketched something already." He spread his sheets of paper on the counter and tried to flatten them with his hand.

I glanced at the drawings, not immediately sure what I was looking at. I was starting to say "We should figure out the math before we draw anything" when I realized Calvin had already designed a roller coaster.

"You drew this?"

His coaster began by catapult-launching the cars up a sharp incline and into the first drop before whipping into a looping corkscrew and finally ending with a camel back. He'd scribbled calculations I couldn't pretend to understand near each section of the ride. On the other papers, he'd broken the roller coaster into smaller sections and included notes about speeds and g-forces.

"I had some spare time at lunch," Calvin said.

I looked from the sketches to Calvin and back. "You did this during lunch?" While Calvin had drafted a kick-ass roller coaster, I'd been chugging chocolate milk.

Calvin shrugged. "It's only math."

"Only math," I muttered. I read over his calculations, which seemed to indicate the ride, if built to scale, could reach a top speed of 82 mph. Not the fastest roller coaster, but the impressive twists and turns were theoretically capable of producing five positive Gs of force in some sections. "Can we actually build this?"

"Yeah," Calvin said. He pointed at the first steep hill. "This is the trickiest bit. We'll need to devise a way to propel the cars up the incline. Most roller coasters tow the cars to the top of the first drop and allow their momentum to carry them through the rest of the ride." He scrunched his forehead. "But if we slingshot the cars up the hill, they'll hit the drop with greater speed."

A couple of customers interrupted, two of whom bought the Apocalypse Diet book. The other was a regular who usually loitered in the graphic novel aisle but never bought anything, who wanted to know if we had some YA book about ants and aliens I'd never heard of. When I returned, Calvin was busy working out more calculations. Without a calculator.

"This is incredible, Calvin. Fuentes will crap her pants if we pull this off." He may not have known anything about Tommy, but he was clearly a genius when it came to roller coasters.

"Whatever."

"Whatever?"

"Yeah," he said. "It's only a grade."

"Maybe to you."

Calvin didn't smile; he seemed bored by the conversation. Like rather than play video games or watch TV or scour the web for porn to fill his empty hours like a normal person, he crunched complicated math problems.

"Did you tell anyone what happened in the restroom yesterday?" he asked.

Calvin stood quietly, the counter and his question between us. I'd honestly been so focused on learning what he knew about Tommy that I hadn't given much thought to catching him cutting himself.

After a moment I said, "Do I need to?"

Calvin shook his head. "I wasn't trying to kill myself, if that's what you're worried about."

"Then why?"

"I told you," Calvin said, slowly, like he was explaining differential equations to a toddler. "To trigger the release of endorphins and inhibit amygdala function."

Calvin's bright blue eyes unnerved me. One was slightly wider than the other, and he didn't blink often, making me feel like he was constantly studying me. Everything about him—his headphones, his black hoodie, his inscrutable Sphinx face—seemed intentionally tailored to repel people and their silly questions.

"That doesn't make sense," I said. "You know that, right?"

"Actually, it does. The pain caused by cutting causes the central nervous system and pituitary gland to release endorphins, which inhibit pain signals and produce feelings of euphoria. Simultaneously, the pain also hinders amygdala function, suppressing emotional overactivity."

Calvin's explanation did nothing to clear up why he'd cut himself. It sounded scientific, but it also sounded like bullshit, and it begged two questions: Why did he need to suppress his emotions, and what would he do if cutting stopped being enough? "It's dangerous," I said.

"Nah. It's harmless." Calvin shrugged, brushing me off. "I used to get hurt worse during wrestling practice."

"If you say so," I said, though I remained unconvinced.

Calvin fidgeted with his earbud cord, looking at the register and his papers and not at me.

I turned my attention back to our assignment, so we could finish and Calvin could leave. I shuffled the papers and said, "I should copy these so I can go over them at home."

"Sure," Calvin said. That and nothing more. I was angry at him for messing with me, but I also felt sorry for him.

Yeah, he was a dick for making me think he'd remembered Tommy, but, though I didn't know why he'd done it, I didn't get the impression he'd acted out of malice.

I spread the pages on the floor and snapped pictures of them with my phone. Calvin stood close to me—too close—and each time I scooted away, he edged even nearer. Clearly he lacked a basic understanding of personal space. When I finished, I returned his papers.

"I should go," Calvin said. "It's a long bike ride home."

"You rode your bike here? How far is that?"

"A few miles. No big deal." He stood near the door but didn't leave. "You doing anything over the break?"

"Not really," I said. "I'm trying to forget it's almost Christmas."

"You should take my number."

"Why?"

"In case you want to work on our roller coaster."

Against my better judgment, I unlocked my phone and handed it to him. When he returned it, I said, "Have a good Christmas," though I was thinking, *Try not to cut yourself.*

"Hey, Ozzie?" Calvin called as I turned back toward the register; Mrs. Petridis would kill me if I didn't finish shelving before we closed.

"What?"

"I'm really sorry about Tommy."

Calvin stood half-in and half-out of the store, wearing his baggy jeans and hoodie, his hands shoved in his pockets, and his face angled down. His messy hair looked weedy, like he hadn't bothered to brush it in weeks, and he looked up at me through his lashes.

"Whatever," I said. "Just . . . don't pull anything like that again and we won't have a problem."

"That's not . . ." Calvin shook his head. "I mean, I'm sorry he's gone."

Calvin looked like such a lost soul. His hunched back and bent shoulders and drooping head gave him away. Like in a world of seven billion people, he felt completely isolated from everyone. Calvin stared at me for a long, strangled second before walking out of the store. I watched him through the windows as he mounted his bike and peddled away.

5,560,000,000 LY

I FOUND MY MOM SHARPENING KNIVES IN THE garage when I got home from work. I'd always thought my mother was the most beautiful woman on the planet. Straight dark hair; intelligent, slightly devious eyes, like she was smarter than you and knew it. My anger at her over the divorce hadn't dulled that feeling, though she did look sinister sitting in a lawn chair next to her sedan, dragging a long carving knife across the surface of the whetstone in silence.

"Feeling stabby?" I asked. Since my parents had announced their divorce, I'd tried to avoid my mom whenever possible. Maybe I was treating her unfairly, but she was the one who'd pushed Dad for the divorce, and blaming her took less effort than trying to understand her.

Mom looked up. I thought she'd heard me pull into the driveway, but she froze like I'd snuck up on her. "What?"

She glanced at the knife in her hand. "Oh. They needed sharpening."

"Right. Well, if Dad winds up dead and full of holes at the bottom of a canal, the police might find this moderately suspicious."

Mom rolled her eyes and continued working on the knife. She drew the blade slowly and precisely across the whetstone, the measured sound hypnotizing. "I'm not planning to murder your father, Ozzie." She paused for a moment. "At least not today."

Maybe I would've laughed if she weren't surrounded by an arsenal.

"Why aren't you working inside? It's hot as balls out here."

"I was enjoying the peace and quiet," she said, her tone implying that I'd interrupted her. Whatever. I was sweaty from unpacking the extra stock Mrs. Petridis had ordered for the holidays and answering stupid questions posed by deliberately clueless customers, and all I wanted at that moment was to take a shower.

"What's for dinner?"

"Leftovers."

"Oh boy."

Mom tested the edge of her knife against her thumb. Satisfied, she set it aside and chose a delicate paring knife.

"You and Renny are welcome to prepare your own meals if you're unhappy with mine."

I figured it unwise to challenge my mother while she was armed. "It's fine. Pot roast is always better the third time." I watched her work and had to admit there *was* something soothing about the repetitive motion and the soft scrape of metal against stone. "Besides, remember what happened the last time Renny tried to cook?"

Mom pursed her lips. "There's *still* chicken stuck to the ceiling."

This was our longest conversation in weeks, and I couldn't wait to end it. I edged toward the door. "Yeah, so enjoy your nonmurdery knife sharpening. I'm off to wash away the retail stink before it sticks permanently."

Mom paused. "Oh, Ozzie, I almost forgot—"

"To tell me we've won the lottery and you're buying me a new car? Gosh, Mom, thanks!"

"To talk to you about your therapy."

I stopped my hand on its way to the knob and stared at my mother's bare feet. "Sorry, those discussions are confidential."

Mom set the knife and stone aside and leveled the full power of her guilt-inducing stare at me. My mother had two superpowers: the ability to be in two places at once, and that glare. She didn't have to remind me that she'd carried me for eight months and clothed me and fed me for seventeen years. Her stare said it for her.

"You need to stop playing musical psychologists, Ozzie."

"It's been a long day. Can we talk about this another time?"

"We're not talking," she said. "I'm telling you that if you don't find a permanent therapist to stick with, I'm going to select one for you."

My mother and I may not have had much in common, but the one quality we *did* share was our stubbornness. "It's not my fault every doctor you send me to is incompetent."

"Now I *am* feeling stabby," Mom said, mostly to herself, and I was grateful she'd set her knives down, though they were still within easy reach. "Enough excuses, Ozzie. Choose a doctor. We will not have this discussion again."

I snorted. "A discussion implies a two-way stream of words in which my input is equally valued."

Mom shook her head. "Your grandmother is laughing in her grave right now."

"Because Nonna's a zombie?"

"When I was your age and made her angry, she would tell me that karma would repay my behavior by giving me children as willful as me." Mom paused, staring at me thoughtfully.

"I'm nothing like you," I said. "I don't give up on the people I care about."

Sadness crept into my mother's eyes. She touched her bare ring finger with her thumb. "I'd hoped you would inherit your father's and my best qualities, but I fear we've given you the combination of our worst."

She might as well have thrown her sharpened knives at me. A knife in my eye, one in my heart, and one in my back as I turned around and walked inside.

TOMMY

TOMMY'S NOSE IS SWOLLEN AND PURPLE, AND HE can't open his left eye. He sits on a stool at the kitchen counter while I fill a gallon-size plastic bag with ice from the freezer.

"I'm calling the cops," I say.

"No you're not, Oz."

"Stop me." My hands tremble; I can't zip the bag shut. Tommy reaches across the counter and takes it from me, closing it and pressing it gingerly against his face.

"One of these days he's going to kill you," I say.

"No he won't."

"How can you say that?" Shouting at Tommy isn't helping, but I can't stop. "Last year he broke your wrist. This time it's your nose. What happens when he cracks your skull? I won't sit around waiting for a call telling me you're dead."

"That's not going to happen." Tommy's swollen nose makes his *voice froggy. I tried to force him to go to the emergency room, but he refused, because nurses ask questions and doctors call police. He's worried about what will happen to his mother if the cops lock up his father. And as guilty as I feel for keeping the secret, I'm more afraid of what Tommy will do if I betray his trust.*

"We should leave now," I say. "Run away somewhere no one will find us." It's difficult to keep my thoughts straight when all I want to do is drive to Tommy's house and kill his dad. "We could hide in the mountains or something. My uncle lives alone in a cabin with no electricity. I bet he'd let us stay with him. I mean, we'd have to find him first and—"

Tommy takes my hand. "One more year, Ozzie," he says. "We have to stick it out one more year so we can graduate."

"We can take the GED. Your life is more important than a stupid piece of paper."

"Ozzie . . ."

I can't look at Tommy without imagining his father looming over him, punching him. Slamming his face into a wall. "You're the only thing in my life that matters, Tommy."

"Don't say stupid shit like that, Oz. Your folks love you, and so does Renny, in his own weird way."

"But they're not you."

Tommy glares at me. I'm not used to seeing anger in his eyes. Not directed at me, anyway. "You know how much I'd give for your life? For parents that love me, a house with a roof that doesn't leak, a bedroom with a real door? You act like you have it so rough." He pulls the bag of ice from his face and points at his swollen eye. "Your pops ever do anything like this to you?"

I shake my head, unable to speak.

"No," Tommy says. "He wouldn't. Because your pops is a saint. He'd never hit you or your mom or Warren." He presses the ice against his face again, wincing. I want to kiss him, hold him. "You have a great life, Ozzie, and you know what hurts worse than a broken nose?"

"Tommy . . ."

"That you don't fucking appreciate it."

Tears roll down my cheeks. I don't notice them until they reach my lips and I lick them away. "I know I'm lucky, Tommy. But I'd give up everything to be with you."

Tommy nods. The anger drains from his eyes, replaced with disappointment. "Then you're an idiot."

2,010,567,000 LY

I LAY ON MY BED STRUGGLING TO READ *ON THE ROAD*.
Kerouac's manic thoughts ran together on the page like he'd
written them in a drug-fueled race to exorcise them from his
brain, which I suppose he had. I preferred books that trans-
ported me to strange places and distant times, but Tommy
had given me *On the Road* before he'd disappeared, and
told me it would change my life. That copy had vanished
with Tommy, so I'd borrowed one from work. I might have
enjoyed Kerouac's adventures more if Tommy was around to
argue about them with. It was the kind of book that might
once have inspired me to hitchhike across the country, but
in my present state of mind, Dean Moriarty struck me as an
asshole, and Sal an even bigger asshole for believing Dean
worthy of idolization.

Still, I kept reading, because Tommy had given it to me,

and there was nothing I wouldn't do to hold on to some piece of him.

A week had passed since I'd met with Calvin at the bookstore, and nothing had changed. He continued sleeping through class. Every time I saw him, I wondered whether he was still cutting himself, and if I should tell a teacher or the police. I even considered talking to Renny about it, but he was too preoccupied with his preparations for basic training to deal with my problems.

I kept waiting for at least one of my parents to realize Renny was making a huge mistake and padlock him in his bedroom until he abandoned his fantasy of becoming a soldier, but that scenario grew less likely with each passing day.

I needed to talk to someone. Lua had been skipping class more often than not, and hardly answered when I texted, and Dustin and I didn't talk about personal stuff often.

Oh, and the last time I'd checked, the universe had contracted to a size of barely two billion light-years across. Ninety-eight percent of the known universe . . . gone. At its current rate, I worried it would collapse entirely before graduation, and I still had no idea why it was happening.

My most recent theory, which had come to me during class while Mrs. Nelson recounted embarrassing stories of her awkward teenage years in an attempt to help us relate to *The Metamorphosis*, was that reality was a lie. That in a distant, dying future, the desperate remnants of humanity had sought refuge in a simulated world, but my future-self's subconscious mind had rejected the illusion. Tommy's disappearance, Flight 1184, the shrinking universe. All symptoms of the truth intruding on my dream of a better life.

As implausible as it sounded, it was no less reasonable than any of the other theories I'd concocted. And if it *were* true, I wondered if Tommy was alive at the crumbling edge of the universe, dreaming some other version of me.

When I realized I'd read the same page of *On the Road* three times, I tossed the book aside, stood, and pressed my ear to my bedroom door. Mom and Dad had been fighting when I'd come home from school, but I didn't hear yelling and hoped it was safe to forage for food.

On my way downstairs I noticed a strange man looking mighty comfortable on the couch in the living room. His brown hair was parted neatly to the side, and that was all I could tell from the back of his head.

"Who are you, and why are you in my house?" I asked. I was holding my phone, ready to call the police.

The man stood and turned around. He was wearing a *Game of Thrones* T-shirt and khaki shorts that revealed tan, hairy thighs. He looked about Renny's age, maybe older, but not by much. I continued down the stairs. The stranger didn't look like a crazed psycho killer, but neither had Norman Bates. The man walked toward me, smiling, and held out his hand.

"Hey, bro. I'm Ben Schwitzer." A sun-and-moon tattoo decorated the underside of his wrist. "You must be Ozzie."

I looked at his hand, but refused to shake it. My parents had taught me the importance of politeness, but that didn't extend to strange men who'd possibly broken into my house with the intention of robbing and/or killing us.

"Am I supposed to know you?"

Ben Schwitzer, if that was his real name, looked like the kind of guy who spent hours at the gym, sitting in front of a floor-length mirror, admiring his broad shoulders and thick arms while he lifted weights. I figured I couldn't take him in a straight-up fight, but I could've probably outrun him if necessary. Still, his youthful red cheeks and his purposely haphazard stubble screamed beer-pong aficionado rather than serial murderer.

"I work with Kat at Entropie," Ben Schwitzer said. "*For her*, I guess you could say. But not directly. I'm in the IT department."

My mom had started working at Entropie—a medical software company—a few months after I was born. I'd been delivered prematurely, and the weeks I'd spent in NICU had demolished my parents' savings. They'd needed the money, but I also think Mom had regretted giving up her career to take care of Renny. She'd started in the logistics department and had worked her ass off to eventually become the COO.

I wondered if Ben Schwitzer was the man Renny told me she'd gone on a date with a couple of weeks ago.

"First job after college?" I asked.

Ben cocked his head to the side. "How'd you know?"

"Lucky guess." I glanced out the bay windows that framed the staircase for Dad's car, but it was gone. "Are you dating my mom?"

Ben shoved his hands into his pockets. He looked as uncomfortable as I felt. "Kat and I are just hanging out."

Hanging out. A mental image of my mother and this man-child on a date crashed through my thoughts. Her leaning forward as he regaled her with stories of his not-so-distant college escapades. Them trying to figure out where to go at the end of the night because she couldn't take him back to her house, where her legal husband and two children slept, and they couldn't go to *his* house because he didn't want to wake up his parents. Laughter bubbled out of me and self-replicated.

Ben frowned. "Did I miss something?"

"The seventies and eighties," I said. "Unlike my mother." My entire body shook. I held on to the banister for balance. "Are you even old enough to drink?"

"I'm twenty-four, bro."

Being "bro'd" by Ben Schwitzer made me crack up harder. Mom walked into the kitchen wearing tight gray jeans and a sleeveless blouse. She looked forty-two going on twenty, which made it impossible to stop cackling. She stared at us, her face hardening to marble.

"Ozzie," she said. "I see you've met Ben."

I held my stomach, trying to swallow the laughter. "You know how old he is, right? You were a year older than he is now when I was born."

Mom's eyes narrowed. Ben forced a smile. "I think I'll wait in the car," he said. "Nice to meet you, Ozzie."

"Don't forget to buckle into your child seat," I called after Ben as he left through the garage.

The moment the door shut behind him, Mom rounded on me. "You think this is funny, young man?"

I tried to wipe the smirk off my face but couldn't. "You're old enough to be his mother," I said. "It's hilarious." Even when my words smacked Mom and I could see I'd hurt her, I couldn't stop laughing.

"I know this is confusing, Ozzie, but your father and I are

through. We will not be reconciling." Her composure amazed me. She gritted her teeth and the muscles in her neck bulged, and I didn't know how she kept herself from slapping the stupid grin off my face. She took a deep breath and let it out. I recognized the technique, because one of the therapists I'd test-driven had encouraged the practice to help me handle stress. "Maybe when you're older you'll understand—"

"Older?" I said. "I'm practically your date's age."

"You have no right to judge who I spend my time with while you carry on this foolish charade of having an imaginary boyfriend."

"Whatever," I said, partially because I knew she was right—my parents' marriage was over, and she was free to date any strange man she wanted—but mostly because, even though I wanted to argue with her about Tommy, it was pointless, since I had exactly no proof he was real.

Mom stopped herself from doing or saying whatever she'd been considering, plucked her purse off the counter, turned, and walked out the door, slamming it behind her.

"Wow," Renny said. "Way to be an asshole."

I found my brother leaning over the railing at the top of the stairs.

"Shut up, Warren."

2,008,389,000 LY

I LOVED MS. NOVAK ONLY FRACTIONALLY LESS THAN I loved Lua. She answered the door at Lua's house wearing the run-down look of a person whose life was all work and responsibility, but who refused to let it break her.

"My second son," she said as she wrapped me in a hug. "How are you, love?"

Before I could unleash the torrent of all my problems on her, the sound of glass shattering from inside the house cut me off. "Jaime's here," she said. "I think they're fighting. Or making up. Who can tell? I should probably check on them."

"I'll do it," I said.

Ms. Novak stood aside to let me in. I followed the shouting voices past the Novak's cheerfully silly Christmas tree to Lua's room, and momentarily debated leaving and spending the evening driving around Cloud Lake. But I wanted—no, I needed—to talk to Lua, which meant refereeing another fight between my best friend and Jaime.

When I opened the door, I saw Lua standing beside the bed, holding a crystal rose over his head. His hair was no longer platinum blond, but electric pink. Jaime stood on the other side of the bed, his arms outspread, his eyes panicked. It was like by opening the door, I'd frozen the moment. I cataloged every detail. Jaime's oily, shaggy hair plastered to his forehead with sweat; the shattered remnants of a lamp on the floor by the closet; the word "No!" paused on Jaime's lips.

Then time unfroze.

Lua threw the rose against the wall, and Jaime flinched as the crystal shards exploded.

"Stop it, Lu! You're acting crazy!" he said.

"Crazy? *I'm* acting crazy?" Lua's eyes grew wide and he launched himself at Jaime, even though Lua was six inches shorter and fifty pounds lighter, and beat Jaime's chest with his fists. "You fucked Birdie Johnson!"

I entered the fray to pull Lua off Jaime. Lua struggled— he was deceptively strong—and I strained to keep him from busting free and attacking Jaime again.

"You broke up with me!" Jaime said. He shook the fight out of his arms and headed for the door. "I'm outta here."

I let Lua go as soon as I thought it safe, but he looked

around the room, grabbed a wooden jewelry box off his dresser, and chased after Jaime. I followed. Jaime was already in his car, backing out of the driveway, and Lua shouted, "Don't forget this, asshole!" and lobbed the jewelry box at his windshield. The box fell short, smashing into the hood of Jaime's Jetta, spilling rings and bracelets and coins. Jaime didn't stop.

We stood outside until Jaime was gone. Then I said, "Wanna tell me what that was about?"

Lua folded his arms over his chest. "Just a minor disagreement."

"A minor disagreement, huh?" I draped my arm over Lua's shoulders. "I guess you're not going to prom together, then."

"With any luck, Jaime won't make it to prom with his dick still attached to his body."

"My mom recently sharpened all the knives in our house, if you need them."

"What?" Lua said.

"Nothing." I felt like I should do or say something, but I wasn't certain how to help Lua. After a minute, I said, "Wanna get coffee?"

"Sure."

I drove us to Prufrock's, a fairly new, trendy coffee bar in Calypso, the next town over. Despite the self-important artist crowd that usually frequented the place, I enjoyed its cozy atmosphere. I wasn't sure it'd survive a year, but I hoped it would. Worn and comfy chairs and couches were arranged haphazardly—nestled in dark corners for those who desired privacy, set up in circles for those who wanted to socialize and hoped to be seen—and the dark wood counters and industrial light fixtures gave the café a moody, dissociative vibe. Even the holiday decorations—mistletoe crafted from metal and gears, a mix of black and silver stockings, and green garland—were muted to match the atmosphere. Capping off the indie ambiance were a few paintings hanging from the walls, some of them pretty good. I was especially drawn to one depicting two boys with raven wings flying into outer space.

Lua claimed a couch in the back while I stood in line to order our drinks.

The cute guy behind the counter laughed and smiled as he spoke to each customer like they were the most important person in the world. His name tag read DIEGO. When it was my turn, I ordered myself a mocha, and Lua a frozen mocha.

"Can you make the frozen decaf?" I asked. "But don't write it on the cup."

Diego raised his eyebrow. "We consider secretly withholding caffeine a capital offense around here."

I glanced over my shoulder at Lua. He was stabbing his phone screen with his finger, either composing a profanity-laced rant to Jaime that I'd need to intercept before he sent it, or deleting every picture of them together. Possibly both.

"My friend's already a little overstimulated. Any more caffeine and he may rack up a body count."

"Got it." Diego winked at me, which made me blush, and prepared our drinks himself.

Lua was still torturing his phone when I returned, carrying our coffees. I settled in, leaning against the arm of the couch, and pulled my legs underneath me.

"I don't understand how you can drink cold coffee," I said.

"It's frozen, not cold." Lua tossed his phone down and focused on his drink. "And it's, like, eighty degrees outside. It hardly feels like Christmas."

My drink tasted more like hot chocolate than coffee; I'd really only ordered it for the delicious whipped cream. "So," I said. "You want to talk about Jaime?"

"No."

"Right."

Lua didn't handle his emotions well. He bottled them up, pushed them down, until the pressure grew too great and they erupted in a geyser of profanity and violence.

Lua and Jaime had dated on and off since freshman year and had spent more than half of their relationship engaged in screaming matches, usually instigated by Lua. I'd never cared for Jaime—he'd hardly made the effort to get to know me or Dustin or Tommy—but he treated Lua well for the most part and genuinely loved him. Jaime had stood by Lua when he'd begun questioning his gender, and Jaime had even punched one of his friends so hard he'd knocked out one of the guy's teeth because the guy had made a rude comment about Lua. But two people can love each other and still not belong together, even if neither of them wanted to admit it.

"My mom's dating a guy from her office," I said.

Lua froze with the straw still in his mouth, then slowly lowered the cup. "What? Seriously? Go, Kat."

"It's weird. He's twenty-four."

"Would it be weird if your dad were hooking up with some younger woman?" Lua asked, and then didn't wait for my answer. "Don't be that guy, Ozzie."

I hadn't expected Lua to take my mom's side. "Logically, yeah, I get it. But she's my mom. And the guy is, like, Warren's age."

Lua shrugged and made me feel like I'd overreacted about the whole thing, which I probably had. "Speaking of Renny.

He still planning to run around the globe and murder inno-
cent people under the dubious banner of democracy?"

"He ships out January second."

Lua slurped her "coffee." "That soon?"

"Yeah." Christmas was only a week away—though it
certainly didn't feel that way at my house—and New Year's
would arrive shortly after. Then Renny would disappear.
Even if he returned, he wouldn't be the same person who
left. I wondered if everyone would forget him as completely
as they'd forgotten Tommy. "I just can't picture him taking
orders from some bull-necked drill sergeant and—"

"He said it was my fault we broke up," Lua said, cutting
me off. "That I spent too much time with the band."

I tried to balance my coffee on the side of my shoe. "We're
talking about Jaime now, right?"

Lua flashed me a "duh" face. "I mean, the band's on the
verge of something huge, Ozzie. Poe scored us time at her
uncle's studio so we can record a demo. And a record label
scout e-mailed me last week. He watched a video online of
one of our shows and wants to see us play live." He squeezed
his hands into fists. "This could be it—everything I've ever
wanted—and Jaime's acting like a needy little bitch."

"He *is* your boyfriend, Lu."

"Was."

"Fine," I said. "Was. And you broke up with him, remember?"

Lua pulled the lid off his drink and used his straw to scoop out the chocolate-drizzled whipped cream. "Yeah, well, I didn't think he'd stick his pickle dick in Birdie Johnson."

"Let me get this straight: You don't want him, but you don't want him to date anyone else?" I frowned, doing my best impression of my mother's dreaded face-of-disapproval. "How's that fair?"

"Nobody wins playing fair."

"Your music's important. I get that." I took a deep breath. "That's why I don't get upset when you disappear for days to practice, but relationships are about compromise, Lu. Jaime told you what he needs. If you're not willing to give that to him, even if you think he's being unreasonable, cut him loose before you wind up hating each other."

Lua rolled his eyes. "Like you're one to give advice."

"What's that supposed to mean?"

"You know what it means, Ozzie," he said. "You treat the rest of us like we don't exist while obsessing after some guy who really *doesn't* exist, and expect us to hang around waiting for you to come back to reality."

I'd wanted to talk about Tommy—needed to, really—but not like this. Not when Lua was angry about Jaime and lashing out at me because I was the only person within easy reach. "I thought we were talking about you and Jaime."

Lua stared into the bottom of his plastic cup and swirled the dregs of his drink with his straw. He was quiet for so long I almost would've preferred the yelling.

"Lua?"

"I love him, Oz."

"I know."

"But I love music more."

I kissed his knuckles. "There's nothing wrong with that."

Lua's anger bled out. His shoulders fell. He looked like a busted tire worn to the treads.

It's impossible to let go of the people we love. Pieces of them remain embedded inside of us like shrapnel. Every breath causes those fragments to burrow through our muscles, nearer to our hearts. And we think the pain will kill us, but it won't. Eventually, scar tissue forms around those twisted splinters like cocoons. They remain part of us, but slowly hurt less. At least, I hoped they would.

Lua smiled, shy and tiny. "That guy behind the counter's pretty cute," she said. "You get his name?"

I glanced toward the register. Diego was talking to a skinny kid with wavy hair, grinning like mad. "I can only deal with one of our love lives at a time. Today we're focused on yours." I watched Diego and the other kid. Their fingers touched across the counter in a way that was too intimate. The way I'd once touched Tommy.

I motioned at Lua's hair with my chin. "Pink, huh?"

Lua shifted on the couch and tucked one leg under his butt. "I wanted to try something new."

I held up my hands. "You don't have to explain yourself to me."

"I know . . . I just . . ."

"What?"

Lua touched his hair. "It's like I keep waiting to look in the mirror and recognize the person staring back."

I stretched out my legs and jiggled my feet, which had fallen asleep. I liked the pins-and-needles feeling as the blood rushed back in. We spend so long in our bodies that we take for granted the myriad parts and pieces of it that work in harmony to keep us alive. Any one of them could fail and we'd die. It's crazy, really.

"Your hair, the clothes you wear. None of it matters. I always see you. You're always Lua to me."

"What if I weren't?"

"How do you mean?"

Lua sighed and shrugged like I'd asked him an impossible question. After a minute he said, "What if I were different?

What if I changed so radically you didn't recognize me anymore?"

"Impossible. You could step into a matter transportation device and come out the other end as Lua-Fly—all compound eyes and spindly legs—and I'd still know you."

"I'm not going to turn into a fly, Ozzie."

"But if you did—"

"I'm not."

"I know."

Lua snaked his hand into mine and squeezed it. "Do you ever wonder if you're the person you're meant to be?"

"I don't know."

"How about when you came out? Didn't you wonder if you'd made a mistake?"

When I'd told Lua I was gay, he'd said he'd known since the day we met, and we moved on with our lives. We rarely discussed it; it was simply a fact of my life. But the truth was, I *had* worried I wasn't gay. Or not gay enough, since the only boy I'd ever loved was Tommy. But I didn't think that's what Lua needed to hear.

"Not really," I said. "Intellectually, I understood what being gay meant, but until Tommy kissed me, I'd never wondered if it meant something to *me*. But he *did* kiss me, and it was like the first time I'd put in contact lenses: The world just came into focus."

Lua pulled away. "Tommy, huh?"

"I'm not crazy, Lu."

"I never said you were."

"You didn't have to," I said. "Tommy *is* real, and it doesn't matter if you don't believe me. It doesn't make him less real."

Lua let out another sigh. She seemed even less interested in getting into a fight about Tommy than me. "I don't know, Ozzie. Sometimes I wish I'd find a zipper on the back of my head so I could unzip my skin and find the real me underneath."

It wasn't like Lua to dance around what he was trying to say, but maybe he didn't know what he was trying to say. So I let him dance. "Whoever the real Lua Novak turns out to be, I'll love him no matter what."

He hugged my arm, squeezed it so tightly that he threatened to cut off my circulation. "Thanks."

We hung out at Prufrock's for a while. It was getting late, but it was the last week of school before winter vacation, and most of my teachers had resorted to showing movies or giving us "fun" assignments to kill time, so I could easily catch up on any missed sleep during class. And I definitely wasn't anxious to go home.

"Did I tell you I met up with Calvin Frye at the bookstore?" I said.

Lua sat up straight. "Uh, no. You most certainly did not."

I nodded. "For our physics project."

"And?"

"And nothing. He's kind of a freak."

"What happened?"

"We talked about our roller coaster." Which was only part of the truth, of course, but Lua had threatened to call DCS every time I'd cried on her shoulder after Tommy's father had hit him, even if she didn't remember it, and I wasn't sure how she'd react to Calvin cutting himself. Besides, it wasn't my secret to tell.

"That's it?" Lua said. "You worked on your roller coaster?"

I shrugged. "Were you expecting me to jump him in the history aisle?"

"Jump him? No. But he *is* cute, in a dreary, the-world-is-unimaginable-pain kind of way. And I've heard he's got a talented tongue."

"Gross," I said. "Also, he's not my type."

"But at least he's real."

"Maybe," I said. But I wasn't so sure.

2,000,349,000 LY

I THOUGHT I WAS STILL DREAMING WHEN I OPENED MY eyes and found Renny sitting cross-legged on my floor, staring at me. Which was at least as creepy as it sounds. Probably creepier.

"Merry Christmas, Oz."

"Were you watching me sleep?"

Renny nodded. "Nothing else to do."

"You could go downstairs and cook me breakfast."

"Fat chance," Renny said. "You're not going to believe this, but Mom and Dad are downstairs making breakfast. Together." A cautious grin broke across his face.

"That's unexpected."

"And they haven't yelled once. I spied on them from the balcony for a while."

I knuckled my sleepy eyes. "Well, damn. I figured Christmas was canceled."

Renny stretched his legs, flexing his hairy feet. He was practically part Hobbit. "Don't get your hopes up. It's not like they bought a tree or put up decorations."

By the time I'd turned ten and Warren twelve, Mom had taken over Christmas-decorating duties. Each year she sent Dad to buy a fifteen-foot-tall tree that barely fit in the house and spent over a week hanging her expensive Lennox ornaments carefully and precisely. Mom had worked hard to transform the house into a delicate winter wonderland we weren't allowed to touch or breathe near. When I needed my kindergarten-crafty-ornament-and-multi-colored-blinking-lights fix, I hung out at Lua's house.

But even though I didn't care for Mom's holiday aesthetic, I'd grown accustomed to our traditions, and the last couple of weeks without them had killed my Christmas cheer. If Mom and Dad had joined forces, even just to prepare breakfast, I'd consider it a Christmas miracle.

"Did you get them a card?" I asked. "I wasn't sure if we were doing presents, so . . ."

Warren winked at me. "I got you covered." He pulled a glittery card and a blue pen from behind his back and tossed me both. Our parents believed gifts should flow from parent to child, not the other way around, so cards were the only thing we were allowed to buy them.

The cartoony smiling people on the front of the card looked too happy to be real, and the poem inside was mushy and not at all what I would have chosen. "Could you have picked a lamer card?" I asked as I signed it and stuck it in the envelope.

"Don't think I didn't try," Renny said. "But that's the price you pay for not buying one yourself."

My brother had a point. I licked the envelope, wondering if my morning breath would adhere to the paper, and tossed it aside. "You think Mom's boyfriend will make an appearance?"

"God, wouldn't that be weird?"

"I can't believe how young he is," I said. "And he 'bro'd' me."

Renny rolled his eyes. "Our mother's a cougar."

"Please never say that again."

We laughed even though we were both mortified.

"Do you think Dad has a girlfriend?" I asked.

"No way."

"How do you know?"

Renny's smile faded. "Are you blind, Ozzie?" When I didn't answer, he said, "Dad's still totally in love with Mom. He's going to be lost without her."

Mom and Dad had met while attending the University of Florida. Dad had been a teaching assistant in a Renaissance literature course, Mom the student from hell—smarter than him and not afraid to call him out when he was wrong. Dad had made the fatal error of giving her a B on a paper about *Doctor Faustus*, which she'd challenged in front of their professor. And won.

Most men would have been too ashamed at being shown up by an underclassman to ever speak to her again, but Dad was shameless. The last day of class, after the final exam, Dad followed Mom into the hall and asked her on a date. She turned him down. That might have been the end of it, but the following semester they ran into each other at a party neither had wanted to attend. They started talking—though depending on which of my parents told the story, they might have also been arguing—and stayed out until dawn. Dad proposed two years later. Mom said no to him that first time too.

Mom used to say she'd given him a second chance because she hadn't met anyone better. I'd always figured she was joking, but maybe she hadn't been. Maybe she'd spent the last twenty-four years waiting for someone better, though I seriously doubted Ben Schwitzer was that guy.

"I don't know," I said. "It's not like Mom's the only one who's been unhappy."

Renny played with the hem of his pajama bottoms. "I didn't say he wasn't unhappy. You can love someone and still hate your life."

"Do you think Mom still loves Dad?"

"You know how Mom is," Warren said. "When she's through with someone, she's through. Remember when Nonna died and she and Aunt Mary fought over the antiques?"

"Who could forget?" Even though Nonna had left a will, Mom and Aunt Mary had still waged a bloody war over every belonging in Nonna's house, and even over the house itself. They hadn't spoken since. "But that doesn't mean she doesn't love him."

Renny nodded. "You know they're not getting back together, right? Dad'll pine for Mom until he dies, but their marriage is toast."

"I know," I said. "But it's hard seeing Mom move on before their divorce is official. That's got to be killing Dad."

"Dad's a big boy," Renny said. "He'll survive."

I understood something about surviving. I understood the person Dad loved disappearing from his life and having to go on as if he wasn't gutted and bleeding out. Only, that isn't living, and I wanted more than for my father to simply survive.

But I couldn't explain that to Warren without bringing up Tommy, and I wasn't in the mood to start *that* conversation on Christmas morning.

"Planning any last hurrahs before basic?" I asked.

"Not really. Brent and Kris and Emilia set up a couple of gaming nights to finish the Orb of Lokaðdyr. Don't want to leave the campaign unfinished, you know?"

"Dungeons & Dragons? That's how you're spending your last days of freedom?"

"What? You think I should party and get shit-faced?"

"Well, no. I guess not." Warren was not a "get shit-faced" kind of guy. As far as I knew, he'd avoided parties during high school. He'd skipped prom and would have bailed on graduation if Mom and Dad hadn't forced him to walk so they could live their dream of spending four hours sitting in cramped seats in a sweltering hot auditorium while they snapped a couple of faraway, blurry shots of Warren accepting a sheet of paper and shaking the hand of a principal he'd never spoken to before that day.

"I just thought you'd want to do something exciting." The smell of bacon and sausage had crept upstairs and into my room, and my filmy mouth began to water. "You might not have the opportunity to do much of anything for a few years."

"I'm shipping off to the army, not prison."

"Spend some time alone with Emilia," I said. "You've had a crush on her forever, right? You should tell her before you leave."

The tips of Warren's ears flushed red. "Do you even live in

the real world, Ozzie? You think I'm going to spill my guts to her and she'll tell me she's felt the same and has been waiting for me to make a move, and then we'll do it the night before I ship out?" He sneered. "That's not even a good fantasy; it's bad porn."

"I just don't want you to leave . . . you know . . ."

"A virgin?" Renny forced a chuckle. "What? Because all the sex you had with your imaginary boyfriend makes you an expert?"

"Tommy's not imaginary—"

"I'm not going to ruin my best friendship to cross off a to-do on some bullshit how-to-be-a-real-man list." Renny didn't raise his voice, but his words still stung. "I don't care about sex, Ozzie. When it happens—if it happens—it'll happen."

"I'm not judging, Renny."

Warren didn't say anything. His breathing slowed and the red drained from his cheeks. Sometimes I didn't understand my brother at all. It's not like I hadn't heard him playing his online games, calling his teammates "faggots," and hooting when he scored a kill. He wasn't as enlightened about everything as he was—at least pretending to be—about sex.

"So," I said, trying to change the subject. "The universe is shrinking. Bet you didn't know that."

"What?" Renny stared at me a moment before he busted up laughing. "You're nuts, you know that, Ozzie?"

"So everyone keeps saying."

Renny pushed himself to his feet and slapped my shoulder. "Come on. Let's go bask in the familial bliss before it all goes to shit."

"Five bucks says they don't make it to noon without fighting."

"I suspect I'm going to lose that bet, but you're on."

Warren slid a five-dollar bill across the table before I'd eaten half my eggs. Mom had mentioned going on a business trip to Chicago after Renny shipped out, and Dad had asked if Ben would be joining her. Cue the yelling.

But they pulled themselves back together long enough to open presents. Without Mom's decorations, it felt like the Christmas spirit had taken one peek through our windows and hell-no'd it to somewhere less hostile. Mom hadn't even hung our stockings. Instead of sitting around the tree to tear the wrapping off our gifts, we sat at the kitchen counter, where Mom and Dad handed them to us unwrapped.

From Mom, Renny received a journal, sunglasses, and a new phone—which he told us he'd need to earn time to use while in basic. Dad gave him a new laptop, which briefly ignited another argument when Mom accused Dad of trying to bribe Renny.

"See," Warren said, elbowing me in the ribs. "There are advantages to the divorce."

"This is an advantage?"

Warren motioned at the laptop. "Obviously." Then he held the *Doctor Who* shirt I'd bought him against his chest and said, "Thanks, Oz."

Since I wasn't leaving home to learn how to kill people with my bare hands, my parents hadn't expended as much thought or money on my presents. Mom bought me a gift certificate to the mall, and Dad got me a new wallet, inside of which he'd slipped a couple hundred dollars. I'd be lying if I said I wasn't a little disappointed by my haul, but my disappointment fled when Renny gave me his gift. It broke my heart and put it back together.

He waited until our parents had retreated to opposite ends of the house before telling me to follow him to his room, where he disappeared into his closet and dug through piles of dirty laundry to retrieve my mystery present.

"Here." Warren handed me a flat rectangle wrapped in baby-shower wrapping paper.

"Cute," I said. "I almost don't want to open it."

"Trust me; you do." Renny was grinning, and I couldn't

begin to guess what he'd gotten me. Usually he bought me a book I inevitably exchanged for one I actually wanted, but the size, sharp edges, and weight gave away that it wasn't a book.

I tore the paper, peeling it back. That ripping sound was the sound of Christmas, and I hadn't realized until that moment how much I'd missed it.

But then I saw Warren's gift, and I nearly dropped it.

"Well?" Renny asked.

I stared at him for a moment, my mouth agape. Then I stared at the present. A framed colored-ink sketch of Tommy sitting on the beach, his back to the water. His gold-speckled eyes, his crooked smile, his round nose. He sat in the sand with his knees pulled to his chest. Behind him, tangerine and violet fingers spread like an open hand against the sky and outlined Tommy like a full-body halo.

"Renny? How?" He didn't remember Tommy, and no pictures of Tommy existed. The drawing wasn't exact, but it was so clearly Tommy.

"Don't be mad," he said. "But I read your journal on your computer to find descriptions of Tommy." When I didn't flay Renny for breaking into my computer—again—he said, "I copied a bunch of the stuff you wrote about him and gave it to Emilia. She's seriously badass, right?"

I wanted to murder Warren a little for invading my privacy, but how could I when he'd given me back Tommy?

When Tommy had vanished, he'd disappeared from every photo and poorly lit phone video we'd recorded. He'd even been erased from my journals, which I'd had to read to learn how my life without Tommy had unfolded, and I'd spent countless long nights rewriting my memories—the way I remembered them—so Tommy would never fade.

I hugged my brother, pinned his arms to his side so he couldn't even hug me back. His head barely reached my chin.

"So, you like it?"

When I let Renny go, I touched the drawing, tracing Tommy's strong jaw. "I love it, Renny," I said. "But I thought you didn't believe me?"

Renny offered a halfhearted shrug. "I've spent years masquerading online as a female half-elven priestess named Dvāra. Who the hell am I to judge?" He motioned at the drawing with his chin. "And, hey, at least your imaginary boyfriend is good-looking."

"Thank you, Renny."

"Don't mention it. Now get out so I can tear shit up on my sweet new laptop."

I turned to leave but stopped at the door. "Warren, I don't want you to go."

I expected him to make a joke or call me stupid. But he said, "Don't worry, Ozzie, I'll come back."

"You'd better," I said. "But just to be safe, if you see a rocket equipped with a saddle, run far, far away."

Renny laughed. "You are so weird."

2,000,081,000 LY

TWO DAYS AFTER CHRISTMAS I STOOD IN THE SHOWER thinking about the Salem witch trials.

Sophomore year my American history teacher, Mrs. Barnes, taught us the story of Giles Corey, who'd been accused of witchcraft. When Corey refused to renounce Satan and admit he'd cavorted with black-magic demons, the self-righteous mob subjected him to pressing in an effort to force the "truth" from him.

Pressing was a barbaric method of execution in which increasingly heavy rocks were loaded on the accused's chest until they pled guilty to their crime or suffocated to death. The French called it *peine forte et dure*—hard and forceful punishment. Mrs. Barnes, with her limited imagination, tried to describe the process of being pressed to death. Of the air being driven from Corey's lungs by the immovable weight balanced atop his chest. The panic as he struggled to draw a breath and realized his chest and lungs lacked the strength. The parched, dry-mouthed gasps as his defiant but futile efforts earned him barely a wisp of air—enough to keep him alive, though few would call it living. And then, another stone pushing Giles Corey's soul inches closer to the infinite void beyond.

According to Mrs. Barnes, Giles Corey took two days to die. I hadn't thought about him since we'd completed the unit on the Salem witch trials. Back then he was little more than the answer to an exam question that, once bubbled in, became irrelevant in my world. But standing in the shower, thinking about my life—about Tommy and Lua and my parents and Renny and even Calvin Frye—I remembered poor Giles Corey.

Tommy was gone, and I had no idea how to find him; Lua was preparing to launch into her glorious new future; my only hope of escaping Cloud Lake rested in the hands of faceless admissions officers scattered across the country, and I wasn't sure I even wanted to go; my brother was days from marching toward danger when he should have been running from it; my parents' marriage was irredeemably broken; the universe was shrinking; and the only person I thought might understand my problems sought relief from his own unknown-to-me problems by cutting himself.

Despite my efforts, my life had become a hard and forceful punishment. Troubles rose from the quarry of my mind—a metric ton of failure and fear—and stacked atop my chest, each worry heavier than the last. A stone for my parents, a stone for college, a stone for Tommy, a stone for Calvin and Lua and the shrinking universe. I stood in the shower, just me and Giles Corey, buried under all those stones, struggling to breathe.

Except, I refused to quit. I was determined to find Tommy and leave Cloud Lake, I would not allow Lua and I to drift apart, Warren was going to survive the military and come home, and my parents' divorce would not destroy our family. Those stones crushed me, and I fought for every inhalation, but they were *not* going to kill me. Not if I didn't let them.

Giles Corey remained brave until the end. He said to his executioners what I stood in the shower and said to life: More weight.

Mom had left early for the office, and I hadn't heard Dad come home the night before, but their constant fighting had polluted the house. The echoes of their anger remained, and I needed a break from it before it permanently seeped into my bones.

Lua was busy rehearsing with the band for her show at

a/s/l on New Year's Eve and didn't have time to hang out, and Dustin's parents had dragged him to upstate New York for their annual guilt trip to visit his grandparents, which left Calvin Frye as my only viable option. If I could've hung out with anyone else, I would have. I'd texted him under the pretense of working on our physics project, half expecting him to not reply, but he'd messaged me his address and invited me over.

Calvin lived in a cookie-cutter subdivision filled with rows of identical townhouses nestled so closely together they looked like dominoes set up to be knocked over. Almost nothing distinguished one from the other, and I drove past Calvin's unit twice before finding it. I parked in the empty driveway and sat in my car debating whether to stay or bail.

In the span of six months my boyfriend had vanished from his home and from the minds of everyone who knew him, I'd tried to run away to find him and had nearly died in a plane crash, and the universe was shrinking. Spending time with Calvin meant the possibility of inviting his problems into my life, but I couldn't carry the weight of my own alone anymore, and I thought maybe Calvin was desperate enough for a friend that we could bear them together.

I made up my mind, grabbed my backpack, and walked toward his house.

Calvin answered the door wearing swim trunks and a tank top. I'd never seen him out of his jeans-and-hoodie uniform. It was like he'd molted. His skin was pasty white, but his arms—which were lined with scabs and scars—and legs were braids of taut, wiry muscle. I wasn't a wrestling fan, but I found it difficult in that moment not to imagine him in his tight spandex uniform.

"Sorry about the mess," Calvin said when he stood aside to let me in. "It's just me and my dad, and we both hate cleaning."

The inside of the townhouse wasn't exactly filthy, but no sane person would have called it clean—half-empty cups stood on the coffee table, and heaps of unfolded laundry lay on the kitchen table. Lua's house was messy too, but where the Novak house felt lived in, Calvin's felt neglected.

"Whatever," I said.

"Want something to drink? I could make coffee."

My brain reminded me I hadn't slept well the last few days, and I nodded. "That sounds great, actually."

I hung around the kitchen while Calvin brewed a pot of coffee in a dirty machine that looked older than my mother—definitely older than her boyfriend. A mountain of dirty dishes rose out of the sink, threatening to topple, and I kept my arms at my sides because the one time I touched the counter, my hand came away sticky.

Armed with plastic tumblers of black coffee—all the mugs were dirty—Calvin led me upstairs to his room.

I'm not sure how I'd expected Calvin's bedroom to be decorated. Maybe like a cross between Renny's room—without the comic books and action figures—and Tommy's—which had been more of a closet, with a mattress on the floor and his belongings piled in a corner—but with black walls and depressing poems or song lyrics framed and hung for all to see. The reality was something of a letdown. The walls were flat white and his twin bed sat perpendicular to the far wall, a nightstand on one side. A clean desk stood in front of the window, with a rolling stool to sit on. And nothing else. Calvin's room was spartan, ascetic. No trinkets or posters or anything to indicate his hobbies or dreams, which was still depressing but in a different way.

"Did you just move in?" I asked, trying to make a joke.

Calvin shook his head. "Possessions are distractions."

"Are you a Buddhist or something?"

"Or something." He sat on the stool. "You said you wanted to work on our project?"

I *had* said that, and it was partly true. We needed to make some progress on our roller coaster to show Ms. Fuentes when we returned from Christmas break. Besides, I still wasn't certain I should discuss my problems with

Calvin. I'd been worried about inviting his troubles into my life, but maybe he had enough issues without me burdening him with my own.

"Yeah." I dug the crumpled pages I'd worked on out of my backpack and handed them over.

Calvin studied them, nodding as he traced the lines with his fingers. "These are good." He stopped at a barrel roll I'd added and said, "I'm not sure this will work. Let's test it." He grabbed his laptop and wheeled to the bed, where he popped it open and started working. A few minutes later he turned the laptop toward me to show off a 3-D wire-frame replica of our roller coaster.

"Whoa!"

"It's an open-source animation software with a sophisticated physics engine that can accurately simulate the real-world conditions of our coaster." Calvin clicked the touchpad, and we watched as the wire-frame car—complete with little wire-frame people—shot up the first hill and proceeded to fly through the loops and turns. When it reached my addition, the car broke away from the track and careened into empty space.

"See," Calvin said. "The cars are entering your roll too fast. Since we don't have time to design brakes, maybe we should find a better spot to include it."

We worked for the next hour, rearranging the track, experimenting with different configurations. It took some rejiggering, but we finally squeezed my barrel roll into the ride without killing the passengers. Though, based on the information provided by Calvin's program, our coaster still exceeded safe speeds. The cars remained on the track, but the theoretical g-forces could cause sensitive passengers to black out. Ms. Fuentes would definitely ding us for a car full of unconscious imaginary riders.

I stood and stretched my arms over my head. "This is tough. I'm pretty sure Fuentes is a sadist."

"We'll solve it," Calvin said.

I pointed at the corkscrew on the screen and said, "Removing part of this would reduce the speed."

Calvin shook his head. "We'll never get an A taking the safe route."

"I thought you didn't care."

"I don't." He kicked off, spinning on his stool.

The thing was, I didn't believe him. His Fortress of Apathy felt manufactured.

"What happened to you, anyway?" I asked.

"Come again?"

"You used to have a boner for school and homework, and now you're kinda limp."

Calvin stopped spinning. His shoulders slumped like I'd flipped a switch and shut him off. I prepared to change the subject, but he said, "When Neil Armstrong and Buzz Aldrin first stood on the moon, they looked at Earth and realized our wars and petty issues were pointless. Experiences like that change people. They realize the things they believed mattered are actually inconsequential. That *they* are inconsequential."

"Is that what you think? That we don't matter?"

Instead of answering, he said, "Can I ask you a question?"

"Only if you agree to answer one first." Calvin nodded, which I took as agreement. "Why were you cutting yourself? And don't give me that bullshit about your amygdala again."

Calvin licked his dry lips. He touched his arm absently, ran his finger over one of the scabs. "Feelings are intangible," he said. "You can't see them, can't touch them. You can hurt and no one would know. But physical pain is real. You can see blood and broken bones. It's simple in a way feelings are not, and cutting makes the abstract pain of feelings substantial."

"But it's messed up," I said. "You get that, right? It's seriously dangerous, and what if you cut too deep?"

"I won't."

"And I'm just supposed to believe you?"

"Yes."

Only, I didn't believe him, and I wasn't going to give up

trying to convince him not to cut himself anymore, but I didn't want to push him too hard when we barely knew each other. So I said, "All right. For now."

"My turn," Calvin said. "Why were you on the plane that crashed?"

I liked that he said "crashed" instead of some stupid euphemism. "I already told you: I was going to find Tommy."

"The boyfriend who vanished?"

"We only agreed to one question."

Calvin nudged me with his bare foot. "You got to ask more than one."

Wasn't talking about Tommy why I'd wanted to go to his house in the first place? I hadn't even needed to maneuver him into the conversation. Calvin wanted to know. But I hesitated. Not just because Calvin had basically admitted he cut himself because he was burdened by emotional pain too big to cope with, but because we were starting to get to know each other, and I didn't want him to judge me. For some reason, his opinion mattered more than I'd expected it to.

But I needed a confidant as much as Calvin seemingly needed to cut himself.

"July third, Tommy was my boyfriend. July fourth, he ceased to exist. And not like he died or ran away; he just vanished and no one remembers him other than me."

"How is that possible?" Calvin asked.

I shook my head. "I don't know."

"Got any theories?"

"Yeah. I doubt you'd understand."

"Try me."

I stared into Calvin's eyes, looking for some indication of his motives. Was I merely an oddity to study, or something more? But his eyes, his face, gave nothing away.

Then he said, "I don't have anyone to talk to either." And that simple statement changed everything. He'd seen through my bullshit story about wanting to work on our project right to the truth of why I'd called, and he was still there; he hadn't kicked me out. That had to count for something.

"Remember Fuentes's lesson on particle-wave duality?" I said.

"Yeah."

"Okay." I rubbed my hands together, trying to organize my thoughts. I'd never said any of this out loud to anyone that mattered—my shrinks didn't count—and I hadn't realized how badly I'd needed to until the words came pouring out. "So we know that photons can act as either particles or waves depending on observation. That video Fuentes showed us about the double-slit experiment proved photons act as particles when no one's watching, and as waves when they are."

"Did you hear about the scientists in Australia who took the experiment further?" Calvin asked.

"No."

"They ran tests using helium atoms proving that not only are objects affected by observation, but that observation can cause them to transmit information backward through time to change their behavior in the past."

Yeah, Calvin was definitely smarter than me. I'd read a few books on quantum physics, though little had made sense, but Calvin seemed to actually understand it.

"Anyway," I said. "So we know this stuff, right? But we don't know *why* atoms act this way."

"There are theories," Calvin said.

"Well, my theory is that particle-wave duality is a shortcut."

"A shortcut for what?"

"Have you ever played Alien Worlds: Kill 'Em All?"

"No," Calvin said. "But I've heard of it. It's an MMORPG, right?"

I nodded. "My brother's a fanatic. The game is made up of hundreds of planets, divided into different solar systems. At any given moment, there are thousands of players exploring those worlds, killing the aliens they find. But they can't be everywhere all the time. Still with me?"

"I think so."

I cleared my throat. The theory sounded even crazier when I said it out loud. "What happens to those solar systems and worlds when no one's in them? Time still moves forward in the game, but what players see when they enter them changes depending on their circumstances."

"Yeah," Calvin said. "Now I'm lost."

I bit my lip, trying to think of the best way to explain it. "It's my fault. I'm probably screwing this up."

"You're doing fine." Calvin smiled.

"Okay, so part of quantum theory is that until we observe something, it exists in all possible states. That's why a photon can act as a wave in one instance and a particle in another. It would be a waste of processing power to keep the unused portions of Alien Worlds running perpetually, so when no one is around to see what's going on, they exist as all possibilities, and then the computer chooses one when someone enters that part of the map, changing to fit the player's expectations."

Calvin stared at me. He hardly blinked. Then he said, "So your theory is that we're living in a game?"

Yeah, it definitely sounded crazy, but I couldn't back down now that I'd put it out there. "Yes. And particle-wave duality, as well as other weird aspects of quantum physics, are shortcuts used by the computer running the simulation."

"That's . . . interesting," Calvin said.

"It's only a theory. One of many."

Calvin pursed his lips. "But how does that explain your boyfriend going missing?"

"Well, that's not the only weird thing that's happened," I said. "There's Tommy vanishing and Flight 1184 crashing and the universe shrinking—"

"Wait. The universe is shrinking?"

I nodded. "A lot."

"And you think it's because we're living in a simulated world?"

"Brains in jars," I said.

"Brains in jars?"

"It's a philosophical thought problem. If a crazy scientist scooped out your brain, kept it alive in a jar, and hooked it up to a computer, feeding it sensory data, your brain would be incapable of telling the difference. You wouldn't know you were a brain in a jar. The world fed to you by the mad scientist would feel real."

Calvin perched on his stool, hugging his knees to his chest. I wished *he* were a brain in a jar, so I could poke and prod at him and figure out what he was thinking.

"You're far more interesting than I expected," he said after a few moments.

"You expected me to be boring?"

"No," Calvin said, flustered. "It's just . . . I'm used to hanging out with guys like Trent, whose thoughts exclusively orbit his dick." He paused. "I like that you think about weird stuff."

Now *I* was flustered, so I changed the subject. "What's the deal with you and Trent, anyway? He came by the bookstore and warned me you were a pathological liar or something."

Calvin's head drooped again. "We have a complicated history." When I raised my eyebrows, he said, "Not like that."

I wanted to ask him more, but a deep voice echoed up the stairs, calling, "Cal? You home?" followed by heavy footsteps.

"In my room," Calvin called back. He grabbed his black hoodie off the floor and pulled it over his head. "My dad," he whispered.

"You okay with Chinese tonight?" Mr. Frye said as he lumbered into view, stopping when he saw me. "Oh. Didn't know you had company." Calvin's father was squat and dense, like God had meant for him to be taller but had been forced to squish him into a smaller package. His blond hair—curly like Calvin's—was thinning on top, and his sunburned face was covered with pale stubble.

Calvin motioned at me. "Dad, this is Ozzie. Ozzie, my dad."

Mr. Frye waved a filthy hand. "You're welcome to stay for dinner, Ozzie, but I gotta work tonight, so you boys'll be on your own."

"Thanks," I said, "but at least one of my parents probably expects me home to eat."

"Sounds nice. Wish I could get Cal to come out of his room for dinner more often."

Calvin grinned. "I would if you were ever around."

Mr. Frye shook his head. "How about you work two jobs and I'll stay home and futz around on the computer all night?"

"Nice try, Dad."

Mr. Frye stood in the doorway for another couple of seconds before saying, "Well, it was good meeting you, Ozzie." He looked pointedly at Calvin. "Maybe you could clean up some tonight? The dishes are out of control."

"But if I leave them in the sink a couple more days, they might walk themselves into the dishwasher."

"Smart-ass."

After Mr. Frye left, Calvin said, "He's a firefighter. One day on, three days off. He also works the stockroom at Walmart."

"Oh. He seems cool."

"He's all right." Calvin didn't seem to know what to do with his hands. He kept wringing them over and over. "He's had a rough time of it since my mom took off. Said she wasn't cut out for being a wife or mother."

"That sucks." I wanted to ask him if her leaving was the reason he'd gone dark side, but it wasn't my business.

The conversation died. I didn't know what else to say, and Calvin had this far-off look on his face. The silence grew uncomfortable, and I was about to leave when Calvin said, "So you really think the universe is shrinking?"

I mumbled "Yeah" and hung my head.

"I don't know how we'd go about it, but if you want help looking for Tommy or proving we're living in a game—a shitty game, by the way—count me in."

His offer surprised me. "Why?"

Calvin glanced at the floor. He fidgeted with the hem of his shorts. "I had a crush on you in tenth grade. Did you know that?"

"Me? What?"

"I did," he said. "You were cute and shy, and I fantasized about you asking me to sit with you and your friends at lunch, and we'd joke and laugh, and you'd hold my hand under the table." He flicked his eyes at me and then back at the floor. "Stupid, right?"

I hadn't suspected Calvin Frye had a thing for me. I hadn't suspected he liked guys. And he was definitely cute, but . . . "I love Tommy."

"I know," Calvin said. "That's why I want to help you."

I checked the time on my phone, trying to cover how uncomfortable Calvin's admission had made me. "I should get going."

Calvin stood as I gathered my papers and stuffed them into my backpack. "I'm around all break if you want to work on the project some more. Or on other stuff."

We walked downstairs. The house felt even lonelier now that I knew Calvin was going to be spending the rest of the holidays alone. I stopped at the door and said, "Lua's band is playing another show at a/s/l on New Year's Eve. Wanna go?"

A smile split Calvin's face, and it was beautiful.

"Definitely. And I can make you a fake ID, by the way."

"Seriously?"

"Sure. It's easy."

"Thanks." I lingered at the door another second before turning to leave.

"Hey, Ozzie?" Calvin called after me.

"What?"

"If we're living in a game, that means none of this is real, right?"

"I guess. Why?"

"No reason. See you Sunday."

1,998,000,000 LY

THE PART-TIME HOLIDAY HELP MRS. PETRIDIS HAD hired didn't know Harry Potter from Langston Hughes. And one of them—usually Chad—stopped me every ten seconds to ask for help locating a book because apparently the alphabet confounded the hell out of him.

I hadn't seen Mrs. Ross come in, but I was at a table eating my lunch when she approached, carrying a stack of GED prep books. She stopped when she saw me. Her eyes widened slightly, and she looked like she didn't know whether to run or pretend like I was invisible.

"You don't have to leave," I said. "I know you don't remember Tommy."

Mrs. Ross didn't respond, but she didn't run away either. She set her books on the table farthest from me and sat facing the window.

After Tommy disappeared, I'd scoured my journals for traces of him. But instead of my history with Tommy, I'd found one without him. Instead of me approaching Lua in sixth grade at Tommy's urging, we'd met because she'd stolen five dollars from me and had gotten into a fight when I'd called her out on it, earning us both detention. According to my journals, I *had* taken Sonia Jackson to the eighth-grade Halloween dance. And afterward we'd gone with a group of her friends to see the newest movie in the Dr. Deadeyes franchise where, in the dark of the theater, Sonia had held my hand and kissed me.

Tommy had slipped out of some parts of my history easily. Parties we'd attended together became parties I'd gone to with Lua or Dustin or alone. Dates Tommy had taken me on had simply never happened. I'd even apparently dated a boy named Erik Bode in tenth grade whom I'd met through Dustin. It hadn't lasted, because Erik's father, who hadn't known Erik was bi, freaked when he caught us making out on Erik's bedroom floor and transferred Erik to military school.

But other events, pieces of my history in which Tommy had been tightly intertwined, made less sense without him. The first weekend after I got my car, we drove to Orlando for no other reason than that we could. I got us lost in the city and we stopped in front of a phone company to figure out where we were and how to get home. Without warning, Tommy had run inside the building and returned less than a minute later with an armful of Orlando phone books.

We'd laughed about it the whole drive back to Cloud Lake.

Without Tommy, I'd taken the trip alone. For no reason that I had explained in my journal, I'd driven to Orlando, stolen a stack of phone books, and driven home.

My journals were filled with a hundred memories like that. Events that lost all meaning without him.

If my memories had been replaced with ones that made sense, I might have eventually come to believe I'd dreamed him. But whoever or whatever had erased Tommy had left behind too many inconsistencies that defied explanation. Like the phone books. That's what convinced me I hadn't imagined Tommy.

Even if I tried to explain all that to Mrs. Ross, I doubted she'd believe me. Instead, I watched her while I ate my lunch and wondered what had filled the Tommy gaps in her life. Tommy had blamed himself for his mother's situation. He'd believed if she'd never gotten pregnant with him, she wouldn't have married and stayed with an asshole like Carl Ross, and she would have finished high school and gone to college. I knew from when I'd called the police on the Fourth of July that she didn't have any children, and that she was still married to Mr. Ross—and the faded bruises on the backs of her arms were evidence enough he was still an abusive prick—but why had she dropped out of high school if not to have Tommy? Who or what, if not Tommy, had kept her from leaving her husband?

I doubted she would have responded favorably to me asking, so I kept my questions to myself.

Twenty minutes remained of my lunch break, but I overheard Chad arguing at the register with a customer, so I gathered my trash and trudged back into the war zone.

Hours later, at closing time, Mrs. Ross was still working. I approached her table and cleared my throat. She flinched but didn't look up.

"Sorry," I said. "It's just that we're closing."

"What time is it?" she mumbled.

"Nine."

Mrs. Ross's eyes flew wide. "Nine?" She rubbed her eyes with the balls of her hands. "Do you know anything about binomial equations? I swear it must've been the devil who invented algebra."

"Actually, algebra's roots go all the way back to the ancient Babylonians."

"Either way, anyone who says they love math has got to be soft-headed."

I knocked my skull with my knuckles. "Ten on Mohs hardness scale."

Mrs. Ross laughed and her cheeks glowed, and I hadn't realized how much I'd missed them—and how much she reminded me of Tommy—until that moment.

"You're a weird young man."

"You'll get no argument from me. I suck at math, but if you need help with the writing sections, I'm your guy."

Mrs. Ross opened her mouth to speak, but whatever she'd been about to say was lost when Mrs. Petridis yelled at me from the back room to lock the doors and bring her the till to count.

"I should get home," Mrs. Ross said. She scooted back her chair and stood. "My husband will be wondering about his dinner."

I wanted to stop her. To ask her about Tommy and find out what her life had been like without him and dig through her memories for any stray scraps that might remain. Even if my friends and family had forgotten Tommy, I couldn't believe his own mother had. But I didn't want to scare her away again.

So I said, "FOIL."

Mrs. Ross stopped at the door. "What?"

"FOIL," I said again. "It's a mnemonic for solving

binomial equations." It was also the only thing I remembered from Mrs. Alley's freshman algebra class. "First, outside, inside, last. You multiply the terms in that order. FOIL."

Mrs. Ross stared at me like I'd spoken Akkadian, but a hint of a smile tugged at the corners of her lips. "FOIL," she said, nodded, and then slipped out the door.

1,780,000,030 LY

WARREN'S GOING-AWAY PARTY FELT MORE LIKE A
"go away" party. Mom, Dad, Renny, and I sat at the breakfast nook wearing party hats and eating gyros and mushy
saganaki from the Greek place up the road. I'd positioned
myself between my parents to act as a buffer, and every
time they looked like they were headed for a fight, I
changed the subject. I refused to let them ruin one of our
last nights with Renny.

He wasn't leaving for four more days—January second—
but this was the only time Renny, Mom, Dad, and I could
coordinate our schedules.

"Where's training, again?" I asked right after Dad
remarked about the dryness of his gyro, an obvious knock at
Mom's decision not to cook Renny's last meal at home.

"Fort Benning," Renny answered with his mouth full.

"Fun."

"I seriously doubt that," Dad said. "Your drill sergeants won't let you sleep until noon."

Mom had barely touched her dinner, because she was waiting for the éclair pie in the fridge—which was the only reason we ordered takeout from the Greek place. Seriously, the pie was amazing.

"Maybe the army will give you some direction," Mom said.

I'd spent the last few days waiting for one of my parents to beg Renny not to leave. He would have listened to them where he ignored me. But my mother and father were incapable of cooperating, not even to save their eldest son from making a huge mistake.

"Basic's ten weeks, then infantry AIT for five weeks. If I'm lucky, I'll get a few days' leave to come home before my first posting."

I didn't understand how Renny could treat this so casually. Like he was leaving for a gambling cruise to the Bahamas instead of the army.

"Listen to your drill instructors," Mom said. "And try to make friends with the other recruits."

"Christ, Mom. It's the army, not kindergarten."

"I know that, Ozzie," Mom snapped.

"Do you?" I could barely stand to look at my parents. Their indifference had killed my appetite. Even for éclair pie. "Look at us. We're wearing party hats, celebrating Renny's idiotic decision to run away from his problems instead of tying him to a chair to make him stay."

Warren set his fork down and folded his hands in his lap. We were talking about him but not to him, and I'd been in his position before. Sitting in the cafeteria while the other kids talked about me and the plane crash like I couldn't hear them. It was a shitty thing to do, but right then I cared less about Renny's feelings than about possibly saving his life.

Dad clenched his jaw. His already too-thin lips became barely more than pink face slits. "Warren's certainly not the first of our sons to run from his problems. We haven't forgotten about your little misadventure."

"Misadventure?" I said. "You mean the one where the plane crashed and exploded?"

Mom tagged in. "Your brother's an adult, Ozzie. Your father and I may not agree with his choices, but they're his to make." She glanced at Dad. "If it turns out Renny's made a mistake, he'll just have to live with the consequences like the rest of us."

"Real nice, Kat," Dad said. "Are you actually bringing that up *now*?"

"I didn't sleep with one of my students' parents."

"Wait," I said. "What?"

But they'd taken up their weapons again and dragged me and Renny into the trenches with them. "No," Dad said. "Just someone young enough to be one of my students."

Mom slammed her fork on her plate, chipping the ceramic edge. "At least I waited until our marriage was over, Daniel."

Dad snorted. "Keep acting as if our marriage hasn't been over for years. You checked out long before I did."

"I'm done." Mom stood and marched upstairs, slamming her bedroom door behind her.

Dad hung his head, pushing strips of fallen lamb around his plate with his fork.

When I couldn't take the silence anymore, I said, "You cheated on Mom?"

"It's complicated, Ozzie."

"Either you did or did not have sex with another woman while still married to my mother. It's really not that complicated."

Dad wouldn't look me in the eyes. "Maybe you'll understand better when you're my age. Or maybe you won't." He wiped his mouth with his napkin and draped it over the remains of his dinner like a shroud. "People drift apart, and sometimes they don't notice soon enough to fix it."

"That's your excuse?" I said.

Dad left the table and walked outside to the back patio.

"Still think I'm crazy for wanting to get the hell out of here?" Renny said.

"Did you know?"

"About Dad?" he asked, and then said, "Yeah."

"Why didn't you tell me?"

Renny shrugged. "Dad needed an ally, and you've always worshipped him."

I couldn't process the new information. All this time, I'd thought my father the victim in my parents' war, but he'd cheated on Mom. I'd been on the wrong side this whole time.

"What about that stuff you said about Dad still being in love with Mom?"

"Him cheating doesn't make it less true," Warren said, but I didn't know how it could be. If he'd loved her, he wouldn't have slept with another woman.

"Everything's changing," I said.

Warren sighed heavily. "No shit, Ozzie." He pulled off his party hat and tossed it onto the table, grabbed his Styrofoam container of éclair pie from the fridge, and headed upstairs.

"Don't go, Renny."

He paused on the landing. "Party's over."

1,675,009,220 LY

I PASSED BELLA DONNA THE FAKEST FAKE ID OF all time outside of a/s/l. I thought Calvin was joking when he'd handed it to me in the parking lot behind the club, but then he'd smiled sheepishly and shrugged. My picture was crooked and the plastic felt flimsy. Worst of all, he hadn't even made me twenty-one. All he'd done was shift my birthday back a couple of months so I could pass for eighteen. Bella Donna smirked at my ID but drew an *X* on my hand anyway.

"See you found your boy," she said. She let her eyes crawl up and down Calvin, lingering in some places more than others. "I can see why you chased him, baby."

I pulled Calvin inside by the arm, not giving him the opportunity to ask what Bella Donna had been talking about.

Your Mom's a Paradox was scheduled to perform early in the night—they were the opening band's opening band—but a/s/l was already crowded to capacity with drunken revelers eager to rock in 2018.

During the week before the show, Lua had been busy rehearsing, so I'd split my time between working at the bookstore and hanging out with Cal. We fought about our roller coaster and argued about the universe. It was the most fun I'd had since Tommy disappeared. I gave Calvin Plato's *Republic* to read and told him to focus on the allegory of the cave. Calvin convinced me to watch *Donnie Darko*, hoping the concept of the tangent universe from the movie might spark some ideas about Tommy's disappearance, though I didn't like how the movie seemed to suggest Donnie was schizophrenic, because it made me think Calvin was insinuating that everything might be in *my* head when I knew damn well it wasn't. But I kept that to myself because the time I spent with Cal was the most normal I'd felt in ages.

When I'd picked up Calvin to go to the club, I'd had to convince him to change into an outfit that wasn't a black hoodie and jeans. He'd compromised by wearing a long-sleeve black T-shirt and different jeans, but had refused to brush his hair, which grew wilder with each passing day.

I, on the other hand, had dressed for the occasion in a sleek black velvet suit Lua had convinced me to buy a couple of months ago but which I'd never had the opportunity to wear. I hadn't dry-cleaned it, and a few spritzes of odor remover had failed to camouflage the old-cigarette-smoke stink, but no one could deny I looked pretty damn good.

Lua had hitched a ride with the band, so I didn't see him until the lights rose and he took the stage wearing a silver-sequined tuxedo. He'd gelled his pink hair into chunky spikes and applied dramatic dark makeup to accentuate his eyes and lips. The rest of the band looked painfully drab in comparison.

Calvin and I hollered loudly for Lua, our voices joined by the enthusiastic crowd. I'd missed spending time with Lua, but by the end of the first song it was clear the practice had paid off. The band tore through each song with an unparalleled intensity and theatrical flair. The only thing missing was a bucket of pig's blood for dramatic effect.

It was near the end of the set, during a soulful, acoustic cover of two Taylor Swift songs mashed together, that I realized I was witnessing the precise moment Lua transformed from an unknown singer in a local band into an honest-to-God rock star. He owned the stage and every one of our souls. His confident fingers skated along the strings of his acoustic guitar, gliding through paragraphs, making the whole thing look like magic, while he melded his voice with Poe's haunting, raspy contralto, and mesmerized the entire club for three minutes and twenty-seven seconds.

Conversations died, the bartenders stopped serving drinks. Every face in the packed club was tuned to Lua.

In that moment I glimpsed Lua's future.

I realized I'd lost Lua as surely as I'd lost Tommy and would soon lose my brother. Lua was going to leave Cloud Lake. Hell, he was already gone. I didn't want to watch him go, but I couldn't turn away. I'd never been so sad to be so happy.

After the band's set, Lua joined me and Calvin on the dance floor. I hadn't told him I was bringing Calvin, and he didn't question it when he saw us, but I was certain he'd grill me about it later. Lua was magnetic, and kept attracting random strangers who couldn't stop gushing about the show, and when a tall tattooed woman with platinum-blond hair dragged Lua to the patio to talk, that left me and Calvin to entertain ourselves.

"Want to get out of here?" I shouted into Calvin's ear. The band that had taken the stage after Lua played screeching, spastic punk that sounded like puppies in a blender. Actually, I think that was their name. Plus, the air in the club was suffocating, and I was sweating through my velvet suit.

Calvin nodded.

We still had over an hour to kill until midnight—I'd

considered going home, but I looked hot and refused to let my suit go to waste—so we walked down Clematis Street, becoming just two more party people on the already crowded sidewalks.

"Lua was amazing," Calvin said. "I mean, really amazing. He's going to be famous, isn't he?" There was something different about Calvin. He seemed more at ease. His limbs were looser, his face more relaxed.

"Probably."

"You don't sound thrilled."

As we walked east from the club, the throngs of midnight-anticipating revelers waxed and waned. Starbucks was booming ahead of us, as was the wine bar across the street, but it was quiet near the railroad tracks.

"I am," I said. "But it means I'm going to lose him."

"How so?"

"He'll sign with a record label or become an Internet sensation and go on tour. I can't follow the band like some obsessed groupie, so when that happens, we probably won't see each other a lot."

"But aren't you planning on going away to college anyway?"

"Maybe. I don't know." I stopped at the intersection and waited for the light to change so we could cross. "But that's not important. I'm happy for Lua, but I'm sad at the same time. Does that make sense?"

"I guess. It just seems like a waste of time to miss someone before they've gone."

We walked in silence until Clematis dead-ended at the intracoastal. We sat on the seawall and dangled our legs over the side, but we weren't alone. Families and couples and groups of friends had gathered to wait for the fireworks. Some sat on the wall like us, others lay stretched out on blankets in the grass. A few boats drifted past, their passengers shouting "Happy New Year!" to us from the water.

But even surrounded by all those people, I still felt like it was just me and Calvin.

"There are so many stars out tonight," Calvin said.

I looked up at the sky. At the nearly full moon hovering over our heads. At the twinkling stars. "Not as many as there should be," I muttered.

"What?"

"Nothing."

Tommy had once told me that astronomers believed it possible that the Milky Way might contain forty billion planets capable of supporting life. If even one tenth of one percent of those were populated by sentient beings, then our galaxy alone could contain over four million life-sustaining worlds. I didn't know how many stars had already vanished, but I couldn't help feeling their loss.

"Ozzie?" Calvin rested his fingers on my hand. I flinched but he didn't pull away. "Are you okay?"

"What if I never find Tommy? What if the universe shrinks until Cloud Lake is all that's left?"

"That's not going to happen."

"But it *is* happening."

Calvin scooted closer. Our arms touched and I shivered.

"After my mom took off," he said, "my dad went through a religious phase. It didn't stick, but for a while he was all about going to church and reading the Bible. He even guilt-tripped me into getting baptized at the beach. The one by the pier."

"I know it," I said.

Calvin cleared his throat. "Anyway, so it was my turn. I waded into the ocean toward Pastor Luke. He said a prayer before he dunked me under. I started to panic, thinking he was trying to drown me. But then God spoke to me."

I arched my eyebrow, trying to hide my are-you-kidding-me-with-this look. "What'd God say?"

"He told me I could breathe."

"Well, that's anticlimactic."

"Underwater," he added. "And when God says you can

do a thing, you do it, right? So I opened my mouth and I breathed." Either Calvin was such a good actor he should have been auditioning for the lead in the school play, or he actually believed God had spoken to him.

"Come on. You're messing with me now."

"I swear I'm not."

"So, what? You're Aquaman?"

Even as more onlookers waiting for the fireworks to begin crowded in around us, I still felt like the night belonged to me and Calvin alone.

"You asked me what had changed. Why I quit wrestling and let my grades slip."

"You gave up because God said you could breathe underwater."

"Yes, but no."

"I don't understand."

"We think we're supposed to drown when we breathe underwater, but we don't have to. We just have to believe."

"That's fine," I said. "But what do *you* believe in?"

Calvin shrugged. "I'm not sure yet."

"I remember people and things that no one else does, and you talk to God." I smiled at Cal. "We're the lamest superhero duo ever."

Calvin's clear laugh rang through the night, drawing eyes

to us. "Just, if we start fighting crime, you have to wear that suit."

"Deal."

A light streaked across the sky. Just a faint flare that disappeared so quickly it could have been my eyes playing tricks on me.

But it wasn't.

"Falling star," Calvin said. "What'd you wish for?"

I glanced at Cal and tried to smile. "Don't tell me you believe in wishes."

Calvin smiled impishly. "No . . . but, okay: What *would* you wish for?"

"To find Tommy. For my parents to get their shit together, to not know my father is a cheating prick, for someone to tell me what I'm supposed to do with the rest of my life, for Warren to come home safe and intact. I could go on."

"You miss him a lot, huh?"

"Warren? He's not even gone yet, but I wouldn't say I miss him, so much as I don't want him to die."

"Tommy," he said. "I meant Tommy."

"Oh. Yeah. I really do."

"I figured." Calvin sounded disappointed. "We should probably start walking back."

I looked around. The number of people had doubled

since we'd arrived. "You don't want to wait for the fireworks?"

"Not really."

We returned to a/s/l with less than five minutes to spare before midnight. Lua found us and planted a sweaty, sloppy kiss on both me and Calvin when the digital clock over the bar turned twelve. He begged us to stay and dance until dawn, but Calvin said he needed to go home, and I wasn't feeling the loud and drunk crowd that had squeezed into the nearly filled-to-capacity club anymore. Despite what I'd said about missing Tommy, I found the one thing I wanted at that moment was to spend more time alone with Calvin, even though that thought made me feel simultaneously guilty and giddy and a little sick to my stomach. Either way, I was grateful to him for providing me with an excuse to escape.

As I drove, Calvin sat so quietly and so still in the car I thought he might have fallen asleep. I shuffled through one of Lua's playlists to cover the silence. When we reached Calvin's house, I parked in his empty driveway.

"I guess my dad got called into work," he said. "Wanna come inside?"

"I don't know." I definitely didn't want to go home, but I wasn't sure I wanted to spend the rest of my New Year's Eve with Calvin either. I turned off the headlights but left the engine running.

Calvin was looking out the windshield at the sky. In the quiet between the end of one song and the beginning of another, he turned down the stereo and said, "Want to know what *I* wished for?"

"What?" I turned to Calvin, and he kissed me on the mouth. It happened so fast—all lips and tongue and minty freshness—and ended before I could properly kiss him back.

"I'm sorry," he said. "I shouldn't have done that."

But as I stared at his face, his lips, his wild hair—as our arms touched, and I took his hand—I realized I wanted him to kiss me again.

I reached my hand around Calvin's neck and pulled him toward me. I kissed him, gentler but with more intensity than the first time. Neither of us spoke as we groped each other, and he pulled me over the armrest and emergency brake into his seat, and it seemed like only seconds later that he'd unbuttoned my shirt and I'd pulled his over his head, and we'd tugged our pants down around our ankles.

Calvin kissed my chest and stomach and hips, teasing me, and I thought about how there might have been a million billion other teenage couples having awkward almost-sex in cars on far-off planets if the stars they orbited hadn't disappeared. But then I pushed those thoughts away and squeezed onto the floor between Calvin's legs.

Before I went down on him, I looked into his eyes and said, "You okay with this?"

He nodded, unable to even speak it seemed, which made me smile.

Despite the buildup and our playful teasing, we rushed to and through the savage crescendo, and then quickly retreated to our own seats—sweaty and sticky and panting—as the inevitable postorgasm embarrassment crept in.

"Sorry," I said as I shimmied into my underwear and pants. "It's been a while and—"

Calvin shook his head. "No, it was good."

Now that I could think clearly without my head clouded by hormones, Tommy barged in and demanded to know what the hell I thought I was doing. How could I claim to love him and then do what I'd done with Cal? I was a hypocrite for judging my dad and then cheating on Tommy. It didn't matter that Tommy was gone for everyone else, he wasn't gone for me. I'd betrayed him, and he wouldn't want me when I found him because of what I'd done. I wished I could take it back. All of it. Go back to the beginning of the night and tell Calvin he couldn't come. Except, I *was* glad he was there. My head and my heart were so full of conflicting feelings that they threatened to overwhelm me.

Calvin startled me when he spoke. "Well, this night certainly didn't turn out the way I'd expected." He'd managed to mostly redress, but hadn't buttoned his jeans, and his shirt was on inside out.

"Understatement of the decade," I muttered.

I was so confused. Part of me did feel like I'd cheated on Tommy, another part thought I might genuinely like Calvin. Still another part wondered if I only liked Calvin because he seemed to believe me about Tommy. Either way, I needed Calvin to get out of the car so I could go home and think without him sitting beside me all beautiful eyes and gorgeous smile, the smell of sex radiating off his skin.

"That's obviously not the first time you've done that," Calvin said, breaking the silence.

I rolled my eyes. "The first with someone I hardly know."

Calvin shrugged. "We know lots about each other. For instance, now I know you're kind of a slut."

The words ripped through me, like Calvin had reached into my mind and pulled out the truth I'd been thinking about myself but hadn't wanted to admit and rammed it down my throat. My guilt would be branded into my skin for Tommy to see when he returned, and how could I face him then? He'd come home and reject me, and I wouldn't be able to blame anyone else for my inability to keep my stupid dick in my pants.

"Get out."

Calvin's smile faded. "Ozzie? I was only joking."

"Get. Out." I flipped on my headlights and shifted the car into drive.

Calvin fumbled with the handle and scrambled out of the car. He stood in the grass, the door still open, and said, "Seriously, Ozzie, it was a joke."

I jammed my foot on the gas and tore down Calvin's street. The force drove the door partially shut. As soon as I was free of Calvin's subdivision, I pulled over and went around to the passenger side door. I opened it and slammed it shut. I slammed it over and over and over, but it wasn't enough.

I drove to the beach and stumbled down the dunes to the edge of the water. I yelled at the sky to give me Tommy back even though I didn't deserve him. But the sky was empty. The stars, all the stars, were gone. I didn't even need to check my phone to know that the universe had shrunk again, and the stars had vanished.

No. They hadn't vanished. I'd given them away to someone who hadn't deserved them, and I'd never get them back.

TOMMY

"SORRY THE CONDOM BROKE, OZZIE."

I stand on the front steps of the unfinished house—abandoned midconstruction when the real estate market bottomed out—holding Tommy's hand, watching the sun punch through the clouds, stretching its arms across the sky with a yawn that feels like forever.

"What?" Everything looks watercolor through my bloodshot eyes. My tie is long gone, as are the top two buttons of my dress shirt, which was neatly pressed once upon a time. I want coffee, but there's the sunrise and there's Tommy Ross.

His eyelids are heavy over his amber eyes, and the tail of his own shirt hangs untucked, covering his khaki pants. And when he smiles, all white teeth and too-much gums, there's nothing else. No world, no sky, no sun. Just me and Tommy and all of time.

Tommy kisses the tops of my knuckles. "The condom. I should've brought more than one."

"Whatever," I say. "It's not like we're worried about getting pregnant."

"I love you, Oswald Pinkerton."

"I love you, too."

"I never want this moment to end."

"Who says it has to?"

Tommy pulls me against his chest and wraps his arms around my stomach. Strong arms. Not like my bony ones. His could move mountains. "And I'm sorry about dinner. I wanted it to be special."

"It was *special," I say. "Everything was."*

"No, I should've taken you somewhere fancy." Tommy shivers in the cool morning air. "But I didn't have the money and—"

I face Tommy and look into his beautiful eyes. I should be freezing, but Tommy's my radiator. "I don't need a fancy restaurant, Tommy. All I need is you."

"Tonight was supposed to be perfect." His voice cracks. "I wanted our first time to be perfect."

I can't keep from blushing. "It was."

Tommy shakes his head, tries to pull away, but I hold tight. "It shouldn't have been on a sheet in an abandoned house, Ozzie. You deserve better."

God, he's everything. "This isn't some abandoned house. It belongs to us tonight. And I wouldn't have done anything different. Not one damn thing."

"I don't deserve you."

"You're amazing, Tommy. The homecoming dance was amazing, dinner was amazing, and that thing we did back there, on that sheet? I can't wait to do it again and again and again and—"

Tommy kisses me. His tongue slides into my mouth, filling it with the taste of garlic. He claws at my belt, digs his thumbs into my hips, and pulls me closer.

"Why are you crying?" I ask.

"I'll love you for always, Ozzie. Until my skin rots and my hair falls out, I'll love you." *His lips brush mine. His hands barely touch me, and I shiver.*

"We should get some sleep before we go home," Tommy says. "My dad's going to kill me for staying out all night." *He turns toward the house, but I catch his hand and pull him back.*

I know Tommy's joking about his father, but I also know he's not. Still, the damage is already done. "Let's stay and watch the sunrise."

"Aren't you cold?"

"A little," I say. "My jacket's inside. I'll go grab it."

Tommy rubs his thumb along my cheek and down the

back of my jaw. *"I'll get it."* He walks into the house, not letting go of my hand until he absolutely has to. I only turn back to the sun when Tommy has disappeared, but the sun is nothing compared to him. Still, I stay to watch a while longer.

263,715 AU

DR. HAMISH LEGGE WAS A QUACK—PRACTICALLY
part duck—and I knew it before he opened his mouth. I'm
not one to discount the value of therapy, especially seeing
as Renny, my parents, and Calvin all could have benefited
from a good psychologist, but Dr. Legge was *not* a good
psychologist.

The motivational posters on his wall betrayed him.
Pictures of penguins with sayings like, "Problems are not
stop signs, they are guidelines." Only a simpleminded fool
believed the secrets to surviving life could be condensed into
bullshit quotations.

"Tell me why you're here, Oswald," he said.

I resisted the urge to roll my eyes. "Because it was this or
jump off the nearest bridge."

I wasn't in the mood for therapy, but Mom had scheduled the appointment and had made it clear skipping wasn't an option.

Dr. Legge typed a note onto his tablet, pecking at the digital keys with only the first two fingers of each hand. He wore a bow tie tied so tightly it was cutting off the blood flow to his brain. His wispy more-gray-than-brown hair was combed neatly, and his beard precisely trimmed.

"Do you often think about hurting yourself?"

"Only when I'm in a useless therapy session."

For some reason, Legge smiled at that. "How was your holiday vacation?"

"Let's see," I said. "I found out my father is a cheater, my brother left for the army yesterday, my best friend is about to achieve her dream and leave me behind, and I gave a blowjob to a guy I thought was my friend but who followed it up by calling me a slut, which I deserved. How was *your* holiday vacation?" I didn't mention losing all the stars or the universe shrinking to just over four light-years because I still couldn't believe it had happened. I mean, rationally, I knew it had, but my brain couldn't process it. Also, I was already pushing my luck with that joke about jumping off a bridge, and I didn't want to give the doctor any additional ammunition he could use to lock me up.

Dr. Legge shifted on his couch. "Quite nice. I took my children to Paris. We toured the Louvre."

"It was a rhetorical question," I said. "You're the worst therapist ever."

"You're not a particularly wonderful patient."

I stood up. Sitting, I'd still been taller than Legge, but standing, I towered over the man. "Christ, I'm not even going to have to make up a reason not to see you again. You're a jerk."

"Sit down, Oswald."

I sat.

"Now," he said, "the one thing you need to understand about therapy is that I can only help you if you want me to." Legge stared me down. "Do you want me to help you?"

"I don't think you can."

Dr. Legge nodded and made a note in his tablet. "Then I believe we're done. It was nice meeting you, Oswald."

He'd dismissed me. No doctor had ever dismissed me. Even when I'd ridiculed them, they'd still tried to figure me out, to force me to open up. I didn't know what to do.

After a moment I stood and walked toward the door.

Before leaving, I stopped, turned to Dr. Legge, and said, "The guy I mentioned. Was he right for calling me a slut?"

Dr. Legge didn't look up from his tablet, but he said, "Sometimes when people lash out, when they call others names, it's themselves they're putting down." His two-finger typing was infuriating. "That answer was free. The next will cost you. Good-bye, Oswald."

255,024 AU

I WASN'T SURE WHETHER I WAS ANGRIER AT CALVIN
for calling me a slut—even if he was only joking—only minutes after I'd blown him, or at myself for so easily forgetting
about Tommy. Either way, I'd deleted Calvin's texts unread
for the rest of winter break, though I didn't know what I was
going to say to him now that we were back in school.

Thankfully, Dustin arrived to physics before Calvin and
regaled me with tales of his vacation at his grandparents'
house.

"So then Bubbe runs out of her bedroom, flapping her
arms, yelling like the house is on fire about how the toilet's
overflowing, and Zayde marches in, suited up with yellow
dish gloves and armed with a plunger, and comes out ten
minutes later holding three wet Barbie heads, asking Bubbe
what the hell she's been eating."

It felt good to laugh, and I loved hearing stories about Dustin's crazy family. "Barbie heads?"

Dustin nodded. "Apparently, Sasha didn't like the way Avi's Barbies were looking at her, so she decapitated them and flushed the heads down the toilet."

"Your cousins are so weird."

"You have no idea, Pinks," Dustin said. "Graeme's going through this phase where he wants to be a comedian, so he spent the entire vacation telling the worst jokes."

"Come on. That's kind of adorable."

"Did you hear about the man who stole a calendar?" Dustin said, deadpan. "He got twelve months."

I busted up laughing.

"Seriously, two weeks of that crap," Dustin said. "It actually made me look forward to working with Ortiz. *If* he shows up." Dustin looked over his shoulder at his still-empty lab table. "What'd you do? Anything good? Renny shipped off, didn't he?"

"Yeah," I said. "Fifteen weeks. If he survives that long."

Dustin clapped me on the back. "You worry too much. He'll be fine."

I didn't expect anything too terrible to happen to Warren—other than possibly having to spend fifteen weeks cleaning latrines with a toothbrush as punishment for oversleeping.

It was what happened after basic that scared me. But I didn't want to talk about that, so I changed the subject. "You missed an amazing show on New Year's Eve. Lua and the band blew a/s/l away. For real. Their set was hands-down the best."

"I don't doubt it," Dustin said. "Our Lua's gonna be famous one day."

"Other than that . . ." I considered telling Dustin about Calvin, but the final bell saved me from oversharing. Anyway, Dustin had never had a girlfriend, so I doubted he would have had any useful advice for me. He left for his table as Calvin slid into class at the bell and took his seat. Ms. Fuentes dove into the next chapter, hinting she'd be quizzing us on the material sooner rather than later.

I refused to look at Calvin. What we'd done had definitely been a mistake. Maybe. Definitely probably. I'd been lonely and horny, and I couldn't even begin to guess what kind of demented thoughts had been going through *his* brain that night. For all I knew, Trent had been right and Calvin was a pathological liar.

All morning I'd half expected to find out Calvin had told the whole school what we'd done, the way Alex Molitor had done to Shay Kristoff after she gave him a hand job in the theater during rehearsals for *And Then There Were None*, but I would've heard about it by now if he had. Calvin kept his head down and his mouth shut throughout class, and he ran off when the bell rang.

I made it through the rest of the day, though I couldn't remember anything that my teachers had talked about during my last two classes, since all I could think about was going home, locking myself in my room, and sleeping until the weekend. When the last bell *finally* rang, I grabbed my bag and headed toward the parking lot.

Lua caught up with me in front of the library. She was decked out in striped leggings and a black dress that skirted the school's rule on appropriate length.

"I've been dying to talk to you," Lua said.

"About what?"

"I would've told you at lunch, but Dustin was there and I wanted you to be the first to know."

Lua's coyness was bordering on annoying. "Is this about Jaime? You've broken up and gotten back together so many times, I'm not sure I want to hear it if it's about Jaime."

Lua grabbed my hand and pulled me to a stop. "It's not about that," she said. "But I did break up with Jaime for good."

"Oh."

"I didn't want to string him along, since I'm going on tour."

I started to tell her I was glad she'd been straight with

Jaime—finally—but I stopped when the last thing she'd said registered in my brain. "Tour?"

Lua nodded, grinning madly. "The lead singer of Cinderfellas invited the band to open for them on their tour at the end of the summer."

"You're going on tour?"

"We're going on tour."

"You're going on tour!" I grabbed Lua's other hand and jumped up and down. She screamed and we laughed and I didn't even care that it meant I'd soon lose her, because how could I stand in the way of her dreams?

"Holy shit, you guys are fucking losers." Trent Williams stood in the grass sneering at me and Lua.

"Go fuck yourself with a power drill, asshole," Lua said, still smiling, still grinning her face off.

Trent muttered something and trudged away.

"He totally wants you."

Lua rolled her eyes. "As if."

"I can't believe it's really happening," I said. "We should celebrate. We'll get Chinese and you can tell me everything. I want all the details."

"I can't tonight," Lua said. "Rehearsals. I've got to write some new songs and we only have a few months to practice." She stopped for a moment. "Shit, Ozzie. This is real."

I held my smile even though it was already starting. Lua was leaving. "Whatever. This weekend, then. And don't say no."

"Yes," Lua said. "This weekend. You and me and MSG."

We kept walking toward where I'd parked, both of us repeating some version of "I can't believe this is happening" over and over until I saw Calvin Frye leaning against the hood of my car. Lua flashed me a questioning look.

"Leave me alone," I said when I got near enough.

"Ozzie, just listen, all right? Give me one minute to explain."

"If you want to discuss our roller coaster, fine. Otherwise I have nothing to say to you." I opened the door and threw my backpack in the backseat. Lua stood to the side all narrowed eyes and jutting hips, like she might beat the crap out of Calvin if she had any idea what was going on.

Calvin straightened and turned toward me. "What I said . . . it was a joke. A bad one. I didn't mean it. I'm so stupid and I ruin everything and I shouldn't have said it." His shoulders drooped. "I'm sorry, Ozzie. I really am."

I stood in front of the driver's side door, clutching the handle, gripping it so tightly my fingers hurt. "Fine," I said. "Thanks for the apology." I opened the door but didn't get in.

"Can we at least meet to work on our project?" Calvin sounded so pathetic, I almost believed he was actually sorry.

"Sure. The quicker we get it done, the quicker we never have to speak again."

Calvin nodded. "Okay. I'll wait for you to call me." He walked away. I watched him until he turned the corner at the end of the sidewalk by the library before getting in the car and starting the engine.

"Do I want to know what that was about?" Lua asked.

"No," I said. "You really don't."

Mrs. Petridis disappeared the moment I walked into the bookstore to work. I might have worried she'd snuck out the back door and run away if I hadn't heard her swearing in her studio.

I busied myself shelving books, letting the rhythmic clicking of Skip's Royal Quiet De Luxe lull me into a trance. My mind wandered back to earlier in the day, to Calvin's face as he stood in front of my car. I tried to imagine how I would've reacted if Tommy had said what Calvin had. I probably would've laughed about it—we would've laughed about it together—but I hadn't laughed when Calvin said it because, whether he'd been joking or not, I thought it was true. Maybe not in the most literal sense, but I *had* cheated on Tommy, which made me feel like dog shit smeared on the bottom of my shoe, and maybe it wasn't fair to blame Cal for my own mistakes.

I was trying to decide whether to stay mad at Calvin or forgive him when someone tapped me on the shoulder. Mrs. Ross stood over me, wearing a cautious smile. Thick makeup hid most, but not all, of the bruising around her eyes. Unlike when Calvin cut himself, I doubted Mrs. Ross thought much about her amygdala when her husband was wailing on her.

"You know where the books on American history are?" she asked. "I need one that deals with the Adams administration."

"Sure." I led her to the history section and helped her pick out a couple that looked promising.

"That FOIL thing worked," she said as I walked with her to a table.

"I'm glad." I motioned at her stack of GED books. "If you want, I can keep those behind the register so you don't have to find them every time."

Mrs. Ross blushed. "I feel bad enough as it is coming here and not buying anything."

I shook my head. "Mr. Petridis wouldn't have minded."

"Mr. Petridis?"

"The owner. Well, he died, so he's not technically the owner anymore, but he wanted to create a place where people could enjoy books, whether they bought any or not."

Mrs. Ross settled at her table and started flipping through

the pages of one of the thick history books. She'd brought along a set of index cards and a marker.

"Can I ask you something?" I said.

Mrs. Ross froze. Her muscles tensed. "I know you think—"

"It's not about Tommy," I said quickly. "I was just wondering why you dropped out of high school."

"That all?" Mrs. Ross relaxed slightly. I figured I'd crossed a line. I was talking to her like we knew each other, but we didn't. The woman I'd known, Tommy's mother, didn't exist. But then she blew out a sigh and said, "I got pregnant."

"You did?"

Mrs. Ross nodded. "My folks kicked me out of the house. I spent some time living in a shelter and working at McDonald's until Carl and I could afford a place of our own. School's not a priority when you can barely afford food."

A seed of hope sprouted fragile tendrils in my chest. I'd heard the story before. But how would *this* story end? Did she give Tommy up for adoption? Was he still out there with a different name, waiting for me to find him?

"What happened to the baby?" I asked, careful not to use Tommy's name or push too hard and risk spooking her.

"Stillborn." Mrs. Ross breathed shallowly, and she blinked more than normal. "I tried going home, but my parents wouldn't take me back."

The same but different. Mrs. Ross had gotten pregnant and dropped out of school, but instead of giving birth to Tommy, her baby died and she wound up stuck in a shitty life with an abusive husband anyway. But at least it proved Tommy wasn't to blame for the way his mother's life had turned out.

Too bad he wasn't around for me to tell him.

"And you were going to name him Thomas, after your grandfather, right?

"Nope," she said. "Carl was pretty insistent we name the baby after him."

"You were going to name him Carl Jr.? Maybe it's better he—" I stopped myself and coughed to cover what I'd nearly said. "Do you still make art?"

Mrs. Ross's head whipped up and she stared at me with narrow eyes. "How do you know about that?"

Shit. I *shouldn't* have known. I scrambled for an explanation while Mrs. Ross bored into me with her eyes.

"Look," I said. "I know you don't believe me—and why should you?—but I grew up around your house. You were like my second mother." I was doing a terrible job of explaining, and, judging by the way Mrs. Ross's nostrils flared, I was screwing things up worse.

"You take your coffee with honey," I said. "And the only book you've ever finished is *Their Eyes Were Watching God.*

You sing Lauryn Hill songs when you wash dishes, and you've seen every episode of the original *Star Trek*. You never cuss, your favorite flower is redring milkweed because it reminds you of your grandmother, and you hide money from your husband in a tin you keep in the toilet tank."

Mrs. Ross looked like she wanted to flee, but she didn't move. "Have you been snooping in my house or something?"

Skip had stopped typing. I caught him with his fingers poised over the keys, eavesdropping. I knew I sounded crazy, but Mrs. Ross had a right to know the truth.

"In another life," I said, "your baby didn't die. You had him and raised him, and I met him and he became my best friend. How else could I know all those things about you? There's no way I could learn your favorite flower by peeking through your windows."

Mrs. Ross pushed her chair back and stood. "I have to go. And don't worry about hiding the books for me. I won't be coming back."

"Please don't leave," I called futilely after her.

She didn't stop or look back, and all I could do was watch her leave.

"You mind if I use some of that for my book?" Skip asked after the door closed behind Mrs. Ross. "It's great stuff."

"Sure," I said. "Fine. No sane person would believe it's true."

253,221 AU

I HATED BOWLING. ANY GAME A TODDLER CAN BEAT you at by granny-throwing a ball down the lane is automatically stupid. Of course, I wasn't playing against a toddler—unless you counted the one two lanes over who kept throwing strikes, which I didn't—I was playing against Dustin, and he was kicking my ass.

"Damn, Pinks," he said. "You really suck at this." He waited for his ball to return so he could pick up the spare. Which he did.

"You don't. Though I wouldn't go putting it on your college applications."

I munched cheesy nachos from the greasy paper container on the table and checked out the score. Even if I threw nothing but strikes for the remaining four frames, I couldn't catch up to Dustin.

Mrs. Petridis had given me Friday night off—she'd given me the whole weekend off, actually. She'd decided to keep Ana on full-time, which had meant cutting my hours, not that I'd minded too much except that I hadn't known what to do with my night until Dustin guilted me into going bowling.

"I feel like we haven't hung out in forever," Dustin said.

"We haven't." I stuffed my fingers in the holes and hefted my ball. While I understood the mechanics of the game, I couldn't translate that into meaningful action. I threw my ball down the lane, and didn't bother watching to see how many pins—if any—I knocked down.

My final score was pitiful, even for me, and we decided to give pool a try. Dustin racked the balls.

"What's new with you, Pinks?"

"Uh . . . nothing?"

"Hear from any colleges yet?"

"If I had, you'd be the second to know." I selected a pool cue at random and waited for Dustin to break. "What about you?"

Dustin scattered the solid and striped balls across the table, knocking one of each into different corner pockets. Seriously, the kid didn't know how to suck at anything. "I got into UF."

"Congratulations," I said, though I wasn't surprised. Any school that rejected Dustin Smeltzer was stupid. "That's your safety school, right?"

Dustin shook his head. "Nope. UF's my school." He lined up the cue ball and sank the fourteen. "You should go. We could room together."

"Wait. What about Princeton? And Duke and Cornell?"

"Too expensive." Dustin scratched. He waited for the cue ball to drop, retrieved it, and handed it to me. "Your turn."

But I just stood there holding the ball. I would've kept standing there if one of the girls at the next table hadn't asked me to move. I didn't understand what Dustin meant by "too expensive." His parents were both lawyers and loaded. After the problems they'd experienced adopting Dustin when he was a baby, they'd started a successful family law practice specializing in helping other couples navigate the adoption process. But they made the bulk of their money handling wealthy couples' divorces.

I placed the cue ball at the end of the table, lined it up to take out the three ball, which was right in front of the side pocket, cocked my cue, and still missed, sending the three ricocheting off the side, where it scattered a cluster of balls.

"Tough break, Pinks."

How could Dustin act so casual? He'd spent the last four years of high school killing himself so he could attend any school he wanted. It didn't matter that he didn't know what he wanted to study, because there was nothing he wasn't good at. Brain surgeon, teacher, theoretical astrophysicist? He could've done anything, though that last one might've been a waste of time if the universe continued collapsing.

"What's going on, Dustin?" I said, finally. "UF's a good school and all, and congratulations, but you're better than a state college."

Dustin cleared two more striped balls from the table like it was nothing. When he finally missed a shot, he stepped back and leaned against the table. For a stoner, tidy had always best described the way he dressed. Navy shorts, short-sleeved plaid shirt. Like he was on his way to a polo match and had wandered into a trashy bowling alley by mistake.

"My dad made a couple of bad investments," he said. "No big deal. We probably won't lose the house."

"Probably?"

"Don't make it a thing. Come on, your turn."

Clearly he didn't want to talk about it, so I held the hundred questions I was dying to ask. By the time Dustin won the game—eight ball, side pocket—I still had four of my balls on the table.

"You hungry?" Dustin asked. "I'm hungry. Let's swing by Denny's."

I'd driven to Dustin's house, but we'd taken his Jetta to the bowling alley. He fired up his glass bowl in the Denny's parking lot, filling the car with thick clouds of smoke, before we went in. The hostess stuck us at a still-damp but hardly clean booth in the corner. Most of the other tables sat empty, but the night was young and creepy.

"How're things working out with you and Frye?" Dustin asked. I sipped shitty coffee while he destroyed a chocolate milkshake.

"Nothing's going on," I said, before I realized he'd probably been referring to our roller coaster.

Dustin grinned. "Which means something is *definitely* going on. Spill it, Pinks."

I dumped the bowl of creamers onto the table and started stacking them. "Isn't it weird how these things sit out all day but don't go bad?"

"Not really," Dustin said. "Bacteria causes them to spoil, so the packages are sealed and then heated to kill it all off." He set both hands on the table and raised his eyebrow. "You're avoiding the question."

Of course I was avoiding the question. Just like he'd avoided discussing why he was throwing his future away at a state university—sure, UF was the top-ranked school in Florida, but it was no Princeton. Our discussions rarely ran deeper than school or our families or our favorite pizza toppings, but maybe talking about Calvin with Dustin wouldn't be terrible.

"We sort of fooled around."

Dustin broke out his stoner grin, highlighted by his bloodshot eyes. "I knew it! When? Where? Does it bother you he's dated girls? Is he your boyfriend now?"

"New Year's Eve." I ticked the answers off on my fingers. "In my car, parked in front of his house. Why would it bother me? And no."

"Was it bad?" Dustin asked. "Does he have a tiny dick? Because I've seen him wrestle and I would've guessed he was packing some serious meat."

"First of all," I said, "gross. Second: How shallow do you think I am?"

Dustin shrugged. "I don't know. If television and movies have taught me anything, it's that size matters."

Coming from anyone else, I probably would've been offended, but Dustin didn't know how to be properly mean. It wasn't in him to demean people. It was still weird, though. "Well, it doesn't," I said. "And, for the record, Calvin's dick is dick-sized, and that's all I'm prepared to say about it."

"Do you like him?" Dustin asked.

"He called me a slut," I said. "Right after we . . . uh . . . finished."

"Harsh. Why?"

"I wish I knew. He tried to tell me he was only joking, but it didn't feel like a joke."

Our waitress delivered our food. Scrambled eggs, pancakes, bacon, sausage, and hash browns for Dustin, and a BLT and fries for me. I wasn't hungry, but Dustin's munchies demanded greasy satisfaction.

"Maybe I overreacted," I said, picking at my fries.

"Your reactions do tend toward the extreme." Dustin talked with his mouth full. "Not quite Lua territory, but you definitely overthink shit, Pinks."

Of course, Dustin probably thought everyone overreacted about everything, but only because he possessed the emotional range of a potato. If I'd found out my parents were broke and couldn't send me to college, I probably would have burned my house down, or something less destructive but equally terrifying. Not Dustin, though. He was either the most Zen person I knew, or he was going to implode one day soon.

"Isn't sex supposed to be special, though?" My only other experience had been with Tommy, and it *had* been special.

"Don't know," Dustin said. "Don't think about it much."

"Sex?"

"Yeah."

"For real?" I said. "I think about it all the time. Like, since I first popped wood, my brain has been stuck on sex overdrive."

"Weird."

"How can you not think about sex?" I asked.

Syrup dripped over the side of his pancakes and pooled near his eggs. He scraped together a mouthful of both, mixing the salty and sweet, which was practically anathema to me, and ate them. "Just don't."

This was a side of Dustin I'd never known. "What about when you need to fire off a few practice shots?"

"Yeah," he said. "I whack it sometimes. It's like flossing, though. Necessary but tedious."

"Wow. Is that why you've never dated anyone?"

Dustin had cleaned his plate while I'd barely eaten half my sandwich. Denny's was starting to fill up with the Friday night after-club crowd, but Dustin and I existed in our own world. "I guess. Like, I'd be down to spending time with someone cool, cuddling and shit. But then there'd be all that pressure to have sex, and I'm just not into it."

I had difficulty understanding where Dustin was coming from. Even though Calvin had ruined it at the end, I still remembered kissing him, and the feel of his hands on my chest. If I were weaker, I might have forgiven him so we could do it again. The idea that Dustin didn't care for or think about sex intrigued me.

"Maybe you should give Frye a chance to explain," Dustin said. "He's not a bad guy."

"How do you know?"

"We had economics together last year."

"But that was normal Calvin, not emo Calvin from the darkest timeline."

"People go through shit," Dustin said. "Some handle it better than others."

"Like you?"

Dustin pushed his plate away and then wiped his mouth with his napkin. "Nah, I'm a mess."

"Yeah, you're a five-car pileup."

I'd tried to bait Dustin into talking about college, but he didn't bite. "Look, all I'm saying is that maybe Calvin wasn't actually after sex. Maybe he just wanted to feel close to someone—that someone being you—and thought sex was the way to get what he wanted."

"He could've just told me he wanted to talk."

Dustin shrugged and looked down at his empty plate. "Let's be honest, Pinks. You're not exactly the easiest person in the world to talk to, and you've been pretty focused on other things the last few months."

I would've been pissed if anyone other than Dustin had said it, but he wasn't wrong. I'd been so concerned with my own problems—my parents and Renny and finding Tommy—that I'd been ignoring everything else. It was entirely possible Calvin had needed something from me, I'd missed it, and he'd thought sex was the only way to get it.

"The real question," Dustin said, "is whether this was a one-time thing between you and Calvin or if you want more."

It was easier to hate Calvin for being a jerk than talk to him. It was easier to think I'd made a mistake—the kind of mistake Tommy could forgive me for when he came back— than that something real had happened between me and Calvin.

"For someone who doesn't think about sex," I said, "you seem to know a lot about it."

Dustin shook his head. "I don't know anything about sex. But I know you, Pinks. Stop overthinking it and talk to the guy. Just, you know, keep your clothes on this time."

"You're an ass."

"I know."

I abandoned my BLT, and we paid and left. When we reached Dustin's house, I stood at my car and we stared at the empty sky. I still couldn't fathom that the stars no longer existed, and found it even more difficult to believe that I was the only one who knew they ever had. The sky felt desolate without them, but it also felt heavy. Like it might fall and crush us under its weight. The whole thing was difficult to even begin to wrap my brain around. I kept hoping I'd look up and find all the stars back where they were supposed to be. Like with Calvin, it was easier to ignore the problem than to deal with it.

"Are you going to be okay?" I asked Dustin.

"We're all going to be okay."

"With the college thing," I said. "You could get scholarships."

Dustin waved me off. "So what if I can't go to an expensive school? I'm luckier than most. UF's a good college, and I'm still the smartest guy you know. I'll be fine."

"I wish I had your confidence."

"You can choose to be happy with what life gives you," he said, "or spend your life miserable. I choose happiness. It's really that simple."

239,924 AU

I LAY IN BED UNTIL NOON ON SATURDAY THINKING about Calvin. Wondering if Dustin was right and I was over-thinking what had happened. Maybe what Calvin had said had been more about him than about me, and he'd explain if I gave him the chance. I just wasn't sure I wanted to give him that chance. Because if Calvin *did* have a good reason for what he'd said, and I forgave him, I'd have to deal with what we'd done. I'd have to deal with what hooking up with Calvin meant for me and Tommy.

I was certain I loved Tommy, and I refused to accept that he was gone and might never come back, but Calvin was here and Tommy wasn't. It was possible that I actually liked Calvin, that something real might have happened between us on New Year's Eve. And if it had, well, I doubted I could forget about Tommy and jump into a relationship with Calvin, but I at least owed him the opportunity to explain.

I finally texted Calvin to see if he wanted to get together to work on our roller coaster. He answered "yes" almost immediately, which meant I needed to get out of bed.

I stumbled downstairs in my boxers. A realtor had been holding open houses while I was at school, and the house was cleaner than normal. It already looked like we'd never lived there. They hadn't just swept away the crumbs on the floor, they'd swept up the memories we'd made. Swept them up and dumped them in the trash.

My mom walked into the kitchen as I reached the bottom of the stairs. She was wearing a black bikini with a flower-print sarong wrapped around her waist, and she'd tied her hair into a ponytail.

"My eyes!" I yelled. "They're burning!"

Mom pursed her lips. "Don't be dramatic, Ozzie. You breast-fed until you were two. Besides, I'm not the one wearing underwear."

I glanced at my Super Mario boxers. "They're more shorts than underwear."

Mom pulled out a pink water bottle and a yogurt from the fridge, setting both on the counter.

I sat at the kitchen bar, hoping she'd leave soon so I

could make myself brunch in peace. "Going to the beach?"

"Yes."

"With Ben Schwitzer?"

Mom shook her head. "I'm not seeing Ben any longer. Not that it's any of your business."

"Did you realize you had more in common with his parents than him?"

Mom rested her hands on the counter and leaned forward, her arms straight. "This isn't easy for me, Oswald."

"How would I know? None of you talk to me. *And* you keep secrets from me."

"I'm forty-two," Mom said. "I'm forty-two and I never thought I'd be dating again. When I married your father, I believed we'd stay together until we died."

"Then tough it out. I know he cheated on you, but Ben Schwitzer makes you even now, right? Don't give up."

Mom's anger lines receded, replaced by a weariness that made her look older than forty-two. "We've changed too much, Ozzie. People can begin on the same trajectory only to wind up, twenty years later, so far from one another that it's impossible to chart a course back." She sniffled, and I thought maybe she was crying, but it could have been allergies. "That's just life, Ozzie. It happens. It'll happen to you."

I thought about Tommy, and wondered if we would have

eventually grown apart. I couldn't imagine a life where I didn't love Thomas Ross. "Does it have to?"

"I don't know." Mom grabbed her water but didn't go anywhere. "Just . . . don't get so focused on where you're going that you forget the people you're traveling with. There's no point reaching a destination if you arrive alone."

"Okay," I said, though it sounded inadequate.

"I'm going to the beach. Don't mess up the house."

"I won't." I wanted to hug her. Tell her I understood, even though I didn't. If two people loved each other enough, it shouldn't matter how far their paths had diverged. Instead, I let her walk out the door.

My appetite left with Mom, so I showered and changed and drove to Calvin's house.

Calvin was sitting in his driveway when I arrived. He waved and popped up, and I parked beside his father's truck.

"Hey! I wasn't sure you'd actually come."

I got out of the car. "Should we head inside and get started?"

Calvin kept his distance. "Actually, I thought we could go for a walk first." He spoke so quickly his words ran together. "Dad's off from both jobs, and he decided to work around the house, which started with light cleaning, but now he's taking apart the garbage disposal."

Calvin's suggestion felt like a ploy to get me alone, but judging by his run-on sentences and manic hand gestures, we probably wouldn't get any work done on our roller coaster until he said what he needed to say.

"Sure," I said. "Let's go."

We walked to the end of his cul-de-sac and veered into the grass, which turned out to be a dog-poo minefield, until we reached a series of boardwalks and gazebos that crisscrossed a large retention pond infested with stalkery, bread-hungry ducks. It was one of those mild breezy days that convinces northerners Florida is a paradise. But no one can truly understand Florida until they've survived a couple of summers where the air is thick enough to drink and the heat index hovers somewhere between sweat-through-your-undershirt and even-Satan-cranked-up-his-AC hot. Where, for five months out of the year, every tropical system is a potential house-slaying hurricane. Where the roaches fly, you can only drive as fast as the ancient snowbird in front of you, and the mosquitos suck every last drop of blood from your body.

But that day it *did* feel like paradise, and I found myself glad Calvin had suggested we spend it outside.

Calvin stopped at a gazebo and parked his butt on a bench, looking across the pond at a fountain spraying misty water into the air.

"I had this whole speech," Calvin said. "I've been reworking it in my mind since New Year's. It's what I was trying to tell you at your car at school, which I'm sorry about, by the way. I didn't mean to ambush you like that. Well, I mean, I guess I did; I just expected to catch you alone."

I climbed onto the railing and hooked my legs through the wood beams to keep from tumbling backward into the water. "We can pretend New Year's Eve never happened, and just work on our project. We don't have to be friends."

"Is that what you want?"

"Yes," I said. "No. I don't know. Just say what you need to say already."

Calvin bobbed his head. "Obviously, you can tell I've got some problems."

"Don't we all."

"There was this guy. He really messed me up."

"So that's why you called me a slut?"

"Yeah," Calvin said. "But no." He fidgeted with the cords hanging from his hoodie's neck. It was like he was wearing a suit of fire ants under his regular clothes and couldn't stop squirming. "The guy . . . he was my first, and I loved him, all right? He said to me what I said to you after the first time we had sex. And the second time and the third—"

"I get it," I said.

"It fucked with my head, and I think he did it so that I'd never feel like I was good enough for anyone else."

Finally, I had nothing to say.

"I was serious when I told you I was joking, but I think I also kind of said it because I was scared you wouldn't want to be with me after what we did, and it was easier to strike first." Calvin met my eyes with his. "Does that make any sense?"

"I know it shouldn't, but it kind of does."

Calvin rocked on the bench, and I wanted to freeze him in place. "I think you're awesome, Ozzie. We haven't known each other long, so it's not like I'm all in love with you because we got off together, but I *do* like you. You're weird and funny and I know I've probably screwed everything up, but I hope you can forgive me for being an asshole."

I wanted it to be as easy as believing Calvin was sincere and accepting his apology. I wanted to be like Dustin and just choose to be happy, but it felt dangerous to like Calvin the way he'd said he liked me. Dangerous for both of us. I think I'd only seen the surface of his problems, and getting involved with him could end badly for everyone involved. And I would definitely hurt him if—no, not if, *when*—I found Tommy.

"We can be friends," I said after a while. Calvin's back straightened and his shoulders lifted. He even smiled. "But I don't think it's a good idea for us to be anything more."

Calvin held up his hands. "You don't have to explain."

"I still love Tommy," I said. "And I'm not giving up on finding him."

"I understand."

I laughed. "I'm glad someone does." I wasn't in the mood to talk about Tommy, though, so I changed the subject. "Tell me about this guy of yours. He sounds like a dick."

Calvin's fragile smile faded. "You don't know him. He's older. A teacher."

"You were hooking up with a teacher? Holy shit! Who?"

"It's not important."

I could tell Calvin didn't want to discuss it, but he couldn't dangle information that juicy in front of me and then withhold the details. "Does he teach at our school? Is he the reason you quit wrestling and started sleeping through all your classes?"

"Yes," Calvin said. "And no." He stood and walked toward me. "I don't want to talk about it."

"Yeah. Obviously. I'm sorry." I shook my head. "It's just . . . a teacher? That's definitely not what I was expecting you to say. "

"Listen. You can't tell anyone."

"I won't."

"Not even Lua."

"Promise."

Calvin stared at me like he was a human lie detector. I guess he decided I was trustworthy, because he said, "We should go work on our roller coaster now." He headed back toward his house.

I hopped off the railing and jogged to catch up. "Hey," I said. "Since we're friends now, why don't you eat lunch with me and Lua and the others? They're weird, but you should come anyway."

"Thanks, Ozzie. I think I'd like that."

248,011 AU

TO MY SURPRISE, CALVIN ARRIVED TO PHYSICS EARLY,
wearing a new black hoodie and clean jeans. We barely talked,
but I felt pretty certain I'd made the right decision about us
just being friends. Between me looking for Tommy and trying to figure out why the universe was shrinking, and Calvin
cutting himself and sleeping with a teacher, I kind of figured
we had enough problems between us that it made sense not
to complicate our lives further. Besides, I was still trying to
wrap my head around Calvin's revelation that he'd had sex
with a teacher. I mean, based on his behavior since the beginning of the school year, it had obviously screwed him up, and
I both wanted to know more and wished I could forget he'd
ever told me.

When the bell rang, I told Dustin to go on ahead, and
Calvin and I walked to the cafeteria together. I hadn't warned

the others I'd invited Calvin to sit with us at lunch, because I wanted to see the looks on their faces when he showed up.

"Where do you normally eat?" I asked as we stood in line with our trays to sample Cloud Lake High's finest culinary delights.

Calvin chose two slices of flat, greasy pizza. "You know the retention pond across from the agriculture building?"

I nodded. Since I'd had pizza for dinner the night before and still felt bloated, I ended up grabbing a sad, wilted salad.

"That's where I eat."

"Oh." No wonder Calvin was excited to eat lunch with us. The thought of him sitting by himself beside a fake pond was about the saddest thing in the world.

"You ready for this?" I asked after we paid for our food.

"Is there any reason I shouldn't be?"

Yeah, I could have clued him in that Lua was probably going to be possessively hostile, and that Dustin would probably attempt to prove he was smarter, but I didn't want to scare him. It was best to send him in blind. Either he'd survive or he'd never speak to me again. Honestly, it could have gone either way.

"Nah," I said. "You can breathe underwater, remember?"

Lua spotted us first. She was wearing a revealing white blouse with suspenders, and her hair was pinned with crystal butterfly barrettes. I was actually glad that she was hanging out on the feminine end of her spectrum. Not that I cared, but I didn't have to worry about Calvin accidentally using the wrong pronoun.

I think it took Lua a moment to register that Calvin and I were walking toward the table together. Like, maybe for a moment, she thought we were just walking in proximity to each other. But as soon as she realized what was up, a suspicious grin split her face. I probably should have been more nervous than I was, but I was committed to doing this, and it was too late to run away.

"Hey," I said. I set my tray down next to Lua. "Calvin's gonna sit with us, all right?"

Priya Soni—a gossip with a massive unrequited crush on Dustin—was standing at the table, and her eyes bulged out of her head when she saw us. I hoped she didn't stick around.

Dustin cast me a quick, knowing smile, and offered Calvin a bro nod. "I saw you wrestle last year. You were a beast. What happened to you? I thought you were going to make me work for valedictorian."

Before Calvin could answer, Priya opened her mouth and released a raging deluge. "I heard you had a brother that shot someone? Is that true? Did you really quit the wrestling team? Because Mindi Bowers said that she heard from Wryan

Jenkins that you tested positive for steroids and you were actually kicked off. Those are *so* gross. Maria said she heard Bobby Yu took steroids and his balls got really small. Did that happen to you?"

"His balls are definitely not small," I said, and then immediately wished I hadn't.

Lua's jaw dropped and she stared at me. I could actually see the chewed-up pizza in her mouth.

"Can we not talk about balls while I'm eating?" Dustin said.

Calvin cleared his throat, pulling the attention away from me and onto him. "Half the school knows how big my balls are. Those wrestling uniforms leave nothing to the imagination. But you want to know what's really awkward? Trent getting a boner while I'm trying to pin him."

"Trent's gay?" Priya said, and before the question had left her mouth, she'd already gotten her phone out and was tapping away.

Lua rolled her eyes. "Don't you have somewhere else to sit, Priya?"

Priya looked up from her phone, glared at Lua, and stomped away.

"Trent's not gay," I said. "He's obviously into Lua."

Lua had regained most of her composure, but I could tell

I was in for the Inquisition later. "Why are boys so uptight about their sexuality?"

Calvin nibbled his pizza. "Because guys are idiots."

"Everyone knows that," Lua said.

"It's like this," Calvin said. "For the majority of guys, sexuality is black or white. There's no spectrum, no in-between. You're either straight or gay. Even bi guys are considered 'bi now, gay later.' If you check out another guy, you're gay. It doesn't matter if you have a girlfriend and ten other girls on the side, all it takes is one rumor and you're branded for life."

Lua pointed at Calvin with her pizza crust. "That's the stupidest thing I've ever heard, and I've spent years listening to stupid shit come out of Ozzie's face hole."

"Thanks?" I said, but Lua kept rambling like I hadn't said anything.

"Guys can be bi. They can experiment. I mean, what if a boy just wants to see what it's like to kiss another boy?"

"Gay."

"Are you serious?" Lua glanced at Dustin. "Is he serious?"

Dustin nodded. "I can confirm."

"It's stupid," Calvin said. "But that's how a lot of guys are."

"Insecure guys," I added, but Lua and Calvin didn't seem to hear me. Lua had been cool with Calvin joining us at a/s/l on New Year's Eve—we hadn't discussed it and I think she assumed I'd invited him as a pity date—but bringing him to lunch was serious business, which meant she had to test him to make certain he deserved to be there.

"So you're saying," Lua said, "that if Dustin wanted to know what making out with a guy was like, even if he's one hundred percent straight—"

"Gay," Calvin finished.

Lua huffed. "You're right: Boys are idiots."

I wasn't sure whether Lua's statement was in indictment of Cal or a roundabout approval, but she hadn't thrown any food at him, so that was a good sign.

Dustin spent most of the rest of lunch complaining about how he was having to build his roller coaster without any help from Jake, whose only contribution had been to attempt to name it the Funky Trumpet, which Dustin had vetoed. But he made sure to humble-brag about his awesome design.

"So," Lua said, motioning at me and Calvin when Dustin finally stopped ranting about Jake. "What's this thing going on with you two?"

"We're just friends," I mumbled.

Lua sighed, her entire face a frown. "Friends who know how big each other's balls are? Right."

Perhaps I'd been too hasty to think Lua was okay with me inviting Cal to sit with us.

Calvin glanced at me, panic beginning to creep onto his face. "We really are just friends," he said, a little too defensively.

"Come on. You came to my show on New Year's Eve, where you and Ozzie mysteriously disappeared, and now you're eating lunch together. Something's going on." Lua refused to let it go. That's just how she was. Usually, it was one of the things I loved about her, but I didn't love it so much right then.

Calvin was back to keeping his hands in his lap and his eyes on the table. I knew if I didn't say something, Lua would keep prodding and scare Calvin off.

"If something's going on, and I'm not saying anything is, it's our business. Is that okay with you?" My voice held an edge, a defiant tone daring Lua to challenge me.

Lua crossed her arms over her chest. "Whatever. It's not like anyone cares."

The tension at the table was suffocating. I couldn't tell whether Lua was mad at me for standing up to her or for bringing Calvin to lunch in the first place.

After a moment of awkward silence, Dustin raised his hand and said, "Uh, I care. If you guys are a thing now, who the hell am I going to take to prom?"

• • •

I chased Lua down after my last class and offered her a ride home, which she grudgingly accepted. I didn't know what to say to her. It was especially difficult because I didn't know why she was so angry at me. And she was definitely angry, because she didn't even try to change the music on my stereo.

Finally, I said, "Are you going to tell me what's going on?"

"I didn't think I needed to."

"I can't read your mind, Lu."

Lua shifted in her seat. "When were you going to tell me about Calvin, Ozzie? I thought we told each other everything."

I braked for a red light. "There's nothing to tell right now. We fooled around. Once. But I don't know what, if anything, is going on with Calvin. And why are you even so upset about this? Weren't you the one who told me I needed to meet people?"

Lua didn't answer. She pouted instead. The light changed to green and I gunned it off the line.

"Come on, Lua. I wasn't trying to keep it from you, but you've been so busy and I honestly don't know what's happening with me and Calvin. I'm sorry I invited him to eat with us."

"I don't care about lunch," she said, her voice so low that I could barely hear it over the sounds of traffic.

"Then what?"

She flared her nostrils, breathing heavily. Finally, she threw her hands up and said, "You're mine. You belong to me. For the last six months you've been all about finding Tommy and missing Tommy and living in a delusional world where you had this life the rest of us can't remember. All I wanted was my friend back, but you haven't come back, you've just replaced Tommy with someone else. Someone who isn't me."

I hadn't expected Lua's words to sting so badly. Not just what she said, but how she said it. There was venom in her voice, and it got into my blood and infected my heart.

"I'm not replacing anyone," I said. "You're still my best friend."

"Right."

"You are!" I couldn't have this conversation and drive at the same time, so I pulled into a gas station and parked in front of the coin-operated vacuum. I unbuckled my seat belt and faced Lua, looking her in the eyes.

"Listen, I'm sorry about Tommy. I mean, I'm not sorry— even if no one else in the world believes he's real, I know he is—but I'm sorry you felt like I was ignoring you." My thoughts were jumbled, and I knew I was doing a poor job of explaining, but I had to try. "I haven't replaced Tommy, and

I haven't forgotten about him. I don't know what this thing with Calvin is. He's weird—really weird—and maybe I like him, I don't know, but even if Calvin and I *were* more than friends, which we're not, no one—not Tommy, not Calvin—could replace you. You're my Lua. You will always be my Lua."

Lua still refused to look at me. I wanted her to scream. I wanted her to yell at me and punch me and throw things at me. Those things might have looked scary to someone on the outside, but she only went nuclear on people she genuinely cared about. But when she was really upset, when she was truly and righteously angry, she cut me off—locked away her emotions and froze me out—and that was scarier than ten collapsing universes.

"Come on, Lu. Talk to me. Don't shut down."

"What do you want from me, Ozzie? What do you expect?"

"I don't know. Honesty?"

"Fine," Lua said. "You want the truth? Here goes: This was supposed to be our year. You and me, Oz. But you wasted the first half pining for an imaginary boy, and now, regardless of what you say, you're going to lose yourself for the rest of it in Calvin, and then you're going to go off to college and I'm never going to see you again. Isn't it easier to just end our friendship now?"

Lua wasn't pulling her punches, and I didn't know whether that was better or worse. "How many times do I have to tell you Calvin and I are just friends?"

"Are you going to take Calvin to prom?" she asked. "Because we were supposed to go together. Remember?"

Honestly, I didn't. I remembered me and Tommy sitting at the edge of the ocean talking about prom, discussing how we were going to rent a limo and wear matching tuxes and dance all night long. I'd assumed Lua and Dustin would join us, but in my memories, it was always me and Tommy.

"I'm not taking Calvin to prom."

"Sure."

Every time I thought I was drawing Lua out, she slipped back into silence and one-word replies. "What do you want me to say? That we'll go to prom together? Done. You and me. Prom. No one else. Is that what you want?"

"It's not just prom."

"College? I haven't gotten in yet, and I'm probably not even going. You can't be pissed about something that hasn't happened yet." I slammed my palm against the steering wheel. "Anyway, you're the one who's leaving. You're the one who skips classes to rehearse with the band and is going on tour at the end of the summer."

Lua rolled her eyes. "Maybe I won't go. Maybe the

universe will shrink so much that there won't be anywhere *to* go on tour."

"Fuck you, Lua." My confusion and hurt turned to indignation. "I know I sound crazy, but you're supposed to be my best friend. You're supposed to be the one person who believes me. Have you considered that the only reason I've been spending time with Cal is because, of all my friends, he's the only person who doesn't treat me like I've lost my mind?"

"Everything's not about you, Ozzie!" Lua fumbled to unbuckle her seat belt and shifted around to face me. Only, where I expected to see fight, I saw something worse: fear. "Do you get that? The whole fucking universe doesn't revolve around you and your problems. Some of us have our own shit to deal with, but you wouldn't know that, would you? No. Because Tommy's gone and the universe is shrinking. You care more about some boy who doesn't exist than the people in your life who are here and trying not to drown." She clenched her fists and her jaw, and her body shook like she was crying but had turned her tears inward.

Her words smacked me so hard that I almost wished she'd stayed quiet and angry. "Lua, I—"

"I'm drowning, Ozzie!" she shouted. "I'm drowning."

I got out of the car and walked around to her side. I

opened the door and crouched in front of Lua. I took her hand and held it to my chest and waited for her to look at me.

"I'm sorry, Lua. I didn't know."

"You didn't know because you didn't ask."

"What can I do? Just tell me what to do."

Lua sniffled and wiped her nose with the back of her free hand. "Stop being such a shitty friend, for one."

"Done."

"And be *here*. Be present. Stop living in a past that never existed."

Give up Tommy. That's what she was really saying. That I should stop looking for Tommy, stop missing him, stop loving him. I couldn't do that. I didn't want to. And it wasn't fair of her to ask me to, but at the same time, it wasn't fair of me to expect her to care about someone she couldn't remember.

"I'll try," I said. It was the best I could offer. Sometimes I wished I could forget Tommy the way everyone else had. It would have been easier. "And, if you want, I won't bring Calvin to lunch anymore."

Lua slapped my arm. "That's not what I'm saying. Of course you can bring him to lunch. Just don't forget that we're there too."

"I won't." I reached into the car and hugged Lua like I was trying to squeeze the last breath from her lungs. I never wanted to let go. Fighting with Lua was like fighting with myself.

When I let go, Lua said, "Come on, I've got rehearsal in an hour."

I nodded and got back into the car. As we neared Lua's house, she said, "I'm glad you put yourself out there, Oz. But Calvin Frye? Really? I didn't think you'd go for someone like him."

I laughed a little. "He certainly wasn't at the top of my list of guys I expected to hook up with. But, seriously, for the last time: We're just friends."

"Keep telling yourself that," Lua said. "Is he a good kisser at least?"

"Not nearly as good as you."

"That happened *one* time."

"And you loved it," I said. "The memory of my awesome kiss will haunt you for the rest of your life."

"Whatever."

I parked in front of her house. Before she got out, I said, "You know, Calvin told me that he thought *he* was drowning once, but he realized he could breathe underwater. Who knows? Maybe you can breathe underwater too."

Lua paused with her hand on the door. "No one can breathe underwater, Oz."

"I guess you're right," I said, but I hoped she was wrong.

231,507 AU

MRS. ROSS SAT HUNCHED OVER A LEGAL PAD, WRITING furiously. Despite what she'd said about never returning, she'd been sitting at her usual table by the window when I showed up for work, and I ignored her so she wouldn't run off again.

The evening passed slowly. Ana had volunteered to shelve the new arrivals—she was quiet, but getting the hang of the job—so I killed time pretending to reorder the science books while I actually read through some of them hoping to come up with a new theory about why Tommy had vanished. Calvin had floated an interesting idea that there was no single true reality, that we each created our own realities. He'd tried to explain it as each of us living in a bubble, and sometimes those bubbles overlapped and interacted, but that they still remained sovereign. He said it explained how two people could know each other but still view the world in radically different ways. The theory made as much sense as anything else I'd come up with, though I wasn't sure it explained why Tommy had disappeared. If I was shaping my own reality, then it seemed unlikely I would have crafted one in which Tommy didn't exist.

My favorite theory so far, though also unlikely, was that all of this was an experiment. Scientists from the future had discovered how to move people between alternate universes, and had accidentally thrown me into an unstable one—one where Tommy had been stillborn—and while the scientists, back in their own universe, couldn't communicate with me directly, all the weird things that had happened, like being partnered with Calvin and Flight 1184 crashing, were their warped way of influencing my actions and helping me figure out how to get home. I wished they could have sent me a text with clear, easy-to-follow instructions because, really, I had no idea how anything they'd done was going to lead me back to Tommy, but I guessed it didn't work that way. Assuming this theory was even correct, which it probably wasn't.

My head was swimming with possibilities, and I didn't notice Mrs. Ross approach until she cleared her throat.

"Good book?"

I looked down at the book I was holding—Brian Greene's *The Hidden Reality*—and shrugged, trying to remain nonchalant.

Mrs. Ross held out her legal pad. The pages were filled with wide, loopy cursive. "I was wondering if you were still willing to help," she said. "I'm no good at essay writing."

I allowed a cautious smile to emerge. "Sure," I said. I told Ana I was taking a quick break and sat with Mrs. Ross at her table. She chewed on the end of her nails while I read her essay. The practice topic had asked her to describe the happiest moment in her life. Mrs. Ross wrote in straightforward but sincere style about the day she found out she was pregnant. She'd been sixteen and had already taken a couple of home pregnancy tests but had needed to know for sure, so a friend drove her to Planned Parenthood. She described sitting in the doctor's office waiting for the results. How her friend had tried to comfort her by stealing a latex glove and blowing it up like a balloon. The mixture of panic and joy when the doctor confirmed her pregnancy. She was too young to have a baby, and she knew her parents would disown her, but it was still the happiest day of her life.

I wondered if Tommy had known this story. If he'd known how much his mother had wanted to bring him into the world. I made myself a promise to tell him when I found him.

I reached the end and set the legal pad down. "It's good," I said. "A little muddled in the middle, but good."

"Yeah?"

"Yeah."

"How can I make it better?"

A piece of advice Tommy had given me when we'd taken speech together popped into my head. I think he would have liked the idea of me passing it along to his mom. "The simplest way to structure an essay like this is: Tell 'em you're gonna tell 'em. Tell 'em. Tell 'em you told 'em."

Mrs. Ross pursed her lips dubiously. "Say again?"

"In the first part of your essay, you state the essay topic and briefly describe your argument—tell 'em you're gonna tell 'em. The happiest day of your life was the day you found out you were pregnant. In the second part, you dive into the details that support your argument. The happiest day of your life was the day you found out you were pregnant *because* . . . Tell 'em. Then in the third part of your essay, you reiterate your argument and briefly list the supporting reasons from your second part. Tell 'em you told 'em."

Mrs. Ross pulled her pad toward her and wrote down what I'd said. "I like that."

"Just something I learned from a guy who was on the debate team at school."

"Anything else?" she asked.

"Your spelling's good, and you've got a great vocabulary."

Mrs. Ross blushed. "I won the spelling bee in middle school. Beat Monique Heston by spelling 'vertigo' correctly. My mother kept the ribbon on the fridge at home until it was frayed and falling apart."

I wanted to know more—to ask her about her life without Tommy—but after scaring her off the last time, I thought it best not to push.

"Well, I bet you're going to ace the GED," I said.

"The math part's still tripping me up."

"I'll be glad when I never have to take another math class again."

"You going to college?" she asked.

The question surprised me. It was the first Mrs. Ross had asked me about myself. "Maybe. I don't know."

Mrs. Ross stared down her nose at me, the same way she used to when Tommy and I would show up at the trailer covered in mud from running around in the woods, playing at being superheroes. But she'd never yelled. Just laughed and made us wash up outside under the hose.

"If you have the opportunity to go, you best take it." She paused, looking over my shoulder out the windows, before returning her focus to me.

"My dad teaches at the community college, and I was thinking about going there for a couple of years." I shrugged. "It's just that I don't know what I want to do with my life."

"Isn't that why folks go to college in the first place?"

"Yeah, but—"

Mrs. Ross waved her hand and cut me off. "Don't 'but' me. I grew up north of here, a place called Winter Garden, but these little towns are all the same. They're parasites that'll devour your potential. You stick around a place like this and you'll wake up one fine morning realizing you wasted your life."

"But what if I'm waiting for someone?" I asked. "What if I leave and he comes back, and I miss him?"

I couldn't tell if Mrs. Ross had guessed I was referring to Tommy. "So what if you do? If he's important, you'll find each other again."

"It's more than that. Every decision I make narrows the choices I can make after. It's like, if I decide to study literature, I close the door on becoming a lawyer or a doctor."

Mrs. Ross snorted. "Says who?"

"Everyone?"

"Look at me," Mrs. Ross said. "I'm thirty-three years old, getting my GED. The only thing I've ever known is being a wife and flipping burgers at McDonald's, but that's going to change. I'm going to change it. The only thing in life that's forever is death. You can change your mind about everything else."

"I just don't know how to decide."

"You ever eat at Sunrise Buffet?"

"Yeah." I didn't mention the only time I'd gone was when she'd taken me and Tommy to celebrate Tommy winning his first debate tournament.

"You don't load your plate with just one thing on the first go-around, do you? You have to sample a little of everything. And if you *do* decide to eat a whole plate of whatever, and you get halfway through and change your mind, you simply push your plate to the side and grab a new one."

I also didn't mention that the food at Sunrise had given me food poisoning, or that I'd spent two days suffering from cramps and couldn't go anywhere that was more than a few feet from a toilet. "I guess," I said. "But life's not really that easy."

Mrs. Ross laughed. "You're young, white, and male. Life doesn't get any easier."

Ana called me to the register to help her handle a return. Before I stood up, I said, "Thanks, Mrs. Ross."

She smiled. "Just remember: If it isn't too late for an old lady like me to change, it certainly isn't too late for you."

224,618 AU

CALVIN HADN'T SHOWN UP TO SCHOOL ON TUESDAY,
and he wasn't answering my texts. I thought about driving to
his house after school to check on him, but I wasn't sure he'd
appreciate me just showing up.

Dad was walking out the door when I got home, and we
narrowly avoided colliding.

"Sorry," he mumbled. "Your mom's working late and I
probably won't be home for dinner."

"Whatever."

Dad stopped in the doorway to the garage. "I know
you're mad at me, Ozzie, but what happened is between me
and your mother."

"You let me blame her," I said. "But this whole thing is
your fault."

"Look, I'm not defending what I did—"

"Because you can't. You cheated; end of story."

"*But,*" Dad said, "our marriage would have ended whether or not I cheated on your mom."

"Sure. Keep telling yourself that."

Dad gritted his teeth, but his anger flickered and faded. His shoulders fell. He walked out the door and shut it behind him.

I could accept that my parents weren't going to reconcile. They'd fallen out of love and their divorce was as good as final. I'd even seen the official papers sitting on the counter, waiting for them to sell the house so they could sign them and dissolve our family. But my father had been the one man in my life I'd looked up to, and he'd let me go on thinking it was all my mom's fault, when he was the one who'd cheated. I didn't know if I could ever forgive him.

I ate a sandwich and then walked to the mailboxes at the end of the street. It was still early for college acceptance letters to begin arriving, so I was surprised when I shuffled through the stack of bills and other junk and found an envelope from Amherst. The crest stood out, bold and burgundy on the upper left-hand corner, emblazoned with the school's motto: *Terras Irradient.* Standing there in front of the bank of mailboxes and the notice board covered with pleas for dog owners to pick up their pets' poop, and invitations to the next homeowners' meeting, my heart sped up. It beat so rapidly my ribs rattled like the storm shutters covering the windows during a hurricane. And then it stopped. Just like that. It'd been beating so hard I could feel my pulse throbbing in my neck, and then nothing.

Is this what death feels like?

No, I wasn't dead. I was still standing. If I'd died, my legs would've buckled and I would have fallen and remained on the ground until some minivan-driving neighbor found my cooling corpse in the middle of the road.

I was still breathing. And then my heart began beating again. It sputtered to life and I lurched to the side, my vision dimming and then everything becoming too bright. I needed to sit. I stumbled to the grass behind the mailboxes and plopped down right beside the begonia bushes everyone in the neighborhood hated but refused to spend the money to dig up and replace. The grass cooled my bare legs, and I held the Amherst letter in my trembling hands and just stared at it.

The letter held my future. My decision to stay or leave was purely hypothetical until I found out whether any of the colleges I'd applied to accepted me. If they all rejected me, it wouldn't matter whether I wanted to stick around Cloud Lake or leave. If I decided to wait for Tommy, I needed to know it was because I'd committed myself to that path and not because it was the only path available.

It didn't matter how big or small the universe was right then; that slender envelope contained the entirety of *my* universe.

I lacked the courage to open the letter. I needed Lua, but Lua and the band were working on their demo. I didn't want to call Dustin, because if I'd gotten in, it would only remind him that he was stuck going to a state school. I would've even settled for Renny.

But the only person I could count on was Calvin. I needed to see Calvin.

I drove straight to Calvin's house without calling or texting first, hoping he was home and would answer the door. The Amherst envelope lay on the passenger seat, and I kept glancing at it as I drove, expecting it to disappear or explode, blowing me and the car to flaming bits and leaving a crater in the middle of Calvin's subdevelopment. I held the letter like it was radioactive as I walked to the front door. I barely remembered the drive over. Had I run a red light? Maybe. The minutes between leaving my house and arriving at Calvin's existed as a dreamlike blur.

Mr. Frye opened the door a moment after I knocked,

almost like he'd been waiting for me. He wore dark blue pants and a Cloud Lake Fire Department T-shirt that revealed his hairy, tanned arms.

"Hi, sir," I said, surprised I remembered how to form words. "Is Calvin home?"

"Ozzie, right?"

"Yes, sir."

"Enough with the 'sir.' Call me Pete." He opened the door all the way to let me in. The house was the cleanest I'd ever seen it, and the smell of bleach lingered in the air. "As a matter of fact, I'm glad you're here, Ozzie."

All I wanted to do was climb the stairs to Calvin's room and show him the envelope. He'd know what to do. He'd know what to say. "You are?"

Mr. Frye nodded. "Come on and sit for a second."

I didn't want to sit and talk to Mr. Frye, but I sat in the recliner perpendicular to the couch anyway, still clutching my envelope. "What's up, Pete?" I felt weird calling him by his first name. He probably wouldn't have been so nice to me if he'd known what his son and I had done in my car in front of his house on New Year's Eve.

Mr. Frye sank into the couch. He held his hands together like he was praying. I waited for him to speak, because I had no idea what all this was about. What if he *did* know what we'd done? Oh God, please tell me he wasn't about to give me some kind of sex talk. I couldn't handle that right now.

"I need to ask you something, Ozzie, and I need you to answer honestly. Can you do that?"

"Sure."

Mr. Frye took a moment, sighing and scrunching his face. I saw little pieces of Calvin in him. His hair and eyes and the way the space between his eyebrows wrinkled when he was thinking hard.

"Have you noticed anything odd about Cal lately?" he asked when he was ready.

"Like what?"

"Strange behavior? Him doing or saying things out of the ordinary?"

"Honestly, sir," I said, "I haven't known Calvin that long. To me, he's always been odd."

Mr. Frye chuckled, but it came out forced. "Yeah. Yeah, that's Cal." He paused, then said, "But I'm talking about more specific stuff. Like, has he seemed angrier or more withdrawn? Has he tried to hurt himself that you know of?"

I didn't think Calvin had cut himself since we'd begun working together—I hadn't noticed any fresh scabs—and I'd believed Calvin when he'd told me he hadn't been trying to kill himself. The cutting was a pressure release valve, nothing more. If I told Mr. Frye the truth, I didn't know what would happen to Calvin, but I suspected it wouldn't be good. I'd pieced together that Calvin's change in behavior over the summer probably had something to do with the teacher he'd been having sex with, and maybe that was something Mr. Frye ought to know, but it'd mean betraying Cal. He'd probably hate me, and he'd definitely never speak to me again, and I needed him too much to risk it.

"No, sir," I said. "Nothing."

Mr. Frye stared into my eyes for so long he made me nervous, and I nearly forgot why I'd come over in the first place. Then he blinked. "Good. That's good, Ozzie. Just, if you notice anything like that, you let me know, all right?"

"I will." I felt weird agreeing to spy on Calvin for his father.

Mr. Frye stood and clapped me on the shoulder. "You're a good kid, Ozzie." He motioned toward the stairs. "Cal's in his room. He was a little under the weather today, but I have a hunch he's well enough for a visit from you. I have to head to work. There's some money on the fridge if you boys get hungry."

"Thank you, sir. I mean, Pete." I stood, anxious to get away from Mr. Frye and his intrusive questions, and bounded up the stairs. Calvin's door was shut, so I knocked.

No answer.

"Calvin?" I called through the door. "It's me, Ozzie." I knocked again. "Cal?"

"What?" His voice sounded muffled and irritated.

I assumed his "what" was an invitation to enter, and I opened the door a crack to peek through.

Calvin was huddled in bed, his black comforter pulled up to his ears. The only part of him sticking out was his blond hair. I opened the door wider. He'd drawn the curtains closed and it was almost too dark. The air was still and stale, the way Warren's bedroom had felt since he left for basic training, and it felt oppressively claustrophobic.

"You sleeping?"

"No," he said, but didn't sit up or throw back the covers. He was a lump on the bed, unmoving.

"Everything all right?"

"Yeah." His voice, that one word, sounded like a long, exasperated sigh.

"I got my letter from Amherst," I said. "I'm too afraid to open it." I stood inside the doorway, waiting for Calvin to say something. To sit up and brush back his wild hair and smile while I opened the letter. "You don't mind if I open it here, do you?" Nothing, not even a grunt. "All right then."

My heart revved into overdrive again, and I forced myself to breathe slowly. It didn't help.

I read the motto one last time. "Let them light up the world." That's what it translated to. Would I light up the world like Lua, or dim and fade away like the universe? Did I even want to know?

Yes. Yes, I wanted to know. I *needed* to know.

I flipped the envelope over and slipped my index finger under the flap. I tore it open slowly, neatly, afraid of ripping the letter inside. There was only one sheet of paper. I pulled it out and unfolded it.

"Dear Mr. Pinkerton: Thank you for your interest in Amherst College. After careful consideration of your application, I am sorry to inform you . . ." I read the rest silently, though those twenty-three words were the only ones that mattered.

The letter fell from my hand.

I looked up. Calvin had raised an arm and pulled back the comforter. I crawled into bed beside him and he wrapped his arm around my chest, and we lay there without a word between us until dark finally fell.

TOMMY

THE WALLS BREATHE. THE WINDOWS, HIDDEN
behind hastily hung plywood, creak and bow from the pressure.
Beyond the walls, Hurricane Rita howls and spits, and she hasn't
even reached the apex of her fury.

"You think Big Apple will deliver?" Tommy asks.

I shake my head. "All signs point to no."

We lie in my living room, under the sheets we hung like a
tent over our heads. I wanted to sleep in my room, but Mom and
Dad scuttled that plan. They were fine with Tommy spending the
night, because his parents had to leave the trailer to stay with his
aunt, who didn't have enough room for him, but they sure as hell
weren't going to allow us to sleep unsupervised in my bedroom.
We built a blanket fort instead, and had spent the early part of
the evening repelling Renny's attempts to destroy it.

"How long do you think this storm's going to blow?"

I try to pull up the weather on my phone, but our Internet is dead and I can't get a cell signal. "Most of the night, last I heard."

"No way I'm getting any sleep."

I wink at Tommy. "There's lots of ways we can kill time in here."

Tommy throws me this frown that reminds me of the faces his mother makes to tell us that whatever shit we're selling, she ain't buying. "Like I can think about that knowing Renny or your folks could pop in any second and catch us. You're crazy, Ozzie."

Kissing him, touching him, feeling his hands on my skin is all I can think about. I can't be this near to him and not. When it comes to Tommy, I'm a junkie. "Well, if we're not going to fool around, we have to do something. I'm bored."

"We could play cards," he says, though not enthusiastically.

"Strip poker?" I grin and nudge him with my shoulder.

"Is sex the only thing you think about?"

I pretend to ponder his question, then nod emphatically. "How can I not when you're so damned irresistible?"

Tommy rolls his eyes, and we lie silently for a while, listening to the wind blow.

"Tommy?"

"Yeah?"

"How much do you love me?"

His stomach tenses. He skips a breath. "A lot."

"You ever think about kissing anyone else?"

He hesitates, which scares me a little. "Do you?"

"I kissed Lua, does that count?"

"No," he says. "Unless you liked it."

"I didn't."

Tommy drums my chest with his fingers. "Why are you asking, Oz?"

"Bored," I say. "Curious, I guess."

"Truthfully," Tommy says. "I have *thought about it."*

It's not the answer I want. I know he's never been with anyone else, but it hurts that he's considered it. And, as if he can read my thoughts, he says, "There are billions of folks in the world, and, yeah, sometimes I think about kissing some of them. But you're the only one I do *kiss."*

"I just thought . . . I guess if you loved me a lot like you said, you wouldn't want to kiss anyone else. But I guess that's dumb."

Tommy doesn't speak for the longest time. I know he didn't fall asleep, because I can hear his jagged breathing and feel him flinch every time thunder cracks. All around us, Rita wails. She's supposed to make landfall as a Category Two—these are just the feeder bands passing over us—but meteorologists had predicted she could stall off the coast to suck up some of our warm Atlantic water before crashing into us as a Cat. Three or Four. Mom wanted to evacuate, but Dad talked her out of it. She was sixteen and living in Homestead when Hurricane Andrew tore across Florida. I doubt she's sleeping much tonight either.

Without warning, Tommy squirms out from under me and crawls toward the fort exit. I follow. I poke my head through the sheets, and he's already pulled his shirt over his head and is working on his belt buckle.

"What the hell are you doing?" I ask.

But he doesn't answer. He drops his jeans and then his boxers so he's standing stark naked in the living room. The only light beams from the camping lantern inside the fort, and it's barely bright enough to make out more than the dim outline of Tommy, but my imagination fills in the details.

"My parents!" I whisper, praying they don't choose this moment to check on us or grab something to drink.

Tommy marches toward the front door, opens it, and dashes into the storm. I scramble after him. The wind blows the door in and I catch it before it slams into the wall. With no barriers between us, Rita's yowls stab through me like forked lightning. If these are just the bands, I'm not sure the house will survive the eyewall.

"Get in here!" I holler. I shut the door behind me to keep from waking Renny or my parents, but I huddle under the awning where it's dry. Palm fronds ripped from the trees pinwheel across the yard. An empty garbage can tumbles down the road until a nasty gust of wind catches it like a sail and lifts it into the air, tossing it a dozen feet. The driveway is already flooded; our street's a river. And in the middle of it is Tommy, naked. Water past his ankles. His arms raised over his head. He sways like a reed as the wind blows.

"This!" shouts Tommy. "This is how much I love you, Oswald Pinkerton! This much!"

Enough to stand in the middle of a hurricane. That's how much Tommy loves me. There are no units of measurement for love. No yards or kilograms or degrees Kelvin. No way to compare the love of one person to that of another. Love defies quantification. Maybe it doesn't matter that he sometimes thinks about kissing other people. He loves me.

I step off the patio to retrieve my idiot boyfriend, and he collapses. I sprint across the grass. My foot sinks into mud, and I twist my ankle, but I ignore it because I'm thinking what if Tommy fell face forward and is drowning. It'll be my fault if he dies trying to prove how much he loves me.

Tommy's already starting to sit up when I reach him. He's holding the side of his head. Rita yanks the trellis on the side of the house out of the ground and flings it across the yard.

"Come on," I say. "We need to get inside." I pull his arm around my shoulders.

But Tommy doesn't move. "Do you get it?" he yells. "This is only a fraction of how much I love you."

"I get it! Let's go!" I haul him to his feet and half drag him inside. I have to lean all my weight against the door to shut it. It's a wonder no one's come to investigate.

Inside, I grab the lantern and Tommy's clothes and lead him into the kitchen. When he's got his boxers and shirt back on, I check him over. He's bleeding from a cut on the side of his head. It probably needs stitches, but butterfly bandages will have to do.

"Are you stupid or what?" I clean the cut, which is as long as my thumb, with iodine, ignoring Tommy's winces.

"Stupid for you, Ozzie."

"You could've been killed!"

Tommy catches my wrist and pulls my hands into his lap. He looks me right in the eyes. Tommy's brown eyes are evening sunlight. "There are exactly two people in my life worth dying for: my mom and you."

"That's sweet, but idiotic. And just because you're willing to die for me doesn't mean I want you to."

"I'm not looking to die either," he says. "I just want you to know there's nothing I wouldn't do for you. That's how much I love you. Don't ever forget it."

219,764 AU

I PICKED UP CALVIN FOR SCHOOL ON FRIDAY SO WE could bring in what we'd completed of our roller coaster for Ms. Fuentes to evaluate. We hadn't talked about my rejection from Amherst or why he'd skipped school and spent the entire day in bed. And I hadn't told him that his father had asked me to spy on him. Sometimes it seemed the list of things we *didn't* talk about was longer than the list of things we did.

When Calvin walked outside, carrying the half-finished track, I barely recognized him. He'd shaved his unruly blond curls, leaving behind pale stubble on his scalp. My first thought was that at least he had a nicely shaped skull.

"Did you get into a fight with an electric razor?" I asked when I got out of the car to open the trunk. I was trying to make a joke, but Calvin didn't laugh.

"I needed a change," Calvin said. And it was all he said.

He didn't speak on the drive to school, and we parted ways in the parking lot. I wondered if this was the type of behavior Mr. Frye had asked me to watch for. The hair on its own wasn't a big deal—Lua changed hairstyles and colors more frequently than most people changed their underwear—but I couldn't help wondering if the drastic transformation was a sign of a larger problem. I'd always felt guilty for not telling someone about Mr. Ross beating on Tommy, and I wondered if I was letting Calvin down the same way by keeping his secret. But I'd already lost Tommy, and I was scared I'd lose Calvin too if I ratted him out.

When Calvin arrived at physics with our project, the other students whispered.

I nudged him with my elbow when he sat down. "Is everything all right?"

Before he could answer, Dustin waltzed in. "Nice cut, Frye." He nodded at me. "What's up, Pinks? That your project?" He set his own roller coaster, which was a little further along than ours, on our table. "Damn. Pretty good. Not as good as mine, of course."

"It was mostly Calvin's idea," I said. "But I bought the wood."

Dustin rolled his eyes. "Why does that not surprise me?"

I gave him the finger, and caught Ms. Fuentes frowning.

The bell rang, and while Ms. Fuentes walked around to each team, I tried to get Calvin to talk to me. I was the one who should have been sullen and mopey. Yeah, I'd applied to other colleges, and I held out hope that at least one would accept me, but that first rejection had wounded me more than I wanted to admit. It stood as proof that some choices were beyond my control, and that, despite my best efforts, my life might not turn out the way I wanted.

"Hey," I said. "What's wrong?"

Calvin tinkered with the track, working on a section of the corkscrew that we hadn't gotten quite right. "I'm fine."

"You're a terrible liar, you know?"

"It's nothing, Ozzie. I promise."

Ms. Fuentes chose that moment to approach our lab table. She tilted her head to the side and circled our roller coaster, viewing it from different angles. "How do you intend to move your roller coaster up this first incline?" she asked.

As far as I knew, we hadn't figured out that part yet. Calvin's simulations just shot it up the slope, but I hadn't devoted much thought to how we were going to implement it on the model.

Apparently, Calvin had. "I've been working on a spring-loaded propulsion system," he said. "With a latch and release mechanism."

"And have you calculated the strength of the spring required to launch the cars?"

"I think so," Calvin said.

Ms. Fuentes nodded. "Interesting. Are you confident it will provide the necessary momentum required to maintain speed through these loops?"

"We ran some simulations," I said, because I didn't want Fuentes to think I hadn't helped with the assignment.

Calvin pulled his laptop out of his backpack to show Ms. Fuentes the program. For a moment—talking g-forces and momentum with Fuentes—Calvin returned to life. I understood physics conceptually, and I could do the math well enough to pass the exams, but Calvin lived and breathed the stuff. He understood it like a language he'd grown up speaking. It reminded me of the way Tommy had understood . . . well, everything.

"Interesting," Ms. Fuentes said again. "It seems like you boys have a great start here. But your entire ride hinges on your ability to launch the cars up that first incline. Simulations are well and good, but I'd suggest not waiting much longer to design that feature. If you can't make it work, you'll want to have enough time before the due date to figure out an alternative."

We thanked Ms. Fuentes, and she moved on to Dustin's

table. Jake Ortiz was absent, again, and the first thing Dustin did was complain about how he'd done all the work.

"I don't think I can do lunch today, Ozzie." Calvin examined the track, conspicuously *not* looking at me.

"Oh."

"It's not you." Until he'd said it, I hadn't thought it was. But now I did.

I didn't know how to help Calvin. Something was obviously wrong, but he wouldn't give me a hint as to what it might be. Tommy had always been happy. Even after his dad beat the crap out of him, Tommy would keep smiling, looking for the shiny sliver of gold in the muddy pile of shit. Sometimes his eternal optimism annoyed the hell out of me, but I could've used some of it right then.

"Wanna ditch?" I asked. I only had one class after lunch—Latin—and in my four years of high school, I'd only skipped once. With Tommy.

Calvin shrugged. "Where would we go?"

It was a good question, and one I hadn't considered. "We could catch a movie. Or go to this coffee shop Lua and I like."

"I don't know. I've missed enough classes already."

Calvin's words felt inert. I struggled to think of a place I could take him that would cheer him up, and then the perfect place sprang into my mind. "I know where we can go."

"Where?"

"It's a surprise, but it's not too far."

Calvin glanced at me, his chary eyes heavy lidded, his lips pursed on one side like he was trying to figure out a way to shoot me down without hitting any vital organs.

"Come on," I said. "Trust me, all right?"

"I guess."

It wasn't the enthusiastic affirmation I'd hoped for, but it was better than nothing.

212,933 AU

SNEAKING OFF CAMPUS WAS BOTH TOO EASY AND a letdown. I'd expected Calvin and I would need to go all Mission Impossible to escape, but we carried our roller coaster to the admin building and told Mrs. Niven we were going to put it in my car. She was busy on the phone and waved us past without even asking our names. The security officer had opened the gates to let the students on work program leave, and we drove off campus without a single challenge. Like I said: total letdown.

Calvin didn't ask where I was taking him, and I wouldn't have said anyway. He scrolled through my phone while I drove, looking first at my music, then at my pictures. Normally, etiquette says you don't go through another guy's photo album, but all of my embarrassing pictures of me and Tommy had vanished with him, and it's not like

I spent my free time snapping dick pics for no one to see.

"Is this your brother?" Calvin turned my phone toward me. A shot of Warren mid-cannonball, about to splash into our pool, filled the screen.

"Yeah. That's Renny."

I hadn't told Calvin much about Warren. There were still so many things about each other we didn't know. It used to bother me when I read books where the main characters fell in love or became best friends after only knowing each other a short time. I'd complained about it to Tommy once, and he'd said that's how it happens in real life. Everyone we meet begins as a stranger, so we project onto them who we need them to be until we get to know them. He said we have to fall in love with the idea of a person before we can fall in love with the actual person.

It sounded like bullshit to me.

Tommy and I had known nearly everything there was to know about each other, because we'd grown up together, while Calvin remained a mystery to me, and I to him. We could change that, but it would require talking about all those things we kept *not* talking about.

"Do you guys get along?" Calvin asked.

I snorted. "Depends on your definition." Before Renny left, I thought I'd had him all figured out. I thought he was just my jerk older brother whose sole mission in life was to torture me. But then he'd given me that drawing of Tommy, and I had to admit he knew *me* better than I'd thought, and I didn't really know him at all.

"Sometimes I wish I had an older brother or sister," Calvin said. "Someone to scout ahead into the future and report back to me."

We were driving down a long, empty stretch of highway toward my secret destination. The ocean on our right, Florida scrub brush on the left. It felt like we were driving through a wasteland, without a soul around for miles to spoil the serenity.

"When I started high school, I was terrified of gym class." I cleared my throat, not sure whether I wanted to tell the story and subject myself to potential embarrassment, but this was how people got to know each other, and I wanted to know Calvin. I wanted him to know me. "I hadn't really developed."

"Developed?" Calvin said.

"No hair under my arms or on my balls."

Calvin cracked a smile. The first I'd seen all week. "Got it."

"Tommy was the only person who'd ever seen me naked, but we'd grown up together and I didn't think of him the way I thought of other people. He never made me feel weird." I kept my eyes on the road, but every once in a while I glanced at Calvin to gauge his reaction. "Renny had told me horror stories about gym. That I'd have to shower and change in front of other guys, and how they picked on kids who were different. So the night before the first day of school, I asked him if it was normal not to have hair on my balls. He told me every guy had hair on his balls by the time he started high school."

"That's an odd thing to worry about," Calvin said.

"You never thought about that stuff?"

Calvin shook his head. "Not really."

"Well, I did." Just thinking about it again gave me anxiety like I was right back in that moment. Anyone who says time travel is impossible has never had to relive the memories of past traumas or mistakes. "So the night before the first day of school, I dug the wig and mustache I'd worn for Halloween out of the attic. I'd dressed up as Sirius Black."

"From Harry Potter?" Calvin asked. I nodded. "Interesting choice."

"Yeah. Warren went as Bellatrix Lestrange and spent the entire night fake killing me." It had actually been an awesome night, but I decided to save that story for another time. "Anyway, I cut up the wig and superglued the hair under my arms and all over my junk."

Calvin covered his mouth his with hand. "You didn't."

"I did. And Warren assured me that real guys didn't just grow hair on their balls, but all up and down their dicks." Calvin was laughing so hard his ears had turned radish red. "There I was in the locker room, believing that not only did I not have to worry about being made fun of for being as smooth as a sand puppy, but that I'd have more hair than any other guy and they'd all think I was super grown-up."

"God. Dear God, I'm sorry for laughing but . . ."

I remembered how mortified I'd been after I'd dropped my pants to change—all proud of my long, lustrous fake pubic hair—and everyone had pointed at me and laughed.

"It's fine," I said. "Enjoy my humiliation. I understand." I grinned at Calvin to let him know I was kidding. "So, yeah, needless to say, Coach Canuso dragged me into his office to explain puberty and anatomy, which fanned the flames of my embarrassment into an inferno of shame. Especially when he pulled out the illustrated pamphlets."

Calvin's whole body was shaking. "I can't believe you superglued wig hair to your balls." I loved seeing him laugh, even if it was at my expense. "We used to prank each other on the wrestling team all the time. Like, once, Trent greased the inside of my singlet with Icy Hot before a preseason match. I don't think I've ever screamed that loud in my entire life."

"That's horrible," I said, even though I was laughing.

Thinking about Calvin wrestling made me curious about something I hadn't worked up the courage to ask before. "You dated Jaya Winslow, right?"

Calvin nodded.

"Are you into girls *and* guys, or did you just not know you liked guys yet?"

"I don't know," he said. "I guess I still don't. Girls are hot, and I didn't hate fooling around with Jaya, but I've always liked guys too."

"So you're bi?"

"Maybe. I'm honestly just not sure yet."

"Was it weird wrestling with guys you might've been attracted to?" We were nearing our destination, and I slowed so I didn't miss the entrance. "I mean, the whole wrestling thing is pretty homoerotic to begin with, but how'd you keep from—you know?—getting excited?"

Calvin's cheeks were still red from laughing, but his expression grew serious. "It's not like that. I get how two guys with nothing but spandex between them rolling around sounds like it'd be a gay fantasy, but when I stepped onto the mat, the guy I squared off against became my opponent rather than a person. I focused on winning and not what he was hiding in his jock."

"But you have to admit, it's kind of hot."

"You took anatomy, right?" I nodded. "Remember dissecting the cats?"

I shivered at the memory. The stink of formaldehyde still turned my stomach. "Yeah."

"There's a point where you stopped seeing it as an animal and learned to view it as merely a collection of skin and muscle and organs."

"You thought about dissecting your wrestling opponents?"

Calvin shook his head. "No, but I stopped thinking about them as people and viewed them as arms and legs and angles to exploit."

"Oh. I guess that makes sense."

I turned into the entrance for Jonathan Dickinson State Park and pulled up to the guard booth. It cost six dollars, most of which I paid in quarters. Calvin watched me curiously but kept quiet until I parked the car.

"Here we are," I said.

"This was your big plan?" He didn't sound impressed.

"Not the parking lot. We've still got a ways to hike."

Neither of us was dressed for hiking, but most of Florida is pretty flat, so it's not like we had to scale mountains. And a welcome cool front had temporarily chased away the heat, though no sane person would call it winter.

Lua and I had visited the park often during her photography phase. We'd spent hours wandering the sandy trails while she snapped hundreds of photos of woodpeckers and scrub brush and palm fronds. The most beautiful picture she'd taken was of a heart someone had drawn in the dirt in the middle of a path, footprints trampling its soft lines. She'd promised to make me a copy, but never had.

Calvin and I walked through the underbrush, while I kept an eye out for snakes—water moccasins and kingsnakes and rat snakes and black racers. The trails held a million places for those beady-eyed death noodles to hide. I couldn't tell if Calvin was enjoying himself. I hadn't brought him to the park to hike, but it was necessary to reach our real destination.

"Can I ask you another question?" I asked, mostly to fill the silence.

"Could I stop you?"

"Probably not."

"Then go for it."

"The guy you told me about, the older one. Was it serious? Was he your boyfriend?"

Calvin sighed like he wished he'd never told me in the first place. "We were friends at first; he was there for me after my mom left. He took me fishing on his boat, and sometimes I helped him work around his house."

"How'd . . . you know? When did things change?"

Calvin dragged his feet, his footsteps heavy and plodding. "We were on his boat. He'd brought beer. I was pretty drunk, lying on the deck getting some sun, and he sat down beside me and started rubbing suntan lotion on my back and . . ." His voice trailed off. Then he said, "You know what? I really don't want to talk about this."

"He took advantage of you, Cal."

Calvin clenched his fists. "I knew what I was doing."

"He was an adult—a teacher!"

"Drop it, all right?"

I didn't want to drop it. But I worried he'd shut down if I kept pushing.

We walked in silence until the trail ended and we broke out of the woods. Ahead of us, at the top of a man-made hill, stood a five-story wooden tower. It was the tallest object around; taller than the trees.

"Come on," I said, leading the way. I was winded by the time we climbed the stairs. Halfway, Calvin had stripped off his hoodie, revealing a white tank top underneath, and tied it around his waist. I walked to the edge and looked out over the park.

"This is what I wanted to show you," I said. "You can see the whole world from up here."

I'd visited the Grand Canyon and seen the Flatirons in Colorado, but the view from the top of that platform was the most beautiful. We couldn't actually see the whole world—we couldn't even see the ocean—but I imagined we could. Standing there, I could forget the universe had collapsed to less than 1 percent of its original size. Standing at the top of the world, everything I saw was everything, and maybe that was enough.

"I come here to think," I said. "I look toward the horizon and imagine Tommy's out there looking back at me."

"What's it like?" Calvin asked. "Being in love, I mean."

I leaned against the railing. "We've all got secrets, you know? We've all got things about ourselves we hate and these dark places inside of us we're terrified to show people. We live in constant fear that someone is going to discover the rotting corpses we keep buried in those dark places, and that when they do, they'll despise us for them." I glanced at Calvin. He was leaning with his back against the railing, his arms folded across his chest. "Being in love with someone is knowing that no matter what you show them, no matter what you've done, they'll never reject you."

Calvin didn't respond right away, and that was fine. I wasn't sure exactly what was going on in his mind, but I sensed he needed space to figure it out.

After a few minutes he said, "If you love Tommy so much, and you're sure he loves you, why are you spending time with me?" He shifted from one foot to the other. "I know you said we're just friends, but you can't tell me there's nothing going on between us."

Calvin's boldness caught me off guard. "I love Tommy, and he loves me. And that confuses the hell out of me—*you* confuse the hell out of me, Cal, because you're here and he's not, and I don't know what to do."

"What if Tommy comes back, Ozzie? What happens to me?"

"You're still my friend. You'll always be my friend."

"But nothing more."

"I don't know."

As much as it must've hurt, I owed Calvin the truth. The laughter I'd mined from him earlier had disappeared. I leaned against the railing next to him. So close we were nearly touching.

"Listen, Calvin. I like spending time with you. But I can't tell you what's going to happen next. You might learn something about me you don't like, or school will end and we'll go to different colleges and never see each other again, or the universe may collapse and swallow both our lives. I just don't know."

Calvin turned and looked out over the park. "The guy—the teacher—I thought he loved me."

"People are assholes."

"You're not an asshole, Ozzie."

"Neither are you, Cal."

201,833 AU

DR. DIXIE McCRANEY LOOKED LIKE SHE'D SPENT THE
morning making out with Pennywise the clown. She nursed
a thirty-ounce iced coffee like it was a baby bottle, and she
was literally the first therapist I'd seen who sat behind a
desk. I sat on the other side in an uncomfortable modern
pleather chair.

She was reading my file—she'd *been* reading my file for
the last five minutes. Nodding occasionally, her lips moving
silently. She finally set it down and said, "You sure have
plowed through a lot of doctors, Oswald Pinkerton." Then
she had the nerve to smile like she'd made a hilarious joke.

"What can I say? I'm indecisive."

"How about you start by telling me a little about why
you're here?"

Why didn't they ever know? I thought the whole point

of seeing a therapist was to get answers, not waste my time providing them with obvious ones.

"Let's see," I said. "My boyfriend vanished, and I'm the only one who remembers him; I tried to run away to find him, and the plane I was on crashed only minutes after a cop pulled me off of it; the universe is shrinking; and I gave a blowjob to a guy who cuts himself, had a fling with a teacher, and who I may like but can't date because I'm definitely still in love with my 'imaginary' boyfriend." I snapped my fingers. "Also, my parents are getting divorced and my idiotic older brother joined the army and will probably shoot himself in the foot."

Dr. McCraney's mouth formed an O. "Heavens!" she said. "Your life is heaps more interesting than mine. All I've got is a cat with six toes."

"Fascinating."

"But I think we should set those issues aside for the time being."

"We should?"

McCraney nodded. She slurped her iced coffee. She actually slurped it. The sound made me want to stab her with her straw. "I want you to tell me about the future, Oswald."

"I'm psycho, not psychic."

"Oh, Oswald," she said. "You're a comedian, aren't you?"

"No."

Dr. McCraney bulldozed ahead. "What does the future look like for Oswald Pinkerton—great name, by the way. Do you have any plans for college? Anything you're passionate about? Tell me where you see yourself in ten years."

"I don't know," I said. "I don't know if I'm going to college. I don't know what I want to do with the rest of my life. I'm not even sure the universe is going to survive long enough for me to graduate." I clenched my fists. I couldn't stop fidgeting. "The only thing I know for certain is that I need to find Tommy."

"Your boyfriend?"

Dr. McCraney was the first doctor to refer to Tommy as my boyfriend and not my imaginary boyfriend.

"My future was Tommy. My future *is* Tommy."

"I see," McCraney said. "And you're worried any choice you make regarding your future now necessarily excludes him."

"Yes!" I said. Hallelujah. Finally! A doctor who understood. "Tommy was my everything. All my friends are leaving: Lua's going on tour, Dustin's heading to the University of Florida, even Calvin will probably get out of Cloud Lake, but I don't know what to do without Tommy. If I stay in Cloud Lake, I might be wasting my life. But leaving means admitting I may never see him again."

"Except he isn't real, Oswald," McCraney said. "It's obvious you're scared of the future, and this boy you've conjured is a convenient cover you're using to avoid making a choice."

I'd been wrong. Dr. Dixie McCraney didn't understand at all.

I didn't even finish our session. I stood and walked out the door.

386,097 KM

NOTHING EVER HAPPENS THE WAY WE EXPECT IT ought to.

I pulled into Lua's driveway to pick him up for a show at a/s/l and honked. He ran out the front door, guitar case slung over his shoulder, wearing leather pants and something that looked like a straitjacket. After he tossed his gear into the back, he climbed into the passenger seat and held up his arms. Rust-colored buckles dangled from the sleeves.

"You like it?" he asked. "Dinah helped me make it."

I didn't answer. He could have gone on and on about anything and everything, and I wouldn't have said a word because of the two envelopes sitting in my lap. Two envelopes that held my future.

Lua snapped his fingers in front of my face. "Ozzie? Are you listening?"

I picked up the envelopes and shoved them at Lua, who immediately quit talking.

"You have to open them," I said. Letters from UC Boulder and New College had both been waiting for me when I got home from school. Not my parents, not the realtor or some unknown family feigning interest in buying our house. Just those two letters. I'd taken them to my room, sat on my bed, and stared at them. But after my rejection from Amherst, I hadn't been able to open them alone, so I'd brought them to Lua.

Lua took the envelopes. "Which one first?"

"Doesn't matter."

"You're gonna get in," he said.

Maybe I would have believed him before, but the first rejection had proved nothing was certain.

"Just do it," I said through clenched teeth.

Lua tore open the first letter, unfolded it, read it, and set it on his lap. Then he repeated the process with the second. All while I sat there fighting the urge to puke.

"Oh, Ozzie," he said. "I'm so sorry . . ."

My gut twisted. I ground my teeth together so hard I thought they would shatter.

Then he said, ". . . you're gonna be stuck in school for another four years. You got in!"

"What?"

"You're going to college!"

"Which one?"

"Both, Ozzie. You got into both."

Lua burst out of the car, ran around to my side, and pulled me out. He squeezed me and we jumped up and down in the middle of his driveway.

"I got in?" I said.

"You got in!"

Ms. Novak must've heard us shouting, because she came running out of the house in a robe with her hair in curlers asking what happened, and Lua said, "Ozzie's going to college!" And Dinah screamed and jumped up and down with us, our hands joined like the points of a star.

Lua hugged me and whispered into my ear, "I'm so proud of you, Oswald Pinkerton. I always knew you were too big for Cloud Lake."

"I got into college!" I said to Bella Donna as she drew a fat black *X* on the top of my hand.

"Good for you, baby," she said. "Now all the boys are gonna be chasing you."

I rolled my eyes, but I was still grinning.

Lua hadn't invited me to the show solely to watch. He

and the band had finished recording their EP and had copied the songs onto flash drives shaped like skeleton keys for me to sell. I set up a table in the back corner of the club. Five bucks for the flash drive, ten bucks for a T-shirt. Each shirt was emblazoned with the band's logo on the front—a cracked clock with a silhouette of Lua over it—and on the back was a list of tour dates, each set in the far-flung past or distant, imagined future.

I hadn't spent much time with Lua lately—I'd been busy with Cal and Lua had been busy with the band—but I promised him we'd go to IHOP after the show to catch up, and not only was I desperate to spend time with my best friend and find out what was going on in his life, I really needed to talk to Lua about Calvin.

I couldn't think straight around Cal. Kissing him filled my thoughts, though we'd managed to keep our lips firmly to ourselves. Sometimes we stayed up all night on the phone debating why the universe—the boundaries of which now extended barely farther than the moon—kept shrinking. I asked Calvin to explain where daylight came from without the sun, but he didn't recognize the word, which made the discussion difficult. Everything was happening so quickly that I hadn't had time to process what it all meant. Getting into UC Boulder and New College was an amazing feeling, but it meant I would have to make a decision about whether to leave or stay.

Should I stay in Cloud Lake for Tommy? Leave for myself? Could I admit that I had feelings for Calvin that I found increasingly difficult to ignore? Too many choices. Too many decisions.

"I'll take a shirt."

"Ten bucks," I said without looking up from my phone. Calvin had texted me a picture of the Thai food he and his dad were eating, and I was trying to think up a witty reply.

"This piece of shit isn't worth ten bucks."

I glanced up, and the last person I expected to see was Trent Williams. He looked so out of place, wearing a Miami Dolphins jersey and khaki shorts, a sneer cutting his ogre face. I snatched the shirt back from him and returned it to the pile.

"What're you doing here, Trent?"

"Came to see the show. What else?"

Trent was eighteen, but he must've had a fake ID that said he was old enough to drink, because he held a beer in one hand.

"So this is what a fag bar looks like," he said. A couple of people nearby glared in Trent's direction.

"I'm surprised I've never seen you here before, considering what people at school say about you."

Trent's smirk transformed into a snarl. "Was it you? Whatever Frye told you about me is a lie. He's a fucking liar."

"Calm down, Trent," I said. "I'm sure it's totally normal to get a boner while wrestling with another guy. Especially if you're gay."

"Fuck you, Pinkerton." He inched closer to the table, but a line had begun to form behind him, and a woman said, "Move it, creep."

Trent bristled and sneered. I doubted he'd start a fight in a club full of people who'd kick his ass for using the word "fag," but pride makes people do stupid shit.

"Whatever," he said, and backed away.

But I actually felt bad about what I'd said. I didn't know whether Trent was gay or straight or fell somewhere in between, and it didn't matter. Trent was an asshole, yeah, but no one deserved people talking shit about them.

"Trent," I called.

"What?"

"Lua and I are going to IHOP after the show. Why don't you come with us?" It had to be getting into college and my preoccupation with Calvin. Those were the only reasons I could think of that I was being nice to an asshat like Trent.

"I'd rather choke on a shit burrito," he said, and disappeared into the crowd. Whatever. I'd tried.

I sold out of the flash drives before the stage lights rose on Lua and the band.

Your Mom's a Paradox grew more confident every time I watched them play. It was only a matter of time before they graduated from opening band to headliner. And I was awed by them. By Lua.

There was a moment midway through the show, during the song "Corporal Jackie, the One-Legged Monkey," when Lua cut his finger. Instead of stopping, he smeared it across the front of his straitjacket and played on. It was gross, yeah, but it was so badass.

I had no idea what my future held, but I saw Lua's crystal clear, and it shone brighter than I could have possibly imagined.

385,972 KM

"HOLY SHIT!" LUA SAID, HOLDING HIS HAND OVER the table for me to see. "I'm an idiot." The cut ran down the pad of his swollen middle finger. "But I couldn't stop playing. I mean, I didn't even feel the pain until the end of the set. It was amazing."

"It was endorphins," I said, thinking about Calvin and his explanation for cutting himself.

Lua wrapped a napkin around his finger and cradled it to his chest. "Whatever it was, I want more."

IHOP was brightly lit and loud. A bawdy group that had come from a showing of *The Rocky Horror Picture Show* occupied most of the other side of the restaurant, still dressed in their fishnets and corsets and skin-tight gold shorts.

Our server dropped off our grilled cheese sandwiches, and we dug in.

"So," Lua said with his mouth full. "What's going on with you and Calvin, college boy?"

College boy. I still couldn't believe it, and I definitely wasn't ready to think about what it meant for my future. "Honestly?" I said. "I have no idea."

Lua rolled his eyes. "He likes you. Obviously. And you're a damn liar if you say you don't like him, too."

I avoided answering by stuffing my face with sandwich. The bread was perfectly toasted and the cheese just warm enough to ooze over the crust and drip onto the plate. It was maybe the most perfect grilled cheese I'd ever eaten. But I couldn't avoid answering all night. Eventually I'd run out of sandwich.

"Yeah, all right. I like him."

"I knew it!"

"But," I said, "it's complicated." I still hadn't told Lua the whole story of New Year's Eve, and I figured that was the best place to start. "So we sort of had sex in my car on New Year's Eve, but he's messed up and I'm messed up and we decided we should just be friends."

Lua stopped with a fry halfway to his mouth. "Aren't you supposed to friend-zone a guy *before* you sleep with him?"

"Like I said: complicated."

"If this is about Tommy, I might strangle you with that guy's feather boa." Lua motioned to the Rocky table.

"It's a nice feather boa," I said. "All violet and fluffy. If you ever strangle me with a feather boa, that's the one I'd choose."

"No changing the subject, Mr. College Boy Subject Changer."

I set my sandwich aside. Not even it could save me now. "All right. You can't tell anyone. You can't even let Calvin know you know." When I was certain Lua understood and agreed to my terms, I said, "Calvin was sleeping with a teacher." I immediately regretted breaking Calvin's trust, but I needed Lua to know Tommy wasn't the only complication between me and Calvin.

"Whoa," Lua said. His mouth hung open. "Do you know who?"

I shook my head. And since I'd already spilled one of Cal's secrets, I kept talking. "And he cuts himself. He used to. I don't think he's done it in a while. He might be depressed. Maybe."

"But this isn't all about him," Lua said.

"What do you want me to say? That I still love Tommy and I don't even know if I want to go to college, much less start something with Cal, because what if Tommy comes back?"

"Pretty much."

"Fine. I said it."

I'd lost my appetite. I wiped the buttery grease from my

fingers and tossed my napkin on my plate. "Look," I said. "I don't care if you don't believe me about Tommy, or that you can't support me because you consider doing so enabling what you perceive to be my delusion, but could you not shit on me for it?"

Lua's hard edges faded. He looked at me like I was one of those sad old dogs in a shelter that no one wanted to take home and would probably wind up euthanized. "I'm not shitting on you, Oz, but I don't want you to trade your happiness now for some slim-to-nonexistent chance of happiness in a nebulous maybe-future."

"Do you think you're telling me anything I haven't already considered?"

"Ozzie." Lua reached across the table and took my hand. "Do you like Calvin?"

"Yeah."

"Do you want to go to college?"

"Maybe?"

Lua rolled his eyes. "Don't 'maybe' me, Oswald Pinkerton. You know you want to be one of those snooty intellectuals showing off your mad smarts by lecturing your classmates about the homoerotic subtext in Hemingway's pompous shitty books. You're the only person I know who gets boners writing term papers."

I couldn't help laughing. Also, Lua wasn't wrong—not about the boner thing; writing essays didn't actually make me hard—I loved books and learning, and I thought I'd love college and the freedom to study subjects I was passionate about, which included pretty much everything.

"Fine. I want to go to college."

"Then do it!" Lua said. "Fall in love with Calvin and then dump his ass and go to college. We'll take a road trip over the summer before I go on tour. Be happy, Ozzie. You deserve it."

"But what about Tommy?"

Lua bit back the first reply that popped into his head—probably about how I was stupid and Tommy didn't exist—and I appreciated his restraint. "If Tommy comes back, and he loves you the way you obviously love him, he'll understand." Lua squeezed my hand. "You've waited long enough."

Lua made it sound so easy. Just stop waiting for Tommy and live my life. Maybe that included Calvin and college, maybe it didn't. But my decisions had consequences, even if I couldn't see what they were at the moment.

"I'll think about it," I said. "Good enough?"

"Not really. But it's better than moping."

Our waitress cleared our plates and replaced them with slices of wobbly chocolate cream pie and thick chocolate milkshakes, which consumed Lua's and my attention until we'd devoured both, leaving nothing behind but empty plates and glasses.

"So," Lua said. "How was it?"

"Delicious, obviously."

Lua laughed. "Not the pie. Sex. With Calvin."

"Oh." I suddenly became interested in drawing lines with my fork through the thin smear of whipped cream left on my plate. "He's got nice equipment, and it's all in working order."

"Nice equipment? That's all you're going to tell me?"

"You want a blow-by-blow account?"

Lua's eyes grew wide and he nodded his head like I should have known better than to even ask. "Duh."

"It was nice. And Calvin was really sweet."

"Puke. Gross. That's not what I meant."

"What? You want to hear how he went down on me and I went down on him but we didn't go all the way because we were in my car in his driveway, which made things logistically awkward?"

Lua's fingers were covered with chocolate and he eschewed his napkin to wipe his hands on his jacket, which was already stained with blood. "That's a decent place to start."

"It's a better place to end." I refused to divulge all the gory details. "Sex is weird, isn't it?"

"How so?"

"Well, I mean, when you're into it, when you're naked and kissing and doing all that stuff, it seems normal and awesome. But then, after, when you're sweaty and sticky and exhausted, it's like you just spent an hour in some bizarro world where it's totally natural to stick your mouth in places you wouldn't stick it under regular conditions."

Lua might not remember, but he'd been equally inquisitive the night after Tommy and I slept together the first time. Lua had practically shoved metal slivers under my fingernails to force me to reveal the tawdry particulars.

"Calvin laughed when he . . ." I mimed an explosion. "You know."

"He laughed?"

"Like a crazy person."

"Is that normal? Are you sure you did it right?"

I shrugged. "I hope so."

Lua nodded knowingly. "Jaime was all 'don't stop, don't stop,' and then he'd come and freak out if I even looked at his dick."

"Hey, it's sensitive down there."

"Yeah, well, Jaime was a little too sensitive," Lua said. "Most of the time I had to wait for him to leave so I could finish my business alone. You guys have it so easy. A couple of tugs and you're done. For me, getting off feels like cracking a safe. Sure, I can let someone drill the lock and hope they pop it, but it usually takes time and finesse to do the job properly."

Many lengthy and graphic conversations with Lua had given me more insight than I'd wanted into female anatomy, but it still seemed abstract to me. While there were definitely downsides to wearing my genitals on the outside—random classroom boners being one of the worst—Lua made the alternative sound much less appealing.

"Anyway, his laugh was demented," I said. "I don't know if he does it every time because we've only done it once, but it was funny. And his body did this weird spasm thing. It was cute and a little unnerving." I'd decided *not* to tell Lua about Calvin also calling me a slut, because we'd sorted that issue and I didn't want to give Lua a reason to hate him.

"Let me guess," Lua said. "You're all stone-faced and serious when your soldiers break formation."

"I don't really know what my face is doing. I'm usually too focused on what other parts of me are doing."

"Well, I suppose I'm happy you finally got laid. You should do it more often, even if the thought makes me want to vomit up my perfectly delicious pie."

"Thanks?"

Lua shook his head, his eyes tinged with sadness. "It's not you. I miss Jaime."

"You regret breaking up with him?"

"Sometimes," Lua said. "I still think it was the right thing to do, and I think I miss the idea of Jaime more than I actually miss *Jaime*, but it was nice knowing there was one person in the world who loved me more than anyone else."

"*I* love you, Lu."

Lua pursed his lips. "Yeah, I know, Oz."

He let his thought trail off. I understood what he was thinking, though. It's how I felt about Tommy. Lua was my best friend, and he would always be part of my life, even if he went on tour and I went to college and we didn't talk for months at a time. We were on planets in different galaxies, and Jaime was for Lua, as Tommy was for me, the sun around which we orbited. Ours, and no one else's.

"Oh!" I snapped my fingers, hoping to change the subject. "Speaking of Jaime . . . well, not Jaime, but of guys we hate who totally love you and want to have sex with you. You'll never guess who I saw at the club."

"If you're going to say Mr. Blakemore, I saw him there a few weeks ago." Lua leaned back in the booth and stretched his arms over his head. "I watched him twerk. High school teachers should not twerk."

"No one should twerk," I said. Lua's fun fact should have surprised me, but it didn't. Any person as persnickety as Blakemore was probably repressing some serious freak tendencies. Still, it was weird to think about teachers having lives and doing things other than grading papers and getting high on the smell of red ink. "But that's not who I'm talking about."

"Don't toy with me, Ozzie. Spill it."

"Trent Williams."

Lua's mouth dropped open, which was exactly the response I'd hoped for. I grabbed my phone off the table and quickly snapped a picture. He slapped at me. "Asshole!"

"That one's going on SnowFlake," I said, and I was already uploading it.

"Trent was really at a/s/l?"

"He tried to buy a shirt," I said. "No, correction: He tried to steal a shirt."

"What'd he say? Tell me everything."

So, of course, I did. When I finished, Lua said, "You invited him to IHOP?"

I poured myself another cup of the World's Shittiest Coffee from the carafe our server had left on the table. "Come on, Lu. You know he's into you."

"I don't think Trent knows what he's into." Lua blinked rapidly, still shocked at learning Trent Williams had gone to a/s/l of his own volition.

"Who are we to judge? We certainly don't fit the textbook definition of normal."

"I know for a fact he hooked up with Aja Shapiro, though she is pretty hot. I'd hook up with her if given the chance." Lua's eyes seemed unfocused and far away. "Do you really think Trent's got a thing for me?"

I stirred three single-serve creamers and eight packets of sugar into my coffee. "He showed up at a gay club on the night you were playing." I narrowed my eyes at Lua. "The real question is: Do you have a thing for him?"

"Even if I thought he was good-looking, which I'm not saying I do, he probably only sees me as a novelty act in his perverted mental circus."

"You don't know that."

"Yeah, Ozzie, I do." Lua bit his lip. "Jaime never cared what was under my clothes. He loved me for me. Do you honestly believe Trent Williams is that enlightened?"

"No," I said.

Lua nodded authoritatively. "Remember that list going around last year? The one that assigned points to each girl in our class."

"And the guys earned the points by having sex with the girls? I remember. Unfortunately."

"Trent started that list."

"Sometimes guys overcompensate," I said.

"Bullshit excuse. Overcompensating for insecurity and a tiny penis doesn't give guys the right to treat girls like shit."

I held up my hands. "I'm not excusing him, but it's like Dustin said: There's a lot of pressure on guys to be one thing or the other. Girls can experiment with other girls, and it's cool—"

"What a crock of shit!" Lua sputtered, and shook his head. "You're an idiot if you think that's true."

"It's a little true."

"No, Ozzie, it's not. Girls don't get a free pass to experiment. That's a fiction cooked up by men and played out in television and movies so they can fetishize girls hooking up, but it's nowhere even close to reality."

"Fine, but if a guy even thinks about experimenting with a guy, he's definitely gay and no one will ever believe otherwise." I sipped my coffee, which was basically milky brown sugar water, and grimaced. "Plus, Trent's dad played professional football, so I bet he puts insane pressure on Trent to be this übermacho, bang-all-the-girls guy's guy."

"Boo-fucking-hoo," Lua said. "Lot's of people whose lives suck don't grow up to be assholes." Lua's attention wavered when the Rocky table spontaneously burst into song. For a moment, I thought he was going to join them, but then he said, "Enough about Trent. Tell me more about Calvin and the teacher. Was it Mr. Bergen? I've always gotten I've-got-candy-in-my-van vibes off of him."

I shook my head. "Calvin didn't give me a name."

"Well, that's not fair."

"I think the guy is the reason for his dark-side transformation."

"Can you blame him?" Lua licked his lips. Most of his glitter lipstick had worn off, leaving them pale and somewhat shimmery. "Being in love is tough enough without the person you're in love with being an adult who took advantage of you."

Which was true. Thinking about losing Tommy was enough to make me want to curl into a ball in the corner of my room and never leave. I couldn't imagine what Calvin was going through. "I think it's more than that, though," I said. "I think what happened with the teacher was just the trigger."

"Maybe he *is* depressed. Maybe it was always inside of him, and this just brought it to the surface." Lua paused. "Like how Dinah gets. Sometimes I think if she didn't work, she'd lie on the couch all day and eat pickles."

Ms. Novak had never hidden her depression. Lua had lived with his grandparents for a few months in seventh grade because Dinah had checked herself into a psychiatric hospital. When she got out, she'd talked to me and Lua about it, explaining her illness and how she was fighting it. I'd always admired Dinah's openness.

"Either way, I think that teacher definitely screwed him up," I said.

"Do you think the teacher molested him?"

"Calvin says it was consensual, but how could it be? He's only sixteen."

"I thought Calvin was seventeen?"

I shook my head. "He skipped a grade in middle school."

Lua formed an O with his mouth. "Yeah, well, I can definitely see how having sex with a teacher could have fucked with his head."

"I just wish there was something I could do."

"Have you considered telling his dad?"

"I thought about it," I said. "But if I rat him out, he'll hate me. Besides, he promised he wouldn't cut himself anymore, so I don't think he's a danger to himself or anything."

Lua rolled his eyes. "Is that your expert opinion, Dr. Pinkerton?"

Maybe Lua was right. I'd always felt guilty I hadn't called the police about Tommy's father beating on him, and getting Calvin the help he needed might have been my chance to make up for that, but Calvin's situation was more complicated, and I wasn't prepared to make any decisions about it at IHOP. "We should probably get home," I said, rather than answer.

Lua and I fought over the bill while the poor waitress stood behind the register unsure what to do. Lua finally won, but I slipped twenty bucks into his jacket pocket while he rocked a victory dance.

When we walked out to the parking lot, Trent Williams was sitting on my trunk with his arms folded across his chest.

"What the hell?" I muttered.

Trent hopped down when he saw us.

"What're you doing here?" Lua asked, his voice defiant.

"Pink Lady invited me."

"Well, you're late, and we're going home." Lua tried to walk to the passenger side, but Trent blocked his path. "You don't want to mess with me, Trent." Lua was barely five feet tall, but he'd never backed down from anyone. I used to think he overcompensated for his lack of height with aggressiveness, but time had taught me that Lua was simply fearless.

When I tried to push myself between Lua and Trent, I smelled booze on Trent's breath. "Go home, Trent."

"What's your problem? I just want to talk to the he-she for a minute."

Oh shit, I thought.

Lua balled his fists and clenched his jaw. He stood straighter and looked Trent dead in the eyes.

I had a good four inches on Trent, but the guy had rocks for brains *and* muscles. If we fought, I'd lose. But I wasn't as worried about Trent starting a fight as I was about Lua starting one.

"Dude, you're drunk," I said. "I'll give you a ride home, but you have to cut this shit out."

Trent shoved me back. "I don't need a ride from the pansy patrol. I just wanna talk to Lua."

I fished my keys out of my pocket and unlocked the car doors with the fob. "Come on, Lua, let's get out of here."

I was worried I'd need to wrestle Lua into the car to keep him from throwing down with Trent, but I was relieved when Lua opened the door and started to climb inside.

Trent lurched forward and slammed the door shut.

A high-pitched wail ripped from Lua's throat, raw and animalistic. I'd never heard a sound that hopeless in my life and I never want to again. He was screaming and screaming, and I felt his pain like it was my own.

Trent was going, "Fuck! Oh fuck! Fuck! I'm sorry!" and he grabbed the handle and pulled the door open again.

Without hesitation Lua kneed Trent in the balls, and

it wasn't some halfhearted move, either. Lua folded him.

"What happened?" I ran around to their side. Lua was cradling his hand against his chest.

"That asshole slammed my fingers in the door!" Lua said. Trent was still moaning on the ground, clutching his balls, and Lua kicked him in the arm with his steel-toed boot.

I tried to coax Lua into letting me look at his hand, but he protected it like a wounded bird. His fingers, from what I could see, were already swelling and bruised.

"Shit, Ozzie. Shit, I think he broke my fingers."

"I'm calling the cops," I said. I already had my phone out and was dialing.

Lua shook his head. "Don't. Let's just go."

"He assaulted you, Lua!"

"I don't care about him!" Lua screamed. "I can't play guitar without my fingers, Ozzie, don't you get it? I need to go to the hospital right now!"

I hustled Lua into the car and left Trent moaning in pain in the parking lot.

Dinah ran into the hospital a little after two a.m., straight from a date and dressed in a short black skirt. Trent had broken three of Lua's fingers. His index was fractured in two places and would require surgery. The whole time we were waiting for the X-rays, Lua kept saying, "How am I supposed to play now?"

I wished I had an answer, but I didn't.

382,011 KM

LUA HELD UP HER PURPLE-AND-GREEN FINGERS FOR
Calvin and Dustin to see as we sat at our usual lunch table.
The emergency room doctor had splinted her fingers the best
he could, but they still looked deformed.

"Do you want me to murder him for you?" Dustin asked.
He looked past me, across the lunchroom toward Trent, who
looked no worse for wear. I'd called the police on the way to
the hospital to report a drunk guy in the parking lot of IHOP
trying to drive home, but he must have either left before the
cops had arrived, or managed to talk his way out of it, and it
made me hate him more.

Lua shook her head. She'd refused my calls over the
weekend and hadn't said much since she'd arrived at lunch.
All the air had leaked out of her. She'd even subdued her

normally flamboyant wardrobe. Wearing jeans and a black blouse, Lua looked so aggressively normal.

"You'll be able to play again, right?" Calvin said. I'd filled him in on what had happened, and he'd spent the rest of the weekend beating himself up for skipping the show, like he could have stopped Trent. Okay, maybe he could have. Calvin was probably the one person, other than Lua, who could've taken Trent in a fight.

Lua shook her head.

"But the doctor said if you get surgery on your index finger, they can put some pins in to make sure it heals properly." Lua had forced the doctor to explain it five times.

"And where the hell am I supposed to get the money for that?" Lua asked.

I hugged Lua, wrapping my arms around her shoulders, but she pushed me away.

"I'm just trying to help, Lu."

"I don't want your help." She looked around the table, challenging each of us. "We don't have insurance. So no surgery, no tour. No music career."

"What about—" Dustin began, but Lua slammed her good fist on the lunch table, causing her tray to jump.

"I can't deal with this right now." Lua stood and walked out of the cafeteria.

"Should one of you go after her?" Calvin asked.

"Let her be for now," I said. "She just needs time."

Dustin started in on how expensive hand surgery would be without insurance, but I'd stopped listening and stared at Trent with his friends. He was eating his lunch and laughing like he hadn't ruined Lua's life. The longer I watched him, the louder the monster in my chest growled, clawing at the back of my ribs, demanding I set it free.

When the bell rang, dismissing lunch, I marched across the cafeteria, right up to Trent.

And I shoved him.

"What the hell?"

Trent was surrounded by his friends, but I didn't care if they piled on and beat the shit out of me. I pushed him again. "You broke Lua's fingers," I said. "Did you know that? She can't play guitar now."

Mason Kang grunted something that sounded like "Fuck the kid up," and a couple of Trent's other friends urged him to knock me down, but Trent kept his fists at his sides.

"She was supposed to go on tour at the end of the summer, but you've ruined her chance to get out of this shithole town because she can't afford the surgery to fix her finger."

"I didn't know," Trent said.

"That's because you're an entitled, selfish asshole who doesn't care about anyone but himself!"

I didn't know Calvin had followed me, but now he tried to pull me out of the crowd that had grown around us. "Come on, Ozzie," he said. "Before Mr. Fletcher gets here."

I jabbed Trent in the chest. "I hope you get everything you ever wanted, Trent. And then I hope someone burns it all to the ground."

Mason surged forward, but Calvin blocked his path and said, "Bad idea, Kang."

I don't know. I don't know what I expected from Trent. Remorse maybe? Some acknowledgment that he understood how badly he'd screwed up Lua's life? Instead, he puffed out his chest and said, "Whatever. Her band sucked anyway."

Calvin grabbed me by the back of my shirt before I could attack. He locked his arms around me and half pushed, half dragged me out of the cafeteria.

Dr. Greg Nelson played with his stylus, tapping the rubber nub on his leg.

"How big is the universe?" I asked.

"I asked you why you thought you were here," he said.

"Humor me, all right?"

Nelson pursed his lips, but nodded. "About three hundred and eighty thousand kilometers."

"Three hundred eighty-two thousand and eleven kilometers, to be exact," I said. "It ends just past the moon."

"Oswald, I'd like to talk about you, not the universe."

I shifted on the couch, trying to find a comfortable spot, but the cushions were lumpy and a spring kept poking me in the butt. "Where does daylight come from?"

Dr. Nelson stopped fidgeting. He looked at me, his vague smile frozen. "I don't follow."

"The universe. It consists of Earth and the moon, right? So where does daylight come from?" I didn't wait for him to answer. "There used to be a sun, a star in the center of our solar system. That's what generated the light and heat for our planet. But it's gone, so what warms the planet? Why isn't it dark all the time?"

"Solar system? Star? I'm not familiar with those terms, Ozzie," he said. "Now, I'd like to talk about you. Tell me how you're doing."

Right. Why would there be a word for a thing that doesn't exist? The word "universe" comes from an Old French word, which itself was derived from the Latin word "*universum*." It means: all. Everything. The totality of existence. Which had shrunk to include nothing more than the moon after Trent broke Lua's hand.

"I'm fine," I said. "Everything's fine." I stopped and thought about it, then said, "You know what? No. Everything's *not* fine. My best friend's dream was destroyed by a prick who doesn't give a fuck, and I can't fix it; I can't let myself feel things for the guy I like who's actually around because I refuse to give up on the guy I love who no one else believes exists; my parents suck; my brother's gone; and no one can tell me where the light comes from without a goddamn sun!"

Dr. Nelson retrieved his tablet from beside his chair and wrote something on the screen with his stylus. "I'm going to recommend to your parents that you meet with a psychiatrist."

"You have *got* to be kidding me."

"In addition to our sessions, I believe you would benefit from medication, so I'm referring you to Dr. Taylor Laurie for evaluation." He finished writing and set his tablet aside.

I shook my head. "No. Screw that. I don't need medication. There's nothing wrong with me."

Dr. Nelson's smile smoothed out like he was speaking to a wild animal. "You probably have some misconceptions about psychiatric medications, but they're not going to turn you into a zombie or alter your personality. They might, however, help you strengthen your grip on reality."

"There's nothing wrong with my grip on reality. You all are the ones incapable of seeing what's really going on."

"Why don't you just meet with Dr. Laurie, and we can take it from there?"

"Or," I said, "you could eat a bag of deep-fried dicks. How does that sound?"

Mom and Dad were waiting for me when I got home. They were both sitting at the breakfast nook. And they were talking. The last time I'd seen them in the same room together was Renny's going-away dinner.

"What happened?" I asked. "Is Renny all right? Did something happen to him?"

Dad stood and held up his hands. "Warren's fine."

"Then what's going on?" My heart was racing.

Mom pushed out a chair between her and Dad. "Sit down, Ozzie. Your father and I want to talk to you."

I dropped my backpack by the stairs and trudged to the chair. On the table lay two more letters. One from UF and one from NYU. Without waiting for permission, I tore them open. Yes from UF, no from NYU. I was all grins when I looked up.

"I got into the University of Florida!"

Dad took the letters and read each. "That's good, son. Good for you. Actually, that's part of what we wanted to discuss with you." He glanced at my mom. "Kat, do you want to start?"

Mom nodded. "Ozzie, sweetheart, we sold the house." Whenever she had to tell me something she knew I wasn't going to like, she spoke in a firm but annoyingly reassuring tone, like I was five again and she was telling me my goldfish had died and she was worried I might have a complete melt-down. "It's not as much as we'd hoped for, but your father and I agree we're not likely to get a better offer."

"Good for you?" I knew it was for the best that my parents separated and finalized their divorce, but we were talking about my childhood home. It was the backdrop for all of my memories; the idea of strangers living in it felt wrong.

"I've already bought a three-bedroom condo in Seabrook," Dad said. "It's only a few miles from here."

I wasn't ready to get into an argument over who I would end up living with, because maybe I *would* go to college, and then it wouldn't matter. All I'd need was somewhere to crash on holidays and during the summer, and I wouldn't even need to stay with one of my parents. Ms. Novak would definitely let me sleep on her couch. And if I *did* decide to hang around Cloud Lake to wait for Tommy, well, maybe I could split my time between my mom and dad equally.

Then Mom said, "And I've accepted a job as the COO of a robotics company."

"Okay?" I said.

"They're based in Chicago, Ozzie. I'm moving to Chicago."

"Oh." I didn't think my parents divorcing would mean they wouldn't live in the same state anymore, but the idea didn't upset me. At least I wouldn't have to choose between them.

"It's . . . whatever," I said. "I'm probably going to college anyway. I'm leaning toward UC Boulder, but New College is tempting. And Dustin's going to UF, so that's always an option."

Mom and Dad glanced at each other. They'd spent so long together that they didn't need words to communicate. Maybe that's what had caused the end of their relationship. Maybe they ran out of words.

Also, my father was a cheating asshole.

"Oz," Dad said. "Dr. Nelson called us."

Uh-oh.

"He's concerned about you, and so are your mom and I."

"Listen, I'm not going back to him. I'll find a different therapist. He wants to put me on pills. Yeah, okay, I shouldn't have told him to eat a bag of dicks—"

"You did what?" Mom said, her face darkening.

Clearly Dr. Nelson hadn't told them that part. "That's not important," I said. "Just, I'm not crazy and I don't need to be put on medication."

"Ozzie," Mom said. "Dr. Nelson is concerned that, with all of the changes in your life, leaving your support system might not be best for your mental health."

"What support system? You're leaving, Warren's gone, Lua and Dustin can't wait to escape Cloud Lake, and I don't know if I'll ever see Tommy again." I didn't give them the chance to respond. "I don't *have* a support system."

Dad sighed. "Be that as it may, we—your mother and I—think it would be best if you lived with me and attended community college for a semester or two. You can defer enrollment at one of your other schools for a year, but until you're sorted out, we think this is the right thing for you."

I stood up so quickly I knocked my chair over. "That's not your decision to make!" Mom reached out to me, but I pulled away.

"Ozzie . . ."

"It's not my fault you guys are getting divorced. Don't punish me for your mistakes."

Dad didn't do "serious" often, but he was serious now. "Weren't you the one considering going to community college anyway?" he asked. "Maybe you were right. We think—"

"There's no 'we' anymore!" I yelled. "You're not a we. Whether I stay here or go to college, or join Greenpeace so

I can lob fake-blood-filled balloons at whalers, is my choice, not yours."

Dad's usually soft face hardened. "I hate to inform you, son, but unless you can pay for school on your own, it *is* our decision."

I turned to Mom. "You can't let him do this!"

"It's only for a semester," she said. "Two at most."

My mom and dad hadn't presented a united front on anything in well over a year. It didn't matter whether I wanted to leave or not, they had come together to rob me of the ability to choose for myself. My mouth opened, but I couldn't speak. They'd robbed me of that, too.

I stormed upstairs and slammed my door behind me.

TOMMY

I FIND TOMMY ON THE SWINGS. HE DOESN'T HEAR me approach from behind, or if he does, he doesn't acknowledge me. I stand at the edge of the mulch perimeter and watch. Tommy kicks higher and higher; his back arches and his arms straighten as he strains to gain momentum.

I don't understand the appeal of swings. It doesn't matter how hard you kick or how much effort you expend; you never actually go anywhere. All that work is futile, but Tommy tries anyway. I imagine him swinging so high his feet touch the moon. He lets go at the top of his arc and sails into the starry sky.

But that's not what happens. Eventually Tommy drags his feet through the rust-colored wood chips and stops.

"Hey," I say, kicking at the ground to make sure I don't startle him.

Tommy turns around. Even in the fading daylight the bruises

around his right eye and on his neck are visible. Blood cakes his upper lip under his nose. He doesn't smile when he sees me.

"I tried the trailer, but your mom said you'd gone for a walk."

"Sorry," he says. "I had to get out of there."

"I get it." I sit in the swing next to his. The chains groan. I doubt they're meant to hold the weight of teenage boys. "Your dad do that?"

Tommy nods. "I forgot to put the lid on the trash, and raccoons got into it."

"Oh."

"It looks worse than it is."

I twist in the swing, catching glimpses of Tommy from the corner of my eye. "You've got to get out of there," I say. "When we go to college—"

"I'm never getting out of Cloud Lake," Tommy says. "I'm going to wind up stuck here like Pops and there's nothing I can do about it."

"You can do anything you want. Maybe we can talk to my parents about you living with us until we graduate next year."

"Right," Tommy says with a bitter laugh.

"And with your grades, I bet you can get a scholarship—"

"I'm not going to college, Ozzie!" Tommy stands, leaving the swing shaking. He walks to the slide and sits at the bottom. "You don't get it. You'll never get it."

"Then tell me."

Tommy scrubs his face with his hands. *"You think everything is easy. You think anything is possible because you're white and your parents have money and all your life people have told you there's nothing out of your reach."*

"I know it's harder for you—"

"You don't know shit," he says.

"We can figure this out, Tommy."

Tommy falls silent. I wish I could read his mind. Cloud Lake isn't exactly diverse, and Tommy's always been one of the few black kids in town, but I didn't think it bothered him.

"People see me," Tommy says. "And all they see is my skin. Most of them don't even take the time to get to know me before passing judgment. I'm black first, everything else a distant second."

"Not to me."

"Fuck you," he says. "I don't need you to save me, Ozzie." Tommy looks at me, his eyes so intense. *"You know why my mama sticks around?" he says. "Why she puts up with him beating on her and on me?"*

I shake my head.

"Because no matter what he does to her, he's not as scary as the unknown. She has no idea who she is without my pops, and she's terrified to find out." Tommy hugs his knees to his chest. "I don't want to end up like that, but I don't know how not to."

"Please just let me help."

"No," Tommy says. "Whatever I do, I need to know I did it on my own, even if I don't know who I am yet."

"You want me to take you home?" I ask after a while.

"Can we just drive around?" he asks.

"Sure."

Tommy doesn't talk while we drive, so I turn on some music and roll down the windows. I drive all the way to Calypso before Tommy tells me he should get back so he can check on his mom.

When I drop him off in front of the trailer, he leans back in through the window and says, "Do you ever wonder who you'd be if we'd never met?"

I shake my head. "I don't even want to think about it."

Tommy shrugs. "Don't you think maybe you should?"

381,705 KM

MS. NOVAK WAVED ME DOWN AND HELD UP A PLASTIC tumbler of iced tea. I tried to shout I'd be done in a couple of minutes, but she couldn't hear me over the lawnmower's choppy growl. The grass was thick, and sand spurs clung to my shoelaces, though they were probably about the most benign things hiding in the weedy overgrowth. By the time I finished the front yard, my shirt was soaked through with sweat, so I tugged it off and threw it on the trunk of my car to dry.

"Thanks for helping, Oz," Ms. Novak said when I walked over to take the iced tea. It was a rare day off for her, and she was using the time to clean the house. She wore a Smashing Pumpkins T-shirt she'd gotten from a concert she'd attended before I was born.

"No problem." I hadn't realized how thirsty I was until I finished the tea in three big gulps.

"Sorry Lua's not around to help." Ms. Novak paused. "I'm worried about her."

"She's not really talking to me." Lua had started skipping school again and had stopped answering her phone. I'd driven to her house Saturday morning, determined to confront her, but Ms. Novak had answered the door instead, which was how I'd ended up mowing the lawn.

"Me neither." Ms. Novak had hardly touched her own iced tea and handed it to me to finish. "Mr. Hightower called from the guidance office. Said Lua's in danger of not graduating."

I believed it. At the rate Lua was going, I wouldn't have been surprised if the principal barred her from attending prom. "Have you ever heard her play?"

Ms. Novak nodded. "Yeah, but Lua doesn't know. I snuck into one of her shows a few months ago. My girl's talented."

"I think she broke more than her hand that night."

"She can still go on her tour," Ms. Novak said.

I shrugged. "Maybe. They could hire another guitarist or something, but right now I don't think Lua's willing to consider that. Playing is just as important to her as singing."

Ms. Novak furrowed her brow and looked at me. "Didn't she tell you? That boy, the one who slammed her hand in the door. He came by with his parents, and they offered to pay for her surgery."

"Are you serious?"

"Lua didn't tell you?"

"No."

"She turned them down. Said she didn't want handouts from nobody."

Normally I would have said that sounded exactly like Lua, but her music meant everything to her. I never imagined she'd put her pride over her band. And it wasn't even a handout; paying for the surgery after breaking her fingers was the least Trent could do.

"Sometimes I think I did Lua wrong by teaching her to only rely on herself. I wanted her to be independent, but I forgot to tell her it's okay to ask for help." Ms. Novak fell silent for a moment and then shook her head. "Enough about my stupid mistakes. How're things with you, Ozzie? Lua tells me you've got a new boyfriend."

"Calvin," I said. "But he's not my boyfriend."

"Why not?"

Even though I'd never explicitly spoken to Ms. Novak about Tommy since he'd vanished, I knew Lua must've told her. "I'm hung up on someone else."

"There's nothing wrong with that."

"But if I start a relationship with Calvin, I'm giving up on Tommy. And if I keep looking for Tommy, I might miss out on something great with Cal."

Ms. Novak chuckled again, like my pain, my indecisiveness, was a joke. "I've dated a lot of men since Lua was born, I even fell in love with a couple, but I never stopped loving her father. I doubt I ever will."

"How's that fair?"

"Fair to who?"

"To you?" I said. "To the other guys?"

Ms. Novak shrugged. "I don't suppose it is, Ozzie. But the world's going to offer you an endless array of what-ifs over the course of your life, and the only choices that matter are the ones you make."

I finished off the second tumbler of iced tea. I understood what she was trying to tell me, but she was talking about making one choice that shut the door on all those other possibilities, and as much as I was starting to like Cal, I couldn't close the door on Tommy.

"Thanks for the tea. I should cut the back before it gets dark."

377,092 KM

I STOOD IN FRONT OF THE MAILBOX, HOLDING THE
envelope, trying to decide whether to stuff it into the out-
going slot or fold it up, stick it in my back pocket, and walk
away.

I'd chosen UC Boulder because they had a great medie-
val literature department and mountains I could have driven
up into and watched the stars from without the lights of the
city obscuring them, if there'd still been stars to see. But I
wasn't sure if I was ready to make this decision. Accepting
my place at UC Boulder didn't have to mean I would actually go, it didn't mean I was definitely making the choice to
give up on Tommy, it just meant I was leaving the option
open to choose later. Of course, I'd also have to figure out
how to convince my parents to change their minds. My
visit with Dr. Laurie hadn't gone well. She'd spent fifteen

minutes with me, asking if I had any allergies and did I hear voices and had I ever taken psychiatric medication before, and then wrote me a prescription for a bottle full of little peach squares I was supposed to swallow each morning. I hadn't decided whether I was going to comply with my new doctor's orders—doing so would be admitting I thought there was something wrong with me, and other than a severe case of chronic indecision, I didn't believe there was—but I hoped at least pretending to go along might help convince my parents I didn't need to stick around Cloud Lake.

But regardless of what they'd said, this wasn't my parents' decision. It wasn't theirs or Lua's or Dustin's or Tommy's. It was mine. The future—*my* future—belonged to me and no one else.

I slid the envelope through the slot and stood back. I'd done it. I was going to UC Boulder.

If there was still a Colorado left by the time I graduated.

361,448 KM

CALVIN GRUNTED "HELLO" WHEN HE GOT INTO THE
car and then didn't speak for the rest of the drive. I'd picked
him up to go to a party at Dustin's house. Mr. and Mrs.
Smeltzer had traveled to New York for a wedding, and Dustin
had decided to throw a party—the first and only grand bash
before his parents lost their house.

I'd grown used to Calvin's quiet moods, but this one
was different. His silence was louder than a plane's rumble.
I'd offered to stay home with him, watch movies, and order
Chinese, but he'd mumbled that we should go to the party.

I only wanted to go because Dustin told me Lua would
be there. I wasn't looking for a fight, but I wasn't about to let
Trent derail Lua's dreams, even if that meant launching a full
verbal assault on my best friend.

I pulled up to Dustin's house and led Calvin inside.

Dustin's house wasn't huge, but it was big enough to comfortably fit a few dozen of my fellow Cloud Lake High seniors, most drinking, some dancing.

Calvin followed me closely as we searched for Dustin.

Dr. Laurie had warned me I would need to avoid alcohol with my medication, and since I hadn't decided whether I was going to take it or not, I grabbed a red cup of vodka and juice and downed half in one gulp.

We found Dustin in the living room, lounging on the couch with a dozen other people I mostly knew around a three-foot-tall bong. Clouds of sweet, sticky smoke clung to the walls and floated in the air, and I could tell by Dustin's lazy grin and heavy eyes that he was super high. No air freshener existed strong enough to eliminate the smell before his parents came home on Monday, and they were going to kill him, but, right then, I doubted he cared.

"Ozzie! Cal! I'd get up, but I can't get up." Dustin had spent the last four years focused on earning the best grades and becoming valedictorian so he could attend an Ivy League school, only to see that dream crumble because his parents had made a couple of bad decisions. I'd worried the loss would crush him, but Dustin was stronger than Giles Corey, and definitely stronger than me.

We made our introductions, and Dustin rattled off

everyone's names, which I promptly forgot. There was a Sabrina, a Joel, two Austins. Too many names to remember. I called everyone "dude" or "hey, you" out of necessity, and no one seemed to mind.

"Drink up, guys," Dustin said.

"Lua here?" I asked.

Dustin took a hit off the bong and blew a jet of hazy smoke toward the ceiling. "Not yet. Maybe. Honestly, I don't know. This couch is my entire universe tonight."

"I know the feeling," I said.

"I'll help you look," he said. "Am I standing up? I'm definitely standing, right?"

"Still sitting."

Dustin patted the couch. "You should join us."

"Maybe later," I said. "I want to find Lua first."

Cal nudged me. "Mind if I . . . ?"

"Yeah!" Dustin said, and shoved some guy with blond dreadlocks aside to make room for Calvin. "Calvin's cool, Oz. How did we never know he was so freaking cool?" He grinned at Cal.

"I'll be back?" I said.

"And I'll be here." Cal flopped down on the couch beside Dustin, who was already packing the bowl.

I rarely understood Calvin. It was like his emotions were

controlled by a single switch he randomly flipped on and off. We'd spent enough time together for me to recognize a few of the triggers that shut him down—college, wrestling, his mother—but sometimes we'd be hanging out in his room and he'd be talking furiously with his hands, arguing with me about a new theory I'd floated for why the universe was shrinking, and then he'd stop cold and go monosyllabic for the rest of the day.

I figured so long as he wasn't hurting himself, I didn't need to tell his father, but I still worried about him.

Besides, Calvin's behavior wasn't that unusual when compared to the rest of the senior class. As we neared graduation, and floods of college acceptance and rejection letters rushed toward mailboxes throughout Cloud Lake, a lot of students had started freaking out. The other day at lunch, Jocelyn Nash had thrown a plate of meatloaf at Devi Chad and then stormed out of the cafeteria because Devi got accepted to FSU while Jocelyn had been wait-listed, but who the hell throws meatloaf over something like that? And Stephen Malik showed up to school with a giant tribal tattoo on his neck, telling everyone it didn't matter since he wasn't going to college and would probably end up working at a convenience store. The tattoo turned out to be temporary, though I wasn't as sure about Stephen's nihilism.

So it wasn't just Calvin who was stressing over the great looming unknown. Only, I suspected the source of Calvin's behavior ran deeper and was connected to the teacher he said he'd had sex with, which I hadn't worked up the courage to press him for more details about. I wanted to help him, but he needed to tell me on his own terms.

I wandered through the house, checking each room for Lua. I found Jaime and Birdie Johnson making out in the kitchen, and kids in other rooms drinking and talking. Dustin's party was quieter than the one party I'd gone to at Trent's. No one had trashed Dustin's house—yet—and the neighbors hadn't called the cops. We were just a bunch of soon-to-be sort-of adults enjoying our last days of wasted youth.

I was heading back to the living room to check on Calvin when I spied a lone figure on the patio by the pool. I peeked my head out the sliding glass door, and Lua's bright green hair—because pink was so yesterday—shone like a neon beacon.

"Lu?" I called.

"No Lua here."

The floodlights illuminated the patio and pool, but Lua kept to the shadows. He stood at the edge of the pool, wearing board shorts and a tank top, and I noticed that he'd stopped shaving his legs. I closed the sliding glass door behind me so we could talk uninterrupted.

"You haven't been answering your phone," I said.

"And yet you keep calling. Funny how that works."

"I talked to your mom today while I was mowing the grass."

"Good for you."

I walked toward Lua but kept my distance. "Listen, you told me not too long ago that you were drowning. Well, Trent's throwing you a life jacket, and you seem hell-bent on ignoring it. Tell me why."

"Because fuck Trent, that's why." Lua glanced at me.

"Fine," I said. "Fuck Trent. But accepting his parents' money to fix your hand doesn't make you indebted to him. It's not charity, it's restitution."

Lua snorted. He sat on the deck and slipped his legs into the pool, and I sat beside him.

"Look, if you're afraid of going on tour, that's fine, but don't use your fingers as an excuse."

"It's not an excuse!" He held up his hand. Even splinted, his index finger was bent at an unnatural angle. "I can't play guitar with this."

"Then let someone else play," I said. "The band will still kick ass without you on guitar."

"Yeah right."

I threw up my hands. "Then get the damn surgery."

"I will . . . eventually. But Trent's not paying for it."

"It's okay to be scared."

Lua laughed. "I liked you better when you only thought about yourself."

"I'm serious, Lu," I said. "Maybe it was all too much. Maybe the tour and the album and the attention were overwhelming, and Trent messing up your hand gave you an excuse to take a step back. That's fine. But if you want this, if you really want to be a musician, don't let your pride or fear stop you."

"At least the things I'm afraid of are real, Ozzie."

"What's that supposed to mean?"

"Universe still shrinking?"

I looked up at the sky. There should have been stars, planets. The sky should have shone so bright, but it was empty. "The moon's gone," I said.

"The what?"

"The moon." I shook my head. "Forget it."

Lua pushed himself to his feet. "Just leave me alone, all right?"

"I still see you, Lua. No matter who you are, I see you."

"That's great, Ozzie. Too bad half the shit you see isn't real."

● ● ●

Calvin was stoned when we drove home from the party. He'd wanted to stay at Dustin's longer, but after my conversation with Lua I'd just wanted to go home. His dad's truck sat in the driveway, so I sneaked Cal up to his room. He fell across his bed while I stripped off his shoes and pants. He sat up long enough for me to pull his hoodie over his head.

Calvin's arms were covered in a latticework of fresh cuts. Long gaping mouths that silently screamed.

"What did you do, Cal?" I reached out to touch one of the cuts, but stopped short. I couldn't make myself do it.

"You really think we're living in a simulation?" Calvin's voice was slurry; his words ran together.

"I don't know. What does that have to do with you cutting yourself?"

Calvin collapsed in on himself, like his bones had liquefied. "'Cause if it is, then none of this is real. None of the good. Especially none of the bad."

I stared at the gashes, at the fresh red ones, at the raised white scars of past hurts. "You should tell your dad what's going on. He's worried about you."

Calvin pulled me down on top of him and kissed me. It happened so quickly, I kissed him back instinctually. I'd wanted him since New Year's Eve, but I wanted him sober and lucid.

I twisted out of Calvin's embrace and backed away from the bed. "Let's talk about this when you're not high."

"Whatever." Calvin rolled over, his back to me. "He used to give me pills. Dulled everything. Didn't feel the pain."

"Who was he, Cal?"

Calvin said, "I still don't feel nothing," and I wasn't sure if he knew I was even in the room. "We're meant to feel, but not me. Too numb."

"Look, Cal, if this guy—whoever he is—drugged you to have sex with you, that's rape. You know that, right?"

Calvin burrowed deeper into his covers. I thought he'd fallen asleep, and I was turning to leave when he mumbled, "I never said no."

359,270 KM

GOOD-BYE, MOON. SO LONG, STARS. ALONG WITH
Tommy and 99 percent of the universe, I remained the only
person who knew they'd ever existed.

I pored over science books at work looking for mentions
of the moon, but found nothing. None of the Apollo space
missions had ever taken place. No country on the planet had
attempted a single manned space mission. Instead of the
Space Race in the sixties, the United States and Russia had
fought over who could first construct a base on the bottom of
the ocean, and President Kennedy's speech at Rice University
in 1961 was no longer remembered as one of the greatest
speeches in recent history, because "We choose to go to the
ocean" hadn't inspired the same level of patriotism as "We
choose to go to the moon" had.

Even though the shrinking universe continued rewriting

history, most things remained the same. The technological achievements we'd discovered while trying to explore space still existed. Tommy and I had both gone through a period of obsession with space exploration, and we'd read dozens of books about the missions to the moon and the inventions NASA—which no longer existed—had created for space travel. Take the modern smoke and carbon monoxide detectors found in virtually every home across America. They were originally developed in the 1970s for use on the Skylab space station. But history had compensated for the changes to the universe, and I learned that the DOEA—Deep Ocean Exploration Agency—had invented the detectors during the construction of Atlantis, the first deep ocean base, built in the late 1960s.

Despite the universe shrinking, history seemed intent on protecting the integrity of the timeline. Like how Tommy's mother had still dropped out of high school even though he'd never been born.

Sometimes thinking about it pushed me to the edge of sanity. The damn universe was disappearing and I was the only person who realized it. If other people knew the truth, there would have been riots and mass suicides and total chaos. But it was a problem I didn't understand and couldn't even begin to conceive of how to solve, so I focused on my other problems, the problems I could actually fix. Like Lua's hand or Cal cutting himself or packing my room for the move, which my parents had scheduled for the following weekend.

When it came to Calvin, I hoped being there was enough to keep him from doing anything permanent, but I worried I wasn't a good, or even a reliable, anchor for him. I seriously considered telling his father about the cutting, but it'd been a week since Dustin's party and Calvin had kept his word not to hurt himself again, and I'd checked his arms and legs each time we were alone together to make sure. I still felt like my life was splintering, though, and I was terrified I couldn't keep it all from flying apart.

Next Sunday was our last day in the house. Mom, who'd started her new job in Chicago, had flown home for the weekend to help pack. I'd begged Dad to hire movers, but he remained obdurately determined we do the work ourselves.

The soon-to-be new owners weren't planning to move in for a few months, but Dad said they wanted us out quickly because they intended to gut the house and remodel everything. I was glad I wouldn't have to watch the home I'd grown up in torn apart and transformed into a place I wouldn't recognize.

I'd spent Saturday morning cleaning out my closet. A

pile of too-small clothes lay in a heap across my bed, and I'd gotten sidetracked sorting a box of papers, mostly old homework. The drawing of Tommy that Renny had given me for Christmas stood propped up against the wall, like he was watching me. My memories and the drawing were all I had left of him. Sometimes I wondered if they were enough.

"Ozzie!" Dad called from downstairs. Between working and babysitting Calvin, I'd managed to avoid my parents, especially my dad, whom I was still mad at for cheating on my mom. I hadn't switched sides, but had instead decided there were no winners in this war and that I was better off hating my parents equally. I continued to play nice, however, because I still hoped to change their minds about letting me go away to college. A plan that had, thus far, met with no success.

I wondered if my parents had any control over their decisions; if they were being subtly influenced by forces they couldn't perceive. I still thought it likely Flight 1184 had crashed to send me a message to stay in Cloud Lake, and was forced to consider the possibility that my parents' renewed unity was merely another warning shot fired from the great beyond.

"Ozzie!" my mom called. "Ozzie, get down here now!"

Her panicked voice echoed through the house and into my room.

I pulled on a shirt and headed downstairs. I stalled at the railing, watching Mom and Dad zip through the house like bumper cars. Mom's suitcase sat by the door even though she wasn't supposed to leave until tomorrow.

"What's going on?" I asked.

Dad looked up at me, his face pale and drawn, holding his phone to his ear. "Oz, come down here."

I walked down the stairs and noticed Dad's duffel bag open on the counter.

"Is someone going to tell me what's going on?"

Mom stopped running about, but Dad walked into the other room to talk on the phone.

"Ozzie," she said, "it's Warren."

"What's Warren? Did something happen to Warren?"

"No," Dad said, but to the phone, not to me. Tentacles of frustration tightened around his words. "Don't put me on hold again. This is an emergency, and—"

Mom rushed me and hugged me so tightly I thought I might break. "Renny's been hurt."

I pushed her away. "Is this a joke? Early April Fools'? Ha-ha? It's not funny."

Tears ringed Mom's eyes; she wiped them away with the

back of her hand. "We don't know the details yet. Something happened during a training exercise, and Warren's been injured. He's at Martin Army Community Hospital. Your father and I are flying to Georgia as soon as we get tickets."

"I'm going too," I said. My heart was pounding. I felt each beat in my throat and nearly choked on them.

Mom shook her head. "I'm sorry, Ozzie, but you can't miss school."

Dad hung up the phone. "Okay. We're flying out of Miami, but we've got to leave now if we're going to make it."

Everything was happening too fast. "I don't care about school!" I said. "I want to go with you."

"Listen, Oz," Dad said. "I'll call the realtor and explain what's happened, and I'll hire movers to finish packing."

"Do you think you can stay with Lua while we're gone?" Mom asked.

I shook my head. They weren't listening to me. "Yeah, but—"

"Good," Mom said. "I don't know when we'll be back, but I'll call you as soon as we know how Renny is."

Dad had grabbed an armful of clothes and threw them into his duffel bag. I wasn't even sure he knew what he was packing.

"You're not leaving me behind," I said.

Dad zipped his bag shut. "We don't have time to argue about this, Ozzie. You're not going, and you're not staying here alone. Go to Lua's house and I'll call her mother on the way to the airport. Understand?"

I didn't know what else to say, and they didn't give me the time to compose an argument. Before I could process what was happening, they were out the door and gone.

I didn't drive to Lua's house. Not right away. I went to Calvin's instead. I showed up on his front step crying, and he didn't ask why. He just hugged me until I stopped. Eventually we wound up at the beach, sitting in the sand, watching the tides roll out. It was weird that there were still tides without the moon to push and pull them.

Calvin probably had a million questions, but he kept them to himself. We sat beside each other, my head on his shoulder, until the light in the sky faded. I didn't know where that came from either, nor did I care.

"I never really saw the stars before," Calvin said out of the blue.

I'd been thinking about Warren, about how stupid he'd been to join the army. He didn't belong there. He wasn't a fighter or a killer. He was just a stupid kid who didn't know what else to do with his life. And then Cal brought up the stars. I'd tried to explain them to him after they disappeared, but I don't think he really understood what they were. Even the word sounded foreign when he said it.

"What?"

"The stars," Cal said. "I don't think I ever saw them."

I shook my head. "You don't remember them, that's all."

"No . . . I mean, yeah, I don't remember them, but I think that even when I could remember them, I must not have seen them. Not really." He shivered in the cool air. "I think the sky was always empty to me."

I wasn't in the mood for one of Calvin's philosophical discussions. Half the time I didn't understand what he was saying anyway. Moments like that, I thought he and Tommy would have liked each other.

If they'd met before Tommy and I had, they might have fallen in love and I'd never have known either of them.

"That thing I told you," Calvin said. "About being baptized? It wasn't true."

"It doesn't matter."

"Yeah it does." Calvin was quiet for a moment. Then he said, "I *did* nearly drown, and God *did* speak to me and tell me I could breathe underwater, but it didn't happen at the beach, and I definitely wasn't being baptized. It started on a boat—*his* boat. He'd given me beer. I was a little tipsy and I fell over the side. He laughed at me because he thought it was funny, and maybe it was, but I sank beneath the surface and didn't float back up. I thought if I let the air out of my lungs and drifted to the bottom of the ocean, everything would be different."

"Cal, I don't—"

"But God told me to breathe, so I breathed. And then he hauled me out of the water."

"God?"

"Coach Reevey."

I pulled away from Cal to look him in the eyes. "Your wrestling coach? He's the teacher you were sleeping with?"

Calvin nodded. "I thought he loved me, but then he said he'd found someone new. That I wasn't special anymore."

"You have to tell someone," I said. "Your dad or a guidance counselor. Anyone."

"He called me to his office last week." Calvin kept talking like he hadn't heard me. No one, it seemed, was listening to me today. "Told me he was sorry. That he could help me get into college if I . . ."

"If you what? Did he do something to you again?"

Calvin's voice cracked. He buried his face in his hands. "The pills he gave me, he said they'd relax me. But then he'd do things to me, and I couldn't stop him. My brain would scream at me to fight back, but my body just couldn't."

"My brother's hurt, and he might die. Why are you telling me this now?"

"Because you deserve to know."

"Listen, Cal. What Coach Reevey did to you isn't your fault. We can tell someone and they'll fire him or arrest him or something. But it's not your fault."

"The funny thing is," Calvin said, "I thought I'd been breathing underwater this whole time, but I guess I've been drowning."

I stood and brushed the sand off the back of my shorts. "I can't do this, Calvin. I can't. Not with my brother . . . not with Renny hurt."

"I know. I'm sorry. You deserve better than me."

"Better than you? Who's better than you, Cal?"

Calvin shrugged. "Everyone."

TOMMY

MY PHONE RINGS. ITS DISTANT CHIMES BORE THROUGH
my dreams and manifest as thunderous peals from the stars. Each one a different note in the heavens that flares when it sounds. I reach out, try to touch them, but they're so distant. And then they fall silent.

My phone rings again, and this time I pull the stars from the sky. My hands ignite and burn sapphire blue. My skin melts and drips to the sand, my bones char and turn to ash. But I hold on to the sound. I unspool it and follow it out of the dream.

"Hello?" My voice is groggy.

"Ozzie?"

Tommy's voice clears the sleepy fog, and I check my hands to make sure they're not burned. I still remember the pain. I sit up in bed, glance at my alarm clock; it's 3:03 a.m.

"Tommy? What's wrong?"

"Nothing," he says. "I just needed to hear your voice." He's lying, I always know when Tommy's lying, but I also hear other voices in the background. Yelling.

"Your dad?"

Tommy grunts. "They shut off our water. Pops blew the bill money on booze."

"Can you get out of your house? I'll pick you up." I only have my learner's permit, but I know how to drive well enough to steal Dad's car and get to Tommy.

"I'm fine," he says. "I'm in my room. Blocked the door with my dresser." Tommy's "door" is a sliding accordion divider, barely thicker than a sheet of cardboard, and definitely not enough to keep his father out. "Just talk to me, all right?"

"What about?"

"Tell me where we'd go if we ran away."

I whisper to avoid waking Renny or my parents. My dream of the stars is already fading, but their clear notes linger longest. "I think we'd run to Colorado. Somewhere in the mountains. Or maybe the desert. Either way, we steal a car and drive west. It takes hours to get out of Florida, but we shed our troubles at the border, and at night we sleep under the open sky." I stop when I hear something crash on the other end of the phone. "Call the police, Tommy."

"Ignore it. Do we stop anywhere on the way?"

"Sure." It's difficult to dream up a story about running away when I'm worried Mr. Ross is going to break through Tommy's door and kill him. But I try anyway. "We don't take the interstate because the cops are looking for us. We drive the back roads instead, and we pull over at every little stand that sells boiled peanuts."

"I love boiled peanuts," Tommy says. "Then what?"

"We reach Boulder and stop in this cute café for breakfast. There's a woman working who keeps looking at us like she recognizes us. Before we leave, she asks if we know where we're going. We tell her we don't. She says the only way to figure it out is to stop searching."

I don't hear anything on the other end of the phone, so I say, "Tommy? You still there?"

Nothing for a moment. Then, "I'm here. Keep talking."

"So we head into the mountains with no destination. We drive until we run out of gas. We abandon the car and keep walking. It's winter, and we're cold, but we keep walking. And then, when we're too tired to take another step, we find a log cabin hidden in the trees. Smoke's rising out of the chimney, and there's a mat at the front door that says 'Welcome Home,' and we know we are home. We stay there and no one ever finds us."

"Is it real?" Tommy asks.

"It's real," I tell him. "As real as you and me."

Mr. Ross bellows in the background, and I hear something heavy break. "I gotta go, Ozzie."

"Tommy, wait—"

"Ozzie, I can't—"

"We'll get out of here, Tommy. I love you."

I wait for him to say it back, the way he always does, but the line goes dead.

337,902 KM

RENNY LOOKED LIKE SHIT. HIS IMAGE ON THE
screen kept freezing, and his voice cut out because the Wi-Fi
at Lua's house sucked. But I could see him, which made me
both feel better because he was alive, but worse because half
his head was shaved completely to the skin revealing a squiggly
line of staples, puckered and raw, and his face was a mass of
cuts and bruises.

But his injuries couldn't account for all the changes in
my brother. Renny was leaner, his cheekbones more prom-
inent, his eyes deep and hollow. He didn't smile, didn't call
me names, didn't joke around. He looked like someone who'd
nearly died and wished he hadn't survived.

"You look good, Renny."

"So everyone keeps saying," he says. "You're all liars, of
course."

Warren had waited until Mom and Dad had gone to their hotel to catch some sleep before calling me. They'd refused to leave his side since they'd arrived and were getting on his nerves, so he'd yelled at them until they agreed to give him some space.

"What happened?" I asked. "All Mom and Dad would tell me is that you fell." They'd also informed me the fall had partially severed Renny's spinal cord at the T6 vertebra, and that he would probably never walk again, but I wasn't sure how to bring that up.

Renny shut his eyes. I didn't know what kind of drugs the doctors were pumping into him, so it was possible he'd fallen asleep. But then he said, "There was this guy—Lucas Prieto—everyone called him Fapper. Don't ask why."

"Gross. I won't."

"Yeah." Renny frowned. "Me and Fapper didn't get along. He thought I was a suck-up because I was good at being a soldier." He looked directly at the camera. At me. "Ozzie, I was *really* good."

"I'm not surprised," I said. Another lie.

"Anyway," Warren said. "We were running the obstacle course, and Fapper hated me because he could never beat me." A small smile crept onto Renny's face. "So we're running the course, and we get to the Skyscraper, which is this tall wood tower we had to scale one side of and rappel down the other, and I'm kicking ass, right? I'm probably going to beat my own best time. But Fapper's right on my tail. I'm hauling myself over the top, Fapper's beside me, and he kicks out, like he's trying to use my face to boost himself over the ledge. Only, he kicks too hard, and I lose my grip."

Renny touches the staples on the side of his head. "I don't remember the actual fall, but Lindley said I cracked my skull on one of the beams on my way down and landed on a log at the bottom." He blinked back tears. "I won't ever walk again."

I wished I hadn't called him. It hurt to see Renny so broken. Not his body, but his spirit. "Mom and Dad said your doctors are waiting for the swelling to go down. That the damage might not be as severe—"

"Don't," Renny said. "Mom and Dad and the doctors keep trying to feed me that bullshit, but I can't take it from you."

Mom told me Dad spent every second he wasn't with Warren in the hospital chapel praying. I doubted he'd do that if he had faith in the doctors' abilities to fix my brother. And Mom hadn't even tried to give me hope Renny would recover the use of his legs. I guess she'd spent so much time sugarcoating the situation for Renny she had nothing left for me.

"Fine," I said. "So maybe you're paralyzed, but I researched these stem cell treatments that are showing a lot of promise. And they have exoskeletons now that could help you walk. You could have bionic freaking legs."

"Do they make bionic dicks, Ozzie? Because I don't give a fuck about my legs."

Renny was hurting, and I wanted to help him. I wanted to get in my car, drive to Georgia, and sleep on his floor. But none of that would fix him.

"That's the worst part, you know?" Warren said.

"What is?"

"Knowing I won't ever have sex."

"You don't know that. I read a bunch of articles about how paralyzed men can have sex." My browser history would've looked so weird if anyone had snooped, but what I'd said was true. I just didn't mention he'd probably have to use pills or inject this stuff into his dick to get an erection because the descriptions had sounded horrible.

Warren shook his head. "Why bother? Even if I could get it up, I wouldn't feel it. And what girl's going to want me now?"

"There are specialists. I bet Mom and Dad could find a doctor who—"

"There's nothing they can do! Shut up about it already!"

I thought maybe the video had frozen because Warren had stopped moving—he didn't even blink—but a light continued flashing on one of the hospital monitors behind him.

I wanted to say something to make Renny feel better, but I could hardly begin to imagine how my brother was suffering. I wondered how I would feel if I woke up one day and couldn't walk, couldn't control my bladder or take a dump without help. Whatever I imagined was nothing compared to Renny's reality. He wasn't ready to think about how to move on from his accident, so I gave up trying to force-feed him hope.

"Mom and Dad driving you crazy yet?" I asked.

"Yeah," Warren mumbled. "I wish they'd go home."

I shrugged. "At least they're getting along. I think this is the most time they've spent together in a year."

"Great. All it took was one of their kids suffering a nearly fatal accident." Renny's chin fell to his chest and we sat there together, not speaking for a while. I didn't know whether he was trying to indicate he wanted me to cut the connection and leave him alone or if he simply needed me there even if we didn't talk.

Just when the silence began to veer into uncomfortable territory, Warren said, "I lied when I said I didn't care about sex. I'm going to die a loser virgin."

"You're not a loser."

Renny ignored me. "You've done it, right?"

I wanted to tell him I'd never had sex either so he didn't have to be the guy whose little brother had done it before him. And the funny thing was that technically, with Tommy gone, I *hadn't* actually gone all the way with anyone, but I remembered sleeping with Tommy, so I figured it had to count.

"Yeah," I said.

"What's it like?"

"Renny . . ."

"Come on," he said. "At least tell me what I'm never going to have. You owe me that."

I sat quietly for a moment, wishing the Wi-Fi *would* cut out so I wouldn't have to explain sex to my older brother. Aside from being totally mortifying, I wasn't sure my experiences were common. Lua had told me sex with Jaime had felt like an endless battle in a war she could never win, Dustin was still a virgin, and I didn't want to think about how Calvin would have explained sex. I didn't know if he'd slept with any of the girls he'd dated, and he'd said Coach Reevey was the only guy he'd done it with other than me, but Reevey had drugged him, so for Calvin, sex had probably felt like an ambush.

"For me," I said, "sex was like reading an epic story. Kind of confusing at first, but when everything began to make sense, the world disappeared—I lost myself in something bigger than me—and when it was over, all I could think about was going back to the beginning and doing it again."

"Only you could make sex sound boring."

But it wasn't. It hadn't been. Sex with Tommy had been the single most beautiful experience of my life.

"Yeah," I said. "You're not missing much."

This time the connection really did stutter, and Warren and I spent a minute calling back and forth to each other. When the video cleared up, Renny said, "Can I tell you something?"

"Anything."

"I'm not sure I can live like this. I'm not sure I want to."

"Don't you even think about hurting yourself, Renny," I said. "There's more to life than sex."

"Says the guy who can stick his dick anywhere he wants to the guy who can't feel his." Warren clenched his jaw, and I wasn't sure if it was from the pain of his injuries or from thinking about what he'd lost. "You were right. I should have told Emilia how I felt before I left."

"You still can."

Renny scoffed. "I can hardly sleep. Not even the drugs

help. And when I lie awake in the middle of the night in this stupid fucking hospital, all I can think about is how I wish the fall had killed me."

My parents shouldn't have left him alone. I touched my phone in my pocket, reminding myself to call them when I was done with Renny and tell them to never leave him alone again.

"Please don't say that, Warren. I need you."

Renny fired off a bitter laugh. "Don't bullshit me, brother. You don't need me. You never needed me."

"That's not true."

"It is, and you know it." He closed his eyes and I thought he was going to fall asleep, but then he opened them again. "I've always kinda hated you, Oz."

"Tell me how you really feel," I said with a halfhearted smile.

"I'm serious," Renny said. "Everything comes so easily to you. Whenever you want to do something, you go out and do it. And the worst part is that you barely have to try. Do you know how great you could be if you put in the tiniest bit of effort?"

I'd thought Warren hated me the way older brothers always hate their little brothers, but I never considered that he *actually* hated me.

"Everything's not easy for me."

"Bullshit," he said. "Remember in third grade when you were in that musical? You'd never sung before, but they gave you a solo anyway. There wasn't a dry eye in the audience by the time you were done. And then you never sang again. I finally found the one thing I was good at, and now it's gone. You're good at everything. You could be *great* at anything."

"I'd cut off a couple of toes to have someone tell me what to do with my life, Renny," I said. "Look at Lua. She's knows what she's passionate about, and she pursues it with this tireless determination that blows my mind. You say I can do anything, but no matter what I choose, there will always be a hundred other things I'll miss out on."

"Boo-fucking-hoo." Warren gave his head a little shake and flinched. "Mom and Dad told me they don't want you going away to college." I started to reply, but he cut me off. "I told them to stop being assholes."

"I'm sure that went over well."

"You'd be surprised at the shit you can get away with when people feel sorry for you."

"Maybe you could guilt them into not getting divorced."

I waited, hoping the joke would elicit at least a wan smile, but Warren's face remained blank.

"Renny—"

"Look, if you don't go away to college, I'll never forgive you."

"And how am I supposed to pay for it without Mom and Dad's help?"

"You can have my college fund," Renny said. "I'm never going to use it."

I rolled my eyes. "I'm not taking your college fund, but if it'll make you happy, I already accepted my spot at UC Boulder. I'll figure something out. Just don't tell Mom and Dad." I wasn't lying to Renny, but even if my parents changed their minds, I still wasn't sure I'd go. And it wasn't just because Tommy might return or Lua might not go on tour. Renny needed me. I had a hundred reasons to stay in Cloud Lake, but I didn't want to argue with my brother while he was in so much pain.

"Good," Renny said. "Go to school, Ozzie. Study something ridiculous. Join a frat and bang a ton of dumb hot guys. Become one of those conceited college kids nobody likes, who bores everyone by spouting pedantic nonsense. Go to grad school because your degree is worthless in the real world. Fuck the real world. The real world took my legs and my dick, Ozzie. The real world took my future. Don't let it take yours."

Warren rendered me speechless. For someone who hated

me, he sure seemed to love me. I wanted to tell him he could have all the things he wanted me to have—that I'd take out soul-crushing loans for my own education so he could have any future he wanted—but I didn't. Because, in a way, he was right. I knew his life wasn't over because he couldn't walk, it just wouldn't be the life he wanted.

"I promise, Renny."

"Good." He sighed and his eyelids fluttered. "Look, I'm getting tired, kid."

"Okay," I said, not wanting to let him go. "When you get home, we'll have wheelchair races on the roads in front of Dad's new place."

"Sounds good." Renny's voice drifted farther away.

"And don't expect me to feel sorry for you either," I told him. "I'm not ceding my chance to call you 'numb nuts' to spare your feelings."

"Shit, Oz, if 'numb nuts' is the best you can come up with, you're not as smart as I thought."

"I love you, Renny."

There it was. A smile. Fragile and newborn, but still a smile. "Ugh, you're such a wuss."

"Wuss? Really? Is that all you got?"

"Don't make me roll over there and kick your ass," he said, which seemed like the funniest thing in the world. He started laughing, and I laughed because it was good to see Renny smiling again. But laughing must've hurt because he winced and held his sides.

"Ow," he said, but he kept grinning.

"Walk it off, Renny."

"You're an asshole, Ozzie. And I love you, too."

211,581 KM

DR. MAKALI SAYEGH HAD BEEN STARING AT ME FOR the longest five minutes of my life. We'd exchanged pleasantries after she'd called me into her office, and then she just sat there, staring and smiling. She didn't ask why I thought I was there. She didn't ask how I was feeling. She hadn't asked me anything other than whether I'd like a glass of water.

I didn't know what her game was, but I didn't like it.

Dr. Sayegh was a tiny woman—barely five feet tall—with gleaming white teeth, an overabundance of laugh lines, and wavy black hair shot through with gray. I admired her for aging gracefully rather than attempting to dodge time with harsh dyes or skin creams made from leftover baby foreskin. Besides, Sayegh didn't act old. She seemed like the kind of woman who'd celebrate her fiftieth birthday by climbing to the peak of Mount Everest just to prove she could.

I examined the walls to kill time, waiting for her to start the interrogation. A picture of the doctor grinning from inside a yellow raft, an oar in one hand, white water raging all around her, hung on one wall. An abstract painting that drew me into its chaotic world of red splatters and neat yellow boxes, probably painted by a man who'd cut off some extruding body part and mailed it to an unrequited love, hung on another.

"My brother's paralyzed," I said when I couldn't bear the silence anymore.

Sayegh covered her mouth with her hand and her eyes widened. "Oh, Oswald. I'm so sorry."

"Fell off this tower thing in basic training." Even though I knew Renny would live, I'd been moving through life like everything around me was distant noise. I spent my days sleepwalking through school and my nights sitting with Lua and Ms. Novak, watching bad reality TV. I hadn't seen much of Calvin outside of physics, and he hadn't made an effort to talk to me, either. "Cracked his skull and severed his spine."

"At least he's alive," Dr. Sayegh said. She didn't have a tablet or a notepad to write on.

"I wish Renny agreed."

"How are you coping with all of this?"

I snorted. "Me? I can still walk. Who cares how I feel?"

"I do," Sayegh said. "Your parents do."

"Right." I folded my hands together. "My parents are staying with Warren until the army doctors transfer him back home to start physical therapy."

"And what about you? Where are you staying?"

"With my friend Lua. Which is fine. It's not like I have a home anymore anyway."

"Why is that?"

The downside to seeing a new therapist every week was constantly having to explain the same things over and over. It would've been easier if they'd shared notes. "My parents are divorcing, so they sold the house." I shook my head. "It doesn't matter, though. That house stopped being a home a long time ago, I think."

Dr. Sayegh shifted in her burgundy leather wingback chair and crossed her left leg over her right. "I spoke briefly with your mother before your appointment," she said. "She mentioned I'm the ninth doctor you've seen in the last six months."

"Eleventh, actually."

"Why is that?"

"Why are you number eleven?"

I started to answer with my usual spiel about her being the next name on the list, but she cut me off. "Why do you keep changing therapists? I understand needing to find one you're comfortable with, but eleven is uncommon."

None of the others had asked me that, and I didn't know how to answer. But I was great at avoiding answers, so I said, "The moon's gone, you know?"

"What is a *moon?*"

"Exactly. Don't you think it's strange that our entire universe ends right outside our planet?"

"Not particularly. Do you?"

"Obviously." My attempt to ruffle Dr. Sayegh had failed.

"We were talking about why you can't seem to stick with a therapist longer than one session."

"Were we?"

"Yes."

"Fine," I said. "You want the truth?"

"That would be nice."

"I don't trust you." I leaned back in the peach love seat and spread out, taking up as much space as I could. "Not you specifically; therapists in general."

"You can't shake hands with a clenched fist," Sayegh said. "Indira Gandhi, the first female Prime Minister of India, said that."

I rolled my eyes. "You should frame that and hang it on your wall."

Dr. Sayegh chuckled. "You enter each new therapist's office determined not to trust them, so of course you never will. But if you want help, you've got to try."

She acted like it was just that easy. But the truth was that I *did* want to talk. I wasn't Giles Corey. The weight on my chest was killing me, and I couldn't bear it alone anymore.

"You want me to trust you?" I said. "Tell me something personal. Something no one else knows."

Dr. Sayegh cocked her head to the side. "I bite my toenails. It's a disgusting habit I never outgrew."

"Something real," I said. "If you want my trust, I need yours."

I figured my challenge would go unanswered—that Sayegh would wait out the clock and I'd move onto Dr. Turcotte—but after a pause she said, "I took Adderall throughout college. It was a new drug back then, and expensive, but I had money and friends who supplied me. I wouldn't have been able to keep up with my course load otherwise. I could stay up all night studying. It nearly ruined my life."

I knew a couple of kids at school who took Adderall, but they all had prescriptions. "Seriously?"

Dr. Sayegh nodded. "I might not have graduated without those little pills, but the price I paid wasn't worth it."

It wasn't the kind of secret that could ruin Dr. Sayegh,

but I doubted it was something she would have wanted her patients to learn. I didn't trust her yet, but she was the first therapist who'd trusted me, and that counted for something.

"Can I ask you a question?" I said.

"Of course."

"And it stays between us? You're not going to run and tell my parents or anything?"

Dr. Sayegh rested her hands in her lap. "Unless you pose a danger to yourself or someone else, anything you tell me is confidential."

"It's not about me; it's about this guy I'm dating. Sort of dating. I don't know *what* we are. His name's Calvin Frye." Sayegh didn't say anything, so I went on. "He was in a relationship with a teacher at our school. I think the guy molested him, and it's really messing him up, and I want him to tell someone, but he won't, and I'm scared for him."

Dr. Sayegh pursed her lips. "That is a serious accusation, Oswald."

"It's not an accusation. It's the truth. Calvin wouldn't lie."

"Oswald, I'm obligated under the law to report the suspected sexual abuse of a minor."

"But you said it was confidential."

Dr. Sayegh dry-washed her hands, over and over. She looked sympathetic, but her voice was stern. "If you had admitted to robbing a bank or accidentally running a man over with your car, I would be bound by confidentiality. However, the law requires me to report crimes committed against children and the elderly. I'm sorry, Oswald. I have no choice."

I stood, my body vibrating. Calvin would never speak to me again if he learned I'd ratted him out. "I made it all up," I said.

Sayegh shook her head. "Do you know who the teacher is?"

"I'm not telling you."

"Sit down, Oswald."

I couldn't resist her command, and I sank back onto the love seat. I doubted my knees could have supported me much longer anyway.

"I promised Calvin I wouldn't tell."

Dr. Sayegh leaned forward and rested her elbows on her thighs. "Do you care about this young man?"

"Yes."

"Then reporting this crime and getting him help is the right thing to do, Oswald." She stared hard at me. "If you know the identity of the teacher who is abusing Calvin, you must tell me. I can keep your identity confidential. No one ever need know you were involved."

I thought about the cuts on Calvin's arms. About how he

said he'd never seen the stars. No one should have to go their whole lives believing the universe is empty. But it wouldn't matter if Sayegh kept my name out of it—Calvin would know I'd told, and he'd hate me.

I didn't want to lose Cal, but he was drowning, and no matter what he said, I didn't believe he could breathe underwater. I'd kept my promise to Tommy and hadn't called the cops on his father for beating him, and I'd lost him and couldn't help wondering if things would have turned out differently if I'd broken that promise. Maybe this was my chance to make up for not keeping Tommy safe. I made up my mind. Even if it meant losing Calvin to keep him from hurting himself again, I had to take the risk.

"His name is Reevey," I said. "Calvin's wrestling coach. He's the one."

207,832 KM

I SUPPOSE IT *WAS* TECHNICALLY BREAKING AND entering, even though I still had my key, but it wasn't really a crime unless we got caught. Right?

I held Calvin's hand and led him into my house, hiking my backpack higher on my shoulder to keep it from slipping.

"Don't peek," I said.

"I'm not peeking."

I hadn't been home since the movers had packed up our belongings and carted them away. They'd taken some of the boxes and furniture to my father's new condo and had put the rest in storage. The house didn't belong to us anymore, but the new owners hadn't begun remodeling yet, so it had been sitting empty since the day we found out about Renny's accident.

"Just so you know," Calvin said. "I don't actually like surprises."

"You'll like this one. Now hush."

It had been a couple of days since I'd told Dr. Sayegh about Calvin and Coach Reevey, and the cops hadn't dragged Reevey away in handcuffs, though I figured it was only a matter of time. Despite part of me hoping Sayegh had changed her mind about reporting what I'd told her to the police, I knew she hadn't, and I was determined to make the most of what little time I had with Calvin before he learned I'd betrayed him and he never spoke to me again.

I let go of Calvin's hand. "Don't move, and *don't* open your eyes." I watched him for a moment to make sure he wasn't trying to spy through his eyelids. When I was satisfied, I unzipped my backpack and arranged my supplies. It took about five minutes to set everything up, and I'd done a pretty brilliant job if I do say so myself.

"Careful," I said, taking Calvin's hand again and pulling him to the floor. "Lie back, but watch your head."

We both lay on the cool tiles, and my stomach fluttered, wondering how Calvin was going to react.

"Can I open my eyes now or what?" Calvin said. "This is starting to get not-in-a-good-way freaky."

"Go ahead."

I watched Calvin's reaction as he first opened his eyes, took in what he saw, and opened them wider.

"Are those . . . ?"

"Stars," I said.

The wide vaulted ceiling glittered with twinkling pinpoints of light. When I was ten, I'd had one of those domes with the constellations that beamed onto the ceiling in my bedroom. Since stars no longer existed, those little planetariums didn't either, so I'd had to build my own. I'd bought a pair of blue and white LEDs that dimmed alternately and a sheet of heavy black paper, into which I'd punched a thousand tiny holes, trying to recreate the constellations from memory. I'd put the lights into a cookie tin and arranged the paper over the top in a dome. When the lights blinked, they gave my stars the illusion of twinkling.

I pointed to a series of stars in the shape of a U. "That's the constellation Corona Borealis. And over there is the Big Dipper."

"Ozzie. They're amazing."

"Eh," I said. "They're a poor approximation of the real thing, but this was the best I could do." I tried to imagine what they looked like to Calvin. He'd never seen stars and only knew the word because I'd explained it to him. They must've looked so alien to someone who was used to a dark and empty night.

"And the whole sky looked like this?"

"Yeah. In remote places where there weren't any other lights around, you could sometimes see other galaxies."

"What's a galaxy?"

"Don't worry about it," I said. "It's not important."

Calvin didn't speak for a while. He stared at the ceiling, his eyes lingering on one spot for a moment before moving to another.

"Why did you do this?" Calvin asked. "I mean, thank you, it's beautiful, but why?"

I wasn't about to tell him I'd arranged our DIY planetarium show because I felt guilty about ratting him out to Dr. Sayegh. And, anyway, that was only partially why I'd done it. "I'm worried about you," I said.

"Sorry."

"Don't be sorry." I fumbled for the words. "I didn't say that to make you feel bad. It's just, I thought if I could show you the stars, you might understand."

Calvin glanced at me side-eye. "Understand what?"

"What we've lost."

"You mean what *you've* lost. The rest of us can't miss something we don't remember."

I wasn't sure Calvin was talking about the stars anymore. "Sometimes it's hard to focus on what's right in front of me when all I can think about are the things behind me," I said.

"Like Tommy?"

The wonder in Calvin's voice had vanished, replaced by a density greater than all the stars combined. I tried to think of a way to explain it that would make sense, not only to Calvin but to myself. "You know how adults are always telling us that high school is the best time of our lives?"

"Yeah," he said.

"It's bullshit, right?"

"I guess."

I watched the lights on the ceiling twinkle, knowing my memories of the real stars were filling in the gaps between the reality and what I was seeing. Our memories and experiences are the lenses through which we see the world, and even though Calvin and I were looking at the same exact lights, I knew we were seeing different things, and I wished I could see them through his eyes.

"I think people who believe high school was the greatest only remember their triumphs. They were adored as sports legends or were popular because they were beautiful. They had everything they ever wanted, and then they were thrust into the real world where no one knew anything about them. Their bosses and coworkers didn't give a shit that they'd scored the winning touchdown in the homecoming game or had been surrounded by more friends than they could count.

The real world is a disappointment to them because their past burned so brightly."

Calvin was chewing his bottom lip. "So I'm a disappointment?"

"No!" I said more forcefully than I'd intended. "That's not what I'm saying." I was messing everything up. "Those people ignore the beauty in the present because they can't stop living in the past. Which is stupid."

"Oh," Calvin said. Then, "Are you going to wait forever for Tommy to come back?"

"I don't know. Would I be dumb if I did?"

"Maybe. Maybe not."

I sat up and leaned on my elbow, angling my body toward Calvin. "I like you, Cal. I really do. But I'm terrified of what might happen if Tommy *does* return. Either way, I'd end up hurting one of you."

"You'll hate yourself if we get together and Tommy comes home, and you'll hate yourself if you wait around Cloud Lake forever and Tommy never returns."

"I guess none of it matters if we're just brains in jars, right?"

"We're not brains in jars, Ozzie."

I didn't know what else to say. I'd only planned to bring Calvin to my house to show him the stars to cheer him up. I hadn't expected to discuss Tommy or us or anything. Instead of lifting Calvin from his dark mood, I'd thrust him deeper into it.

"I'd be lying if I claimed to understand what you're going through," Calvin said. His voice echoed against the walls, trying desperately to fill the void my family had left behind. "But how about this: I like you too, Ozzie. Maybe you're right and we're living in a simulation or a false vacuum or some parallel universe. Maybe none of this is real, but *you're* real. This thing between us is real."

"Cal—"

"So let's see where it goes. For all we know, we could end up hating each other."

I couldn't help laughing. "That's a terrible sales pitch," I said. But he was right. My own parents were proof two people could spend half their lives together and wind up strangers.

"I don't know, Cal."

Calvin glanced at me but kept most of his attention on the stars above. "Let's give whatever this is a try," he said. "Go on a couple of dates, maybe go to prom. And if Tommy *does* come back, I'll walk away. I won't make you choose."

"Why?"

"I think you might be worth it."

Calvin was so different from Tommy, but the same in many ways. I didn't deserve either of them.

"Just say yes," Calvin said.

"But it's not fair to you."

Calvin turned toward me. "I know you're afraid no one is going to live up to your memory of Tommy, but you're lucky, you know. *I'm* afraid everyone is going to be like Coach Reevey. At least you know what it's like to be in love. To know the guy you're with loves you more than anything. I don't have memories like that. All I have is a head full of nightmares. So, no, life's not fair, and I'm *still* willing to take the risk. Are you?"

I felt like an asshole. After everything Calvin had been through, he was still game to take a chance, even knowing how bad it could turn out. And there I was, vacillating. I didn't know whether it was possible to love and be loved again the way I'd loved and been loved by Tommy, but I thought not finding out might be the most idiotic decision I could make.

I leaned toward Calvin. He wrapped his arms around me and we kissed under the stars.

My lips were raw by the time we disentangled. All we'd done was kiss, but it had felt more intimate than trading blowjobs in the car on New Year's Eve.

I lay on my back under the stars just grinning, my mind filled with Calvin.

"Your house is nice," Calvin said when he'd caught his breath.

"It's not my house anymore."

"It's nice anyway. Kind of empty, though."

"Yeah, but it's been empty for a long time."

Calvin squeezed my hand, which he'd taken while we'd kissed and hadn't let go. "How's your brother?"

"Okay, I guess." I hadn't talked to Renny since our video chat, but Mom and Dad had given me daily updates. "There's still too much swelling to see exactly how severe the damage is, and it'll be a while before they're ready to move him home, though he might make it by graduation."

"That sucks," Calvin said.

That summed up the situation well. It sucked he'd never walk again and it sucked he'd lost something he loved. It just . . . sucked.

Calvin sat up and wiped the sweat off his forehead with the back of his arm. "I should get home."

"Right." We stared at the stars a while longer before I shut off and dismantled the lights. I hated to lose the stars again, but I could turn these on whenever I needed them.

I drove Calvin home and we made out a little more in his driveway. Now that I'd started kissing Calvin, I never wanted to stop. But we had school the next day and I could see Mr. Frye's shadow standing in front of the windows.

As Calvin opened the car door, I said, "Hey, so earlier, did you ask me to go to prom with you?"

Calvin stopped, turned to me, and smiled. "I guess I did. What do you say?"

"Can Lua come with us?"

"Definitely," Calvin said. "But your lips belong to me."

I smiled my best smile. "I'll let you and Lua fight that one out."

204,616 KM

LUA AND MS. NOVAK WOKE ME UP ON MY BIRTHDAY
with a plate of flaming donuts. They sang "Happy Birthday"
as loudly as they could, and when I blew out the eighteen
candles, I wished I'd never told Dr. Sayegh about Calvin.

A week had passed and the cops still hadn't arrested
Coach Reevey. I hadn't returned to Dr. Sayegh either, but it
seemed she hadn't followed through with calling the police.
That's what I'd wished for, anyway.

You'd think I would have wished for Tommy to return.
It's not that I didn't want him back, but after it'd seemed like
things couldn't get any worse—my parents divorcing, Lua's
hand, Renny winding up paralyzed, the universe shrinking—
they'd actually begun to get better. I'd begun to think my
hard and forceful punishment was nearing its end.

Which was one of the many mistakes I'd made.

• • •

Ms. Fuentes was going over the answers to our homework in physics, and Calvin kept rubbing his knee against my leg. Since the night I'd shown him the stars, we hadn't been able to stop touching each other.

"Wanna hang out tonight?" he whispered. I hadn't told him it was my birthday.

"Sure." I suspected Lua probably had something planned for dinner, but I didn't feel like celebrating. I wanted to freeze the present so nothing else could change.

Calvin winked at me. "My dad's working overnight."

He let my imagination fill in the rest, and I conjured a million things we could do alone in his house, most of them involving a distinct lack of clothing.

I was about to tell him I couldn't wait, when the classroom door swung open. Ms. Fuentes stopped speaking midsentence. Vice Principal Grady stood in the doorway, looking as severe and unhappy as usual. Seriously, I don't think he'd cracked a smile in his entire life. I was willing to bet he hadn't even laughed as a baby.

"Sorry to interrupt, Betsy," he said, "but I need one of your students." Grady waited until Ms. Fuentes nodded. "Calvin Frye? Gather your things and come with me."

When Grady called Calvin's name, he sat frozen for a

second. He looked at me, then at Grady. My stomach knotted. The crease between Calvin's eyes deepened. He had no idea what was happening, but I did.

"What's going on?" Calvin asked.

"Just come with me, son," Grady said. "I'll explain everything in my office."

"Don't forget we have an exam tomorrow, Mr. Frye," Fuentes said while Calvin collected his books and bag.

Vice Principal Grady cleared his throat. He looked uncomfortable, like he'd cinched his tie too tight. "He might need to make up that exam another day, Betsy."

"We'll work it out," she said. Even *she* was curious, and I hadn't believed she'd cared about anything other than physics.

"I'll text you about tonight," Calvin said before he followed Grady into the hallway.

"Yeah. Great." Though I had a feeling once Grady explained why he'd pulled him from class, Calvin would never text me again.

I suspected Priya ran an entire network of gossipy spies who fed her information like a CIA station agent. I wouldn't have been surprised if she'd found a way to tap our phones.

"Oh. My. God. Did you hear?" Priya had barely waited

for us to sit at our lunch table before running toward us and vomiting the latest scandalous news.

Dustin had asked me if I knew why Grady had called Calvin out of class on the way to the cafeteria, but I'd feigned ignorance. I mean, I thought I knew, but I could have been wrong. I prayed I was wrong. Maybe Calvin was being given a special award or maybe something had happened to his father. I felt like a shitty human being for hoping his father had gotten hurt at work, but I could live with that if it meant Calvin wouldn't hate me.

Lua was working her way through a bowl of mac and cheese, holding her fork awkwardly because she couldn't bend her index finger. It was like a crooked tree branch, gnarled and knotty.

"Let me guess," she said. "They've cancelled the prom due to an outbreak of nobody-gives-a-shititis."

I set my tray down next to Lua. I think she was still pissed at me for trying to force her to accept Trent's help with her surgery, but living with her while my parents were with Renny had forced us to call a temporary truce.

"Does it have anything to do with Calvin?" Dustin asked.

Priya's eyes grew wide. "How'd you know?"

"Vice Principal Grady pulled him out of physics." Dustin had barely taken his seat before digging into his plate of green beans and meatloaf, which I suspected was just the recycled hamburgers they hadn't sold from the prior week.

Lua was staring at me, expecting me to answer. "Don't look at me," I said. "I'm just as clueless as you are." Obviously, she knew I was lying.

Priya rubbed her hands together. The only thing she loved more than cheerleading was dishing juicy gossip. It was like it was *her* birthday instead of mine.

"Well," she said. "Calvin wasn't the only person removed from class today."

My stomach hurt so bad I couldn't eat. The mashed potatoes cooled on my plate, but I didn't care. They might as well have been drying concrete.

"Nishay heard from Darnell that Mr. Gugino pulled Trent Williams out of weight training. He didn't even let him shower or change out of his gym clothes."

Trent? Well, that didn't make sense. Maybe I was wrong about why Calvin had been called out of class.

"I wonder why," I said.

"Fuck Trent," Lua said almost at the same time. "I hope someone breaks *his* fingers."

"We get it, Lu," I said. "He's an asshole. But he also offered to pay for your operation, so let it go."

Since the attack, Lua had begun to dress more subdued.

Less rock star and more mopey-emo-teen. Lots of jeans and black T-shirts, which made it difficult to tell whether she was feeling more like a boy or a girl on any given day. I assumed girl that day because her shirt—black with a logo for a band called Slutever, which I was surprised no teacher had forced her to turn inside out—was torn at the neck to reveal cleavage.

"Offering to fix what he broke doesn't absolve him of being a dick. In his case, it's a terminal condition." Lua folded her arms over her chest, daring me to argue, but I didn't. Mostly because I wanted to survive lunch, but also because I didn't want to have to sleep on her floor until my parents returned with Renny.

"You're right," I said. "Forget I mentioned it."

Priya waited calmly for us to finish arguing. But despite her outward serenity, I could tell she was practically ready to explode.

"There's more?" I asked.

"Oh yeah."

Oh no.

"And this is the best part," Priya said. "Brea told me she heard from Avi . . . did I tell you he asked her to prom? He poured hot oil on the grass of her parents' front yard to spell out the question. Mr. Grant was *so* pissed. But she said yes, and—"

Dustin said, "Get to the point," with his mouth full of meatloaf.

"Anyway," Priya continued. "So Avi had to go to the office to pick up his inhaler because he'd forgotten it at home and his mom had dropped it off for him, and he saw police there talking to Calvin."

And there it was. Dr. Sayegh *had* called the cops. I checked my phone again to see if Calvin had messaged me, but his last text was from the day before, asking me if I still wanted to go to prom with someone as screwed up as him. To which I'd replied with a simple "Yes."

I considered texting him to ask if he was all right, but there was only one reason I could think of that the police would be questioning Cal.

"Ozzie?" Dustin asked. He was staring at me. They were all three staring.

"What?"

"I asked if you know what's going on?"

I shook my head. I'd already done enough damage by telling Sayegh.

But Lua was watching me, and I knew she'd put it together. I just prayed she didn't say anything in front of the others.

Then Lua said, "Probably steroids or something. Isn't that what you said a few weeks ago, Priya?"

I could've kissed Lua right then. Priya eventually sat down and spent the rest of lunch spinning theories about how the whole wrestling team was likely hooked on steroids, and that's why Trent and Calvin had been called to the office. Either they'd taken steroids or witnessed others shooting up. By the end of lunch Priya had concocted an entire conspiracy.

I kept my mouth shut and let her believe her little fiction, because it didn't matter. The truth would reveal itself eventually, but I could try not to make the situation worse.

Lua turned down the stereo in my car as soon as we drove out of the parking lot. Like the truth, she was a tidal force.

"It was Reevey, wasn't it?" she said. "The teacher Calvin was banging?"

My eyes widened. "How did you . . . ?"

"It's not that tough to figure out," she said. "He was sleeping with a teacher, something happened, he quit wrestling. Any idiot could've connected those dots."

"Don't tell Dustin," I said. "Or Priya."

"I won't," Lua said. "Did you convince Calvin to go to the cops?"

I shook my head. The muscles in my face felt tight, and I had to keep blinking back tears. After lunch I'd walked past the office and had seen Mr. Frye's truck in the parking lot.

I couldn't speak. I knew the moment I opened my mouth I was going to lose it and probably get into an accident and kill us, so I pulled into the parking lot of an emergency animal hospital.

"I told my therapist," I said, before I broke down crying. My body shook. Tears streamed down my cheeks and snot dribbled out of my nose. I was sobbing so hard I wasn't even certain Lua could understand me. It took me a minute to piece myself back together, and Lua waited patiently. "I was worried. Calvin's been acting weird, and he cut himself again and then he told me Reevey used to drug him and I don't even know what else that asshole might've done to him, but I was scared he was going to do something stupid, so I told my therapist and she said she had to report it." I slammed my fist on the steering wheel. "He's going to hate me so much, Lua."

Lua took my hand and cradled it against her chest. "He won't hate you."

"Of course he will."

"Okay," she said. "Maybe he will."

"Is that supposed to help?" I tried to wipe my nose with the back of my hand, but I just smeared the tears and snot across my face.

Lua sighed. "You did the right thing, Oz. It's better for Calvin to hate you than be dead, right?"

"Yeah." I hung my head. I hadn't felt so low since the Fourth of July.

"Christ. You really like him, don't you?"

"That's not important right now."

"Of course it is," Lua said. "If you didn't like him, you wouldn't have risked him hating you to get him help." She dug into my glove box for a wad of napkins. "Being honest with the people you care about is hard. I'm kind of proud of you, Ozzie."

"I doubt Cal will see it that way."

"Maybe not right away. But give him time."

I finished wiping my nose.

"How do you think Trent's involved? Do you think he knew?" Lua asked.

I'd nearly forgotten that Priya said Trent had also been pulled out of class. "I don't know."

"You don't think Reevey and Trent . . . ?"

"Well, now I do," I said. But I couldn't even think about Trent right then. "I just don't want Calvin to hate me, Lu."

"We'll figure this out. It'll be okay."

"I hope you're right. I don't think I can lose anyone else."

199,207 KM

COACH REEVEY WAS REMOVED FROM SCHOOL THE
day after Calvin and Trent were questioned by the police, and
Calvin didn't show up for the rest of the week or the following Monday, either. I texted him a couple of times, playing
dumb, asking where he was and if I could come over, but he
didn't reply. I'd wanted to go to his house over the weekend,
but Lua convinced me to give him time. I didn't want to give
Calvin time. I wanted to see him—I needed to know if he
blamed me—which is why Lua was right to tell me to stay
away. My feelings were irrelevant. It didn't matter whether
Calvin despised me, only that he was okay.

It took less than a day for the news that Coach Reevey
had also been questioned by the police to travel through
school, and the *Cloud Lake Herald* splashed the story across
their front page on Monday. Reevey hadn't been arrested,

though the article suggested it was only a matter of time, but the school had suspended him with pay pending an investigation.

Calvin and Trent weren't named in the story—it only stated that Reevey had allegedly been involved in relationships with at least two underage students—but it was easy to piece together that Trent and Calvin had been pulled from class the day before Coach Reevey's suspension. The biggest surprise was that Reevey had also been abusing Trent, and I wondered how the police had figured it out. Obviously, they'd learned about Calvin from Dr. Sayegh, who'd gotten it from me, but I never would've guessed Trent was involved.

"Dude, Pinks," Dustin said after physics as we walked to the cafeteria. "Did you know?"

I'd skipped lunch since the day Calvin was pulled from class in order to avoid this exact conversation. I hung my head as we walked through the halls. People knew Calvin and I were friends, and I imagined them pointing at me and whispering. I deserved much worse for betraying Calvin's trust.

"Yeah."

"Whoa." Dustin shook his head. "So was it some Jerry Sandusky rape shit or what?"

"I don't know. Calvin never gave me the details."

"Sick." We entered the cafeteria, and I felt even more eyes. "It totally explains why he quit wrestling. And it happened to Trent, too? That's messed up."

I wanted to emergency eject from the conversation. Talking about what Reevey did to Calvin and possibly Trent made my skin crawl, but I hadn't brought my lunch, so I followed Dustin to the line. As we stood there, Dustin spinning wild hypotheses about what Reevey might or might not have done to Cal and Trent, I spotted a table set up near the far wall. It was draped with a blue cloth and bore a glittery sign that read: PROM TICKETS $32.

"I'll be right back," I told Dustin, cutting him off mid-theory. I made my way to the table and waited in line. Our prom's theme was "A Night to Remember," which was stupid. It would probably wind up a night most people tried to forget. I didn't know if I'd even go, but I wanted to see Calvin, I wanted to apologize, and I thought arming myself with prom tickets might get me through his door.

D'Arcy Gaudet and Thea Castro sat behind the table, a gray lockbox between them. I couldn't stand D'Arcy, but Thea wasn't so bad. We'd been in the same geometry class, and I'd let her copy my English homework in exchange for the answers to our geometry worksheets.

I pulled cash out of my wallet. I'd been saving my pay

from the bookstore to fund another trip to find Tommy, but I think Tommy would have understood and approved of me using it for this. "Two tickets," I said.

D'Arcy's lips rested in a self-satisfied sneer. "Who's your date, Ozzie? Your she-male freak friend?"

I had to grit my teeth to keep from telling D'Arcy exactly what I thought of her. I was pretty certain the only reason she hated Lua was because Trent had a crush on her. "Not that it's any of your business, but no."

Thea tapped a clipboard with her pen. "We're supposed to keep a list." She had the decency to look embarrassed to be sharing breathing space with D'Arcy. We hadn't been friends in geometry, but we'd laughed together over Mrs. Musser's military buzz cut and persistent elbow warts.

I held the cash in my hands. The bills hung limply between us, and I just wanted them to take my money and give me the tickets so I could slink back to my table. "Calvin Frye," I said.

D'Arcy's eyes grew wide, and she feigned shock. "Oh! I thought he was taking Coach Reevey."

Thea flashed D'Arcy a scowl. "Rude."

"What?" D'Arcy said. "I'm only repeating what I heard."

Buying the tickets had been a terrible idea. I should've waited, or asked Lua or Dustin to buy them for me, but now

I was stuck standing there, waiting for D'Arcy or Thea to take my goddamn money.

To my surprise—and for which I was deeply grateful—Thea said to D'Arcy, "Are you still, like, taking that college guy you've been dating to prom? Or did he finally realize you're a shady bitch and rethink his life choices?"

D'Arcy's mouth moved, but no sound came out. While she was trying to reply, Thea took my money and handed me my change and two prom tickets.

"Hey," Thea said as I turned to leave. "Tell Calvin I hope he's doing okay."

"You know Cal?"

"We had world history together last year. I would have flunked without his help."

"I'll tell him. Thanks."

I wanted to throw up. By purchasing the tickets, I'd committed to seeing Calvin, whether Lua or anyone else thought it a good idea.

After Latin I sat in my car in the parking lot until most of the other seniors had cut out, rehearsing what I would to say to Cal, trying to find the right words. Tommy once told me a person doesn't have to be good with words to tell the truth, because the truth is beautiful all on its own. The truth in this situation was that I hadn't known when I told Dr. Sayegh that she'd go to the cops, that everything I'd said to her wasn't going to remain confidential. But those were excuses, ways to shift the blame, and I doubted they'd win me points with Calvin. I'd upended his life, spilled his secrets to the school and everyone in Cloud Lake. No excuse could change that.

When I finally worked up the nerve to drive to Calvin's house, Mr. Frye met me at the front door. I hadn't considered what I'd say to him if he answered; I was used to him rarely being around, but of course he probably hadn't left Calvin alone since the day it all came out.

"Hey, Pete."

"Ozzie." He stood in the doorway. I didn't know what I'd do if he refused to let me in.

"Is Cal around?"

"He's not up for visitors today."

"I get that," I said. "But it'll only take a minute. I just want to give him something."

Mr. Frye seemed to think about it for a moment before he stood aside. I rushed toward the stairs before he changed his mind, but when I started up, he said, "Did you know?"

"Some." When I turned around to look him in the eyes, all I saw was disappointment. He'd trusted me to look after

Cal, and I'd let him down. No. I hadn't let Mr. Frye down; I'd let Calvin down, and that was the worst part.

"Don't stay long," he said.

I nodded and ran up the stairs. Calvin's door, usually closed, stood wide open. Calvin was sitting at his desk in front of his laptop, wearing plaid pajama bottoms with a hole in the knee and no shirt. He looked terrible. His skin was pasty and his eyes sunken and bruised. His hair had begun to grow back unevenly.

"Cal?" I said, and waited for him to look up.

"I don't want to talk to you." His normally spartan room was trashed—papers and books and clothes everywhere.

"Will you at least let me explain?"

"Did you tell someone?"

"Yes, but—"

"Then there's nothing to explain." Calvin's voice was liquid nitrogen. His words froze and boiled and burned. "They made me go to a doctor and found the cuts. Now Dad won't let me wear a shirt in the house or shut my door. When he's at work, he pays a nurse to watch me so I can't hurt myself."

"I'm sorry," I said, and then stopped. "No. I'm not sorry." I stayed in the hallway because I didn't feel welcome in Calvin's room. I figured Mr. Frye was probably at the bottom of the stairs listening, but I didn't care. "Listen, Cal, I was worried. When I told my therapist what happened to you, I didn't know she was going to call the police, but I'm glad she did. Coach Reevey hurt you, and you've been hurting yourself. You need help. If you hate me for telling, I can live with that so long as you're alive."

Calvin kept staring at his laptop, moving his mouse around, though it didn't look like he was actually doing anything. "You know what Will used to tell me?"

Will was Coach Reevey. Calvin had never used his first name around me, but I guess it was silly to think he'd called him Coach Reevey when they'd been alone.

"He said I'd meet a lot of people in my life, but that none would truly understand me the way he did." Calvin glanced at me, his stare ruthless. "How fucked up is it that he was right?"

All the things I'd thought about saying while I sat in my car after school—all the millions of ways to apologize I'd tried to think up since Vice Principal Grady had pulled Calvin from class—vanished, and I was left speechless. Not because what Cal said had hurt, though it had, but because of the possibility he was right. Maybe I didn't understand Calvin. Maybe I never would.

I pulled the prom tickets from my pocket and set them on the floor in front of his door before leaving. Just in case.

168,111 KM

I DODGED A PAIR OF FLYING PLIERS AS I WALKED
into the bookstore stockroom. They hit the wall and skittered
across the floor.

Mrs. Petridis swore. She was standing at her worktable
over a tiny dead mouse. "Sorry, Ozzie." She clenched her fists
and slumped onto her stool.

"At least you didn't throw the mouse." I grabbed an
unopened box of books that needed shelving. "Why do you do
this, anyway?" I'd never asked before, unsure I wanted to know.

"Because I take these dead things that would repulse most
people, and I transform them into something beautiful."

I wasn't sure I'd call her dioramas beautiful, but I couldn't
deny they were interesting. The intricate details and the care
she put into them astounded me. Her current project was a
scene from *North by Northwest*.

"But they're still just the hollowed-out husks of things that used to be alive."

"To you. To me, they're art." She motioned at the pliers on the floor. "Kick those on over to me."

I left Mrs. Petridis to work on her dead animals, and manned the store. Ana showed up later, and I took a break from shelving books to help Mrs. Ross with her essay again, but I had trouble even focusing on that. My mind kept wandering while I read.

"That bad?" she asked. There was something different about Mrs. Ross. She sat with her back a little straighter, and she hadn't worn her sunglasses into the store. It'd been a couple of weeks since I'd seen her, but that was mostly because Ana had taken a lot of my shifts.

"No," I said. "Your essay is great; I'm just worried about this guy I've been seeing."

Mrs. Ross chuckled. "Boys are the root of most problems."

"Tell me about it."

"Well?" she asked. "What'd he do?"

I shook my head. "It's not what he did."

"Then what'd *you* do?"

I felt weird discussing a guy who wasn't Tommy with Mrs. Ross, but I needed someone to talk to, and I wasn't about to return to Dr. Sayegh and have her blab everything I told her to the police.

"He trusted me with a secret and I told someone else and then everyone found out about it." I raked my hair back with my fingers. "But I'm not sorry, because someone had done something bad to him and it really messed him up."

Mrs. Ross nodded along as I spoke. When I finished, she said, "You know what faith is?"

"I guess."

"If you've got to guess, you don't know." She smiled tentatively. "Faith is believing in something even when every other soul in the world tells you you're wrong. Even when all the evidence says you're a fool. No matter what people say or how much they hurt you, faith means you keep believing."

"How's that supposed to help me?"

Mrs. Ross shrugged. "You have to believe you did right by this boy, even if you're the only one. And you never know. Maybe he'll come around. Sometimes what's in people's heads and hearts is too big for words."

I mumbled at the table. She said, "What?" and I said, "You told me that same thing about Tommy once. After we'd had a fight."

I waited for Mrs. Ross to gather her things and run off like she had when I'd last mentioned Tommy, but she didn't.

She folded her hands in front of her and stared at me for a long time.

Then she said, "Tell me about him."

I was so surprised that I looked up at her, and the shock must've shone from my eyes, because she said, "Go on, I'm listening."

"Well," I began, "Tommy was amazing." I hadn't talked about Tommy, really talked about him, in so long that the stories poured out of me. I told Mrs. Ross about the time Tommy and I ran away from home and spent two hours— which had seemed like forever when we were eight—living in a tree. How he could argue with anyone about anything and always win, and how infuriating that was. About the time he stole twenty dollars from our fifth-grade teacher's desk so he could buy Mrs. Ross new paintbrushes. I wanted to tell her everything I remembered—and I remembered everything— but that would take more time than we had, so I gave her the highlights and left out the sexy bits.

And she listened. She didn't interrupt. She laughed at some of the stories, looked like she might cry during others, but she never said a word.

"We talked about leaving Cloud Lake after high school," I said, "but he was worried about you. He was scared of what Mr. Ross would do to you. More than anything, though, he wanted to know you were safe. I think that was the best thing about Tommy. He'd throw himself in front of a train to keep the people he loved from harm."

Ana was tossing me dirty looks because she wanted to close up, but I didn't care, because I felt lighter. I hadn't realized how heavy Tommy's memories were and how difficult it had been to carry them alone for so long. It's not like I'd shed them, but now I had Mrs. Ross to help me bear the load.

"I left Carl," Mrs. Ross said after a moment of quiet.

"You did?"

She nodded. "Got a second job at Target and met a cashier who was looking for a roommate. It isn't much, but it's something."

I couldn't believe she'd left her husband. Tommy had always hoped she would, but he never thought she'd go through with it. "How'd he react?" I asked.

"Carl?" Mrs. Ross chuckled. "He threw some things around and threatened to kill me, but that man doesn't scare me anymore. He told me if I walked out the door, I couldn't ever come back. So I marched outside and slammed the door to that trailer shut for the last time."

"Good for you," I said. "Tommy would've been proud."

"I wish I could've known him."

"Me too."

Maybe some doors that slam shut behind you and can't ever be opened again aren't the scariest things in the world after all. Maybe some doors are better off closed. That way we can focus on the ones still open in front of us.

155,081 KM

THE NEXT COUPLE OF WEEKS SUCKED. CALVIN returned to school, but he refused to speak to me, and he wouldn't sit with me at lunch. He showed up to physics, ignored me, and ran out at the bell. I tried to follow to see where he was eating, but I couldn't keep up. We hadn't worked on our roller coaster project in a while, but all I wanted was for Calvin to talk to me again.

I couldn't count on much lately other than Tommy still being gone and the universe continuing to collapse, so I threw myself back into trying to figure out why. I'd spent so much time wrapped up in Calvin's life that I'd nearly let go of Tommy, and I wondered if maybe all the things that had gone wrong were the universe's way of punishing me for it.

The only good thing that had happened was that Renny was being transferred to a hospital in Miami the next day. I was supposed to pick my parents up at the airport and we were going to drive over there together to see him, which scared me a little. I wasn't sure how I'd deal with seeing Renny broken, but, like with Cal, broken was better than dead.

"Are you going to sit on your computer all night?" Lua asked. He was dressed in ripped jeans and a tight white T-shirt that lay flat across his chest.

I looked up. I'd been working at the dining room table for so long that I hadn't even realized it was night. I rubbed my burning eyes. "This is important."

Lua pulled out a chair and sat beside me. "Look, I've let you mope long enough. I get that you're upset about Calvin, but if he's going to forgive you, he'll do it in his own time."

"And if he doesn't?"

"Then fuck him, all right? I'm not your goddamn therapist."

I rolled my eyes. "Whatever."

"Whatever what?"

I glanced at Lua's crooked finger.

"Oh," Lua said. "Well, for your information, I agreed to let Trent's parents pay for the surgery."

That got my attention. "You did? What changed your mind?"

Lua shrugged. "I talked to Trent."

"And?"

"And, it's none of your business." Lua sighed and shook his head. "Let's just say that after hearing what he had to say, I decided to give him the benefit of the doubt."

"Does this mean I'll have to find a new date to the prom?"

"Ugh, no. He's still a creep." Lua smiled a little, and I kind of got the feeling that he wasn't being entirely honest. "But it does mean the tour's back on. There'll be some physical therapy, and I'll probably need to rework some of the songs so I can play them on my keyboard until I'm one hundred percent, but I'll be killing it again before you know it."

That was the first piece of great news I'd heard in ages.

Then he said, "Anyway, I'm going to a/s/l tonight, and you're coming."

"Lua . . ."

"No excuses, Ozzie. Even my mom's got a date. I'm not letting you sit here and sulk."

Lua bullied me into the shower and fussed over my hair and outfit until he was happy. I suspected the main reason Lua wanted me to go was so I could drive, but I didn't care. We danced until we were both soaked with sweat, and I allowed myself to forget my troubles for a while. Occasionally I caught someone out of the corner of my eye who looked like Calvin, but it was never him.

I kept hoping he'd realize I didn't mean for any of this to happen, that he'd forgive my betrayal, but as the days stretched on without a word from him, I began to think he might never absolve me.

But a night out with Lua turned out to be exactly what I needed. A cute guy with long dark bangs even hit on me. I tried to tell him I wasn't interested, but Lua butted in and wrote my number on the back of his hand. I didn't know whether the guy would call, or if I'd answer if he did, but it was nice to feel wanted.

I checked the time and swam through the crowd to find Lua. "Come on!" I shouted into his ear. "We gotta go."

Lua frowned but let me drag him off the dance floor. When we were clear of the noise, he said, "What's your problem?"

"I have to be up early in the morning."

"Tomorrow's Saturday, Oz. You can sleep in."

I screwed up my face. "My parents are flying back tomorrow. I'm driving to Miami to meet them at Renny's new hospital. I told you all this yesterday."

Lua's brow creased. "What are you talking about, Oz?"

I thought it was the music, that the bass had rendered Lua deaf or something, so I led him out to the patio. "Come on, Lu. You remember. Renny's doctors released him to a VA hospital in Miami? They'll be here tomorrow morning?"

"Listen," Lua said. "I let the whole Tommy thing slide, but now you're taking it too far."

"I don't understand."

"Parents, Oz? And who's Renny?"

No. No, no, no, no, no. "My parents, Lua. Katherine and Daniel. And my brother, Warren? Fell during an army training exercise and wound up paralyzed? He's been at a VA hospital in Georgia for the last few weeks?"

Lua shook his head. "Okay, now you're just making up words. What's a Georgia?"

"The state directly north of Florida!" I shouted. Other people on the patio were staring, but I didn't care.

"Calm down," Lua said. "I know you're upset about Calvin, but this isn't funny."

I sat on a bench along the wall and buried my face in my hands. "What the hell is going on, Lua?"

"You tell me." He sat beside me but kept his distance.

"Are you saying my parents are gone?"

Lua grabbed his phone out of his pocket. "I'm calling Dinah."

I caught his wrist. "Lua. Tell me what happened to my parents."

"I don't know! Why are you doing this?"

"I'm not doing anything. Just tell me about my parents."

"You were left at a fire station the day you were born, Ozzie. All you had was a note with your name. My mom adopted you. You've been my brother since we were babies." I'd never seen Lua so worried. "Look, you know Dinah's always encouraged you to find your birth parents. If you have, just say so."

Lua and I? Siblings? Ms. Novak had adopted me? My entire history had been rewritten while I'd danced. My parents and Renny edited out of my life. I grabbed Lua's phone and pulled up a map of the world. It had shrunk to a sphere with a circumference of only 1,508 miles. Europe, Asia, South America, Africa, 98 percent of the United States: gone. Florida existed as the only landmass on the entire tiny planet. When the universe had shrunk before, all I'd lost were hypothetical planets with theoretical people, but the people who had vanished from Earth had been real. They'd had real families and real histories and had lived real lives. I'd hoped the universe would stop shrinking once it reached Earth, but it was going to continue collapsing until nothing remained but me, leaving me alone in Cloud Lake forever.

"I haven't found them," I said, my voice defeated. "They're gone. They're all gone."

Lua wrapped his arm around me, and I let him. There wasn't anything else I could do.

"Come on, Oz. Let's go home."

I nodded, but I didn't have a home anymore. Everything I had was being slowly stolen from me, and I didn't know how to stop it.

1,491 MI

MY MOTHER, FATHER, AND BROTHER HAD ALL
become casualties of the same Great Whatever that had
stolen Tommy from me. In the new and not-so-much-
improved history of my life, my parents had abandoned
me, and Ms. Novak had adopted me. I'd grown up with
Lua, whose own history had changed so that she'd been
born and raised in Cloud Lake. None of it made a damn
bit of sense, but I had to go on about my life like everything was peachy.

Renny and I used to play this fun-for-him-but-not-
for-me game where he hit me in the arm in the same place
as many times as he could before I told him to stop. The
first couple of punches hurt the worst, but after a while, I
stopped feeling the pain. I grew numb to it even though I
could see the bruise already beginning to form and knew

it'd hurt like a son of a bitch later on. That's how it was losing my family. I was numb. I'd lost so much that I couldn't feel it anymore. The universe was going to keep taking and taking and taking everything I cared about from me, and I was powerless to stop it.

Even with all the theories I'd come up with for why the universe was shrinking, I was no closer to a way to stop it. So I did the only thing I *could* do.

I kept moving forward.

Dr. Sayegh smiled from her chair but didn't rise to greet me. "I didn't expect to see you again."

I didn't bother sitting, as I wasn't planning to stay long. "I just wanted to tell you in person that I won't be returning."

"So you kept your appointment to tell me you won't be coming to any more of your appointments?"

I nodded. "Something like that."

"Have a seat, Ozzie." Dr. Sayegh motioned at the couch. She slipped her glasses off and let them hang around her neck on a silver chain. I considered leaving, but part of me was curious what she had to say, so I sat. "You're an interesting young man, Oswald Pinkerton."

"Don't you mean crazy?"

Sayegh shook her head. "I dislike that word," she said. "And I don't think you're crazy."

That surprised me, and I sat up straighter. "You believe me, then? About the universe?"

Dr. Sayegh paused for a moment. "Do you believe in God, Ozzie?"

"Maybe," I said. "I don't know."

"Neither do I." Dr. Sayegh kept fiddling with her glasses, which was making me nervous, like her anxiety was creeping across the distance between us and seeping into me. "There are things in this world I can't explain, that I may never be able to explain, but that doesn't make them less real."

I wished I hadn't come. I wasn't sure why I had. I hadn't bothered telling any of the other doctors in person I wasn't going to see them anymore, and now that I was eighteen, my mom—or Dinah, now that my parents were gone—couldn't compel me to see any doctor I didn't want to, but I'd felt like I owed it to Dr. Sayegh to tell her to her face. Which, in hindsight, was stupid.

"It doesn't matter whether you believe me or not," I said. "I can't fix it. The whole damn universe is going to collapse into nothing, and I can't do one damn thing to stop it."

"Maybe you're not meant to," Sayegh said. I started to interrupt her, but she didn't let me. "Have you ever considered the possibility that you're not supposed to stop what's happening?"

"No," I said. "Because what's the point of knowing something's wrong if I can't do anything about it?"

Dr. Sayegh's eyes lost focus like she wasn't seeing me anymore. "Maybe the point is to just live your life."

I snorted. "Not sure how much of a life I'm really going to have when the whole world is Florida and will probably keep shrinking until there's nothing left but Cloud Lake."

"And what, exactly, did you do with your life that was so wonderful when the world was larger?"

"I . . ."

"Exactly," Dr. Sayegh said. "You claim that the world used to be much bigger than it is, but did you explore it? Did you take advantage of it? How is your life all that different now than it was before?"

I couldn't answer, because I hadn't *done* much of anything. Even when there'd been a whole universe to explore, Cloud Lake and Tommy had been my everything.

"So that's it?" I said. "I'm just supposed to go on living my life no matter how much the universe takes from me or how small it gets?"

Dr. Sayegh nodded. "It's what the rest of us do, Ozzie."

I stood up but didn't immediately head for the door. I

thought Sayegh would try to stop me, try to convince me I needed to keep seeing her, but she didn't say a word.

"See you around, Dr. Sayegh."

"Good-bye, Ozzie," she said. "Please close the door on your way out."

1,473 MI

ON THE DAY OUR ROLLER COASTERS WERE DUE, I
didn't bother calling Calvin to ask him if he'd bring in what
we'd completed because I knew he wouldn't answer his
phone. His attendance at school had become sporadic, and
I'd heard through the Priya Spy Network that most of his
teachers were allowing him to complete his assignments from
home and take his final exams early so that he didn't have to
return. Once the news about Coach Reevey had gotten out,
seven more boys had come forward with allegations that he'd
tried to coerce them into having sex with him. One was still
a freshman, though his name was kept confidential, and the
other six were previous graduates. I was surprised the school
hadn't given Calvin As for the rest of the semester to keep
him from suing.

As the other students filed into physics class carrying their own projects, including Dustin, whose roller coaster looked amazing, I kept hoping Calvin would walk through the door and slide into his seat, flash me a smile, and that everything could go back to the way it had been before I'd betrayed him. But I doubted that was going to happen.

I kept thinking about what Dr. Sayegh had said about how I was supposed to keep living my life even though everything was changing. But how could she expect me to care about prom, which was only a couple of days away, or graduation, which was a couple of weeks after prom, when I'd lost my parents, Renny, Tommy, and 99.9999 percent of the universe? How was I supposed to move forward when everything I cared about was gone?

I couldn't stand around and wait for the universe to collapse completely. I had to do something, find some way to fix it. It was easy for Sayegh to suggest I might not be meant to stop the universe from shrinking or bring back Tommy and my family, because she couldn't remember the way things had been. The universe had always looked small to her, but I knew differently. I knew what it could be, and what it would be again.

Ms. Fuentes talked excitedly about our projects before launching into her review for our final. I hardly heard any of it, and then time seemed to skip forward and the bell rang.

"Ozzie?" Ms. Fuentes called as I stood to leave. "Would you mind waiting around for a moment?"

"Sure."

Dustin flashed me a what-the-hell-is-going-on look, to which I shrugged even though I knew she probably wanted to ask me where my project was. I figured she'd give Calvin a pass, but she was going to flunk *me* for sure.

When the last student had left, Ms. Fuentes sat on the edge of her desk and smiled.

"About my roller coaster—"

"That's what I want to speak to you about."

Great, I thought. *Here it comes.*

"Remember when I told you I belonged to a group of hobbyists who build model roller coasters and that we meet a couple of times a year to show off our designs?"

"Sort of," I said.

"We're meeting this summer, and I'd like to ask you, and Calvin of course, for permission to take your project with me to show them."

"I'm sorry, what?"

"It's really quite ambitious," she said, like she hadn't heard me. "I know I said you'd have the opportunity to present them in class this week, but I couldn't wait to see yours and Calvin's in action. It's reckless and creative, and it could have failed spectacularly, yet you boys pulled it off. I'm extremely proud."

I wasn't sure I was hearing Fuentes correctly. "You have our project?"

Ms. Fuentes nodded. "Calvin's father brought it in this morning." She walked toward the back of the class, where the other projects were set up and crowded on the tables and shelves and floor. I didn't spot ours at first, but then I saw it on a shelf in the corner. Completed.

I walked past Ms. Fuentes to our roller coaster. Calvin had finished everything. The corkscrew, my barrel roll, the extra loops. He'd even added cheesy ancient-Egyptian-inspired decorations to the mounting board and around the track, and had given our coaster the name "The Ozymandias Orbiter." I watched as Fuentes set the car at the bottom of the first incline. The last time we'd worked on it, we still hadn't figured out how to propel the car up the track, but Calvin had devised a brilliant solution.

"How'd you come up with the idea of using an electro-magnet to repel the cars up the slope?" she asked.

"Calvin did that," I said in awe of him. Even with everything he'd been through, even though I'd betrayed him, Calvin had still finished our project.

"It's ingenious." Fuentes plugged in the magnet and

turned it on. The three linked cars shot up the incline and barreled along the track smoothly. For thirty-eight seconds, I held my breath and waited for the cars to detach and fly loose from the track, but they never did. They reached the end—which we'd discussed coating with a spray-adhesive to slow the cars, and which Calvin seemed to have done—slowed, and came to rest.

"Wow." The word slipped out, and I cleared my throat because I didn't want to clue Fuentes in that this was the first time I'd actually seen the roller coaster in action outside of the computer simulation.

Ms. Fuentes nodded. "Honestly, I was worried this project might be too advanced, but you all, especially you and Calvin and Dustin, proved up to the challenge. Good work."

"Thanks." The thing was, despite what I'd constantly said to Calvin, I didn't really care about the grade. I was caught up wondering what it meant that Calvin had finished the project on his own and had his father bring it in. Had he completed it as a peace offering? Was this his way of letting me know he'd forgiven me?

"So you don't mind if I hold on to it for my group?" Fuentes asked.

"Sure, yeah."

Ms. Fuentes's face lit up. "Wonderful!"

"Thanks, Ms. Fuentes." She probably thought I was thanking her for the praise, but even if Calvin still hated me for betraying him, she was the reason I'd gotten to know him. Regardless of how things turned out—if I found Tommy, if the universe collapsed and swallowed us all—the time I'd spent with Calvin had made the last few months bearable. More than that, Calvin had become part of my life, as real as Tommy.

Ms. Fuentes continued to beam with pride. "So, have you decided where you're going to college? I assume you *are* going."

"University of . . ." I stopped myself. The University of Colorado didn't exist anymore. Colorado didn't exist anymore. "I haven't made up my mind yet."

"Well, regardless of what school you choose, I suspect you'll do great things. My college years were some of the best of my life. There's more to learn than you'll ever know."

"I guess," I said. "But, and I know this is going to sound weird, I think I'm going to miss high school."

"Maybe, but the world is bigger than you can possibly imagine, Ozzie, and you've only just begun to explore it."

The irony of her statement wasn't lost on me. "Ms. Fuentes? Remember when you taught us about particle-wave duality?" She nodded. "And you showed us that video on the double-slit experiment?"

"Fascinating stuff," Ms. Fuentes said. "Some days I think I would have enjoyed specializing in theoretical physics."

"Well, I was wondering: If observing atoms is what causes them to decide how to act, does that mean *we* shape reality?"

Fuentes furrowed her brow and took in a long, deep breath. "That's a somewhat esoteric reading of the theories."

"Is it? If the world around us is in a state of flux until we observe it, how do we know that our intentions and thoughts don't impact what it will become?"

"Because we don't actually change anything, Ozzie," she said. "It's all about perception."

"I don't follow."

Fuentes tapped her lip with her index finger. Then she said, "Let me show you something." I followed her to her desk and waited while she rolled the overhead projector in front of the whiteboard. She hunted around until she found a sheet of paper. She folded it into three even sections.

"When I fold the paper like this," she said, "it forms a triangular prism. Three equal rectangles that connect to form a triangle."

"Uh, okay?"

"Now, when I hold it up to the light, what do you see?" Fuentes positioned the paper on the overhead so that its shadow was projected on the whiteboard.

"Aside from your hand?" I said. "A rectangle."

"Right. And how about now."

"A kind of flattened hexagon."

"Right again." Fuentes turned the paper on its end. "And now what?"

I shrugged. "A triangle. What does this have to do with quantum physics and reality?" Part of me wished I'd never asked, seeing as I wasn't sure I was going to understand her answer.

Ms. Fuentes shut off the projector and set the paper aside. "The point is that if you look at the object one way, it's a rectangle, another and it's a hexagon or a triangle. But none of that changes the fact that it's a prism." I must've looked completely baffled, and I was, because she said, "What we observe as some kind of duality—an atom is either a wave or a particle depending on our observation—may not reveal the entire truth. The atom may be neither of those things. It might exist in a completely different state we're incapable of seeing or comprehending. Someone who only saw the shadows of our prism might deduce that it had changed shape, while we would know it was a prism all along."

Her explanation reminded me of the allegory of the cave. "In other words, there might be a truth out there we don't know yet?"

"That's an interesting way to put it, but yes."

"So then how does that relate to reality?"

"I'm not sure I understand," Fuentes said.

"I guess I'm asking: Do we create reality by interaction and observation, or does it only appear that way because we're incapable of seeing the whole prism?"

Ms. Fuentes sighed. "You're moving into philosophy here, Ozzie, and I'm not sure I'm the right person to help you. What I can tell you is that it probably doesn't matter. It doesn't matter whether we know if an atom is a particle or a wave or something else completely. Not knowing doesn't change the reality of what an atom is. What matters is that we continue searching for the answers." She frowned. "Did that help at all?"

"I think so," I said. "Thanks. See you tomorrow."

1,295 MI

LUA ADJUSTED MY BOW TIE FOR THE TENTH TIME
in an hour. He stepped back and closed one eye, appraising
my appearance. "I guess that's as good as you're going to get."

"Well, no one wears a tux like you, Lu."

"Tell me more."

While I'd gone with a classic black-and-white tux,
Lua wore baby blue with a sequined bow tie and cummerbund that would have looked ridiculous on anyone else,
but which Lua wore with style. He'd even dyed his hair to
match.

"You ready for this?" he asked.

"The dance?" I shook my head. "I don't even know why
I'm going."

"Because it's a rite of passage. It's going to be lame, right?
But if you stay home and mope, you'll regret it. Or you won't.

It's only prom." Then he shrugged. "Actually, though, I was talking about photos with Dinah."

"Oh. I'm definitely not ready for that."

"Tough." Lua grabbed my hand and led me out of my room.

Before the universe had stolen Renny and my parents, Lua's house had only consisted of two bedrooms, but in addition to rewriting history, the universe was also adept at home remodeling and had converted the garage into a bedroom for me. Even as it stole parts of my life, the universe gave me other things in return. It had disappeared my family and replaced it with a new one; it had devoured the stars but given me the opportunity to recreate them for someone who'd never seen them; it had robbed me of Tommy but gifted me Calvin.

I'd managed to lose Calvin all on my own.

I couldn't figure out why the universe bothered. Why replace what it had stolen? Why not just take me too and end the whole thing? From the day I narrowly avoided dying on Flight 1184, it'd seemed as if the universe was trying to tell me something, but I hadn't been able to decipher what. Sometimes I thought it was trying to tell me to get as far from Cloud Lake as possible, other times to never leave. If it were attempting to send me a message, I wished it would be a little less ambiguous. A bright neon sign in the sky would have been far more helpful.

Lua and I endured about an hour of Ms. Novak taking pictures and forcing us to pose in front of different parts of the house. I played along because, in a way, it was her special night too. In this new history, she'd watched us fumble through the world as toddlers, seen us struggle to escape our awkward phases, and now we were getting ready to move to the next stages of our lives. To journey out into the real world—though there wasn't much world left—and become adults, whatever that actually meant. As angry as I'd been at my parents over the last few months for acting like idiot children over their divorce, I hated that they'd been cheated out of these moments.

"You both look so handsome!"

"Come on, Dinah," Lua said. "The limo's going to be here soon."

Ms. Novak lowered the camera. "But it's not here yet, and you're mine to do with as I please until it arrives." She peered through the viewfinder again. "Now, give me old Hollywood glamour."

We posed with silly faces; as spies; I held Lua across my arms; he tried to lift me in his; and we even managed to get serious long enough to give Ms. Novak a photo she could print, frame, and hang on the wall.

Finally—finally!—our limo arrived, but the moment Dustin climbed out in a hideous plaid tux with matching Chucks, Ms. Novak bullied him into pictures with me and Lua, and it took us another half hour to extricate ourselves from photography hell and crowd into the limo.

Dustin passed around flutes of sparkling apple juice—in addition to the scrutiny of metal detectors at the dance, we could be subjected to breathalyzer tests if any of the teachers suspected we'd been drinking—and held them aloft to toast.

"To the last best night of our lives," Dustin said.

Lua shook his head. "I'm not drinking to that. If this is going to be the best night of our lives, we're in serious fucking trouble."

Dustin rolled his eyes. "Shut up and toast!"

So we did.

I hadn't heard from Calvin, so Lua, Dustin, and I had pooled our resources to go as a group. Maybe that was how it was always meant to be. They were my people, after all.

While most of the seniors we knew had planned expensive dinners at fancy restaurants on their parents' dime, we opted for a pizza joint near Cloud Lake High, and I was willing to bet we had more fun than any of them. We spent dinner telling stories about old times. About who we were and who we hoped to become. About the time Dustin had tripped and fallen onstage while accepting an award for perfect attendance. About the time in tenth grade Lua had played Robin Hood in Cloud Lake High's production of *Robin Hood*, and had slipped on an ill-placed plant during a fight scene and given himself a concussion, but had still managed to finish the show. Even though his memory of that night remained hazy, I remembered every detail for him.

I wondered if these last four years really had been the best of my life. It wasn't fair Tommy wasn't with us, able to share his own stories, or that I'd only gotten to know Calvin over these last few months. None of it seemed fair, and I couldn't guess what life would throw at me after graduation. The universe was shrinking so quickly, I didn't know if we'd make it through the end of the year, and I was equally terrified and relieved. Terrified for obvious reasons, but relieved because if the universe collapsed completely I would never have to know whether the choices I'd made had been the wrong ones.

I pushed my plate away and said, "I want you all to know that I'm really glad we're friends. I wouldn't have survived high school without you."

Lua stuck his finger in his mouth and mimed puking.

"When'd you get all sentimental, Pinks?" Dustin said.

"I didn't. I just love you guys, all right? Is that okay?"

Dustin shrugged. "It's not like we're going anywhere."

"Lua is," I said. "Tour starts at the end of the summer."

Lua frowned. "I wouldn't really call it a tour. Sure, the band's booked at just about every club and bar in Cloud Lake, but that's not saying much."

I knew if I checked my phone, I'd see that the world had shrunk to the size of Cloud Lake, but I left my phone in my pocket, because knowing wouldn't make any difference. I couldn't change it. I'd spent months trying to figure out the whys and hows of the universe shrinking, and had absolutely nothing to show for it. Maybe it'd never been in my power to find Tommy and stop the universe from collapsing. Maybe all I could do was enjoy the time I had left.

"Too bad Calvin isn't here," Dustin said.

Lua kicked him under the table. "Topics of conversation explicitly excluded tonight are: Calvin Frye, Trent Williams, Jaime Trevino, and graduation. Tonight is all about the dancing. Right?"

"It's cool," I said. "I wish Calvin were here too, but I'm not going to spend the night crying into my cummerbund."

Dustin, who'd managed to put away an entire pizza on

his own, stifled a burp behind his napkin. "The cops finally charged Coach Reevey."

"About time," Lua said. "I hope they lock him up and some prison dude makes Reevey his bitch." When I glared at Lua, he said, "What?"

"Prison rape: not funny."

Dustin wasn't usually the sort to gossip, but I think he jumped in to keep me and Lua from brawling. "I heard police raided his house and found pictures on his computer of some of the boys. I heard they also found pills. Lots of them. Valium, Rohypnol, MDMA."

Lua lowered his eyes. "Trent told me."

"I thought we weren't talking about Trent tonight," I said.

"We're not," Lua said. "But he did tell me a little of what Reevey did to him, and if you knew what he'd told me, prison rape is the nicest thing you'd wish on that asshole."

Calvin may not have divulged the specifics, but I'd seen their effect on him. Reevey had stolen his life. I doubted Calvin would look back on high school as the best years of *his* life. I still believed the things that had happened to me since Tommy had vanished weren't coincidences, but now that thought made me sick to my stomach. No message could've been important enough to kill a plane full of people. Nothing in the whole universe was so crucial for me to know that it necessitated ruining Calvin's life. In the end Calvin was probably right to hate me, even if he didn't know the real reasons he should.

"Now that we're all depressed," I said, "who's ready to dance?"

The prom committee had spent the first half of the year locked in a contentious debate about whether to hold the dance at the school and spring for a band or to hold it at a fancy hotel and hire a cheap DJ. When they'd decided to go with a live band, few believed any decorations could transform the dank building into something other than a gym. I'd counted myself among the nonbelievers, and it was nice to be proven wrong.

"A Night to Remember" was still stupid, but after I'd been patted down by Mr. Purdue—an ancient math teacher whose eyesight was so bad, he called everyone "son" regardless of gender—because I'd set off the metal detector, passed my breathalyzer test, and walked into the gym, I couldn't believe it was the same place I'd been forced to play basketball and dodgeball and volleyball in. They'd even managed to mostly eliminate the scent of accumulated sweat and humiliation.

Violet and silver balloons crowded the ceiling, and gauzy fabric decorated with lilies hung from the walls. The lights were dim and atmospheric, and the committee had set up tables draped with violet tablecloths. The centerpieces were plastic bouquets that held various pictures of our class taken throughout the year. A stage had been erected where one of the basketball hoops once stood—though I had no idea how they'd managed to remove it—and the band played a cover of an eighties song I only recognized because Lua had forced me to listen to it on repeat over the summer between eighth and ninth grade, when she'd gone through her emo eighties phase.

"D'Arcy's still a narcissistic sociopath," Lua said. "But she throws a mean prom."

I couldn't disagree with either statement. But what amazed me more than the gym's conversion was that D'Arcy and her friends cared so much about prom that they'd expended the effort required to transform it so completely. If I'd been in charge of decorations, I might have hung a couple of banners, hooked up Lua's phone to a speaker, and called it a night. Which was probably why no one had asked me to help.

The moment we got inside the gym, Priya found us and dragged Dustin toward the dance floor. We'd arrived respectfully late, partly because Dinah had held us up with pictures, but also because we hadn't wanted to be the first to arrive.

"Sit?" I said. Lua nodded. I took one step toward an

empty table before Lua took a detour to where Jaime and Birdie were hanging out with a couple of their friends. Lua didn't even ask if we could sit with them before plopping down in a chair.

"What's up?" I said to Jaime, and he held out his fist for me to bump.

"Band's kind of lame." Jaime's voice trembled slightly, and Birdie scooted her chair closer to his.

"They're not bad," Lua grudgingly admitted.

"You should go up there," Jaime said. "Show 'em how it's done."

Lua nodded, but his hand operation wasn't for two more days, and even then it would take a few weeks of physical therapy before he could play. He glanced at Birdie, who was wearing a low-cut, skin-tight black dress, her hair piled atop of her head in crispy curls. "You look really beautiful, Birdie."

Birdie pursed her lips. "What're you playing at?"

"Retract the claws," Lua said. "I'm not after Jaime. Actually, I think you two are better together than he and I ever were."

I shared Birdie's suspicions. Lua was not a graceful loser, and for all I knew, this was Step One of Lua's nefarious plan to break Birdie and Jaime up by drowning them in compliments.

"Uh, yeah," Birdie said. "Thanks?" We sat at the table enduring one of the most awkward silences in the history of awkward silences until Birdie grabbed Jaime's hand and said, "I wanna dance, babe."

Jaime, Birdie, and their friends meandered to the dance floor. Jaime glanced back once and mouthed, "Thank you."

"What was that all about?" I asked as soon as they'd gone.

Lua shrugged. "He looked happy, didn't he?"

"I guess." I was honestly shocked Lua hadn't grabbed one of the picture-holder centerpieces and beaten Jaime or Birdie or both with it.

"I gotta say: This new mature Lua is freaking me out."

"Don't get me wrong," Lua said. "I still want to yank out Birdie's weave and dump a bucket of pig's blood all over her pretty dress, but she makes Jaime happy, and after the train wreck formerly known as our relationship, he deserves it."

Lua was right, I'd just never expected that brand of rational, self-sacrificing logic from him. I wondered if he'd finally looked in the mirror and recognized who he saw. I'd always found it odd that Lua possessed so much confidence when it came to his music and his gender identity, but still seemed so uncomfortable in his own skin. Apparently, that had changed. Lua was still my Lua—I still recognized him—but he was also different.

"Hey," Lua said. "I really am sorry Calvin's not here."

"It's okay."

"I tried to call him a couple of times. He didn't answer, but I may have left some long, rambling messages explaining why he should forgive you and come to the dance."

My eyes shot open. "You didn't."

"I really did."

"Lua . . ."

"You're my brother and my best friend, Ozzie." Lua turned to face me, so close our knees touched. "If you think there's anything I wouldn't do for you, you obviously don't know me well."

I couldn't help myself. I hugged him until he pushed me away.

"Gross! No PDA. I have a rock star reputation to protect."

"I love you, Lu."

"Yeah, yeah. I love you, too, Ozzie."

Eventually we joined the dancers tearing up the floor even though Lua wouldn't stop complaining about how terrible the band was, and we caught Dustin and Priya dancing intimately during an odd slow cover of "Happiness Is a Warm Gun." I wondered how it was possible the universe was only the size of Cloud Lake but that the Beatles still existed. If there was no England, where had they been born? I could've gotten my phone out and searched, but I suspected the answers would simply lead to more questions, like how we had phones and where they were manufactured.

I left Lua, Dustin, and Priya shaking their asses on the dance floor and went to use the restroom. When I returned, the band was playing another slow song. Dustin was standing against the wall holding Priya's purse.

"So . . . Priya?"

Dustin shrugged. "What can I say? She's a champion cuddler."

I couldn't help laughing at the mental image of Priya and Dustin all snuggled up together. "You seen Lua?"

"Yeah . . . about Lua . . ." Dustin pointed at the dance floor. I followed his finger, searching the crowd.

And then I found Lua. Dancing. With Trent Williams. Trent's arms were wrapped around Lua's waist; Lua's head leaned against Trent's chest. I stood there with my mouth hanging open until Lua caught me staring and shot me an I-will-kill-you-if-you-say-one-damn-word look. I smiled in return.

I danced a couple of songs with Priya, a couple more with Lua. Dustin even forced me to dance one with him, and we cracked up the whole time.

I kept hoping Calvin would surprise me. I imagined him

walking through the doors in a black hoodie tux, catching my eye from across the room, his smile all the forgiveness I needed. I imagined us dancing until we were the only two people left on the floor, dancing long after the band had played its last cheesy song. I imagined kissing him.

If my life had been a movie or a book, the night might have ended that way—I might have gotten my happily ever after—but my life was neither of those things. No one's life is. Life is life. It happens, it goes on. Eventually, it ends, but other lives continue, new ones begin. That's just the way of it. My life would keep going on until the day it didn't, and I could either make the best of it or waste it wishing for what I didn't and might never have.

TOMMY

TOMMY DIGS THROUGH THE BAG OF CANDY, PICKING *out the banana Runts for himself, before passing it to me. We walk through the mall with no particular destination. He's been quiet since I picked him up, but I can tell by the way he breathes shallowly and winces that he must've gotten into a fight with his father.*

"You still up for fireworks on Dustin's boat Tuesday?" I cheek a couple of strawberry candies. Tommy chews his candy, but I suck on mine until they disintegrate. "Dustin said he managed to get a bunch of illegal shit—M-80s and stuff."

"Yeah," Tommy says. "Sure. Sounds fun."

I'm dying to ask Tommy what happened, to make sure he's not seriously hurt, but he won't talk about it until he's ready.

Tommy veers toward a tux rental shop. He stands at the window, so close his nose touches the glass.

"Are we shopping for formal wear?"

"Just looking," Tommy says.

The mannequins in the window—rigid and frozen in time—masquerade in various getups. Everything from classic penguin suits to flashy, brightly colored tuxes only Dustin or Lua would wear.

"Just a few months and we'll be picking ours out for prom." I nudge Tommy with my shoulder. "You're going to look so hot I'll probably jump you before the dance."

Tommy nods. "I guess."

I'm pretty certain his father is the source of his mood, but I'm worried. I've spent so many nights considering calling the police or child protective services to get Tommy's father out of their house, but I never make those calls because Tommy would never forgive me.

"Come on." I grab Tommy's hand and pull him into the store. I tell the salesperson a lie about attending a ritzy fundraiser for my father's imaginary company, and before I know it, I'm standing in the middle of the store in a slim-fitting black tuxedo. The salesperson goes on and on about how handsome I look and how it fits like a latex glove. I'm not paying attention because I'm waiting for Tommy.

"I'm not coming out in this," Tommy calls from his fitting room.

"Why not?"

"Because I look dumb, Oz."

The salesperson tries to coax Tommy out of the fitting room, but I shoot the guy a look that shuts him up.

"Don't make me bust down that door and drag you out, Thomas Ross."

I hold my breath to see if Tommy's going to call my bluff. The lock slides back, the handle turns. Tommy walks out of the fitting room. He's wearing a midnight-blue tux with a traditional black bow tie. My mouth falls open.

"Forget it," Tommy says. "This is silly."

"You look . . . wow."

Tommy steps toward me. "For real?" He plucks at the shawl collar and examines himself in the mirror.

I nod because I'm tongue-tied. I can't imagine how anyone— how Tommy—could look at himself and not see how beautiful he is. I drag him to the floor-length mirrors and stand beside him. Thankfully, the salesperson has the decency to give us some space.

"You know what I see when I look at you?" I ask.

"A goof in a suit he can't afford?"

"The most handsome man in the universe, who also happens to be the guy I love." I lean into him. "And next year, when we go to prom and you're wearing this tux, I'll know everyone hates me because you're mine."

Tommy stares at our reflections for a while. Then he says, "Are you really set on doing this prom thing?"

"Don't you want to go?"

"Maybe." Tommy pulls away from me. "I thought you hated all that school shit."

"I do, I guess, but it's prom. We've been talking about going together since freshman year."

"That's the thing," he says. "Haven't you ever thought of going with anyone else?"

"Another guy?" The salesperson is watching us, and I suspect he knows I lied about the fundraiser, but I don't care.

"Not necessarily. We could go with Lua and Jaime, and Dustin and whoever he takes. It's just, we're always Ozzie and Tommy. I don't know how to be anything else." Tommy looks at his shoes before he heads back into the fitting room.

I change into my regular clothes and we leave the shop. I'm afraid to speak, too afraid to ask him to explain what he meant earlier. Whatever is going on with him is bigger than his father. I'm not sure I want to know anymore.

"Is it so bad being Ozzie and Tommy?" I ask.

"You know I love you, right, Ozzie?"

"But?"

Tommy shakes his head and takes my hand. "No but. Just: I love you."

I breathe a sigh of relief. "I love you, too."

3.12 MI

AFTER PROM THE LIMO DRIVER DROPPED US OFF AT
Lua's house so I could get my car, and then I drove us all to
Trent's. Most everyone who'd gone to the dance, it seemed,
showed up at the party. Trent's parents were home, but they
stayed in their bedroom and let us drink and dance and gen-
erally raise hell.

I hadn't wanted to ask Lua about Trent with Dustin in
the backseat, but he'd run off the moment we got to the
party, so, after I made the rounds, I found Lua alone in the
front yard. He'd shed his jacket and was staring at the sky,
which was only partially visible through the trees, but so
dark and empty without the stars that it was difficult to tell
the difference.

"So," I said. "You and Trent?"

"Shut up about it or I'll break your nose, Ozzie." Lua

stood rigid and proud. "There's no me and Trent. He wanted a dance, so I gave him a pity dance."

I held up my hands. "I'm not judging. I have an imaginary boyfriend, after all."

Lua relaxed slightly. "Is Tommy really imaginary?"

I looked around for somewhere to sit, and ended up settling for the ground, which was covered with pine needles. Trent lived out west, with dirt roads and almost as many horses as people.

"Have you ever had one of those dreams that seemed so real you had trouble realizing it wasn't when you woke up?"

Lua sat beside me. "Yeah."

"Tommy's kind of like that. Only, he's not a dream. No one remembers him, but he's real to me. I have these memories; an entire history of him and me. Of all of us." A smile touched my lips. "Like this one time the three of us went skinny-dipping at the beach last year, and some dickhead stole our clothes. We couldn't go home naked, so we drove to Walmart because it was the only thing open at two in the morning. All I had in my car was one of those crinkly silver blankets in my emergency kit. Tommy wrapped it around himself like a toga, went inside, and bought us stuff to wear. You got pissed because he'd picked out a One Direction shirt for you, and you tried to refuse it, but it was too small to fit me or Tommy."

I couldn't help laughing at the memory, but Lua didn't laugh or smile. "I don't remember that."

"I do," I said. "Maybe that's what matters."

"No, this is what matters. You and me, Oz."

"You're right. I know you're right."

"But listen, if you need to find Tommy, I'll help you."

"Why now?" I asked.

Lua sighed. "You're not the center of the universe, Ozzie— you're not even the center of *my* universe—but Tommy is clearly the center of yours, and even though you can be such a selfish asshole sometimes—"

"Christ, Lua, tell me how you really feel."

"I'm trying," he said, and waited to see if I was going to interrupt him again. "Even though you can be a self-centered prick, I want you to be happy."

My anger slipped away. "What if I never find him, Lu?"

Lua was quiet for a moment. Then he poked me in the ribs and said, "Maybe something better will find *you*."

He pointed across the car-littered front lawn to a shadow walking toward us. I didn't understand until the shadow peeled away from the darkness. Calvin had shown up after all. He approached slowly, his hands buried in the pockets of his hoodie.

"Hey," he said.

"Hey."

Lua hopped up. "I think I'll leave you boys alone."

I wanted to stop Lua from leaving, but I didn't. I stood and brushed the dirt and pine needles off my butt.

"You look handsome in your tux," Calvin said. His eyes were bloodshot and bruised. "How was prom?"

I shrugged. "Lame. You didn't miss anything except Trent and Lua dancing."

Calvin wore his surprise openly. "Trent? And Lua?"

"Yep. Lua says nothing's going on, but stranger things have happened."

"Wow." Calvin stalled a couple of feet away, and I felt more uncomfortable than when I'd caught him cutting himself in the restroom at school.

"Listen," I said. "I'm really sorry I told my therapist. I didn't know she'd call the cops, not that that's a good excuse. I shouldn't have told anyone. And while I'm being honest, I also told Lua. She didn't tell anyone, but you deserve to know."

Calvin bobbed his head like he was floating in water, everything below his chin submerged. "It's all right."

"No, it's not."

"You're right," Calvin said. "It's not. But I forgive you. I've been talking to my own therapist. My dad forced me to go after he found out about Reevey and the cutting, and it was either that or a forced stay at a psychiatric hospital."

"Who is it?" I asked. "I've been to a lot of therapists."

"Dr. Sayegh? Makali Sayegh."

I chuckled. "Yeah, I know her. She's not terrible."

Calvin shrugged. "She told me it was a good thing it all came out. That keeping the secret might have killed me."

"I'm glad it didn't."

"Some days, I'm not sure I am."

Calvin started walking, and I jogged to catch him. We wandered down Trent's driveway, onto the dark dirt roads. I wanted to hold his hand so badly, but I didn't know what it meant that Cal had come to the party. He said he'd forgiven me, but you can forgive someone and still never want to see them again.

"It's fucked up, you know?" Cal said. "I saw these pictures of myself—pictures Coach took while I was drugged—and I don't remember them. But I still love him and I think he loved me. Isn't that fucked up?"

"No. *Reevey* is fucked up. He hurt you, and that's not your fault."

Calvin walked with his head down and his back bowed. "I feel like he stole part of my life I'll never get back. I feel like there's nothing left for me."

"I'm here for you, as a friend or more. It's totally up to you. I'll respect whatever choice you make."

"You love Tommy," Cal said. "I know it and you know it. You'll always love him."

"True, but Tommy's not here. I don't know where he is, and I may never find him. But maybe he's where he's supposed to be, and maybe I'm where I'm meant to be too."

We walked for a while, not talking. I wasn't sure whether I believed what I'd said. It was true that I didn't know if I'd ever find Tommy, but I didn't know if I believed never finding him would be okay. I didn't know if I'd ever be able to move on with my life if I couldn't at least tell him good-bye. It was all so confusing, and Calvin complicated my life even more.

"Can we go somewhere?" Calvin asked when we reached the end of the street. He slipped his hand into mine and stared into my eyes. Without the moonlight or the stars, it was almost impossible to see his face, but I imagined I could still see his eyes, and they were beautiful.

"Sure," I said. "I think I know just the place."

1.89 MI

I LAY IN THE DARK ON THE FLOOR OF MY OLD bedroom beside Calvin. Sweat chilled my skin, and my chest rose and fell heavily.

I'd had a feeling that, even though my parents had vanished, my old house would still be empty. That the universe would have come up with a reason to keep anyone from moving into the house in which I'd once lived with people who no longer existed. And I'd been right. I didn't have a key anymore, but the sliding glass door on the far side of the house had been open. It hadn't even felt like breaking in this time.

"You all right?" I asked Calvin.

"No," he said.

I hadn't intended to have sex with Cal—that's not the reason I'd brought him to my old house—but then he was kissing me in my bedroom, and he was unbuttoning my shirt and pants, which now lay in a heap on the floor in the corner. His hands had trembled. He was scared of the drop—we both were—but we'd reached the top of the incline and had fallen together, and we hadn't crashed. We'd survived. At least, I thought we had.

I sat up on my elbow. "Was it . . . was it bad?"

"God, no. It's not you, Ozzie. I just—"

"What?"

"I thought doing it with you would make me happy. That being with someone who cared about me would fix everything. But it's all the same. I'm still the same."

"I'm sorry, Cal. It's my fault. I shouldn't have—"

"It's not your fault, Ozzie. I wanted to do it; it was my decision."

"Do you want to go back to the party?" I asked, because I couldn't think of anything else to say.

"Party?"

"At Trent's house."

"Who's Trent?"

I crawled across the room, dug my phone out of my pocket, and pulled up a map. The entire world, the entire universe had shrunk again. Everything west of my house was gone, and there wasn't much left east, either. Just some of the beach and the ocean. And each time I reloaded the map, the world shrank a little more. I didn't even know where my phone had come from. Who'd built it or where I'd purchased it. I'd thought the universe was confusing before Tommy had disappeared, but the smaller it got, the less it made sense.

"What's wrong?" Calvin asked.

"Everything's gone," I whispered. "I thought maybe it would spare Cloud Lake, but even that's disappearing."

"I want to see." I started to hand Calvin my phone, but he said, "Not the map, the edge of the universe."

We dressed in silence and darkness. Confusion rippled through me. Sleeping with Tommy had brought us closer together, but both times with Calvin seemed to drive us further apart.

"Did you ever figure out *why* the universe is shrinking?" Calvin asked while I sat on the floor and tied my shoelaces.

I shook my head. "No, and I don't think I'll be able to stop it before it swallows everything."

"Oh."

"I saw the roller coaster, by the way. Ms. Fuentes loved it so much she's taking it to show her roller-coaster-building group."

"Ms. Fuentes?" Calvin asked.

"Forget it." My heart broke. He didn't remember Ms. Fuentes or Trent, which meant he probably didn't remember

Coach Reevey either, but he was still affected by what Reevey had done to him. Not even the universe could fix what Reevey had broken.

I stood and helped Calvin to his feet. Our faces were so close and I wanted to kiss him, but I didn't. "Do you think this is my fault? That I'm the reason the universe is shrinking?"

"Maybe," he said, and it wasn't the answer I'd expected. "Honestly, I don't know, but I think it means something that you're the only person who remembers the way things used to be."

"Doesn't it seem weird to you that the whole of existence is just part of one small shitty town?"

"Not really," Cal said. "Though I *do* find it odd I grew up so near the edge of the universe and have never gone to see it."

"Are you sure you want to now?"

Calvin nodded. "Definitely."

The beach wasn't far from my house, so we walked. Outside, in the middle of the night, the universe didn't just feel small, it felt deserted. We saw no people, no animals, no cars. As far as I knew, Calvin and I were the only humans in existence. It should have been comforting not to have to face the collapse of the universe alone, but it wasn't.

I held Calvin's hand while we walked, thinking back to that first night Tommy and I had slept together. I'd wanted to climb to the top of the tallest building and shout about it for the world to hear, but it wasn't the same with Calvin. Instead, I wanted to keep what we'd done to myself. I wasn't ashamed, but I did wonder if it had been a mistake. Maybe whatever invisible hand had pushed us together had only ever intended for us to be friends, and I'd crossed a line by allowing us to become something more. Or maybe it had never been about me at all.

We reached the beach road and found a path through the dunes. I kicked off my shoes and socks, and Calvin did the same. I knew something was different before we cleared the sea oats and bushes. I still hadn't gotten used to the empty sky, but what I saw on the horizon was deeper than emptiness.

"So," Calvin said. "That's it."

Less than a quarter mile off the beach, the sky had disappeared, replaced by a void. That was the only way to describe it. It wasn't black, it wasn't gray. It was the complete and total absence of everything. Even the word "empty" implies something that can be filled, but the vast *nothing* in the sky was bottomless. Calvin and I could have poured forever into it and that boundless zone of negative space would have simply devoured all that we were and remained more than empty.

"It's moving toward us," I said.

"Is it?" The universe must have rewritten Calvin's memory every time it shifted. He could have remained standing at the edge of the ocean until the universe consumed him, and he would've thought it normal.

"It's never going to stop."

Calvin pulled his hoodie over his head and tossed it aside. Then his undershirt.

"What're you doing?" I asked.

He continued undressing. He unbuckled his belt and kicked off his jeans. "Why wait?"

"Calvin, stop."

"I want to know what's on the other side."

"Nothing!" I yelled. "There's nothing on the other side." I grabbed him before he could strip off his underwear, and he pushed me away. I tackled him to the ground, but Calvin was a champion wrestler. He swung his legs, wrapped them around my waist, and held me in a headlock. I struggled, but I couldn't defeat him, so he let me go.

"Do you want to be trapped here forever?" Calvin asked. "What if we're meant to escape? You keep saying you're waiting for Tommy and your family to return, but how do you know they're the ones who have vanished? What if you're the one who disappeared, and they're on the other side waiting for you to find your way home?"

I *didn't* know. Calvin's theory made as much sense as anything else, but I couldn't know for certain.

"I'm scared," I said.

Calvin took my hand, helped me up, and kissed the tops of my fingers. "It would be weird if you weren't."

"But why is this happening?"

"Why does *anything* happen?" he asked. "I sure as hell don't know. The only thing I know for sure is that we can do nothing and maybe we'll wind up taken like you said Tommy and your family were, or we can face the uncertainty and see what's on the other side for ourselves."

"It'd be easier if someone would just give me the answers," I said. "If everything that's happened—Tommy vanishing, Flight 1184 crashing, the universe shrinking—is a message, why not come right out and tell me what I'm supposed to do?"

"That's not how the world works, Ozzie. Some things, you have to learn for yourself."

Calvin was right. Since the day Tommy disappeared, I'd been waiting for him to return, but he hadn't, and now everyone had vanished. Every person I ever knew or loved. And soon, with or without me, Calvin would follow them. I didn't know if the universe was a simulation or a bubble about to burst or even a spooky quantum reality I'd willed into existence. All I knew for certain was that I'd wind up alone if I stayed.

"Okay," I said. "I'll go."

I squeezed Calvin's hand and pulled him toward the ocean. But he didn't follow.

"Come on. We can do this together."

He shook his head and let go of my hand. "I think you should do it," he said. "And I want you to, but I need to do this part on my own."

"You sure?"

"No," he said, laughing.

I didn't want him to leave—I didn't want to face the void alone—but I understood why he needed to do this himself. If he was going to survive what Coach Reevey had done to him, even if he couldn't remember who Reevey was, he needed to face the future on his own terms.

"Whatever happens," I said, "I want you to know that I care about you, Calvin Frye. Maybe this universe was never real, but *you* are. You're the only real thing in it."

"That sounds like a good-bye," Calvin said. "But I think we'll see each other on the other side." Cal stripped off his underwear and turned toward the water. He walked until the waves lapped against his bare feet. The void grew closer. With each second that passed, it devoured more of the ocean.

"You're going to find your way, Ozzie." He took another step into the water.

"Just wait," I called after him. "Wait for it to reach the shore. It's too far out to swim. You'll drown."

Calvin glanced at me over his shoulder. He was smiling. "I won't drown, Ozzie. I can breathe underwater."

He walked until the water reached his waist, and then he dove in and swam. I watched Cal until his pasty skin disappeared under the stygian sea.

Calvin Frye was gone.

I sank to my knees. I thought maybe I would feel the moment Calvin entered the void or was swallowed by it or whatever happened when he reached it, but I didn't. And there was no one left to tell me he no longer existed.

I wished I could've gone with him. I wished I had his courage. I knew if I waited long enough, the emptiness would swallow me. I wouldn't have to do anything but stand on the shore and let it take me. I thought watching Calvin swim to the void would give me the strength to do the same, but I was a coward. The nothingness shuddered and moved closer. I couldn't do it; I'd already lost everything and everyone I ever cared about, and if I died, no one would remember them.

I ran back across the dunes. I stumbled and fell, and when I looked behind me, the ocean was gone. I forced myself to my feet and kept running up the hill to the road. I tripped and stubbed my toe. A flap of skin and blood and gravel hung off the end of my big toe, but I kept running.

I reached my house and slammed the door behind me. I climbed the stairs to my room, and tried to shut that door too, but a force on the other side pushed back. A soundless wind blew into my room, carrying with it a crumpled scrap of paper that floated through the air and landed on the floor. I leaned all my weight against the door and finally slammed it shut. I picked up the paper, crawled into the corner, and hugged my knees to my chest. I didn't know where the paper had come from, but I recognized the writing. It was from my journal. The journal from the world where Tommy had existed.

The nothingness was all around me. I didn't need a map to know that only my house and I remained.

Finally, I was alone, and I smoothed out the paper and began to read.

TOMMY

TOMMY AND I LIE SIDE BY SIDE ON TOP OF HIS *trailer. His father's snores drift up through the thin metal. The Fourth of July is still a couple of days away, but one of Tommy's neighbors is already shooting off fireworks in the distance. The dazzling lights dim the stars for a moment, except there are so many scattered across the sky they can't be outshone for long. The stars look haphazard, though I know they're not. Someone put them there. There's some design. I just can't figure out what it is.*

"Tell me we'll always be together, Tommy."

I expect him to answer immediately. For him to tell me that nothing will keep us apart, that it'll always be him and me against the world.

But he doesn't. And I wait.

"Tommy?"

"I can't," he whispers, even though his father could sleep through a nuclear bomb strike.

"Come on. We're going to be together forever, right?"

"Actually, Oz," he says, *"I was thinking we need some time apart."*

I slap Tommy playfully. "Stop fooling around."

"I'm not fooling."

I tilt my head and search his face, his eyes, for the joke, but don't find it.

"Since the day we met, our lives have been all about each other. I've spent years so focused on you and on us that I haven't given hardly any thought to the rest of my life. I don't know how I'm going to afford college, you don't know what you want to do with the rest of your life." He throws his hands up. *"It's like we've spent the last nine years being one person, and I don't know who I am when I'm not with you."*

"What does it matter?" I say. "I don't even care about college. All I care about is you. Being with you."

Tommy sits up on his elbow. The metal roof groans. "And I care about you, but that's the problem, you know? Being together isn't enough if we're not whole individual people."

"But I love you, Tommy. Don't you get that?"

"I do," he says. "It's just . . . I need to know who I am on my own. I need to figure out who Thomas Ross is, and I can't do that with you stuck to my hip."

My heart is breaking. "I don't know what to do without you."

"I know," *he says.* "That's the problem."

"Are you breaking up with me?" *I already know the answer, but I need him to say it. I won't believe it until I hear him say it.*

"Yeah," *Tommy says.*

There it is. I've known Tommy since second grade. He was my best friend and my boyfriend. And now? Now I don't know what we are.

Tears roll down my cheeks, bile rises in my throat, but I don't move. I don't leave. I can't.

"What happens now?"

"I don't know. Maybe one day in the future, after we've both had time to figure out who we are, we'll find each other again and see if the love is still there."

"But how will I find you?" *I say.* "The world's a big place."

Tommy takes my hand. He's broken up with me, but he still holds my hand. "Trust me: It's not so big."

25 FT

TOMMY HAD BROKEN UP WITH ME.

I'd remembered everything about Tommy—the deep thrum of his voice, the way his hands felt tender when he touched me even though his skin was rough, every fight we'd ever had, every single kiss we'd shared, the dimple on his left cheek, the freckle on his big toe. I could recall the most random details about Tommy and our life together, but I'd forgotten that night. The night he broke up with me. I'd rewritten every memory of Tommy I could recall from my journals, but I hadn't rewritten that one.

I'd spent months searching for him, I'd almost died on a plane crash to find him, I'd waited around Cloud Lake hoping he would return, but Tommy was never coming back, and even if he did, he wasn't coming back to me.

The void waited outside my bedroom walls. I was alone in the universe.

I still didn't know what had happened. Even now that I remembered Tommy breaking up with me, I didn't know whether I'd created this universe from my broken heart or if I was a brain scientists had plopped into a jar and were experimenting on, with Tommy nothing more than a part of the sadistic test, but I still had to decide whether to stay here, afraid and alone, or be brave like Calvin and see what, if anything, was on the other side.

Lua had fought to achieve her dream. She knew she might fail, but she refused to stop. Trent had broken her fingers, but she still moved forward.

Dustin had spent four years killing himself to get the best grades. He'd had a plan, and his parents' bad choices had stolen that plan from him, but he hadn't given up. He'd pivoted. Made a new plan. It might not have been the one he'd wanted, but he kept moving forward.

Coach Reevey had nearly destroyed Calvin, but even he had found the courage to take a stand. To walk into the abyss without knowing what might lie on the other side. He'd embraced his fear, and I knew he hadn't drowned.

I looked at the page in my hand. The memory of the night Tommy had broken up with me, blocked before, throbbed in my mind. It hurt like it had happened just yesterday. I remembered hating him. Crying in my bedroom, swearing I'd never speak to him again. I'd hated him so much, I'd erased him from my life.

But he'd been right.

We'd spent so much time as Tommy and Ozzie that I didn't know who I was or what I wanted without him. I thought Tommy disappearing and Flight 1184 crashing and the universe shrinking were messages telling me to stay in Cloud Lake. I'd spent months waiting for some kind of sign, but I was beginning to think none of this had ever been about me. I wasn't special or important; I was just a boy chained in a cave, too stupid to know I'd been staring at shadows on a wall while the real world was happening behind me. And now the chains were gone, broken, and I had to make a decision. I had to choose.

I opened my curtains. The void had stopped on the other side of the glass, and it waited for me outside my bedroom door. The universe was no longer contracting. I felt certain I could remain in my room until I grew old and died, but I'd do so alone.

Or I could step into the unknown. Maybe I'd find Tommy and Calvin and Lua and my family. Maybe I'd discover the future or nothing at all. I knew what awaited me if I stayed, and there was comfort in that knowledge. My future on the other side of the void was unknowable and frightening. Here in my room, I *was* the center of the universe, the single star around which everything revolved. Beyond the void, I was probably just another insignificant particle floating amongst a vast sea of countless others, and that terrified me.

The scariest thing in life is the door that closes and can't ever be opened again. Once I opened the door and stepped into the void, that door would slam shut behind me and I could never go back.

But maybe it's okay to be afraid. Mrs. Ross hadn't let fear stop her from walking away from her old life and slamming that door behind her, and maybe those slamming doors *are* the scariest things in life, but they're not the worst. The worst is never going through them at all.

I didn't know whether my world was merely shadows on the wall, but it was time to turn around and find out.

I took a deep breath, held it, let it out. I gripped the knob, opened the door, walked into the void, and pulled the door shut behind me.

∞ AND THEN SOME

I'D SURVIVED.

I guess.

The inside of the arena reeked of sweaty bodies, and despite the air conditioners laboring overhead, the air was thick and moist. I sat amongst my fellow classmates. We had all survived. Not just the universe shrinking; we had survived high school. Lua sat a row ahead of me, Calvin way up front where I could barely make out the back of his head.

And Dustin stood onstage in his blue graduation cap and gown addressing the Cloud Lake High class of 2018.

"I went skydiving yesterday. I've been skydiving a lot lately, actually. I didn't tell my friends or my parents—surprise!—and yesterday was my first solo jump." Dustin was so far away that I could barely make out his face, but I knew he was sweating and nervous. I hadn't known he'd gone skydiving, but it didn't surprise me. It was a very Dustin thing to do.

"Falling isn't the scary part. You'd think it is, what with the falling and screaming and plummeting toward the ground. But a moment after you begin to fall, you reach terminal velocity, and you realize that you're not falling. You're flying. Maybe it's an illusion created by wind resistance, but that's okay because you're still flying. You can hold your arms out and soar or pin them to your sides and shoot forward like a rocket. How you descend is totally up to you.

"No, the falling isn't the scary part. Falling is easy. Jumping is hard. Jumping is scary. Until yesterday, I'd made all my jumps tandem, with an instructor strapped to my back. I couldn't really screw anything up because she was there to correct my mistakes—to tell me what to do if my brain froze—but yesterday, I jumped alone.

"I stood outside the open hatch, holding onto the rails, my feet planted on something solid, and I knew that I'd need to push off. To jump into the open and unforgiving air. Alone.

"There was this moment where I was like 'Oh, hell no, I am *not* doing this.' And I could have climbed back into the plane and ridden it down, but I didn't. I'd taken the right courses; I'd listened to my instructors. I possessed all the knowledge necessary to make it to the ground safely. Sure, it was still dangerous. My chute might not have opened or I might have freaked out and forgotten all the things I'd learned. Skydiving isn't without risk, but flying is totally worth it.

"So I took one last breath, I let go of the railing, and I jumped."

Dustin wiped sweat from his forehead with the back of his hand. He paused and stared out at us. I wasn't sure he could pick me out of the ocean of caps and faces, but I liked to imagine he could.

"Graduating seniors of Cloud Lake High: It's time for us to jump."

I stuck my tongue out at the camera as I shielded my eyes from the sun.

"Come on, Ozzie, don't be such a spoilsport." Mom stood with her hand on her hip while Dad tried to snap a picture. "This is for posterity."

"You've already taken a million. How many more does posterity need?"

My parents hadn't fought since Mom had arrived earlier that week for my graduation. She'd tried to get a hotel room, but they'd all been booked by relatives who'd traveled to see their nieces and nephews and grandchildren graduate, so she stayed with me and Renny and Dad. I wound up sleeping on the couch while Mom took my room. I liked to think that their newfound friendship was repayment for my having to camp out on the most uncomfortable sofa bed in existence. But maybe this was the new normal for them. Now that they were no longer husband and wife, they'd found a way back to the friendship they thought they'd lost.

"Ozzie," Mom started, but Renny jumped in and said, "How about one with me?"

I took a knee beside Renny and slung my arm around his shoulders. "This is super lame," I said.

Renny grinned, all teeth, and whispered, "Suck it up, brother. If I had to suffer through this shit when I graduated, so do you."

All around us, kids in blue gowns were being similarly tortured by their parents. Graduation had been a grueling three hours, but now that it was over, I almost wished it had lasted longer. Almost.

Mom and Dad started arguing about how to work the camera, and all I could do was sigh. Okay, so maybe they had a way to go still, but I'd take what I could get.

"When's Mom going back to Chicago?"

"Tonight," Renny said. "You know Dad planned a party back at his place for when we're done here, right? Aunt Lila and the brats will be there. Mom tried to convince Uncle David to leave the cabin, but you know how he is."

"He has a phone now?"

Renny shook his head. "She's been writing letters to him for months." Renny snapped his fingers. "And you'll never guess who else is coming."

"Then save me the effort and just tell me."

"Aunt Mary."

My mouth fell open.

"I had the same reaction," Renny said. "She and Mom buried the hatchet, and neither one ended up with it in her back."

"That's unexpected."

Renny furrowed his brow. "Promise me we'll never stop talking like that."

"Oh lord," I said. "Are you getting emotional? Are you going to cry? I don't think I could deal if you cried. At least not until Mom and Dad get the camera working so I can record photographic evidence of it."

Renny slugged me in the shoulder. "You're such a dick, but promise anyway."

"You're my brother, Renny. My dumbass, gimpy brother. And I'll be around to annoy you until the day you die."

"Yay me." But Renny was smiling. Even though my

brother had only been in the army for a few weeks, those weeks had changed him. He might have lost the use of his legs, but he still looked taller to me. More confident. Skinnier, too, which Mom and Dad seemed hell-bent on correcting.

I bit my lip. "So, about the party," I said. "Think anyone will notice if I don't show?"

Renny's smile morphed into a disapproving frown. "Does this have anything to do with the packed duffel bag I saw this morning?" He waved his hands to cut me off. "Actually, don't tell me. I'd prefer to maintain plausible deniability."

"I'll be back in a few weeks." Renny raised an eyebrow. "Don't worry. I'll call Mom and Dad and let them know when I'm on the road and they can't try to stop me."

"They're going to kill you."

"Maybe. But I still need to do this." I stood and stretched my legs while Mom and Dad continued bickering over the camera. At this rate, I'd never escape. "How about you, Renny? Think you can survive without me for a few weeks?"

"I'll manage." I might not have believed him before, but this new Renny was easy to believe. "Did I tell you I signed up for a couple of classes at community college?"

"I'm surprised you have any space left in your schedule, seeing how much time you spend sucking face with Emilia."

A blush crept into Renny's cheeks. "Shut up about it."

Yeah, Renny was definitely going to be all right.

"Nice speech," I said.

Dustin kept looking over his shoulder at where his parents stood chatting with Principal Brzezinski under a shady palm tree. "Yeah."

"Skydiving?"

Dustin offered a halfhearted shrug. "Let's just say I wasn't handling the news about my parents' financial situation as well as I'd led you to believe."

"No judgment here."

A burst of rowdy laughter erupted from Dustin's parents and stole his attention.

"Doing anything over the summer?" I asked.

"Building houses with Habitat for Humanity before I leave for UF," he said. "I convinced Priya to join me. It's not quite the kind of quality time she was hoping we'd spend together, but she seems enthusiastic." Dustin slapped my arm playfully. "Speaking of UF, did you make up your mind about college?"

"UC Boulder," I said.

"I'm going to miss you, Pinks."

"You could come. Pot's legal in Colorado."

Dustin rolled his eyes. "Which is *so* wasted on you." He glanced at his parents again. "But, no. My parents would sell everything they owned to send me if I asked, but I can make this work. Besides, Calvin's going to UF too, so at least I'll know someone."

I hadn't known that about Calvin, but I was glad. "Good for him."

The stress of not knowing what horrifying stories his parents were telling Principal Brzezinski was beginning to become too much. "I should . . ."

"We had a good run, didn't we, Dustin?"

"The best." Dustin flashed me one last stoner grin before trotting over to join his parents.

I zipped through the crowd looking for Lua, stopping whenever someone I knew grabbed me to tell me how crazy all this was and how they were going to miss me even though we hadn't known each other well. And I let them, because it was the end of one chapter of our lives and the beginning of another, and everyone deserved to leave with happy memories.

I spotted Calvin and his father across the parking lot, hanging out with some older people I assumed were his grandparents or other assorted relatives.

After I'd stepped through the doorway, the next thing I remembered was waking up in my empty room in my old house, and I'd driven immediately to Calvin's place. He hadn't seemed surprised to see me, but he didn't remember anything that had happened between us other than working on our roller coaster. To him I was nothing more than his lab partner in a class he no longer had to suffer through.

Calvin's memory of me wasn't the only thing that had changed. Rather than me spilling his secret to a therapist I'd never visited in this reality, Calvin had been the one to report Reevey to the police. I'd read in my journal that he *had* shown up at a/s/l that first night, but he'd never mentioned Tommy, so I hadn't chased him into the boys' restroom and caught him cutting himself; we'd never made out or had sex or become anything more than friends; and Flight 1184, which I'd never purchased a ticket on, had landed safely in Seattle on August 21 at 7:03 a.m.

Oh, and the universe was expanding.

I watched Calvin pull his graduation gown off over his head. Underneath he'd worn khaki shorts and a bright blue button-down shirt.

Calvin saw me and waved. I waved back.

I missed him. He'd swum into the ocean to find what was

on the other side, and had discovered the life he deserved. I could have told him all the things we'd gone through in whatever bizarro reality I'd spent the last few months living in, and he might have believed me, but he'd earned his happiness and I refused to take it away from him.

"Congratulations, Ozzie."

I turned around to find Ms. Fuentes standing alone. She was wearing a stylish-for-her dress and clip-on shades over her giant glasses.

"Thanks, Ms. Fuentes."

"Sad to leave school behind?"

I laughed. "Not really. But you were definitely my favorite teacher, and I learned a lot in your class."

Fuentes beamed. "That's the best compliment you could have given me. Thank you."

"You're welcome."

"Did you decide on a college?" she asked. "I saw in the program you've been accepted to a wonderful array of schools."

I nodded. "UC Boulder. They've got a great English department."

"Sounds like you've got a plan," she said. "But if you ever grow tired of reading dusty books, I think you have a real knack for designing roller coasters."

"Maybe," I said. "Between you and me, I honestly don't know what I'll end up doing."

"Don't worry about it, Ozzie. You've got the rest of your life to figure it out."

I finally found Lua and Trent hanging out alone. Trent didn't call me any names when he saw me, and nodded when he left.

"Still want me to believe there's nothing going on between you and Trent?"

"Yes," Lua said. "Because there's nothing going on." I frowned and glared down my nose at her. "Look, he needed someone to talk to, and I don't mind listening. Anyway, it's not like either of us is relationship material."

"If you say so." I held up my hands in surrender. "You ready?"

"Not quite." Lua made me endure a few more pictures, this time with Dinah behind the camera, before we finally walked to my car.

The moment Lua climbed into the passenger seat, she plugged her phone into my stereo.

"You sure you want to do this?" she asked. We'd both tossed our caps and gowns into the trunk. She'd worn a glittery corset and leggings under her gown, like she was about to play a show.

"I'm sure," I said. "Are you sure? You don't have to come."

"Fuck that, Oz. You go, I go." She snapped her seat belt into place. "But we have to be back by August first so I have time to practice with the band before the tour." She held up her hand. Tiny pins stuck out of her skin around the stitches that ran the length of her finger. "And I have to do my finger exercises so I can play."

"August," I said. "We'll be back by then." I started the car but didn't put it into drive. I just sat there with my hands on the steering wheel.

"Ozzie?"

"Hold up," I said. "There's one last thing I need to do." I hopped out of the car and dodged through the crowds of smartly dressed students and their families. I searched their faces until I found him.

And I had. I'd found Thomas Ross.

It wasn't the first time I'd seen him since I'd stepped through the void and returned to this world, but it was the first time I'd worked up the courage to speak to him. I still wasn't entirely sure what had happened, but I had a lot of theories. The one I thought most probable was that I'd somehow been sucked into an unstable parallel world shaped by the feeling I'd lost Tommy. I don't know if I created that world, but I did know that even if Tommy didn't want to be with me anymore,

I never wanted to live in a world where he didn't exist.

Tommy stood beside his mom talking to Dr. Eisenhauer, his old debate coach. He smiled when he saw me. I smiled back.

"Hey," he said, after he'd trotted over to where I was standing.

"Hey."

"I wanted to see you, but I didn't know—"

"It's all right, Tommy," I said.

"You don't hate me?"

I shook my head. "Never."

Relief flooded his face.

I'd spent months dreaming of Tommy, dreaming of seeing him again and kissing him. The second thing I'd done after I'd returned was look him up. I found his beautiful smiling face on SnowFlake. Everything had gone back to the way it had been before he'd disappeared. He'd been my best friend and boyfriend. And then we'd broken up. I'd wanted to talk to him since I got back, but I'd been too scared. Only, I couldn't leave without seeing him one last time.

Yeah, I'd found Tommy, but we were traveling separate paths now. Maybe they'd merge somewhere in the future, maybe they wouldn't. For the present we were on our own.

"I heard about Renny," Tommy said. "He okay?"

"He's good." I glanced at his mom, waved. She waved back. "Your dad didn't come?"

"Mama kicked him out. She's divorcing him. Finally."

"Good for her."

"Yeah," Tommy said. "I'm gonna stick around for a while. I got into FSU and got financial aid, but I deferred for a semester to help her get on her feet."

"Maybe you could take my job at the bookstore," I said.

"You quit?"

"Yesterday was my last day. I'm not going to be around much this summer, and then I'm off to UC Boulder in the fall."

Tommy smiled. It was a wistful smile, though. I knew he was happy for me, but he was sad too, if that makes sense. I felt the same. Happy for the future, sad for all I was leaving behind.

"That's great," Tommy said. He bit his lip. "I'm really going to miss you, Ozzie." Before I could reply, he closed the distance between us and wrapped me in a hug I never wanted to leave.

But I had to. I had to let go.

"Lua's waiting for me," I said.

Tommy hiked his thumb back at his mom. "Mama's treating me to dinner to celebrate."

"Take care of yourself, Tommy."

I turned to leave when Tommy said, "Hey, Ozzie? You think we'll ever find each other again?"

I nodded. "I'll always find you. No matter how big the universe is, I will always find you."

I took off without waiting for a reply. Lua was still sitting in the car. I shut the door and buckled in.

"Ready?"

"This is your show, Ozzie. Where to?"

Lua was looking at me, waiting for me to put the car in gear and drive. I'd stepped into the void and survived. The world wasn't what I'd hoped for, but I think it had returned to the way it was meant to be. The universe was vast, and though I might have been just one infinitesimal part of it, the whole of my unexplored life stretched before me. I could go anywhere. I could become anything or anyone I wanted.

"I don't know," I said. "Somewhere we can see the stars."

ACKNOWLEDGMENTS

Books are never written by the author alone. They're written and published by a community. I'm lucky to be surrounded by the very best community any author could hope for, and words alone could never be enough to thank everyone. But here goes anyway.

Thanks to . . .

Amy Boggs, my brilliant, thoughtful, and tireless agent. I would not, could not, be here without her.

Michael Strother, my exceptionally talented editor at Simon Pulse, without whom this book would not exist.

The entire team at Simon Pulse and Simon & Schuster—who have given me a home in publishing and supported me far better than I deserve—which includes: Mara Anastas, Mary Marotta, Liesa Abrams, Faye Bi (who always gets me where I need to be and has the best taste in TV and movies), Adam Smith (my copy editor extraordinaire), Lucille Rettino, Christina Pecorale, Candace Greene McManus, Carolyn Swerdloff, Kerry Johnson, Sara Berko, Michelle

Leo, Anthony Parisi, David Gale, Justin Chanda, and all the amazing and hardworking folks who make this job the best in the world.

Katie Shea Boutillier at Donald Maass for working so hard to help my books reach audiences outside of the U.S.

All the librarians, teachers, and booksellers who put books into the hands of the readers who need them.

My family for supporting me, but especially my mom, who keeps me company on my commutes and lets me ramble about my ideas and is the best cheerleader a son could ask for.

My best friends and first readers: Rachel "Pookie" Melcher, Margie Gelbwasser, and Matthew Rush. How they haven't banished me to a parallel universe is beyond me. I love you guys!

The book bloggers and reviewers who spread their passion for books to every corner of the Internet.

All the readers who have reached out to me to tell me their stories and support these crazy books. I owe you a debt of gratitude that can never be repaid.

And, finally, I'd like to give a very special shout-out to Ryan Sousa, the first (and only) reader to guess the real intentions of the sluggers from *We Are the Ants*. Keep marching on!

AUTHOR'S NOTE

When I published my first book, I never expected that I'd wind up writing books that dealt so heavily with issues of mental illness, though I probably should have. If you know me in real life or online, you know that I'm not shy about discussing my own history with depression or my attempted suicide at nineteen. Those two things, more than any others, have influenced the books and characters I write.

One of the greatest aspects of writing for young adults is that teen readers can smell bullshit from a million miles away. You can't pander to them, you can't talk down to them, and you can't sugarcoat anything. All you can do is be honest, which is what I try to do when writing about mental illness. And what that means is that the characters I write do not always make the best choices. In fact, they often make the very worst choices imaginable. They deal badly with their own depression. They're fearful of doctors and the wrongheaded stigma attached to mental illness.

They often make decisions I would never encourage people to make in real life.

Like Calvin, I cut myself when I was a teen. I was afraid to ask for help, and I didn't know how to work through the pain and anger that had built up inside of myself. I used cutting and punching walls as a pressure-release valve. And, like Calvin's, my decision was the worst imaginable. But I wrote Calvin as honestly as I knew how, not as a role model for how to deal with depression, but simply as a confused, messed-up kid.

There are lessons I hope people will take away from this and my other books—lessons about the value of life and love and the future—because despite my own struggles, those are the lessons *I've* learned. I hope Calvin's story and Ozzie's story, and Jesse and Henry and Diego's stories from *We Are the Ants*, will serve not as instruction manuals for how to deal with depression, but rather as maps of how *not* to deal with it. If I were to write a book detailing how to deal with mental illness, it would be one page and would read: Talk to someone. Seek the help you deserve. Mental illness is *not* something to be ashamed of, and asking for help is *not* a weakness.

So if you find yourself struggling with mental illness or thoughts of suicide (or even if you just need to talk), please tell someone. A parent, a teacher, a psychologist, a friend. If you're considering hurting yourself, tell someone. As Henry said: Depression isn't a war you win. It's a battle you fight every day. But the great thing about life is that it's a battle you don't have to fight alone. Please don't fight it alone.

RESOURCES

The Trevor Project: www.thetrevorproject.org 1-866-488-7386
National Suicide Prevention Hotline: 1-800-273-8255